THE APOTHECARY'S DAUGHTER

THE APOTHECARY'S DAUGHTER

Charlotte Betts

WINDSOR
PARAGON

First published 2011
by Piatkus
This Large Print edition published 2012
by AudioGO Ltd
by arrangement with
Little, Brown Book Group

Hardcover   ISBN: 978 1 445 88337 3
Softcover   ISBN: 978 1 445 88338 0

British Library Cataloguing in Publication Data available

Printed and bound in Great Britain by
MPG Books Group Limited

For my mother and father,

Dorothy and Michael Spooner

The Fading of the Light

January 1665

Chapter 1

Inside the apothecary shop Susannah stood by the light of the window, daydreaming and grinding flowers of sulphur into a malodorous dust as she watched the world go by. Fleet Street, as always, was as busy as an anthill. The morning's snow was already dusted with soot from the noxious cloud blown in from the kilns at Limehouse and the frost made icebergs of the surging effluent in the central drain. Church bells clanged and dogs barked while a ceaseless stream of people flowed past.

Thwack! A snowball smashed against the window pane. Susannah gasped and dropped the pestle, shocked out of her lazy contemplation. Outside, a street urchin laughed at her through the glass.

'Little demon!' Her heart still hammering, she raised a fist at him. She watched him darting away through the horde until her eye was drawn by the tall figure of a man in a sombre hat and cloak picking his way over the snow.

Something about the way he moved amongst the hubbub of the crowd, like a wolf slipping silently through the forest, captured her curiosity. As he drew closer Susannah recognised him as a physician, one of her father's less frequent customers. Stepping around a steaming heap of horse droppings and a discarded cabbage, it became apparent that he was making his way towards the shop.

Susannah pulled open the door. 'Good morning,' she said, shivering in the icy draught that followed him.

He touched his hat but didn't return her smile. 'Is Mr Leyton here?'

'Not at present. May I help?'

'I hardly think that you ...'

She suppressed her irritation with a sigh. Why did he assume she was incapable, simply because she wore skirts? 'Do, please, tell me what you require, sir.'

'What I *require* is to discuss my requirements with your father.'

The man's tone tempted Susannah to make a sharp retort but she reined in a flash of temper and merely said, 'He's gone to read the parson's urine.'

The doctor's dark eyebrows drew together in a frown as he took off his gloves and rubbed the warmth back into his hands. 'This is a matter of urgency. Please tell him Dr Ambrose came by and ask him to call on me when he returns.'

'May I tell him what it is you wish to discuss?'

Dr Ambrose hesitated and then shrugged. 'I have a patient who suffers from a stone in the bladder. Leyton mentioned to me that he'd had some success with his own prescription in cases of this kind. The patient's state of health is not so strong that I can recommend cutting for the stone since he has a chronic shortness of breath. Can you remember all that?'

'Oh, I should think so.' Susannah smiled sweetly and vigorously stirred up the ground sulphur with the pestle until it floated in a choking cloud between them. 'Father usually recommends spirits of sweet nitre for a stone, mixed with laudanum and oil of juniper. Your patient should sip a teaspoonful in a cup of linseed tea sweetened with honey.'

Dr Ambrose coughed and pressed a

4

handkerchief to his nose. 'You are sure of this?'

'Of course. And you might try milk of gum ammoniac stirred with syrup of squills for the wheezing in the chest.'

Dr Ambrose raised his eyebrows and Susannah did her best not to look smug. 'Perhaps you would like to warm yourself by the fire while I prepare the medicines for you?' she said.

'Do you know the correct proportions?'

'I am perfectly used to dispensing my father's prescriptions.'

She retired to the dispensary, a curtained-off alcove at the rear of the shop, and peeped through the gap in the curtains while he, apparently thinking he was unobserved, lifted his cloak and warmed his backside by the fire. Stifling a laugh, she turned to the bench and set to work. As she bottled up the last prescription the shop bell jingled. She pulled aside the curtain to see an elegantly dressed lady enter.

'Please, take a seat by the fire and I will help you in just a moment,' Susannah said.

She handed the two bottles of medicine to Dr Ambrose and, in the interests of repeat business, made the effort to be civil. 'I hope you are warmer now?' She wondered whether to tell him he had a sulphurous streak across his nose but decided against it. 'They say this bitter wind comes from Russia, which is why the frost has barely lifted since December.'

'Perhaps that's as well,' the doctor said. 'The cold moderates the severity of the plague.'

'Except in the parish of St Giles, of course. We must pray that the freeze destroys the pestilence.'

'Indeed. Put the prescriptions on my account.'

5

He nodded and left.

Susannah, wondering if he'd been sucking lemons, watched him set off again down Fleet Street. What a shame his darkly handsome face wasn't matched by more pleasing manners!

The other customer was a fair-haired woman of about Susannah's own age and dressed very finely in a fur-tipped cloak with a crimson skirt just visible beneath. She stood on tiptoe, examining the preserved crocodile which hung from one of the ceiling beams. Her small nose wrinkled with distaste. 'Is it real?'

'Certainly! It came from Africa. My father bought it from a sailor.' Susannah still remembered her mixed fear and fascination when he'd brought it home many years before. She had tentatively touched its hard, scaly body with the tip of her finger, shuddering as it stared back at her with beady glass eyes. Her younger brother, Tom, had hidden behind the counter until their mother assured him the creature wasn't alive.

'This *is* Mr Leyton's apothecary's shop, at the sign of the Unicorn and the Dragon?'

'As you see, the sign hangs over the door.'

'Is Mr Leyton here?'

'Not at present. May I help you?'

Pursing her lips, she looked Susannah up and down. 'I would like . . .' She glanced around at the bottles and jars that lined the walls, frowning a little. 'Yes. A bottle of rosewater will do very well. Tell me,' she said, running her gloved finger along the counter, 'how many hearths do you have in this building?'

'Why, we have three bedchambers, the parlour and the dining room and then there is the shop,

6

dispensary and kitchen,' stammered Susannah, taken aback.

'The house is narrow and crooked with age.'

'But it is also deep.' Susannah stood up very straight, a flare of temper bringing warmth to her face. 'And the parlour is panelled and we have a good yard.'

The woman sighed. 'I suppose it is well enough.' She put a handful of coins on the counter, picked up the rosewater and waited until Susannah snatched open the shop door for her.

Relieved to be rid of the woman with her prying questions, Susannah stood shivering in the open doorway for a moment, glancing up the snowy street beyond the waiting sedan chair. She saw Ned, the apprentice, hurtling along towards the shop, returning from delivering a packet of liver pills to the Misses Lane. His head was down against the bitter wind and she realised that he was on course to collide with the departing customer.

'Ned, look out!' she called.

At the last second he swerved, narrowly avoiding barrelling into the lady as she climbed into her sedan chair.

She gave Susannah an accusing look, put her nose in the air and motioned for the chair to leave.

'Take more care, Ned!' snapped Susannah.

He banged the door behind them and hurried to the fire to warm his hands and stamp the feeling back into his feet.

'For goodness' sake!' Susannah's repressed irritation with both her recent customers made her voice sharp. 'Fetch the broom and clear up all that ice from your boots before it turns into puddles.'

'Sorry, miss.'

'And then you can dust the gallypots.'

'Yes, miss.' He blew on his fingers, collected the broom from the dispensary and began to sweep the floor.

Susannah relented. Sometimes Ned put her in mind of her brother, Tom, now living far away in Virginia. She reached a large stone jar down from the shelf, scooped out a spoonful of the sticky substance from inside and smeared it onto a piece of brown paper. 'Here!' she said, handing him the salve. 'Rub this on your chilblains and it will stop the skin from breaking. And don't forget to dust the gallypots!' She retrieved the sulphurous pestle and mortar from the counter and carried it in to the dispensary to mix up an ointment for pimples.

She had lived in the apothecary shop for all of her twenty-six years and it held her most precious memories. As she measured ingredients and mixed the ointment she hummed to herself as she remembered how, when they were children, she and Tom had learned to add up by counting out pills. She recalled experimenting with the weighing beam, fascinated that a huge bunch of dried sage weighed exactly the same as a tiny piece of lead. In the big stone mortar, the same one she was using now, she'd made gloriously sticky mixtures of hog's lard combined with white lead and turpentine as a salve for burns. She'd learned to read by studying the letters, in Latin, painted on the gallypots which lined the walls and then to write by tracing her father's exquisite handwriting on the labels fixed to the banks of wooden storage drawers.

Now she busied herself setting a batch of rosemary and honey linctus to boil, sniffing at its sweet, resinous scent. Cold weather and London's

8

putrid fog was excellent for business since most of the customers had a perpetual winter cough. Licking honey off her thumb, she glanced through the gap between the dispensary curtains to see Ned lying over the counter, teasing the cat with a trailing piece of rag. Suddenly he slid back to the ground and with meticulous care began to dust the majolica jars. Susannah guessed from this that he'd glimpsed his master returning.

Cornelius Leyton struggled through the door with a large box, which he placed on the counter between a cone of sugar and the jar of leeches. The frost had nipped his nose cherry red.

'What have you bought, Father?'

Taking his time, he began to untie the string.

'Let me!' she said, snatching a knife from under the counter and slicing through the knot.

'Always so impatient, Susannah!' Carefully, Cornelius lifted the lid.

Susannah caught a glimpse of dark fur and gasped. Was it a puppy? But then, as her father lifted aside the tissue paper, she realised with disappointment that she was mistaken.

Cornelius gathered up the wig and shook out its long and lustrous black curls. 'What do you think?' he asked.

'It's ... magnificent. Put it on!'

Eyes gleaming with anticipation, he snatched off his usual wig, a modest mid-brown affair that he'd had for a number of years, to expose his own cropped grey hair. Then, reverentially, he placed the new wig over the top.

Susannah stared at him.

'Susannah?'

Speechless, she continued to stare. Her father

9

was fine-looking; tall, with dark eyes and an air of authority, but she had never thought of him as a vain man. In fact, she'd always had to chivvy him into buying a new coat or breeches and his hat was embarrassingly old-fashioned. But this wig was an entirely different affair. It turned him into an elegant stranger and it made her uneasy.

'Well?' His expression was anxious.

'Astonishing,' she said, at last. She lifted up one of the silky curls which fell near enough to his waist. 'It's very handsome.' She fumbled for words. 'I hardly recognise you. It makes you seem so . . . young.'

A quickly suppressed smile flitted across his face.

Ned said, 'You look exactly like the King, sir.'

Cornelius threw his apprentice a sharp look. 'You have time for idle chatter, Ned? Shall I find you something to do? The copper still in the yard must be scrubbed. Of course the ice must be scraped off it first . . .'

Ned hastily returned to his dusting. 'I was talking to my old friend, Richard Berry,' continued Cornelius, with an amused glance to Susannah, 'and he said a more fashionable appearance will be good for business. Perhaps I should have a new hat, too?'

'I've been suggesting that for months!'

'Have you?

'Father!'

'I have some visits to make. Did you brush my blue coat?'

'Of course.'

'Then if there's nothing that needs my attention here . . .?'

'Oh! I forgot. Dr Ambrose asked you to call on

10

him to discuss a patient of his with a kidney stone. I prepared the prescriptions for him.'

'Good, good.' Cornelius picked up his old wig and went upstairs.

Susannah stared after him. What on earth had inspired him to suddenly start taking an interest in his appearance? Shaking her head, she returned to the dispensary to pot up the sulphur ointment. As always, spooning that particular mixture into jars evoked the familiar recollection of an afternoon eleven years before when she'd helped her mother to do the same thing. Her mother's gentle voice was imprinted on Susannah's memory and she could recall, as if it were yesterday, how her hand had rested tenderly upon the swell of her belly. That was two days before she died and there had been the same sulphurous reek in the air then, mixed with the usual aromas of rosewater and beeswax, liquorice and oil of wormwood, turpentine and drying herbs. Those were the scents of her father's trade and they ran in Susannah's blood.

The shop bell jolted her back to the present and she was pleased to hear Martha's voice. Until her marriage Martha had lived in a neighbouring house and been her closest friend for twenty years, despite her Puritan leanings. Pulling back the curtain, Susannah went to greet her.

Martha, as neat as always in a starched apron and with her dark hair tucked firmly into her cap, recoiled as they kissed. 'Ugh! What is it this time?'

'Nothing dangerous! Merely complexion ointment.'

'It certainly smells dreadful enough to frighten pimples away.' Martha turned bone white and held her slim fingers over her mouth while she

11

swallowed convulsively.

'It's not *that* dreadful, surely?'

Martha smiled faintly. 'The slightest thing turns my stomach, at the moment,' she said pressing her hands to her apron. 'I came to ask for some of that ginger cordial you made for me last time . . .'

'Last time? Oh Martha! Not another one? Little Alys isn't even weaned.'

'I know.' Martha sighed, the shadows under her hazel eyes dark against her pale face. 'I did warn Robert that if he insisted Alys went to a wet nurse it was likely I'd fall again but you know how stubborn men can be.'

'Stubborn and peculiar,' Susannah added, thinking of her father's latest purchase. She pulled the joint stool from under the counter and stretched up to the top shelf for the ginger cordial, then decanted some of the golden liquid into a bottle and stopped it with a cork.

The narrow door to the staircase creaked open and Cornelius appeared, wearing the new acquisition and his best blue coat. He showed more lace than usual at his throat and new blue ribands on his shoes. The air around him carried the distinct aroma of lavender water and self-conscious pride.

'Martha. Are you keeping well?'

Martha's freckled face turned from white to red as she bobbed a curtsy. 'Mr Leyton. Thank you, I am very well.'

Cornelius's eyes flickered to the bottle of cordial and then to Martha's waist. 'And all your little ones?'

'Well, too.'

'Good, good. I shall not detain you.' He picked

12

up his cane with the silver head. 'Susannah, do not wait up for me; I shall not be home for supper.' He launched himself into the hurly burly of Fleet Street, raising his cane to attract a passing hackney carriage.

Martha stared at her friend with wide eyes. 'Your father looks so different. I never realised before what a handsome man he is.'

After Martha had left, Susannah began to wonder where her father had gone, all dressed up in such finery.

*   *   *

Two weeks later Susannah was baking sugar jumbals with the maid, Jennet, when Cornelius came into the kitchen. He stood by the fire, shifting from foot to foot and watching as Susannah pounded the sugar and Jennet washed the salt from the butter. His dead wife's recipe book lay open on the table, a sprig of dried lavender marking the place.

'Was there something you wanted?' Susannah asked after a while.

Cornelius picked up the lavender and twirled it between his fingers. 'Your mother's favourite flower,' he said.

'And we're making your favourite biscuits.'

'So I see.' He replaced the lavender and in so doing knocked the book to the floor.

A dozen scraps of paper flew out and Susannah scrambled to pick them up and tuck them back between the precious pages. 'Father, why don't you go into the parlour and I'll bring you some of the biscuits when they're baked?'

'Yes, perhaps that would be best. There's

13

something . . .'

'Hmm?' Carefully, she broke eggs into a basin.

'Later.'

'He's as jumpy as a cat with fleas!' said Jennet, after he'd gone. She dried her hands on her hips. 'I think he's up to something.'

When the jumbals were ready Susannah dusted them with powdered sugar and carried them up to the parlour where she found Cornelius standing by the window, staring down at the street. He turned, his face taut with worry.

'Father, what is it?' she asked, suddenly anxious.

'You are so like your mother. Sometimes I catch sight of you with your pretty auburn hair and just for a moment I can almost believe Elizabeth has come back to me.'

'I never feel she's really left us.'

'I know.' He sighed deeply. 'But she *has* gone. And it's been eleven long years. You have been a great comfort to me, especially since Tom left too.'

She squeezed his hand. 'We've been a comfort to each other.'

Abruptly he turned again and paced across to the hearth.

'Susannah, I fear I have done you a disservice.'

'A disservice? How could that be?'

'I've been selfish. Your companionship has been so dear to me that I have kept you close to my side . . .'

'But that's where I want to be!'

'You've learned my craft better than any of the apprentices I've taken on over the years and your writing is neater than my own. Even your Latin is as good as any scholar's.' He smiled wryly. 'But you should be married by now, with a brood of little

14

ones, like Martha.'

'I've never wanted babies.' It wasn't true, of course. She wanted children as much as any woman but . . . she shuddered, remembering.

'I have been remiss in finding a husband for you.'

'I'm perfectly happy keeping house for you. Besides, what man would I find who could match up to you?' There had been Nicholas, of course, but Father hadn't considered him good enough for her. And then there had been the young man with the smiling eyes who delivered herbs to the shop from the farm in Essex . . .

'Susannah, times change.'

'What do you mean?'

He took her hands between his, not meeting her eyes. 'I love you as much as any man could love a daughter, but we've grieved for your mother for too long. I have made a decision.' Still he didn't look at her. 'I intend to take another wife,' he said.

She gave an uncertain laugh. 'You should not jest about something like that.'

His mouth tightened. 'I've made myself perfectly clear. I shall be married again. And I have met a suitable lady, a widow.'

'But we manage very well.' Susannah helped to keep the account books for the shop and she knew that they were far richer than anyone might suspect from the simple way they lived. Puzzled, she shook her head. 'Your old age is secure; you have no need to marry to increase our fortune.'

'That has not been a consideration in my decision. Through no fault of her own, the death of this lady's husband has left her in straitened circumstances.'

'This widow has no jointure?'

15

Cornelius studied his shoes.

'Then I do not understand. Why would you want to do such a thing?'

'Because it is time. Because I need . . . companionship.'

'Companionship? But we have each other! We do everything together. What more companionship could you possibly need?'

Cornelius's face flooded as crimson as the phials of cochineal in the dispensary. 'A man needs a wife for . . .' He gestured with his hands, at a loss for words.

Suddenly she realised what he meant and the heat rose up in her own face. It had never occurred to her to even *imagine* that her own father had those particular needs.

'The lady is looking forward to meeting you.'

'I don't want to meet her!' Her fingers tingled and a cold shiver ran through her whole body. 'Father, this is madness! Consider . . .'

'Enough! I shall bring her to dine with us the day after tomorrow. That will give you and Jennet time to prepare a good dinner.' His tone brooked no argument.

Susannah swallowed and stood up very straight. 'Am I to know the name of this widow?'

'Arabella Poynter. A pretty name, is it not? She has two sons and a daughter, Harriet, who is intent upon becoming your friend.'

There was a roaring in Susannah's ears and for a moment she wondered if she might faint. 'Father, you cannot. Everything will change!'

'My mind is quite made up.' He turned his back on her and picked up a book from the table. She was dismissed.

Her knees trembling with shock, Susannah returned to the kitchen.

*   *   *

Determined that Mistress Poynter would be unable to find fault with what was to become her new home, Susannah and Jennet set to the housework. Tight-lipped, they swept and scrubbed the hall, stairs and parlour from top to bottom, obliterating the film of soot that continually settled everywhere from the sea-coal smog.

Jennet, her hands red and weeping from scouring the pans, took the rugs into the yard and beat them until the cloud of dust mingled with the frosty mist of her breath. Susannah polished the plate with horsetail so that the pewter shone with the translucent gleam of still water under a thundery sky. Lost in thought, she stared at her reflection while she tried to understand why her father would wish to change their lives. It cut her deeply that he'd not told her he was lonely. She'd believed they were such close companions that they had no secrets from each other.

On hands and knees, Susannah rubbed the wide elm floorboards in the parlour with her own beeswax and lavender polish, each sweep of the cloth feeding her smouldering resentment. Who *was* this gold-seeking widow who had the temerity to imagine she might take her mother's place? And why did Harriet, the daughter of this interloper, imagine that they might be friends?

The following morning Cornelius counted out a fistful of coins from the locked chest in his bedchamber and placed them in Susannah's palm.

17

'It is my express wish that you do not stint on the quality of this celebration dinner,' he said.

Susannah stared at the coins in her hand. She doubted that she had spent as much on food over the past month. Usually bid to be frugal, Jennet and Susannah argued over what to cook as they trekked through the snow to the market but agreed that a beef and oyster pudding, to Susannah's mother's special recipe, of course, was an essential centrepiece for the banquet.

Nearly two hours had passed by the time they returned with their baskets filled with provisions fit for the feast that Cornelius expected for his future bride. Frozen to the bone, they took off their wet overshoes and built up the fire. Susannah made the pastry while her hands were still cold and Jennet put the mutton on to boil and peeled the turnips. All the while she was rolling out the pastry Susannah was praying to herself that her father would change his mind about this unwelcome marriage.

The oysters took longer to open than expected and they began to worry that they had been too ambitious in their choice of menu for the time available. When the bells of St Bride's chimed a quarter to three Susannah flung off her apron and left Jennet to the greasy work of turning the chickens on the spit.

Upstairs, Susannah put on her best green silk bodice and the skirt with the petticoat of gold damask. Then she lifted the lid of her little marquetry box and took out one of the two most precious things she owned. She slipped the gold chain over her head and kissed her mother's pearl pendant before settling it into place over her breast.

18

The other treasure lay in the box wrapped in blue velvet; a miniature of her mother. The artist had caught the likeness well and she smiled steadily back, her face forever fixed in youth. Susannah suffered again the familiar, aching loss of a mother snatched away too soon. How could Father even *contemplate* replacing Mama?

She wiped her eyes and knew that she could delay no longer. She peered into the looking glass. Would she do? She bit her lips to bring the colour back. The steamy kitchen, as always, had caused her hair to spiral into ringlets and she only had time to smooth them into place and pin on her lace cap before running down to the parlour.

Cornelius, dressed in his new wig and best coat, was peering down the street. 'Mistress Poynter should be here any minute,' he said. 'You look very well, my dear. I always liked you in that shade of green; it matches your eyes.'

Susannah admitted to herself that jealousy probably made her eyes greener than usual. 'All is in readiness,' she said. 'Jennet burned the carp a little but I removed the skin and smothered it in a butter sauce with herbs.'

A sedan chair stopped in front of the house and Cornelius stood back from the window. Susannah wasn't so well mannered and stared, heart galloping in her chest as she waited to catch a glimpse of her future stepmother. She was disappointed though, since the woman was swathed in a dark cloak with a hood. Daintily she picked her way through the slush and snow to the front door.

Downstairs Jennet's clogs clattered across the hall.

Susannah swallowed back a sudden surge of

19

queasiness and hoped Jennet had remembered to put on a clean cap and apron.

Cornelius took up a carefully nonchalant position leaning against the mantelpiece and adjusted the lace at his cuffs again.

Waiting with her shaking hands gripped together, Susannah listened to the footsteps coming up the stairs.

The door opened.

Susannah caught her breath. It was the inquisitive young woman who had visited the shop a few days previously. She stared at her, frowning. 'I wasn't expecting to see you,' she said. 'Are you Harriet? Could your mother not come, after all?' She felt a flicker of annoyance for all the time she and Jennet had spent preparing the house and the dinner, only to find that Father's intended had not appeared.

The woman raised her finely plucked eyebrows. 'My mother has been dead these past five years, may the Lord keep her.'

Cornelius held out his hands to her and she offered her powdered cheek to be kissed. 'Arabella, what a delight it is to have you join us,' he said.

'And for me to be here, my dear Cornelius.'

'Let me present my daughter, Susannah.'

Bemused, Susannah took the small, cold hand and struggled to reconcile her expectations of a forty- or even fifty-something widow with the girlish creature dressed in forget-me-not blue silk that stood before her. Had her father taken leave of his senses?

'We have already met, Father,' she said.

'How so?'

Arabella flushed rosily and fluttered her

eyelashes. 'I confess curiosity had the better of me, dear Cornelius. I came to make a trifling purchase the other day.'

'But why did you not call for me?'

'You were not at home and since it was before you proposed to me I hardly liked to introduce myself. Besides, what could I have said to dear Susannah without appearing too forward?'

The yearning way Father looked at Arabella made Susannah deeply uncomfortable. 'Father tells me that you have a daughter?' she said, to break the spell between them.

Smiling, Arabella turned to Susannah as if she'd just noticed her. 'Harriet is my eldest; eight years old and a sweet child, as you will find out. And then there are my two sons, Mathew, six and John, four.'

'But . . .' Shock ran through Susannah like an icy river. It had simply never occurred to her that her future stepmother's children were still young and would likely need to live under her father's roof. 'But where on earth will we put them all?'

'I am sure we shall manage, shan't we, Cornelius?' Arabella gave him a radiant smile.

'Of course we shall!'

'And you, dear Susannah,' she said, 'will have the pleasure of a little sister and two new brothers.'

Susannah watched her father pat Arabella's arm. This woman had bewitched him! Suddenly, she couldn't bear to be in the same room with them both. 'I shall go and see if dinner is ready,' she said.

In the kitchen, Jennet gave her a wide-eyed look. 'She's not at all what I expected,' she said.

'No, she isn't,' said Susannah, still barely able to comprehend this turn of events. It was bad enough that Father wanted a wife but this girl was hardly a suitable companion for him.

She returned upstairs, carrying the roasted chickens on a platter. She hesitated in the doorway as she caught a glimpse of Arabella encircled in her father's arms, toying with the buttons on his waistcoat.

Cornelius let Arabella go but he didn't look at his daughter as she set the platter on the table.

The dinner made an excellent show. There was the stewed carp, the famous beef and oyster pudding, boiled mutton with turnips and carrots, apple pie, candied quinces and a splendid cheese. Hardly any of it was eaten. Cornelius was too lovesick, his eyes never leaving Arabella's simpering face, and Susannah was too sick with apprehension as she began to appreciate just how much the household was likely to change.

Chapter 2

'Holy matrimony is an honourable estate not by any to be enterprised, nor taken in hand, unadvisedly, lightly or wantonly ...'

The parson's voice rang out clearly but Susannah let her mind drift. She sat at the front of the church of St Mary-le-Bow in a new hat, listening to the silken rustle of a congregation uncomfortably dressed in their best clothes, all there to witness her father's marriage. Most of their friends and the doctors, apothecaries and several grateful patients of their acquaintance had come. Those of a nervous disposition had stayed away, anxious to avoid large gatherings for fear of pestilential infection. The

22

pews on the bride's side of the church were sparsely populated.

Arabella stood at the altar rail with her father and there was nothing Susannah could, or would, do now to change the course of events. She had used every reasoned argument she could to make her father reconsider but in the end she'd had to accept that he had fallen in love with Arabella and would be miserable without her.

During the weeks that the banns were being read, Arabella had joined them for dinner twice and on one occasion they were invited to the house she rented in Wood Street. There they met her children. Harriet's fair hair and delicate features made her a diminutive replica of her mother, while Susannah wondered if the two boys, stocky and dark, resembled their late father.

'First it was ordained for the procreation of children, to be brought up in the fear and nurture of the Lord ...'

The parson's words made Susannah blink. The indecent thought that Father and Arabella might have children together hadn't occurred to her. Surely Father was too old, even though his bride was young? It was shock enough to gain three new step-siblings without the awful prospect of any more children to come.

'Secondly, it was ordained for a remedy against sin, and to avoid fornication ...'

She shut her ears to this and silently sang a psalm very loudly inside her head. The thought of Arabella in her nightshift, in her father's bed, was impossible to contemplate without toe-curling embarrassment.

'Thirdly, it was ordained for the mutual society,

23

help and comfort, that the one ought to have of the other, both in prosperity and adversity ...'

Susannah freely admitted to herself that she was jealous of Arabella for coming between herself and Father but perhaps, in time, they would learn to like each other. After all, there was no reason why she and her father should discontinue their comfortable evenings reading aloud together; the only change would be that Arabella would be sitting on the other side of the hearth.

'Who giveth this woman to be married to this man?'

Arabella's brother stepped back. The parson placed her hand in Cornelius's palm.

And so it was done.

*   *   *

The wedding breakfast was held at the Crown and Cushion in Thames Street and once the chattering guests were seated Richard Berry, who had officiated as Cornelius's best man, banged his knife on the table.

'Pray silence for the pie!' he shouted. He turned his ruddy face to Cornelius, barely able to contain his mirth. 'This is my gift to you,' he said. 'I hope it will amuse you.'

The fiddler scraped a merry tune on his violin as two serving maids carried in a vast pie on a tray balanced between their shoulders. Richard Berry danced a little jig as the pie was placed with much ceremony on the table before the groom.

Cornelius sliced into the pastry and everyone gasped and then laughed as a flock of doves burst through the crust. Frightened by the noise, the birds fluttered about scattering crumbs, and worse, over the gathering.

Chaos ensued. Mathew screamed himself into hysterics when he saw how his mother took fright, flapping her handkerchief at the birds and emitting piercing shrieks. One of the guests came forward with a flask of sal volatile but Arabella was apparently enjoying herself far too much being the centre of attention to be calmed and threw herself sobbing onto her husband's shoulder.

Susannah recognised Dr Ambrose, dressed rather too soberly for a wedding, as the guest who had tried to minister to Arabella.

'How is your patient with the stone in his bladder?' she asked.

'Your father's prescription is effective.'

'More effective than sal volatile is in aiding my new stepmother?'

'So it would appear.' Dr Ambrose turned away but not before she noticed a surprising spark of amusement in his dark eyes.

Arabella had subsided somewhat by then and was being comforted by her new husband, who carefully dabbed at a splatter of bird droppings which had landed amongst her golden curls. Although Cornelius told her that this was a good omen, she refused to be persuaded.

The Crown and Cushion was famed for the quality of its wine and ale and the party became very merry. Susannah retreated to an anteroom and sat on a high-sided settle by the fire, closing her eyes in an attempt to ignore recent events.

She woke a little later to hear voices and glared round the corner of the settle to see her father enter the room, followed by Richard Berry.

25

'Saving all your energy for your wedding night, old man?' asked Richard, poking his friend in the ribs.

'God knows, Arabella has awakened my senses in a way I thought could never happen again,' said Cornelius. 'I don't want to spend the next eleven years as celibate as the past eleven. And I'm too old now to want to risk the pox caught off some light-skirt in Smithfield.'

Susannah clasped a hand over her mouth and shrank back into her hiding place.

'And the new Mistress Leyton with her cream-fed complexion has really caught your fancy, hasn't she? Can't blame you for that.' Richard sighed. 'Ah, young flesh! I dream of it sometimes. But I'm happy enough with my old Bridie, even if she's lost a few teeth and her waist has thickened. She still snuggles up to me nice and warm on a cold winter's night.'

'Bridie is a good woman. My Elizabeth was very fond of her.'

'Ah well! But now we must all make merry while we may,' said Richard. 'Who knows when the Spectre of Pestilence might snatch us away? One sneeze and a day later you could be dead. Live for today, I say!'

*   *   *

It was dark by the time the wedding party left the Crown and Cushion. Headed by Richard Berry's capering figure, it processed along Fleet Street, several of the group distinctly unsteady and singing more raucously than was mannerly. Once the procession reached the apothecary shop it took some time to send the well-wishers on their noisy way and by then Arabella's children were tired and fretful.

Susannah had prepared her brother Tom's bedchamber in readiness for them. She had always hoped that he would return from Virginia, whence he had been apprenticed at fourteen. It had saddened her, as she put fresh linen on the bed, to finally accept this was unlikely to happen and that these new children were to inhabit his room instead.

She had little experience of children, overtired or otherwise, and it was a revelation to her just how long it could take to put them to bed when they had no wish to sleep. Arabella laid them top to toe on the mattress and listened to them say their prayers. The children took fright at the shadows in the corners of the strange bedchamber and screamed when the old tabby cat came to investigate. Arabella kissed their cheeks, promised them that the nasty creature wouldn't nibble their toes while they slept and suggested that their new sister told them a story. She smiled sweetly and said goodnight.

Susannah stared at the children, who stared back. Sighing, she tried to remember the bedtime stories her mother had told to her when she was small.

At long last, the children's eyelids drooped and all became quiet. Exhausted, Susannah retired to the parlour to join the newly married couple.

'What a joyful day!' said Cornelius, stoking up the fire to a crackling blaze.

'Joyful!' said Arabella, making a face. 'But I forget, you were not savaged and despoiled by wild birds. I do not *at all* like your vulgar friend, Richard Berry.'

Susannah flinched, anticipating her father's pain at this sharp remark but he appeared unruffled.

'Come, my dear, it was but a jest.' He took his wife's hand and kissed her fingers, one by one.

Arabella sniffed and they sat in awkward silence by the fire.

Susannah's eyes opened wide as she noticed Arabella dab at her eyes with a handkerchief as she stared into the flames. Surely she should be happy now that she had ensnared Father and secured her future? But what of her *own* future? What changes would her stepmother bring to the household?

Arabella's chin quivered while her hands twisted her handkerchief in her lap. 'So, I am now Mistress Leyton,' she said.

'Indeed you are!' Cornelius smiled encouragingly.

Arabella didn't answer.

'I have asked Jennet to bring us a jug of the Canary wine up from the cellar,' Susannah said, after a while. 'And only a light supper of bread and cold meat, since we had such a good dinner.' She knew she was talking too much in an attempt to fill the awkward silence and was relieved when Jennet came in to set the table.

'A toast to my beautiful new bride!' said Cornelius, holding up his glass.

Susannah forced her face into a smile.

Arabella preened herself. 'I shall have to make the best of it,' she said. Peace returned.

After the supper dishes had been cleared away Susannah took down a book of Donne's poems. She anticipated that the poems of Catullus, in the

28

original Latin, might not appeal to Arabella.

'Shall you read first, Father?' She held the book out to him.

He took it from her but then placed it slowly on the table. 'You must be tired after such a day, Susannah. Perhaps you will wish to retire?'

'Not at all! I have been looking forward to resuming our discussion of *Astraea Redux.*'

'I think not, Susannah.'

'There is something else you would prefer to read?'

'Not tonight. Are you sure you are not tired?' His hand reached out to one of Arabella's silky ringlets and twisted it gently around his fingers.

'Oh! I see.' And she did. She watched her father lay the ringlet onto her stepmother's bare shoulder and allow his hand to linger for a moment on her white skin.

Arabella gave him a sideways glance through her eyelashes.

Susannah recalled Richard Berry's knowing comments and felt her face grow hot. All at once she couldn't wait to leave the parlour. Retiring upstairs far too early was infinitely preferable to watching Father and Arabella making sheep's eyes at one another.

Upstairs, she had not been in her bed for more than a minute before she heard the stairs creak. Then there were whispers and a stifled giggle before the latch of her father's bedchamber rattled and the door clicked shut. The walls in the old house were thin and she could hear movements for a while but then the muffled voices ceased.

She lay wide-eyed in the dark, trying not to hear the sighs and gasps of her father's lovemaking and feeling lonelier than at any time since her mother's death.

She had put the pillow over her head to shut out the rhythmic knocking of the bed against the wall, when a child's wailing cry made her start up. The knocking stopped but the wailing grew louder and she could hear Arabella's protesting voice. Unable to bear it any longer she went to investigate.

Mathew was red-faced and roaring as his brother berated him. Harriet had retreated to the corner of the room and huddled on the floor, whimpering.

'Whatever is going on in here?' Susannah asked.

'Mathew's wet the bed again,' said John, 'and my nightshirt is wet, too.'

Cornelius appeared in the doorway, his mouth set in a thin line. 'Susannah, will you settle the children?'

She noticed that his nightshirt was on inside out and there was no sign of his nightcap. 'Surely Arabella will want to tend to them?' she asked.

'I wish her to rest.'

'But the bedlinen must be changed!'

'Then call for Jennet.' Without another word he hastened back to the marital bed.

Susannah didn't see why Jennet should be disturbed too. Jaw clenched, she stripped the bed and remade it, briskly tucking in the corners and tugging the counterpane straight. She settled the boys firmly back into bed but Harriet flatly refused to join them. Unable to face a battle of wills, Susannah took the girl into her own bed and fell asleep with a sharp little elbow lodged in her back.

In the morning running footsteps and shrieks of laughter came from the boys' bedroom and a door slammed hard enough to shake the house to its very

30

foundations.

Harriet kicked her on the shin. 'Get up! I'm hungry.'

'Has your mother taught you no manners?' snapped Susannah.

Harriet stuck out her tongue and jumped out of bed before Susannah could catch her.

Rubbing at the new bruises on her back, Susannah got up. Her father's door remained firmly shut. There was a trail of feathers across the landing and when she reached the boys' bedchamber she gasped. The entire room lay under a snowstorm of duck down. There was no sign of either the empty pillowcases or the perpetrators of the mischief.

It was mid-morning when Cornelius and Arabella came downstairs to break their fast. By that time the children had eaten all the bread, tormented the cat, and spilled coal on the parlour floor.

'My darlings! Come to kiss your mama!' said Arabella.

'They have been very naughty children,' said Susannah, almost at the end of her tether.

'Nonsense! They are simply high-spirited. Could you not manage to amuse them for a little while? Come children, say good morning to your new father.'

Susannah watched in amazement as, one by one, the little hellions filed up to Cornelius and bowed or curtsied. It didn't surprise her, however, when a few minutes later she saw John stick his tongue out at her father's back.

'Susannah,' said Arabella after she had breakfasted off a beaker of ale and some stale eel pie, 'I will have the household keys and account

31

books, if you please.'

'I beg your pardon?'

'The keys. And the accounts. I shall, of course, be taking control of the household affairs.'

Susannah laughed, incredulous. 'But I have been mistress of this household since I was fifteen years old!'

'There can be only one mistress and I am your father's wife.' Arabella's pointed little chin lifted.

'Father?' Susannah turned to her father. 'Surely you don't really mean to take the keys away from me?'

'My dear, of course you must hand them to Arabella.'

'But . . .' She was unable to speak with the shock of his betrayal.

'You may help Arabella until she finds out how we go on here.'

'That won't be necessary, Cornelius. I have my own way of going about things.'

'As you wish, my dear.'

Susannah watched him drop a kiss onto the top of his bride's head and the foolish, adoring expression on his face made her stomach rebel just as if she had eaten meat on the turn.

Arabella held out her hand to Susannah, a glitter of triumph in her ice-blue eyes.

Shaking with rage and distress in equal measure, Susannah loosed her mother's chatelaine from about her waist and slowly held out the keys.

'I shall start by inspecting the store cupboards,' said Arabella. 'I have no intention of breakfasting on stale pie every morning.'

'That wouldn't have been necessary if your children hadn't been so greedy with the bread,' retorted Susannah, stung by the injustice of her comment.

'I can see that you have a lot to learn,' said Arabella with a flinty smile. 'Of course, since you are a spinster with no children of your own you cannot be expected to know how to manage a family home. Children grow quickly and there must always be plenty of bread.'

'There *was* plenty of bread. Your children ate their fill and then hurled the rest at poor Tibby until she was so terrified she ran up the chimney and burned her tail. Perhaps *you* have something to learn about governing your children?' Susannah clenched her fists as her wretchedness turned to temper.

'Cornelius!' Arabella appealed to her husband, her lip quivering. 'You cannot allow your daughter to insult me like this!'

'I must go and see to the shop,' said Cornelius, retreating. 'Ned is not to be trusted on his own for too long.' He made a hasty exit.

Deep inside her breast Susannah felt a cold, hard stone of disbelief. How could her beloved father, her companion for so many years, suddenly care so little for her?

Arabella waited until the door had closed and then turned to Susannah, hands on her hips and fury in her eyes. 'Don't you tangle with me,' she spat, 'or you'll be sorry for it! I didn't come this far to have a stuck-up miss like you get in my way. I'm telling you now that you'd best do as I bid you if you are to stay in this house. I will *not* be troubled by your tantrums. *Do you understand me?*'

Susannah was so shocked to hear anyone in her home shouting like a fishwife that it rendered her speechless.

'God knows,' muttered Arabella as she turned away from Susannah, 'everything is difficult enough without that.'

Stumbling in distress, Susannah ran from the room.

*   *   *

Some weeks later, Susannah called on Martha.

Martha, six months into her pregnancy and as rounded and neat as a turtledove, ushered her into the parlour.

'It is all far worse than I could have imagined,' Susannah said, cocking her head and listening to the sound of shrieks and stamping feet on the floorboards above. She had been forced to bring Mathew, John and Harriet with her since Arabella pronounced herself far too busy to care for them and now they rampaged about upstairs, picking quarrels with Martha's children.

'Can you not persuade your father to change his mind and allow your stepmother to hire a nursemaid?' asked Martha. She sat with her feet up on a footstool, mending her husband's shirt.

'We have no room for another maid. The house is bursting at the seams as it is. Besides, Father says he cannot see the need for it and as long as Arabella can foist the children off onto me or poor Jennet she has no need of a nursemaid either.' Susannah was fairly burning with indignation. 'He'd soon change his mind if *he* had the care of them. I had no idea children could be so disobedient.'

Martha shrugged. 'They must be taught from the beginning to respect their elders.'

34

'Arabella will not allow the use of the birch.'

'Then I fear you have a hard road ahead of you.'

'It's not just the children.' Susannah heard the quaver in her voice and blinked back tears. 'Arabella begged for a pair of virginals and Father went straight out to purchase them for her. As a child I always wanted to learn but he said it was an unnecessary expense. Now he sits at her side every evening looking down the front of her bodice and caressing her shoulders while she plays.'

'They are newly married, Susannah. Perhaps you should spend more time with your friends and leave them to be alone together.'

'What friends? Apart from you, of course? I've always spent my free time with Father.'

'Then it's time you made more friends of your own.'

'How do you suggest I do that? I'm either in the shop all day or minding those little villains. I can hardly roam the streets at night looking for friends or go into alehouses by myself, can I?' She rubbed her eyes, gritty with exhaustion. 'Harriet has taken up residence in my bed and I'm nearly kicked to death! *And* I'm expected to rise during the night to change the bedlinen. Surely Mathew should be dry at night by now?'

'You must remember that he has lost his father and moved to a new home, which may have upset him.' Martha reached out to squeeze Susannah's hand. 'Poor Susannah! You have all the drudgery of marriage and children, without any of the joy.'

Martha's sympathy was Susannah's undoing. 'It's the way Father looks at her in that doting fashion,' she wept. 'He keeps touching her and kissing her and I feel as if my presence is always a nuisance to them. He has no use for me now.'

'They need time together to learn each other's ways.'

'But we haven't been to a play or one of the lectures at Gresham College for weeks. Father never wants to read with me or have any interesting discussions any more. We're *always* interrupted by Arabella chattering about the colour of the ribbons she is going to use to trim her hat or some such trivial thing. And he listens to her as if she has said the most fascinating thing in the whole of the city. I just want everything to be back as it was before she came,' she sobbed.

'All men are made fools by desire. It won't last for ever.' Martha's hazel eyes were wistful. 'It never does, not even in a marriage made for love.'

'But what can I do? You can't imagine how miserable I am.'

'A woman's life often is miserable and you have to accept that it's God's will ...'

'Please, don't spout your Puritan ways at me, Martha!'

'Puritan or not, there are only three choices in this life for a woman, Susannah.' She put aside the mending and folded her hands over the roundness of her belly. 'You can submit to your family, you can look for a position as a servant in another household or you can find a husband of your own.'

'I *won't* let Arabella push me out of my home! Besides, where would I go?'

'If you were married you would be mistress of your own home.'

'I cannot marry!'

'Of course you can.'

'After what happened to Mother?' Susannah

36

swallowed, pushing away the terrible memories of that time.

Martha sighed. 'What happened to your mother was a very dreadful thing but it in no way means that history will repeat itself with you.'

'Even if I was inclined to marry, I have no suitors.'

'Of course you haven't!' snapped Martha, losing patience at last. 'And it's almost too late. You've passed girlhood and over the years you and your father have chased away all possible suitors so that you could both continue to live in your own safe, bookish little world. And now you're shocked because he has taken his interest elsewhere. If you are so determined to avoid marriage you should consider that if you become a servant in another household you may not be treated kindly.'

'So I am to continue to be Arabella's waiting woman in my own home?' Indignation made Susannah's face burn.

'You have been spoiled by your father and forgotten your place in the world, Susannah.'

'Spoiled? Me?' Susannah wasn't sure what upset her the most: the accusation or seeing such resentment on her friend's usually calm face.

'You cannot deny it! What need has a woman of reading Latin poetry or having opinions on politics? Your father has indulged you too much since your mother died.'

'He has not!'

'Yes, he *has*!' Martha glared at her.

Susannah stared back, shocked by her antagonism.

Upstairs there was a childish shriek of anger and then a thump followed by loud wailing cries. Anger boiled inside Susannah as she ran up the stairs to punish the miscreants. Would her life never be restored to its former ordered and contented state?

Chapter 3

Jennet's pock-marked face was magenta with exertion as she riddled the buck sticks in the washtub. 'I'd like to see the mistress wash the linen for once,' she muttered to Susannah as she tipped in another bucket of water.

'Hah!' said Susannah. 'Such a fine lady cannot be expected to soil her hands with maid's work, can she?' The kitchen was swelteringly hot and steamy and the mere thought of heaving the sodden linen out to dry increased her exhaustion.

'Fine lady?' Jennet snorted. 'She let it slip she come from Shoreditch, like me. There are no fine ladies in Shoreditch.'

It had been three months since the tornado that was Arabella and her children had whirled over the threshold. Washing the linen had become an unwelcome and much greater feature in the household routine. Apart from the almost nightly wet bed, the children dirtied their clothes with monotonous regularity and Arabella refused to wear her chemise for more than three days at a time. Susannah wouldn't have minded if her stepmother had taken her part in the washday drudgery but her housewifely actions didn't extend to participating, merely to finding fault. When Susannah suggested sending the laundry out, Arabella wouldn't hear of it.

'Nonsense! What are a few wisps of children's clothes to the usual wash?'

'It's not just the clothes; it's the bedlinen!'

'Has that maid been complaining again?'

'Jennet works very hard,' Susannah protested. 'She rose at four this morning to put the laundry to soak.'

'That's what we pay her for, isn't it? If I find any reason to suspect she is slacking . . .'

'Jennet has been with this family for as long as I can remember and she has never slacked.' It was true. Susannah's mother had told her that it was sensible to choose a maid whose face had been spoiled by the pox since she would work hard and be grateful for employment and, over the years, Jennet had become a much-loved member of the household.

'Your father is too tight-fisted with the housekeeping money for me to allow maids to sit and twiddle their thumbs while the laundry is sent out.' Arabella's mouth had set in a discontented line. 'It seems Cornelius is not inclined to spend his money on anything at all, except those books he reads, while I am forced to go about in garments worn ragged with use. Your father married me under false pretences! He promised me that he was a man of considerable means and was full of tales of how I would want for nothing, but it's all different now that he has me in his bed, isn't it? I had thought that he wouldn't wish people of his acquaintance to see me in such a shameful state, going about with a darn in my hem.'

Susannah had overheard raised voices the previous night as Arabella pleaded with Cornelius for a new dress of yellow silk. She smiled to herself

39

with grim satisfaction as she helped Jennet to carry hot water from the fire to the washtub. At least her stepmother hadn't won that particular battle, she reasoned, blowing a strand of damp hair off her face. She rested for a moment in the kitchen doorway, watching the children play outside in the yard. The hot June wind gusted over the wall, bearing the stench of the Thames from Blackfriars, and she couldn't help wondering if it carried sickness with it. The plague and the spotted fever had taken a hold in the parish of St Giles. About twenty-five had been buried each week since the spring and by the beginning of May it had spread through the parishes of St Andrew's and St Clement Dane's before reaching the City. Only the week before, as the foetid heat of summer pressed down upon them, she'd seen a house in Drury Lane shut up with a red cross painted on the door. Shuddering, she imagined the plight of those locked inside, left to die a miserable death and to leave an inheritance of infection behind them for their family. She had always loved the city but increasingly she wished for the clean air of the country.

*   *   *

The children, made argumentative by the hot and muggy weather, had finally fallen asleep and Susannah, Cornelius and Arabella had retired to the parlour. Noise from the street clamoured in through the open window along with the humid air. Susannah had covertly loosened the lacing on her bodice but was still stifled by the oppressive warmth.

40

Arabella paced up and down, making it nigh on impossible for Cornelius and Susannah to concentrate on their reading.

'Cornelius, I beg you!' She knelt at his feet, her hands clasped prettily under her heart-shaped chin.

He slipped a bookmark into his volume of sonnets and Susannah watched his face, flushed and shiny in the heat, become entirely expressionless.

'Arabella, I have explained to you, several times, that I cannot simply uproot my business and move us all to the country,' he said.

'You must!'

'I will not. The shop has never been busier and we are making good money. Besides, where would we go?'

'Anywhere!' She pushed herself to her feet and stood over him, hands on hips. 'Are you so selfish that you cannot see that you risk the health of your wife and my little ones if we stay?'

Susannah noticed that she was not included in her stepmother's concerns but was compelled to defend her father's decision. 'We do everything possible to minimise risk, Arabella,' she said. 'Every morning I wash the counter with vinegar. We hold vinegar-soaked sponges by our noses to dispel evil humours when we are talking to customers and we make sure never to stand too close to any of them. And, as you know, I make a fresh infusion of rue and wormwood each day for us all.'

'Nasty bitter stuff! The children can't possibly be expected to drink it. And each and every person who walks into the shop may be the bearer of disease. This hot weather breeds sickness.'

'You must understand, my dear,' said Cornelius, 'that I can be of use here not only to the sick but in providing advice and preventative remedies to those who are well.' He reached for his wife's hand but she snatched it away.

'And what use will you be to any of *us* if the pestilence takes you? I've already lost one husband and you've no idea what it is to be thrown out into the world with children and no means of support. It's pure selfishness on your part, that's what it is!' Arabella's voice had taken on distinctly shrewish tones. 'Well, all I can say is, don't expect me to risk my life by sharing a bed with *you*, Cornelius Leyton! From now on I shall sleep with the children.'

'Calm yourself, my dear!'

Arabella flounced from the parlour, slamming the door behind her.

Cornelius massaged the bridge of his nose and sighed.

Susannah stood up and went to the window, hoping to catch a breeze. The sun was setting and the sultry city air hung heavy and malodorous over the street.

'*Am* I wrong, Susannah? Do you think we should flee to the country?'

She hesitated. Her father's unhappiness made her sad but a small, base, part of her hoped it would open his eyes to Arabella's selfishness. 'How can we go?' she said. 'We're needed here. So many apothecaries have already gone.' A shiver ran down her back. 'Or died.'

Cornelius rested his chin on the top of her head as they stood by the window watching the darkening sky.

*   *   *

'Father, can you spare Ned to go into the yard and amuse Mathew and John for a while? I've spent all morning as nursemaid and there is so much to do in the dispensary.'

'Where is your stepmother?'

'Lying down in her chemise with a megrim,' said Susannah. 'Again. She will not dine with us but has ordered Jennet to take her a tray at three o'clock.'

Cornelius sighed. 'I see. In that case . . . Ned, will you do as Susannah asks?'

'Yes, Master.' Ned, boiling up foul-smelling chopped roots and herbs for a poultice, escaped as fast as he could. Barely more than a child himself, it was little hardship to him to play hopscotch or bowl a hoop for a few hours.

'I'll go up and see Arabella,' said Cornelius. 'She didn't come to church yesterday. This cannot go on.'

Since Arabella had refused to speak to her husband for the last week, Susannah wondered if she would even allow Cornelius to enter her bedchamber. Arabella had amazed her by her ability to maintain a sulk for so long, especially since she was sharing a bed with Mathew. Susannah had mistakenly thought a few nightly soakings would hasten her return to the marital bed.

Although she found them trying in the extreme, Susannah did not wish the children ill and worried about their refusal to drink the infusion she made to ward off the plague. She was taking steps to improve matters. Overnight she had steeped some wormwood and rue in a measure of beer and now she squeezed the juice of a lemon into the strained liquid. She sipped a spoonful but although it was less bitter than the usual concoction she thought

43

it unlikely that the children would find it an improvement.

The shop bell jingled; Susannah glanced up and caught her breath to see a tall figure shrouded in a black cloak and hat standing in the doorway. He carried a long staff, painted red, and wore a white mask shaped like the beak of some fearsome bird of prey. She stood wide-eyed, staring at him, until he spoke.

'Miss Leyton.' He came inside and rested his staff against the counter.

'Dr Ambrose? Is it you? You startled me.' Relief—she supposed it was relief—made her heart flutter in a way that surprised her.

He reached behind his ears and released the strings which held the mask in place. 'It is not my intention to frighten people. I merely wear this mask as a precaution against infection when I visit the sick.' He turned the mask over and removed a small muslin bag filled with charcoal and herbs. 'This is to filter the air I breathe and I wear high boots and swaddle myself in this thick cloak to protect myself.'

'You must be near dying of heatstroke! And you look so terrifying I'm sure anyone who comes across you in the streets will turn and run away faster than quicksilver.'

'Is your father here?'

'He's tending to my stepmother. May I help?'

'It's not a medical affair.'

She repressed a smile, pleased that he now seemed to take it for granted that she was knowledgeable about such matters.

Dr Ambrose shifted from foot to foot and Susannah wondered what made him look so ill at

44

ease.

'My cousin Henry has arrived from Barbados,' he said. 'He has the intention of starting his own importing business and has asked that I introduce him to people who may be interested in his venture. He hopes to sell sugar, rum and tobacco directly from his father's plantation. I know you stock those items.'

'Shall I tell Father that you will bring your cousin with you next time you visit? If his prices are keen I'm sure my father will be happy to discuss business with him. Meanwhile,' she said, 'perhaps you will advise me?'

'I am at your service.'

'The children refuse to drink the infusion I have made to ward off the pestilence. They say it is too bitter and no amount of reasoning with them will make them swallow it.'

Dr Ambrose's face lightened with amusement and Susannah thought how different he looked when he shook off his usual dour and sombre expression.

'The answer is right in front of you,' he said. He pointed to the cone of sugar on the counter. 'I have always found that children will swallow the nastiest medicine if it is well sweetened.'

'That's such an obvious answer that I feel cross with myself for not thinking of it before!'

'There is another remedy that I find successful. Take some toasted bread and spread it thickly with treacle or honey and sprinkle over chopped leaves of rue. I promise you that it is irresistible to children and will disappear in the shake of a cow's tail.'

'I may try that myself. It is difficult to face

wormwood before breakfast, don't you think?'

Dr Ambrose allowed the smallest of smiles to flit across his face.

'And I shall ask Father to make a note of the recipe in the journals that he keeps.'

The doctor had barely disappeared down the street when Susannah heard her father and Arabella on the stairs. Both their faces were wreathed in smiles and she wasn't sure if she was happy or not to see that they were linked arm in arm.

'Susannah, my dear, Arabella is recovered sufficiently to join us for dinner.'

It was quite clear to Susannah as they ate their mutton pie and boiled carrots that her stepmother had succeeded in attaining her latest heart's desire. Cornelius had conceded that he would not wish his friends to think he was a miser and that the yellow silk dress Arabella craved was entirely necessary to her well-being and to his reputation. Her megrim disappeared upon the instant and her terror of contracting the plague did not deter her from making a visit to her dressmaker that very afternoon. That evening she returned to Cornelius's bed and, once more, Susannah had to sleep with the pillow over her head.

*   *   *

Arabella's sunny mood persisted over the next week and Cornelius lost the strained expression that had haunted him. Although it made Susannah uncomfortable to see him fondling Arabella with a foolish smile upon his lips, she was pleased he was happy again. For herself, all she desired was to keep busy, well away from her stepmother's presence.

On the day that Arabella went to collect her new dress the children were left in Susannah's care again. Jennet had been to market early and brought home a large pike, it being a Friday, and herbs from the countryside in Islington together with some new eggs to make a custard. Since Jennet was busy preparing the dinner, Susannah carried the washtub into the yard and filled it with water, stripped Mathew and John of their clothes and encouraged them to jump up and down on the soaking laundry.

'It's not decent!' said Jennet, shocked. 'In the light of day too, as naked as savages. Better not let the mistress catch you!'

The little savages screamed with delight at the cool water on their hot skin and Susannah had every hope that their energetic enjoyment would have the extra benefit of saving Jennet and herself from one of their most tedious chores.

Harriet, considering herself too old to join in her brothers' fun, attached herself to Susannah yet again, like a shadow.

Susannah vacillated between being irritated by and sorry for the little girl. Her residence in Susannah's bed was a constant annoyance and each bruise upon her person from the night-time kicks was a manifestation of the invasion of her privacy.

Susannah had work to do in the dispensary so she gave the child some pills to count and package while she busied herself with the pestle and mortar, grinding sugar and dried rue. Dr Ambrose's suggestion to make the wormwood infusion palatable to children had been most successful and since then she had boiled up copious quantities of the syrup. She called it Leyton's Plague Prevention

47

Cordial and anxious mothers bought it as quickly as if it were hot cakes.

Susannah set the pan on the fire and stirred the powdered sugar into the water.

'I don't want to do this any more,' said Harriet, flicking a pill across the room. 'It's tiresome.'

'It's a job that needs to be done. When you've finished you can help me to stir the pan while the sugar dissolves.'

'Don't want to! I hate it here. Why can't we go to the country like Mama says?'

'Because we are needed here.'

'But there's nothing to do!'

'Of course there is. There's never enough time to do everything. If you don't want to help me you can go and assist Jennet in the kitchen.'

'I'm not a servant!'

'Stop whining, Harriet! We all have to work.'

'Mama doesn't.'

Susannah barely trusted herself to speak. 'Finish packaging those pills and then you can go and sit in the parlour and learn your catechism. I shall examine you after supper.'

'Shan't!'

'You will do as I say, miss!'

Harriet narrowed her eyes and then, with deliberate intent, swept her arm across the counter and scattered several hundred Leyton's Popular Pills onto the floor.

Susannah gasped. Never had she seen such a display of insolence. She grasped Harriet's wrist, ready to give her a good shaking, but the child screeched so loudly that Susannah started, dropping her hand as quickly as if it were a hot coal. Harriet ran from the dispensary into the shop, still shrieking with rage.

Susannah didn't have red hair for nothing. Temper blazing, she sprinted after her.

Ned watched them, his eyes wide, as she chased Harriet round the counter in the shop.

Glancing over her shoulder at Susannah as she ran, Harriet snatched a gallypot off the shelf and dashed it to the ground, quickly followed by another. Powdered liquorice flew up into the air and then Susannah lost her balance as her feet slid through a puddle of oil of turpentine. Still screeching, Harriet ran to the door as Susannah fell headlong, banging her head on the corner of the counter.

She wasn't sure what happened then. The next thing she knew was that she was lying on the floor, the pungent scent of sal volatile was making her nose run and she had a thunderous pain in her head.

'You've had a fall.' Strong arms pulled her to a sitting position.

'My head hurts!' She raised her fingers to her forehead and was shocked to feel the stickiness of blood.

When she saw her stained hands she at once became faint again. Ever since her mother died she hadn't been able to abide the sight of blood.

'Miss Leyton!'

Taking a steadying breath, she opened her eyes and saw that it was Dr Ambrose who had come to her assistance. She struggled to stand but was firmly pushed down.

'Rest still,' he said.

He supported her as they sat together on the floor while he pressed a cloth to her forehead.

Susannah was strangely conscious of the doctor's arm round her back and his warm hand on her forehead. She closed her eyes and leaned against his muscular chest. His skin smelled of shaving soap and his breath was faintly scented with peppermint. After a while, she realised that Harriet's screams had stopped. 'Where's Harriet?' she asked.

'I have her.'

The voice came from near the door and Susannah turned her head to look. A man a little older than herself, with smiling eyes set in a handsome face, held Harriet to his chest. The child was scarlet with rage as she sobbed and sniffed and wiped her nose on her sleeve. The man dabbed gingerly at her face with a lace-trimmed handkerchief.

The shop bell tinkled and Arabella, resplendent in buttercup-yellow silk liberally decorated with lace and rosettes of blue ribbons, saw her daughter in the arms of a stranger.

'Mama!' Harriet kicked her rescuer on the shins, wriggled to the floor and ran to hide her face in her mother's skirt.

If Susannah's head hadn't hurt so much she would have laughed at how quickly Arabella sidestepped to avoid Harriet's runny nose being wiped on her lace underskirt.

'What has happened?' Arabella's voice was sharp.

'Do not alarm yourself, madam.' The stranger smiled winningly. 'There has been a slight mishap and your daughter is upset. She ran out of the door as we arrived and I snatched her up to prevent her from falling into the path of a hackney carriage.'

'Oh!' Arabella gathered Harriet to her bosom,

50

carefully turning her daughter's grimy face away from the precious silk. 'I thank you, sir.'

'May I introduce myself? I am Henry Savage, Dr Ambrose's cousin.'

'Arabella Leyton.' She proffered her fingertips.

Susannah regarded Mr Savage more closely. More unlikely cousins she couldn't have imagined. Mr Savage's golden hair, richly patterned waistcoat and smiling face were full of sunshine, while Doctor Ambrose's severe but darkly handsome looks carried something of the night.

Mr Savage bowed to Arabella. 'I came today hoping to introduce myself to your husband on a matter of business.'

Cautiously, Dr Ambrose lifted the cloth away from Susannah's head and peered at the wound. He was so close she could feel his breath warm on her cheek and she looked away, suddenly discomfited by his gaze.

'The bleeding has stopped,' he said, helping her to her feet.

Arabella shrieked. 'Susannah, what have you done? There is blood all over your bodice.'

'What have *I* done?' She was indignant. 'Harriet smashed a gallypot between my feet and I slipped in oil of turpentine.'

Arabella wrinkled her pretty little nose. 'And what is that terrible smell?'

Susannah sniffed. It wasn't only the turpentine that smelled unpleasant. Then she remembered. 'Oh, no! The syrup!'

The pan was burned black and its contents wasted.

'Your father will be most displeased with your carelessness, Susannah,' said Arabella, tight-lipped.

51

'You know how he hates waste.'

'It was hardly my fault!'

At that moment Mathew and John, stark naked and dripping wet, arrived to see what had caused the commotion.

'What in the name of heaven . . .? I'm only away from home for a short while and when I return it's to Bedlam!' scolded Arabella.

'If you took the time to look after your children none of this would have happened!' snapped Susannah. 'I cannot be left to do everything while you go out buying new dresses. Harriet is ungovernable.'

Mr Savage stepped forward. 'Ladies! Come now, nothing too grave has happened. Your new dress is very handsome, madam, and may I say that only a lady of taste and discernment could have picked the blue ribbons that adorn it to so *perfectly* match the clear blue of your eyes. My cousin will bandage the wound on Miss Leyton's head and so no real harm has been done. And we must all be thankful that little Harriet was saved from a terrible and untimely death.' He pressed a hand to his chest and raised his eyes heavenwards. 'I thank God that I chanced to be here to save her.'

Arabella blanched. 'Was she really in such danger?'

'If I had not been there . . .' Henry Savage shook his head sorrowfully.

'Then I am greatly in your debt, sir.'

He smiled. 'This is true but all I ask in return is that I may be introduced to your husband.'

'He is not at home just now. Perhaps you would come back later? Or . . .' Arabella tapped her cheek while she thought. 'I have a better idea. Since

52

I have such cause to be grateful to you, will you and your cousin do us the honour of dining with us tonight?' She smiled prettily. 'I shall have a chance to show off my new dress and perhaps by then I may have restored some order to the household.'

Susannah's eyes met those of Dr Ambrose and her boiling indignation was instantly extinguished by his incredulous expression. She clasped a hand over her mouth and saw the doctor turn away to stifle his own amusement.

Mr Savage bowed again. 'I am sure I speak for my cousin when I say we will be delighted to dine with two such beautiful ladies. And your husband, of course.'

*　　　*　　　*

The rays of the evening sun slanted through the parlour window making a golden halo of Arabella's fair hair and touching her buttercup silk dress with shimmering radiance. She looked divine, thought Susannah, in spite of the vulgar over-embellishment of the blue ribbon rosettes.

Perfectly aware of the effect she was having on not only her husband but also her male guests, Arabella flirted shamelessly with them all.

Susannah had put on her green silk with her mama's pearl pendant and carefully arranged her auburn curls as well as she could over the bandage Dr Ambrose had wound about her forehead. She knew she was not in her best looks and her head throbbed like a blacksmith's anvil even though she had rubbed oil of lavender onto her temples. She feared she would have a black eye by the following day.

Mr Savage had an engaging manner and, although it was obvious he had no compunction about using his charm to persuade Cornelius to place an order for sugar and rum, it was gracefully done.

'I am determined to make a success of my new life here in London,' he said.

'If you can so easily bamboozle me into doing business with you, there should be no difficulty about that,' said Cornelius, pouring him another glass of wine.

'Unfortunately the plague has caused many merchants to flee to the country and it is not as easy as I hoped to sell even such good quality merchandise as I offer. But I assure you that you will be delighted with the sugar and rum you have ordered, once the *Mary Jane* has docked.'

'And *you* may be assured I will come looking for you if I am not,' said Cornelius.

'Mr Leyton did not amass his fortune by allowing tricksters to cheat him,' said Arabella. 'He is most particularly careful with his money. As I should know.' She smiled at her husband to sweeten the words.

Susannah resisted the impulse to say that Arabella had caused her father to loosen his purse strings more in the past few months than at any time in the previous eleven years and concentrated instead on the way Henry Savage's golden-brown hair curled so attractively against his shoulders.

'Henry won't be hard to find if you are disappointed with your goods,' said Dr Ambrose, 'since he is living with me at present at my aunt's house in Whitefriars, Mr Leyton.'

'I have met Mistress Fygge,' said Cornelius

54

to Susannah. 'A formidable woman; well read and with a lively curiosity. How is your aunt, Dr Ambrose?'

Dr Ambrose's mouth curled into something resembling a smile. 'Aunt Agnes is as she always is.'

Susannah realised that Mr Savage was looking thoughtfully at her, studying her face as if he'd only just noticed her. Discomfited, she tried to meet his gaze with equanimity. She always found it hard to think of something interesting to say to a handsome man. Hastily she remarked, 'It must be a wonderful thing to travel the world. Tell us about—'

'Is London so very different from Barbados?' interrupted Arabella, loathe to have attention placed upon any other woman.

Mr Savage laughed. 'You cannot imagine how different. London is so frenetic. Life moves at a slow pace on a plantation, except in the fields, of course. My father has two hundred acres and over a hundred slaves.'

'I have seen black slaves,' said Susannah, determined not to let Arabella shove her oar in, 'working at the docks or as menservants to the wealthy.'

'I should not care to have one in the house,' said Arabella, making a face.

'I hear they can be schooled,' said Cornelius.

'Indeed they can!'

Arabella sniffed. 'We shall have to take your word for that, Mr Savage. My brother has trained his parrot to speak but it has no real intelligence. I suppose it may be the same.'

Henry Savage's lips tightened momentarily and Susannah was surprised to see he shot Arabella a glance that almost looked like distaste.

'And what other impressions have you of London?' asked Susannah.

'The constant noise and the ever-present black smoke; my face is covered in smuts all the time! The streets are so narrow and dark after the wide-open and sunny space of Barbados. And the drains carry such a stench that I cannot get it out of my nostrils.'

'You will become used to it in time and hardly notice it, unless the weather is hot.'

'I find it strange that such a fine city as this, with the most handsome buildings everywhere, allows the tanning and smoking industries to found their businesses within the city to foul the air and make the inhabitants cough. But on the other hand, there are so many ways to find amusement here. I like the hustle and bustle of a thousand people going about their business and already I have made many new friends in the coffee houses.'

'I should very much like to hear more about your home in Barbados,' Susannah said.

'The sun always shines and the plantation house has high ceilings and tall windows to welcome the breeze. The slaves have their own accommodation and in the evenings after the day's work is done you can hear them singing. It's a haunting sound and I miss it.' His expression was wistful. 'And, of course, there were the house slaves to tend to my every need. Here I have to manage for myself.'

'I wonder that you left this paradise behind and came to noisome, turbulent London, Mr Savage,' Susannah said, thinking that his eyes were as blue as a summer sky.

Mr Savage drank deeply and it was a moment before he replied. 'My cousin will tell you that there is always a serpent in paradise.'

'A serpent?' Arabella's eyes opened very wide. 'How very exciting! As you know, my husband has a dried alligator in the shop but I have never seen a serpent.'

'I think my cousin is teasing you, just a little, Mistress Leyton,' said Dr Ambrose. 'He means that life is not always as perfect as it seems. Indeed, I found that to be true during my sojourn on my uncle's plantation.'

'You have travelled there?' Susannah asked, her eyebrows raised in surprise.

'Some six years ago my uncle needed a doctor to tend his slaves. I stayed for a year.'

'He must be a good master to take such care of his slaves.'

Dr Ambrose shrugged. 'As my uncle said to me, they are a valuable commodity and it does not pay to allow them to sicken and die.'

'Enough talk of slaves,' said Cornelius. 'My wife shall entertain us on the virginals.'

They withdrew to the parlour where Arabella played for them.

It didn't take a great deal of persuasion to encourage Mr Savage to accompany her. He had a fine tenor voice and Susannah couldn't take her eyes off him.

*   *   *

The following day, Ned poked his head into the dispensary, where Susannah was labelling pots of salve. 'There's a gentleman to see you.'

She peeped through the curtain and saw Mr Savage talking to her father. She withdrew hastily,

57

a strange fluttering in the pit of her stomach. As she had predicted, the bruise around her eye was a glorious shade of purple and she didn't want Mr Savage to see her looking less than her best.

Cornelius called out. 'Susannah! Mr Savage has called to see if you are recovered from your fall.'

It would have been ill-mannered to hide and all she could do was to brazen it out. She drew back the curtain. 'How kind of you, Mr Savage. As you can see, although quite well in myself, I have a black eye.'

He winced. 'Poor lady! I have brought you these.' He handed her a bouquet of pink roses. 'Fresh from the country this morning! I came to ask your father if you would like to accompany me on an excursion to Hyde Park. I have hired a coach, which was no mean feat as there are few horses to be had in London any more.'

'I hardly think I'm fit to be seen in public.'

He hesitated. 'Please, do not disappoint me. It would be a change of scene to distract you from your pain and I should so enjoy your company.'

'As long as Arabella is free to chaperone you, a little jaunt would do you good, Susannah,' said Cornelius. 'You are far too pale.'

Half an hour later they were bowling along in the hired coach. They left the leather blinds lowered and the breeze whipped Susannah's curls against her cheek.

'This was a good idea of yours,' she said to Henry Savage, whose own hair was also escaping from its confining ribbon and blowing into attractive disarray. Her fingers curled over her palm as she resisted the impulse to brush a loose strand off his cheek. She laughed as Arabella grabbed at her hat

58

when a sudden gust threatened to snatch it away. 'It has been so hot and still of late that it's marvellous to feel the wind on my face.'

'Hot?' laughed Mr Savage. 'Until you have felt the weight of the Barbadian sun on your skin you cannot know how hot the sun can be.'

'And until you have experienced an English winter you cannot imagine how cold that can be,' said Susannah. 'Sometimes the Thames freezes over and we skate on it.'

'Perhaps I shall see the frozen Thames this winter. I can tell you, I wished the sea had been frozen over when I came to England; then I could have walked here instead of rolling backwards and forwards in my bunk.'

'Was the journey very bad?' asked Arabella.

'Torture! I was confined to my cabin for several weeks in the certain knowledge that I would die.'

'But you arrived safely in the end,' Susannah said.

'By God's will! But after twelve weeks at sea I thought the ground was still rocking under my feet once we docked in London.'

'Then you will not be in a hurry to return to Barbados?' said Arabella.

Mr Savage looked out of the window. When he turned to face them again Susannah could have sworn he had tears in his eyes, but perhaps it was just the wind. 'I shall never return,' he said. 'London is now my home.'

'In that case,' said Arabella, 'you'll be wanting a wife.'

Blushing at her forthright comment, it was Susannah's turn to look out of the window.

Chapter 4

Susannah calculated that Martha's baby would come very soon and she was overcome with remorse. It had been two months since she and her friend had parted with the air as cool as frost between them. Supposing all did not go well with her? She would never forgive herself if Martha didn't survive the birth and they had not made their peace. She would go this very day to visit her friend.

She spent the morning baking biscuits and then put them in her basket with a bottle of Leyton's Cordial for Martha's children. As an afterthought she went into the yard and picked a handful of thyme from the pot by the door, dusted off the soot and tied it up in a thread. She wished that she could make a proper herb garden but nothing thrived in the sour earth of the yard. Returning to the kitchen she found Harriet rooting through her basket.

'What are you doing?'

'Nothing!' Harriet stared at her defiantly.

'You've been eating my biscuits!'

'Haven't!'

'Don't lie to me, Harriet! There are crumbs all around your mouth.' Susannah was beginning to dislike the child for her mean and petty ways.

Harriet stuck out her tongue and flounced out of the kitchen.

Susannah sighed. At least she wouldn't be burdened with her presence while she visited her friend. She let herself out of the shop door and set off down Fleet Street with all haste before Arabella caught her and insisted she take the boys.

The streets were strangely quiet. Each time she went out Susannah noticed that there were fewer and fewer people. Far from being jostled and harried by the press of the crowd as she had been used to all her life, it was possible to walk along with space and air around her. Strangers took care to cross the street when they saw each other coming and each day she saw carriages and cartloads of furniture trundling away towards the west, journeying to the country. In the past month it had become almost impossible to hire a horse since so many had been bought by the wealthy, desperate to escape from a city where plague haunted the streets.

Near St Bride's Susannah passed two houses which had been shut up, red crosses painted on their doors above the words *Lord Have Mercy Upon Us*. The red paint dripped down from the crudely painted letters just as if it were blood. One house was silent but in the other a woman screamed; a high thin wail of terror that went on and on. The sound bored into Susannah's ears like a spike and she began to run as fast as she could to escape from her own fear. Her family had been lucky so far but who could tell who would be the next to sicken?

She reached Martha's familiar door and hammered on the knocker. After what seemed like a long time she heard the bolts scrape back and Martha's servant let her in. She followed the girl to the parlour, where Martha was teaching three of her children their catechism. She looked up and Susannah's heart froze for a second when she thought she hadn't been forgiven but then Martha smiled.

'Sit down. You are very welcome. Bessie, will you

61

bring us a jug of ale?'

Susannah couldn't wait any longer to make her peace. 'I'm sorry. I know you were only trying to help me.'

'We both said what we thought was right.'

Susannah rummaged in her basket. 'For the children,' she said, putting the remainder of the biscuits and the bottle of cordial on the table. 'It's to ward off the pestilence.'

Martha sent the children to play outside. 'I shall be glad of your medicine,' she said, her eyes shadowed with sadness. 'We are mourning my neighbour's family. They were shut up on the Thursday and by the Sunday they had all perished. The cart came for them during the night.'

A prickle of fear ran down Susannah's back. 'Our fishmonger has gone, too. I try not to dwell on the risk of infection except in so far as we are very careful not to stand too close to our customers for fear of it.'

'It's a terrible thing when a house is shut up but I believe the Lord Mayor was right to insist upon it. The pestilence is contained, especially in the poorer alleys where so many live crowded together.'

'I can't bear to think about it.' Susannah reached out for Martha's hand. 'But all goes well with you and the babe? You look so serene,' she said, 'even though it's near your time. Aren't you afraid?'

'What purpose would that serve?' Unconsciously, Martha clasped the silver cross at her neck. 'As with the plague, I place my trust in a merciful God. Fear breeds fear so I do not waste my strength but save it for the travail ahead. Besides, the Lord has smiled upon me. Five babies and only one has been called to the arms of his Maker.'

Susannah envied her friend's calm acceptance of her fate. 'There is a bunch of thyme in the basket for you. When the pains start make an infusion and sip it slowly. It will help you to have a safe and speedy delivery and bring the afterbirth away cleanly.'

'Thank you. Now tell me how the world is with you. What of your stepmother?'

Susannah pulled a face. 'I cannot like her. We had a terrible argument yesterday. We found a mouse had got into the flour crock. Jennet couldn't understand it. Tibby has always been such an excellent mouser that the little beasts never dared to show their whiskers in our kitchen. And then we realised we hadn't seen the cat for two days. It turned out Arabella had called the dog-killer and handed Tibby over to him.'

'Surely Tibby was no threat to your health?'

'Of course not! She never strayed further than the yard. The dog-killer is meant for the dogs and cats that roam the streets and spread the pestilence. It was pure spite on Arabella's behalf, since Tibby scratched Mathew when he teased her.'

'She doesn't sound very kind.'

'She thinks only of herself. I wouldn't mind so much if I didn't believe she married Father for his money.'

'But of course she did!' said Martha. 'What else is a poor widow with children to do? And she makes him happy, doesn't she?'

Reluctantly Susannah nodded. 'So long as she has whatever she desires. I have never known such a greed for fripperies. We have made a new friend and it has given her the frequent excuse that she needs a new dress or a pair of gloves or a silk petticoat, since there are more social occasions.'

'A new friend?'

Susannah's cheeks stained pink. 'Mr Henry Savage, the cousin of Dr Ambrose. He is recently come from Barbados.'

'Is he married?'

'No.'

'Aha!' Martha smiled. 'And is he tall, dark and handsome?'

'Oh! I've hardly noticed,' said Susannah, unable to meet her friend's questioning eyes. 'Not too tall, about my own height. And he has golden-brown hair, which has a natural wave. He doesn't wear a wig.' Susannah smiled a little to herself as she remembered the way the sun brought out the golden lights in Henry's hair. 'His complexion is a little swarthy from years spent in the hot sun but he has good teeth, such blue eyes and a merry smile.'

'Tell me about these social occasions.'

'Well, we took a boat upriver to Barn Elms and had a picnic on the river bank and we went on another excursion to Wandsworth. Mr Savage had to search high and low to hire a horse since they have nearly all left London for the country now and it cost him a great deal. But he said no effort was too much to give me pleasure.' Susannah felt quite puffed up with pride that he paid her so much attention.

'Did he now?'

'We wanted to go to the theatre but it's shut because of the plague so we took the children to see the lions at the Tower. I haven't been since I was a girl and it was such fun.'

'I'm very glad to hear that you are able to put your books away for a little and go out into the

64

world.'

'I do confess I have enjoyed all these social events more than I would have thought possible.'

'And I suspect your Mr Savage has something to do with that?'

'Oh Martha, I cannot hide it from you! Certainly he has distracted my thoughts away from the irritations of life since I'm as wanted as a piece of two-week-old fish by my father and Arabella.'

'Have you thought any more about looking for a position in another household?'

'Of course I have! But I refuse to let Arabella push me out of my home.'

'Marriage would allow you to have your own household, where you would answer to no one except your husband.'

'I've told you, Martha, I will not marry.' Susannah resolutely put aside the thought of Henry Savage's sparkling blue eyes.

'Susannah, for goodness' sake! You *must* forget what happened in the past.'

'I only wish I could.'

*   *   *

Walking home, Susannah reflected upon what Martha had said. *Could* she ever forget what had happened? It was eleven years ago but the events of that time were burned into her memory and she could remember it as clearly as if it were last week.

Mother had seemed well, right until the end. That last baby had been a surprise, a shock even. In the thirteen years since Tom had been born, Mother had miscarried four babies, followed by a long time in which she had not conceived at all. In

65

fact she confided that she had stopped hoping for another child.

'It must be God's will. Besides,' she had said, 'I have my two perfect children. What mother could hope for more?'

When Elizabeth's courses stopped and her waist began to thicken she thought it was the change of life. It wasn't until she felt the baby move that she realised the truth.

'My precious, last chance baby,' she said.

Together, she and Susannah sewed tiny clothes and hemmed sheets for the cradle. Susannah made a little cloth rabbit with lop ears and looked forward to the day when she would sing a lullaby to her new brother or sister while she rocked the cradle.

The first pains started one evening during supper.

'It's too soon to call the midwife,' said Elizabeth.

Susannah banked up the fire in the bedchamber and sat beside her mother through the long night, rubbing her back and murmuring encouraging words.

Cornelius busied himself in the dispensary, at intervals bearing herbal infusions upstairs to ease the pain.

Goody Tresswell called by and pronounced that all was progressing normally. She closed the shutters tight for fear of draughts and stoked the fire until the flames leaped in the grate, casting flickering shadows on the walls.

But the baby was in no hurry.

At last, on the afternoon of the second day, Elizabeth began to push. She heaved and sweated, making deep, frightening groans as she strained.

'It can't be long now, Mama. I'll send Tom for Goody Tresswell again.' Susannah sponged her mother's face, a knot of worry in her breast.

'I'm so tired,' Elizabeth said. She closed her eyes, purple-shadowed with exhaustion.

The midwife broke the caul with a sharp-ended thimble, releasing the waters and making the contractions even fiercer. She pressed down so hard on her patient's stomach that Elizabeth screamed. But still the baby didn't come.

Goody Tresswell's mouth set in a thin line of determination as she kneaded Elizabeth's belly. 'You must push harder, Mistress Leyton.'

'I can't,' mumbled Elizabeth. 'Let me sleep.'

Cornelius, hovering outside the birthing room door, called to the midwife and they had a whispered consultation. Tom was sent to fetch the doctor.

An hour later he returned, not with Dr Quiller, an old friend of the family, but with a stranger, a loud man in a stained coat.

'Dr Ogilby,' he said. His breath carried the pervasive reek of rum. Rubbing his hands together, he belched slightly. 'What have we here?' He peered down at Elizabeth, who lay with her eyes closed. 'Wake up, madam! Your work is not finished yet.'

Staggering slightly, he pressed his ear to her stomach, rolled up his sleeves and prodded at her belly. 'The infant is feet first and must be turned,' he pronounced.

'I've tried that,' said Goody Tresswell, hands on hips.

'It's as dark as the pits of hell in here. Light another candle!' Ogilby said. 'Right, let the dog see the rabbit!' He dragged up Elizabeth's nightgown to expose her swollen belly, with no regard for her modesty. He grasped hold of her, kneading and pummelling until he was red-faced and sweating, while Elizabeth moaned and sobbed.

In tears, Susannah watched him. Ogilby's fingernails were dirt-encrusted around the edge, as if he had been digging vegetables. It seemed indecent to have such rough, dirty hands touch her mother's white skin.

Finally Ogilby gave up and sat on the edge of the bed scratching absent-mindedly at some old flea bites on his chest. 'Little devil isn't having it,' he said. He put his ear again to Elizabeth's belly and listened, holding up a hand and shushing Susannah as she attempted to comfort her mother. 'Still alive. Fetch your father,' he instructed.

Susannah ran downstairs into the parlour where Cornelius and Tom waited with white faces.

'Dr Ogilby wants you.'

Cornelius stood up and Susannah saw that his chin was trembling. Suddenly frightened she ran to him. 'Mama will be all right, won't she?'

He held her tight but didn't answer her question.

Outside the bedchamber, Dr Ogilby waited for them. 'Which one do you want?' he asked Cornelius.

'Which one?'

'Your wife or your child? They may both die but I'll try to save one of them for you.'

Susannah let out a cry.

'My wife,' said Cornelius, his voice catching on a sob.

'You'll need to hold her down. She'll struggle.'

Elizabeth didn't look as if she could struggle. She

68

lay deathly still, her forehead sheened with sweat.

Ogilby took off his coat and directed Susannah to hold her mother's arms while Cornelius and Goody Tresswell pinned her legs wide apart. Then he went to his black bag and took out a number of instruments: a small saw, a long thin knife and a sharp steel hook. He turned away but not far enough to conceal the flask from which he drank.

'Put the basin ready and hold her tight,' he said, wiping rum off his mouth with the back of his hand. 'We'll soon have it out.' Suppressing a belch, he picked up the knife with the long blade.

Susannah gripped her mother's arms with hands that shook uncontrollably.

Elizabeth screamed. Wild-eyed, she reared up.

'I said hold her still, damn you!' shouted the doctor.

'Don't hurt my baby! Don't hurt my baby!' Elizabeth's head rolled from side to side as she fought her oppressors.

'Mama, Mama! You must keep still!' sobbed Susannah as she wrestled to stop her mother from bucking and twisting.

'Don't let him hurt my baby!'

The flickering firelight cast Ogilby's gigantic, hunched shadow onto the bedroom wall.

At last Elizabeth's screams subsided into moans.

Susannah could not bear to look but mingling with the reek of doctor's rum-soaked breath she could smell the metallic tang of blood.

Ogilby reared up. 'It's done,' he said. 'And you might stop that wailing and show a little gratitude, madam. You'd have been dead yourself if I hadn't acted.'

Elizabeth lay still now, her eyes tightly shut,

though that didn't prevent the tears seeping from under her lids.

Susannah, shaking and sobbing, kissed away the tears and smoothed her mother's hair, murmuring endearments into her ear.

Cornelius stood in a shocked daze, staring into the basin.

Ogilby leaned onto Elizabeth's belly with one hand and took hold of the umbilical cord with the other and began to pull on it.

'Stop!' Shocked into action, Cornelius grabbed Ogilby's wrist. 'She'll bleed if you do that.'

The doctor shook off Cornelius's hand. 'Are you questioning me?' He pushed out his chin and balled up his fists.

'You must let the afterbirth come in its own good time!'

'Rubbish! Let's get this whole sorry episode over with and then you can bring your wife some beef tea and she'll soon be sitting by the fire giving thanks that she is saved. And I can be away to my next patient.'

Before Cornelius could argue, Ogilby tugged at the cord again and the placenta came free. Blood gushed from between Elizabeth's legs.

An expression of surprise flitted across Ogilby's face.

'Mama!' Susannah kissed her mother's forehead but her eyes remained closed.

Goody Tresswell hastily stuffed a handful of rags between Elizabeth's thighs but almost immediately they were saturated. She snatched up the bedlinen and wadded it up on top of the rags but in only a few moments that too was scarlet and dripping.

Ogilby took another nip from his flask and

70

watched silently as the midwife bent over Elizabeth and attempted to stop the flow as it cascaded over the edge of the bed and soaked into the floorboards.

Cornelius sank to his knees, buried his face in his wife's hair and began to pray, imploring God to save his beloved.

After an interminable time Goody Tresswell straightened up and shook her head. 'It's no good, sir. She's gone.'

'Damnation!' Ogilby swigged from his flask again and then offered it to Cornelius, who swept it out of the doctor's hand with a bellow of rage before breaking into harsh, racking sobs.

Numbed, Susannah stared at her mother, lying there so white and still. Disbelieving, she put out a finger to touch her skin. It was still warm. Was this really her mother? Dead?

It was then that she looked into the basin on the table beside the bed. A tiny hand was raised, as if saluting her, from a sea of congealing blood. But it was the baby's face which was Susannah's undoing. The eyes were half-closed and the perfectly formed rosebud mouth looked as if it was pursed ready to take its mother's milk.

Susannah started to scream.

*   *   *

Susannah leaned against a wall in Crown Alley, the vomit rising in her throat as she remembered that terrible day. Even after all this time she could remember every dreadful detail. Martha had been lucky so far; she had no idea of how perilous childbirth could be. But Susannah had seen it for

71

herself and the prospect of risking her own life in such a way was unthinkable. Marriage brought children; there was no escaping the fact. She took some deep breaths until the sickness passed and then started walking again.

Further up the alley a man was shouting and it took a moment for Susannah to realise that he was shouting at her.

'Get away! Don't come near me!'

Confused, she stopped in her tracks.

'I saw you struck down. Get you home and bolt the door behind you!'

'I'm not ill, merely a little faint.'

'It's the pestilence, that's what it is, and you're abroad infecting innocent souls.'

'No, you're wrong, I promise you!'

'I saw you taken sick! Get away from me!' The man's voice rose as hysteria took hold of him.

'Truly, I am well!'

The man bent to pick up a stone, threw it at her and then took to his heels and ran away.

There were only a few people in the alley but they began to shout at her too.

As another stone skimmed past her head she turned and fled back the way she had come.

Twenty minutes later, heaving for breath, she arrived at the back gate to the yard. Mathew and John, playing with their bricks in the dust, looked up at her curiously as she let herself in.

'They've been looking for you,' said Mathew. 'Have you been crying?'

'Mama is cross because you didn't tell her where you were going.'

'I'm not obliged to let your mama know my every movement!'

72

Mathew shrugged and turned back to his bricks.

As she went in by the kitchen door Susannah saw the two boys' heads close together, watching her.

'Wherever have you been, Miss Susannah?' asked Jennet.

'I went to see Martha.'

'Well, you'd better get yourself upstairs. The mistress is in one of her moods.' Jennet went to the sink where she dropped a handful of sand into the soup pot and started to scour it vigorously, her broad hips wobbling from side to side as she scrubbed. She glanced back over her shoulder. 'Tidy yourself up first. Your face is dirty and your hair looks as if it hasn't seen a comb since Michaelmas last.'

'I met some people who thought I was sickening. They threw stones at me and I had to run away.'

'Never! People are that nervous right now. Brings out the worst in them. Yesterday I heard of a Dutchman who was set upon and beaten because it was the Dutch who first brought the plague to the city. Anyhow, get yourself upstairs or the mistress will be throwing stones at you, too. The master wasn't pleased he couldn't find you, neither. By the way, there's a visitor.'

'Visitor?'

'Your friend. That Mr Savage.'

'Oh!' A sudden stab of pleasure made Susannah smile.

'Perhaps you should put on your best dress?' Jennet gave Susannah a sly look over her shoulder.

As Susannah hurried upstairs, her father poked his head out from the parlour. 'There you are! Mr Savage is here.'

'Jennet told me. I'm just going to wash my face

73

and I'll join you.'

'Quickly, then!'

In her bedchamber Susannah poured clean water into the basin to remove the dust and tear-stains from her face. Her underskirt was dirty from her dash through the streets and she hastily brushed the hem before running downstairs again. She paused outside the parlour door to pinch her cheeks to bring the colour back and then went in.

'Susannah, at last!' said Arabella with a smile that didn't reach her eyes. 'As you can see, Mr Savage has come to visit us.'

'How kind of you to call,' said Susannah.

Henry Savage, dressed in a gold brocade waistcoat and with a froth of lace at his cuffs, came forward to take her hand. 'I was determined to wait until you returned home and your father and stepmother have been plying me with excellent cakes and ale.'

'Mr Savage has a particular reason for calling upon us today,' said Cornelius, smiling at her.

It was then that she knew why Mr Savage had come. Her heart began to beat as fast as a drum and her mouth turned dry.

Arabella stood up with a rustle of taffeta skirts. 'Cornelius, my dear, I think we should allow Mr Savage a few moments alone with Susannah.' She swept from the room and Cornelius followed with a backward look of encouragement to his daughter.

After the door had closed behind them, Susannah and Mr Savage were left face to face in awkward silence.

'I expect you can guess what it is I wish to say to you?' His teeth were very white when he smiled.

'No, indeed,' stammered Susannah.

74

'Come, there is no need to dissemble with me,' he said. 'You must know that I hold you in high regard? I have been in London for some weeks now and my importing business is going well. My prospects are good and I intend to put down my roots here.'

'Do you have no intention of returning to Barbados?'

'My future is here in London. And to that end I wish to ask if you would do me the honour of becoming my wife?'

Susannah swallowed and looked out of the window. What to say? The thought of escaping from a household where she was little more than a nuisance was vastly appealing. And she liked Henry Savage. She liked him a great deal. He was charming and cheerful with a sense of humour that made her laugh. She didn't love him, of course, but in time she might. But how could she possibly risk . . .

'Miss Leyton; Susannah. May I call you that?'

'I . . . I'm not sure you should, Mr Savage.'

'But if we are to become betrothed it is perfectly allowable.'

She held her breath, her thoughts whirling as if she teetered on the edge of a precipice.

'Susannah?'

'It *would* be allowable, *if* we were to become betrothed.'

His smile slipped and he was silent for a moment. 'Do you not wish it? I had thought . . .'

'I am flattered and honoured, of course . . .' She wondered if he could hear the rapid hammering of her heartbeat.

'Your father was sure you would consider my

proposal favourably. And Mistress Leyton is delighted at the prospect.'

'Of course she is! She cannot wait to be rid of me.'

'I have noticed that your relations with your stepmother are sometimes a little strained and I hoped that the thought of a household of your own might appeal to you.'

'Oh yes, it does! You cannot imagine how much I should like that.'

His face fell. 'Then . . . it can only be that you do not find the thought of me as your husband to be pleasing. I am sorry for that since I thought we had become good friends.'

'We have! I like you very much, Mr Savage. It's only that . . .'

'There is someone else who has captured your heart?'

'Oh no!'

'Are you sure? Someone your father would not approve of, perhaps? Believe me: I do know that Cupid does not always fire his arrows where it is fitting.'

'There is no one else.'

'Then please tell me why my proposal makes you look so unhappy.'

Apprehension made her voice sharp. 'It is not *your* proposal, it is *any* proposal. You see, I am very anxious about . . . the married state.'

Some of the tenseness left Henry's eyes and he gave a wide, confident grin. 'Susannah, my dear, all brides are a little nervous of the married state. I can promise you that I would always treat you with the utmost gentleness in that way.'

'It's not that . . .' She bit her lip and looked at

her feet to hide her blush. 'My mother died in childbed,' she said in a low voice. 'It was the most terrible experience. And . . . and I am frightened to have a child.' Once again she heard in her mind her mother's piteous screams.

'I am sorry for that. But every day thousands of women give birth and live long and happy lives.'

'I will never forget what happened.'

A fleeting expression of impatience raced across his face. 'Naturally. All I ask is that you give my proposal your consideration.'

She resisted the impulse to run from the room and looked back at him with a steady gaze. 'I have, Mr Savage. I'm sorry, but I will never marry.'

'I see.' He shrugged. 'Then I will take my leave of you.' He turned back to her again, his hand on the latch of the door. 'I won't give up so easily, Susannah. I like an independent woman with spirit and you certainly have that. And I would allow you the freedom to follow your own pursuits. I will come again in one month's time and see if you have changed your mind. I bid you good day.'

He was gone.

Susannah sat down and covered her eyes with her hands. Had she made a terrible mistake?

The door burst open. 'You might well snivel, miss!' spat Arabella, her fists clenched. 'How *could* you refuse him? He's handsome and charming; what more could you ask for, at your age? I doubt you'll get another offer like that.'

'I'm not accepting a proposal simply to please *you*, Arabella. I won't let you push me out of my own home!'

'This is *my* home now and there isn't room for both of us. Can't you see that you'd be much happier if you had a household of your own? Though how you'd manage it I can't begin to imagine. Your father and I cannot have you underfoot any more.'

'Then if I am not needed, you had better start looking after your own children for a change instead of leaving it all to me and Jennet.'

Arabella lifted her chin and smiled. 'Well, I can tell you now that there will be a great deal more effort required from you in *that* direction in the future.'

'Are you threatening me?'

'Not in the least. But you should know that your father and I expect a happy event. Our baby will be born in the new year.'

Susannah was unable to contain her gasp of shock. 'What have you done!'

'Made your father a very happy man.'

Arabella's triumphant smile made Susannah feel sick.

Chapter 5

'That child needs a purge,' said Susannah. She was standing in the kitchen doorway and watching Harriet outside in the yard as she defiantly kicked up a cloud of dust perilously close to the drying washing. 'It might dispel some of her spleen.'

'Might not do you any harm, neither.'

'How dare you!'

Jennet raised her eyebrows. 'I've known you long enough, Miss Susannah, to know when I can speak my mind. We can't go on like this. Everyone is out

78

of temper.'

It was true. Despite her earnest desire not to let Arabella win the battle of wills, Susannah had begun to consider seriously what employment she could take up that would allow her to escape from the turbulent household. Her life now was nothing but duty and strife and she was sick of it.

Her mood wasn't improved by the fact that she missed Henry. She had enjoyed the way he had taken her out and about, regularly devising some little entertainment or treat for her. Of course, Arabella had always been there, the thorn in Susannah's side. And irritatingly Henry, like most men, was oblivious to her stepmother's barbed comments, uttered as they were from smiling lips.

Now Henry had gone and there was nothing to amuse Susannah any more. It was only her terror of childbirth that prevented her from changing her mind about his proposal. Why, oh why, could they not simply remain friends? Or be married without sharing a bed? But she knew the answer to that every time she saw her father's melting looks as he caressed Arabella. As Martha had said, all men were made fools by desire. Henry would expect a wife in the fullest sense and that was an end to it.

The morning passed in relative peace. Arabella went to visit her glove-maker in the Exchange, while Jennet attempted to restrain the children from causing complete mayhem. Susannah instructed Ned on the proper use of marigolds in the preparation of a poultice to strengthen the heart in a fever, while all the time she pictured Henry's face and wondered if she'd made a terrible mistake.

Arabella returned from her shopping expedition

carrying an armful of parcels, which she dropped onto the counter in the shop. 'I should have taken Jennet with me to carry my purchases,' she said. 'Fetch me a chair, Cornelius. I'm exhausted.'

'You must take care, Arabella! In your condition ...'

'Susannah, call the maid to bring me a glass of ale. It has never been in my nature to be lazy, Cornelius, which turns out to be your good fortune since you will not allow me to employ a nursemaid.'

'You know we have no room for another servant, my dear. As it is Ned sleeps under the counter in the shop.'

'Nonsense! Jennet could share her bed in the attic with the new girl.'

'Her room is barely more than a cupboard ...'

'You are not listening, Cornelius. I simply cannot manage the smooth running of the entire household, three children and a new baby without any help.'

'But you have Jennet!' said Susannah, unable to contain herself any longer.

Arabella carried on as if she had not spoken. 'If your purse strings are so tight, Cornelius, then there is no option but to take Susannah out of the dispensary and put her to work in the nursery.' She spoke calmly but directed a challenging glance at Susannah.

'You will not!' Horror at the thought of it made Susannah clench her fists as she planted herself in front of Arabella, her eyes blazing. How *dare* she? 'Already I am forced to nursemaid your unruly children while you recline on your bed eating candied apricots or make visits to the Exchange to shop for fripperies. You needn't think I'm going

80

to stop my valuable work simply to indulge your indolent ways.'

'Susannah!' Fury made Cornelius's face white. 'I will not allow you to speak to Arabella in such a manner. Apologise at once!'

To her? Surely he didn't mean it? 'Certainly not!' Anger and betrayal burned inside her chest. 'Has she bewitched you so much, Father, that you have taken entire leave of your senses too? How would you manage in the shop without me?'

Arabella held up her hand as Cornelius opened his mouth to speak. 'You place too great an importance upon yourself, Susannah. Your father has a perfectly good apprentice. I shall be gracious enough to overlook your uncivil behaviour this time but you had better get it into that red head of yours that I am the mistress here now. Your insolent ways will change at once or I shall find you a position as a scullery maid in another household.'

'Father?' Susannah turned to Cornelius for support.

Cornelius's s mouth was set in a thin line and the corner of one eye twitched. 'I . . .' He swallowed. 'I . . .'

'Father?' Her voice quavered in disbelief.

'I am going out to the coffee shop,' he said, looking down at the floor. 'I shan't be back for dinner.' He snatched open the shop door and was gone.

Susannah stared at the door, shaking with shock.

'It's no good you looking to *him*,' said Arabella with a curl of her lip. 'All men are weak.'

Susannah, cut to the quick by Cornelius's betrayal, was unable to speak.

Arabella sighed. 'Let me speak plainly. When I

81

married your father I had not meant to make an enemy of you, Susannah, but you flout me at every turn and I will not have it. The simple truth is that this house will never be large enough for both of us.'

'That is certainly true.' Susannah leaned against the counter, suddenly feeling as if her legs wouldn't hold her up for a moment longer. Below her breastbone a cold, hard knot of certainty began to form.

'I am your father's wife,' continued Arabella, 'and here I shall remain. For the sake of harmony, you must leave. You should have accepted Henry Savage's proposal but you've missed your chance now. I saw him at the Exchange this morning. He had Miss Horatia Thynne upon his arm. She is not so well favoured as you, in fact someone less generous than myself might call her ugly.' Arabella gave a wry smile. 'Perhaps I am not as mean-spirited as you might think, Susannah? I do acknowledge that you are an attractive young woman, if you are prepared to overlook red hair.'

'How very kind!'

Arabella ignored Susannah's comment. 'Horatia is the daughter of Robert Thynne who was an acquaintance of my first husband. Robert Thynne has made his fortune importing silk from the East and if he has to buy his unfortunate daughter a husband that is what he will do. No matter what the price. So if you had any intentions of enticing Henry back to your side, you should give them up now.'

Susannah was silent. In the back of her mind she had toyed with the thought that she could always change her mind if life at home became too difficult.

'In my condition I am not prepared to live in a continual state of discord,' continued Arabella. 'You will leave by Michaelmas. You will find yourself a position or I shall find one for you. I have a friend who may be in want of a companion and I shall make enquiries.'

'Father will not allow it!'

'My dear.' Arabella smiled a smile so dreadful in its self-confidence that it made Susannah blink. 'You can be sure your father will do whatever I wish him to. His life will not be worth living if he does not.'

*   *   *

Susannah put on her plain grey skirt and jacket, hid her curls under her hat and went downstairs.

Cornelius was advising a customer on the best course of action to rid himself of a tapeworm so she waited in the dispensary until she heard the shop bell ring.

'Are you going out?' Cornelius asked.

'I have made up my mind to visit all the apothecaries in Fleet Street and find myself a position.'

Cornelius shook his head. 'My dear, what you hope for is unattainable.'

'You could speak for me.'

'It will make no difference.'

'But why not? Have I not worked beside you since I was a child?'

'It might be different if you were an apothecary's widow; there would be no bar to you continuing with his business then but . . .'

83

'Someone will know my worth and give me work!'

'You were always headstrong, Susannah. But you are wrong about this. By all means humiliate yourself if you must but I promise you that no apothecary of my acquaintance will allow you to work in his dispensary. You had much better seek more suitable employment as companion to a lady.' He turned his back on her and began counting pills into boxes.

Susannah left the shop, slamming the door behind her. She walked briskly up the street, anger burning in her cheeks. Taking a few calming breaths, she stopped outside the first apothecary shop she came to. The shutters were up and by the heap of detritus wedged against the door it looked as if no one had been inside for weeks.

Several other apothecaries were shut up too and she supposed they must have left in the general exodus to the country. She hadn't realised just how many premises had closed. Even more upsetting were the two with red crosses painted upon their doors.

She peered into the gloomy interior of another shop but it looked so ramshackle that she knew this was not the place for her. The one next door, at the sign of the lavender bush, appeared more promising. She had known the owner, a Mr Gordon, for years. Inside the shop was empty but there was a half-mixed concoction in a basin on the counter. She dipped a finger into it and touched it to her tongue. Thyme, fennel, ginger, salts of tartar and magnesia. A remedy for indigestion and flatulence, she guessed. The mixture would be improved with a few drops of oil of peppermint.

Gordon appeared from the back and folded his hands across his chest. He smiled, exposing a fine set of yellowing teeth. 'Miss Leyton, is it not?'

'Indeed.'

'Has your father sent you to collect some ingredient he is lacking?'

'No, not at all. I came,' she hesitated, but it would not do to lose courage now, 'I came to ask you if you have need of some extra help in your dispensary?'

'A new apprentice?'

'Not exactly. As you know, my father has recently married and his bride has three children. There will also be a new addition to the family soon and our house will become too small for so many. Therefore I have taken the decision to seek work in another apothecary's shop. I have considerable knowledge, having worked at my father's side for ...'

'You?' Gordon frowned. 'You cannot mean that you are seeking to practise my profession?'

'Although I have no formal training I already practise ...'

'But you are a *woman*.'

'Yes, but ...'

'It is against God's will to have *female* apothecaries.'

Rage swept over Susannah in a red tide. 'And how do you know that?'

Gordon drew himself up to his full height, puffing up like a toad in self-righteous indignation. 'Are you questioning the doctrine of the Church? What other blasphemous thoughts have you? You will leave my premises at once!'

Susannah stared at the spittle frothing his mouth and hated him. 'One day there *will* be female apothecaries.'

'Not in this world or in my lifetime! May God strike you down for even imagining such a thing! I don't know what your father is thinking of for allowing you out with such ideas. If you were my daughter I'd have you confined to Bedlam. Now get out!'

'Nothing would make me stay! Not if you were the last apothecary in the city.' She shoved the basin of half-mixed medicine towards him, slopping it onto the counter. 'Why don't you take some of your own remedy? It might rid you of some of your hot air!' She took a great deal of satisfaction in slamming the door behind her.

*   *   *

August arrived and Susannah was no further on with her quest for a congenial post. She talked to all the servants who came into the shop, to ask if they knew of any positions in their household, but invariably they shook their heads. So many of the richer sort of people had left London, abandoning many of their servants to scratch a living in the streets. Susannah's frustration and despair increased with the passing of the days and Arabella took every possible opportunity to remind her that Michaelmas wasn't far off.

She decided to visit Martha while she still had the freedom to do as she pleased. She had made a linen swaddling wrap with a drawn threadwork edge ready for the new babe and she set off with it in her basket.

The streets were unnaturally empty in the heavy heat of the August afternoon. There were few horses left in London and the streets were the cleaner for it. Susannah held a bunch of rosemary to her nose as she walked but there was no escaping from the summer reek of open drains. Half the shops were closed and boarded up in Fleet Street, their owners dead or gone to the country. In the walk to Martha's house, Susannah noticed barely fifty people but she did hear the passing bell ringing from St Bride's. The bell sounded nine times, denoting the death of a man, followed by a pause and then twenty-seven times. After another pause the bell tolled again six times, followed by twenty-five. A twenty-seven-year-old man and a twenty-five-year-old woman. Unease made Susannah glance over her shoulder as she hurried on her way, wondering if the dead had been carried off by the plague.

Martha's front door was open and two of her little ones sat on the front step playing with their dolls.

'Hannah. Patience. How are you today?'

'We are well, thank you.'

'Mama is having her baby today.'

Susannah flinched. 'Today?'

'The midwife is here and Father has gone to fetch Grandmother.'

Through the open doorway Susannah heard a groan from upstairs and her heart began to thump. Reluctantly she went inside. At the top of the stairs she peered into the bedchamber and saw Martha in bed, her dark hair freed from the usual confines of her cap.

Martha glanced up and saw her friend hovering in the doorway. 'Susannah! Bless you for coming. I'd so much rather have you than Richard's mother.

I couldn't stand to hear again a minute by minute account of each of her thirteen births again. Come and sit beside me.'

'Oh no!' Susannah backed away, her pulse beginning to flutter with apprehension. 'I simply wondered if you were all right.'

'Perfectly. Though I shall be happy to hold your hand.'

'I . . . I cannot stay,' stuttered Susannah.

'There is nothing to be afraid of, is there Goody Joan?'

The midwife, a round little person with a face crinkled with laughter lines, came forward smiling and drying her plump hands on her clean white apron. 'Nothing at all, my dear.' Her country voice was calm and reassuring. 'Sit you down beside her. It won't be long now.'

Martha gasped. 'Another one.' She snatched hold of Susannah's hand, closed her eyes and began to breathe deeply.

Goody Joan lifted the sheet and peered between her patient's legs. 'Time to get you onto the birthing stool, if I'm not mistaken.'

Susannah, quaking in sudden panic, looked about her wondering how she could run away while Martha was gripping her hand so tightly.

'All right, my dear,' said the midwife after she had assisted Martha onto the stool. 'Push down now.'

Martha took a deep breath and her face turned scarlet.

'Black hair, by the look of it,' said Goody Joan. 'Just like your husband.'

Susannah sat beside Martha, her hand crushed as her friend travailed. The groaning sounds

Martha made carried Susannah straight back to the overheated room where her mother had struggled for life while Dr Ogilby's grotesque shadow had flickered on the wall. But this room was full of sunshine, a gentle breeze came through the open window and Goody Joan encouraged her patient with kind words. Then Martha grunted again before giving a long cry of triumph. Goody Joan caught the slippery little body in a cloth. Wiped clean, he began to cry, loud and demanding.

Susannah heard herself sob as Martha took her son in her arms and kissed his forehead.

'Isn't he perfect, Susannah?'

'A healthy little boy,' confirmed Goody Joan, beaming.

Susannah couldn't speak, her face contorted with tears of relief and joy.

Martha, glowing with maternal pride, touched her gently on the hand. 'See, childbirth isn't terrible at all. It's one of God's miracles.'

*   *   *

When Susannah arrived home Jennet called out to her from the kitchen. 'The mistress wants you,' she said. 'She's in an uncommon good mood.'

Susannah went upstairs to the parlour, where Arabella waited for her.

'Sit down, Susannah. I have some news for you.'

'Oh?'

'You may consider yourself very fortunate. I have found you a position to an acquaintance of mine. She is Mistress Driscoll and has two little girls aged eight and nine and seeks a waiting woman who can do plain sewing and teach the children their catechism. I think you can manage that? You are to present yourself tomorrow morning so that she can take a look at you.'

The day of reckoning had arrived then. Susannah, still in a daze as she relived the events of the afternoon, went to her bedchamber. Carefully she unwrapped the precious miniature from the soft blue velvet and studied her mother's face. 'Why couldn't it have been as straightforward for you as it was for Martha,' she whispered. 'If you were here today, I wouldn't be forced to leave behind me all that I hold dear.'

*   *   *

The following morning Susannah took herself off to Aldersgate and waited in the hall of the imposing town house that might become her home. Before long the maid took her into the parlour. Mistress Driscoll put aside her needlework and looked Susannah up and down.

'I assume you play the virginals?' she asked.

'I am afraid not.'

'I see.' Her pale mouth was thin-lipped and disapproving. 'Can you teach my daughters to draw and to curtsy and how to conduct themselves in polite society?'

'Yes, ma'am. And I can teach them to write a neat Italian hand, translate from Latin and a little Greek and French.'

Mistress Driscoll opened her eyes wide in amazement. 'What possible use can any of that be to a girl? Can you teach them to dance?'

'I'm sure that I could,' said Susannah doubtfully.

'And shell-work and embroidery?'

90

Susannah was mercifully prevented from answering since the door burst open and an immensely fat man in a tight claret-coloured coat strode into the room. 'Ah! Who do we have here? Friend of m'wife's, is it?'

His wife coughed. 'Mr Driscoll, this is the person Mistress Leyton mentioned to me who might be suitable as a companion.'

'Ah! Companion. Yes. Girls need a companion. Have you met them yet? Pretty little things, though I say it myself.'

'No, sir, I have only just arrived.'

'She can't play the virginals,' said Mistress Driscoll.

'Ah! No matter. We'll bring in a music master and they can all learn. What do you think of that, miss?' He beamed at her, his eyes disappearing into his fat cheeks.

'I have always wanted to learn to play. Your daughters and I could practise together.'

'Excellent! Then that's settled. Call the girls down from the nursery, my dear.' Mistress Driscoll pursed her mouth as if she was about to speak, thought the better of it and left the room.

'Been a waiting woman for long?' asked Mr Driscoll.

'No, indeed. My father has an apothecary shop and I have been used to helping him in his dispensary.'

Mr Driscoll sucked his teeth. 'Be able to give my wife a purge, then, if she needs it?' He threw back his head and roared with laughter until his face was as claret as his coat.

Susannah judged it best not to join in.

Mistress Driscoll returned with her daughters,

fat as butterballs and remarkable only for their plainness. They came forward slowly and curtsied as low as their solid little legs would let them, while their father looked on approvingly.

'Poppets, aren't they?'

'Indeed,' said Susannah, thinking that only their father could admire their little pudding faces. At least they didn't look as if they could cause too much trouble.

*   *   *

Arabella wore a gloating face of insufferable triumph at having got her own way but Susannah attempted to ignore it. A strange tranquillity had descended upon her as she accepted the inevitable, almost a sense of relief that she would no longer wear herself out in fighting with her stepmother. There were only a few days before she was obliged to take up her new post and she was determined to make the most of them.

Cornelius absented himself from the shop at every possible moment and avoided being alone with her. Susannah tried to ignore the pain caused by his behaviour by busying herself with turning out the dispensary store cupboards and leaving all in good order. Ned was minding the shop and she ignored the bell every time the door opened since he'd have to become used to managing on his own. She was sweeping the dispensary floor when she heard a voice behind her.

'My, aren't you industrious?' Henry Savage leaned against the wall, watching her as she worked.

'Henry!' Susannah clapped her hand over her mouth. 'Mr Savage! What brings you here?' Her pulse quickened and she hoped her sudden blush didn't betray her.

Henry smiled. 'Take off your apron; we're going out. I want to show you something.'

'I can't ...'

'Why not?'

Why not, indeed, she thought. This might be the last irresponsible thing she ever did now that she had a lonely old age in service to look forward to. She was conscious that she wore her work dress, patched in places and stained with mercury. 'I cannot go out like this! I must at least wash my face.'

Henry took the broom from her hands and rested it against the cupboard. Pulling a handkerchief from his pocket he wiped a smut from her cheek. 'Perfect!' he said, then took her arm and ushered her out of the door.

'Where are we going?' she asked.

'You'll know soon enough.'

They walked along Fleet Street and Ludgate Hill, around St Paul's Cathedral and past Susannah's favourite bookshop and then cut through the maze of alleys until they reached a row of smart town houses in a courtyard off Watling Street. They were new enough that the stonework was still pale, barely touched by the greasy smoke stains that darkened the older, neighbouring properties. Henry escorted Susannah up the steps, drew a key from his pocket and opened the door.

Ignoring her questions, he led her from elegant room to elegant room, even showing her the kitchen. The high ceilings echoed back their footsteps as they explored. There were signs that the previous owners had left in a hurry; dead

93

flowers in a vase, drawers left open and a child's rag doll lying forlornly upon the stairs.

'Well,' he said. 'What do you think of it?'

She sensed he wanted her approval and pushed away the thought that the house seemed lonely, empty. 'It's a wonderful house,' she said. 'So spacious. But why are we here?'

He raised an eyebrow. 'Am I not a man of my word? I said that I'd come back in a month. And I thought you might wish to see the house I intend to make my home.'

'But . . .' Embarrassed, she looked away. 'Miss Thynne . . .'

It was Henry's turn to look discomfited. 'Ah! So you've heard about her?'

'My stepmother tells me she has a large fortune.'

'Indeed. I can see you are too sharp for me to pull the wool over your eyes so I freely confess I have imagined how useful it would be to have a fortune. Oh dear me, yes!' An irrepressible smile twitched the corner of his mouth. 'But I have also imagined how it would be to have Miss Thynne's unfortunate face opposite mine at the breakfast table every morning and how much I would rather it was yours, dear Susannah.' He took her hands in his. 'Please, do tell me that you have changed your mind?'

Chapter 6

Susannah pinned her hair up and allowed it to fall in loose ringlets over her shoulders, in the way she had seen Arabella dress her hair before she went

94

out. She peered into the age-spotted mirror and adjusted one of the curls so that it lay over her décolletage. Anxious green eyes peered back at her from a face as pale as her gown. She pinched the colour into her cheeks and forced a smile. She couldn't see all of herself at once in the small mirror but she knew that the tightly laced bodice made her waist look tiny. She could do no more; it was time to go downstairs.

She closed her bedchamber door behind her for the last time and gathered up the heavy cream silk of her skirts, cool and slippery to her touch.

Downstairs in the parlour, her father waited for her.

'You look delightful, my dear,' said Cornelius, kissing her on the forehead.

'Thank you, Father. Arabella took great interest in helping me to choose my wedding dress.'

'I am glad that you have become friends, at last.'

Never friends, thought Susannah. She had remained steadfast in her refusal to wear the vulgar dress with too many ruffles and furbelows that her stepmother had wanted for her. But they had both made accommodations in their relationship and in the circumstances the outcome was as good as it was ever likely to be. 'I hope that you will be able to return to the quiet life you are accustomed to, Father, now that I am leaving.'

'I fear there is little chance of that,' said Cornelius. 'When the new baby arrives he will doubtless overturn any thoughts I might have had about a peaceful old age.'

'Perhaps Arabella is right and you should employ a nursemaid? The money will be well spent, I assure you.'

Cornelius kissed her again and there were tears in his eyes. 'I do feel as much affection for you as it is possible to feel for a daughter,' he said. 'I am not blind, you know, I do realise that Arabella can be a little difficult at times.' He blinked hard. 'But I still love her in spite of that.'

'I know you do. And I want you to be happy, which is why I am leaving.'

'You are so like my dear Elizabeth. You look at me with your great wounded eyes and it tears my heart to pieces. If I could only have had her back again I would never . . .'

'What's done is done.' She couldn't talk of it any more. As the time to leave drew nearer, a numbness began to descend upon her and it became too much effort to speak. She wondered for a moment if King Charles had felt the same as he made his final walk to the scaffold. In the distance, the bells of St Bride's began to peal.

'It's time. I wish you much happiness, my dearest.' Cornelius took Susannah's arm and led her down the stairs and into the street where the hired carriage waited to carry them to the church.

* * *

There had been only the three weeks while the banns were being read for Susannah to become used to the idea that she was to be married. Entering the shadowy interior of the church she felt as if she was in a dream. This was a day she had never expected to happen. Standing dry-mouthed at the altar beside Henry, with her heart fluttering as if it were a bird trying to escape, she forced herself to breathe deeply as the voices echoed around her.

96

It would never do to faint now.

It wasn't until they all emerged into the sunshine that Susannah really looked at Henry. This man is my husband, she said to herself as a shower of rice landed at their feet. How curious! *My husband.* Until death us do part. And I shall do everything in my power to love Henry and to make him love me, too.

Smiling widely, Henry held her arm and made a great play of introducing her to everyone as Mistress Savage. His dimpled smile endowed him with a great deal of charm, thought Susannah, having the effect of making him seem more handsome than he actually was.

The wedding breakfast was a much quieter affair than at Arabella's marriage to Cornelius. So many of the family friends and acquaintances had left town to avoid the plague but Susannah was pleased that Richard Berry had come with Bridie and that Martha had brought her husband. Henry's cousin, Dr Ambrose, and their aunt, Agnes Fygge, were there too.

Martha, baby James in her arms, warmly embraced her. 'I'm truly happy for you, Susannah. Mr Savage has a most agreeable manner and he's young. You should count yourself lucky.'

'I do.' It was true; she had a future to look forward to now, after the anxieties and unhappiness of the past months. Finally, the numbness of the past few hours began to release her from its grip.

'And there is something I want to ask you. Will you be godmother to James? Since you were there at his birth it seems right that you should keep a special eye on him.'

'I would be honoured!' Susannah tickled little

97

James under his chin and was rewarded with a gummy smile.

Cornelius had spared no expense for his daughter and they dined on steamed bass, roasted quails, tarts of marrowbone and a fricassee of chicken, followed by apple and quince pie, comfits and marchpane sweets washed down with the best wine the Crown and Cushion had to offer. Arabella's children were surprisingly well behaved except for Mathew, who had to be taken outside to be sick since he'd eaten more than his share of marchpane.

Agnes Fygge, a bent and crippled old lady with sharp black eyes and cheeks unnaturally bright with rouge, sat opposite Susannah. 'And how d'you think married life will suit you?' she asked.

'Very well, I'm sure,' stammered Susannah, her gaze fixed upon the old woman's elaborate walking stick with its silver handle in the shape of a monkey's head. Beside her, Henry was deep in conversation with Dr Ambrose.

'Hmm. Not sure I was suited to it myself. M'husband's dead now though.'

Susannah, unsure if this was a matter for congratulation or commiseration, kept silent. Next to her, Henry was speaking in hushed tones to his cousin and becoming increasingly agitated.

'Been a widow for a long time now. Do what I please,' said Mistress Fygge.

Susannah nodded, pretending attention while she tried to listen to what Henry was saying.

Dr Ambrose's eyebrows were drawn together in fury as he answered Henry. 'You must not bring them here!'

'Henry tells me you like your new home?' said

Mistress Fygge, apparently deaf to her nephews' quarrel.

'Oh, yes! It's much finer than I might have hoped for. Henry's importing business is expanding fast, he tells me.'

'Does he now?' Agnes's mouth twisted in an ironical smile. 'Always had a persuasive tongue. Very like his grandfather in that way. Dead now, of course.' She turned away to speak to Richard Berry on her left.

Henry and Dr Ambrose had their heads close together by now, whispering. Then Henry poked his cousin in the chest to press home his point and Dr Ambrose scraped back his chair and reared up.

'*I promised!*' said Henry, striking the edge of the table. 'And now I can fulfil that promise.'

'I'll have no part in it!' Dr Ambrose flung down his napkin and stormed from the room.

Susannah watched him go. 'Henry, what has upset your cousin?

Henry laughed but his face was strained. 'Will always was dour and bad-tempered. Disappointed in love, I'm afraid and it's soured him. But I'll not let him spoil our wedding day.' He banged on the table with his knife. 'A toast! Let us have a toast to my bride!'

*   *   *

That night, by the time Susannah returned from the privy Henry was already in bed and waiting for her. She had delayed going upstairs for as long as possible after their supper, even taking the time to welcome Peg, the young maid Henry had hired, and supervising the priming of the candlewicks and the locking of the doors. A sudden attack of anxiety made her insides churn. But in the end she could put it off no longer.

Susannah's trunk had been placed beside the dressing table. She took out her new embroidered nightshift and hung it over the back of the chair while she loosed the pins and ribbons from her hair. It felt awkward to be alone in a bedchamber with a man, even if he was her husband. She had avoided thinking too much about what was to come, too terrified to consider the possible consequences, but at the same time anxious to please her new husband. As she combed her curls free, she caught sight of his reflection in the looking glass, watching her. She spun round and he smiled fleetingly.

She sent a wavering smile back at him and fled behind the folding screen in the corner of the room. Loosening her bodice with trembling hands and scrambling into her nightshift, she had to fight back a wave of panic. Breathing deeply, she stood behind the screen with her shaking arms crossed tightly over her breast while she gathered courage.

'Susannah?'

'Yes?'

'It's late. Come to bed.'

Reluctantly she emerged.

Henry was pale and for a moment Susannah wondered if he was as nervous as herself.

She kicked off her slippers, climbed into bed and sat up, very straight, beside him with the sheet pulled up tight under her arms. She wondered if he could hear the unsteady beating of her heart. 'Shall I blow out the candle?'

'Not yet. I want to look at you. There's no need to be frightened,' he said, tipping her chin to face him.

Susannah concentrated on his eyes. Eyes as blue as a summer sky.

He smiled at her and lifted her cold hand to his lips. 'My wife!' he said wonderingly. 'We shall do very well, I believe.'

Susannah nodded, a little of her unease slipping away. He reached out and touched her mouth, slowly tracing its curves with his finger and it felt natural to her to turn her head to kiss his fingertip.

She made no move to resist as he slid his hands into the mass of her loosened hair and bent to kiss her.

It wasn't at all unpleasant, she thought. The stubble on his chin prickled a little and he tasted of the Canary wine they had shared at supper. She wasn't sure what he expected of her and sat motionless while he continued to kiss her. His lips were warm and silky. He began to caress her shoulder and then to nibble at the hollows of her neck, which brought her out in goose pimples.

Some of her tension began to seep away and she leaned against him, tilting her head so that he could reach her more easily. His hands fumbled with the drawstrings of her shift and then tugged impatiently at them until she helped him. Her loosened shift slipped down over her shoulders and her fingers twitched as she resisted the impulse to pull it up again and clutch it tightly against her neck. After all, Henry was her husband and it was her duty to be a compliant wife.

'I've never seen skin so very white,' he whispered as he stroked her shoulders. He bent his head and slowly dropped a myriad of kisses on the swell of her breasts. Gradually, her shift moved lower and lower until the tip of his finger touched her nipple. He rolled it gently between his finger and thumb.

Susannah gasped. The most extraordinary sensation of warmth began to radiate out from deep within her.

Henry was breathing hard and his other hand was reaching down to pull up her shift and ease it over her head.

Naked under the sheet, she lay back and watched as he roughly pulled off his own nightshirt and dropped it to the floor beside her own. Wide-eyed, she saw his firm, brown chest with its light covering of golden hair. She bit her lip as she resisted the urge to reach out and stroke him, in case he thought her wanton.

He threw back the sheet and instinctively she curled herself up to conceal her nakedness. She gasped as he kneeled over her. She had never seen a healthy man undressed before and it wasn't at all like the engravings she had seen of Greek and Roman statues. Squeezing her eyes tight shut, she tried to put the picture out of her mind.

'Don't! Let me see you,' he said, uncurling her and pushing her back against the soft pillows. He kissed her again, his mouth hot and his breathing fast.

His hands were all over her, seeking out all her private places, cupping her breasts and even touching her honour, but a delicious languor had descended over her and she lay back, eyes closed and allowed him to do what he wished. An agreeable tension was building deep inside her and she became impatient with him, wanting him to . . . What? She didn't know what it was but she yearned for it.

102

Henry climbed on top of her and pushed her legs apart with his knee. He began to move his hips, trying unsuccessfully to enter her.

Opening her eyes, she was confused to see his teeth were bared in a grimace as he stared at some point over her shoulder.

'Henry?' she whispered.

'Shh!' he hissed. All tenderness for her seemed to have disappeared and his breathing was ragged as he scrabbled between her legs, probing her with impatient fingers and attempting to push himself into her. He had a torn fingernail and it scraped repeatedly against her soft flesh, making her whimper.

He was heavy and the movement of his hips grating against her own became increasingly uncomfortable until Susannah wondered how much longer she could bear it. At last, close to tears, she whispered, 'Henry?'

He froze. 'What?' His voice was hoarse.

'You're hurting me.'

'Don't talk!'

'I'm sorry but you're hurting—'

'Shut up! Don't talk to me *now*!'

He ground his hips against hers again and she let out a sob of distress.

'Damnation!' He became still and sank down heavily on top of her, his breath rasping in her ear.

She felt him begin to soften against her thigh.

'It's no good,' he muttered. 'I must have been mad to think I could do this.'

Shocked, Susannah lay motionless, waiting to see what would happen next.

Henry rolled off her, yanked the sheet from the foot of the bed and wrapped it around his shoulders. He turned his back and lay, unspeaking, in a rigid mound.

Outside the church clock tolled the hour.

Susannah stayed quite still, not daring to wipe away the tears that ran down her cheeks and soaked the pillow. What had she done wrong? She didn't know anything about a wife's duties in the bedroom but surely this wasn't right?

Henry was silent for a long time and Susannah suspected that he was as wide awake as she was.

After an eternity, the church clock rang again and then Henry let out a muffled snore.

*   *   *

In the morning she was woken by the sound of a cart clattering over the cobbles. Light seeped through the cracks in the shutters and cast a pale luminosity over the walls. It took her a moment to recognise the unfamiliar room. Abruptly she turned her head on the pillow. Beside her, Henry still slept, his mouth open and his breath sour.

As the events of the previous night flooded back she relived the embarrassment and failure of the marital act. She had disappointed her new husband in some way and she had no idea how to rectify the situation. She felt gingerly between her legs. She was sore and bruised but there didn't seem to be any lasting damage. She glanced again at Henry, fearful he would wake and she would have to face him. It was a peculiar thing, an act of such intimacy between two people who were not much more than strangers. But in time they would be strangers no longer and perhaps all would be comfortable and easy between them. Meanwhile she was lying there

104

naked and wanting only to rectify that before Henry awoke.

She slipped out of bed, retrieved her nightshift from the floor and quickly pulled it over her head before splashing her hands and face in the bowl on the washstand. Glancing at Henry's still sleeping form, she tiptoed over to her trunk. Taking out the little marquetry box and the pearl pendant, she put them on the dressing table next to her comb, together with a pot of toothpowder that she had made herself, her Turkish toothbrush and a bottle of lavender water. Since Henry still slept, she dressed quietly and crept downstairs.

Peg waited for her in the kitchen. Though willing, she was small and undernourished for her fourteen years, with a freckled face and earnest grey eyes. She wore a vulgar, ruffled and beribboned blue dress with a cheap lace petticoat, which displayed too much of her bony little chest and was entirely unsuitable for a kitchen maid. What had Henry been thinking of to hire such a child as sole servant in a large house, wondered Susannah. 'Does your family live nearby?' she asked.

'They all died, you see,' said Peg, her face crumpling. 'The pestilence, it was. Mam, and Dad and six little ones.'

'When was this?' asked Susannah, taking an involuntary step back.

'Six weeks gone, so it's quite safe, madam.'

'How very terrible for you!'

'Oh, yes, it was! Dad had it first. We'd only come up from the country last year. "To seek our fortune," he said. Terrible sick he was with the purple spots on his legs.' Her fair hair hung in greasy rat's tails around her woebegone face. 'Gone

105

in two hours, would you believe and then the baby and little Georgie.'

Somehow Susannah had the weeping girl in her arms and was patting her knobbly back but there was no stopping her tale of misery.

'Mam was mad with crying and it were a blessing for her when she went, too. The dead-cart took them away by night and the watchmen shut the rest of us up in the house. One by one all my brothers and sisters went and I could only watch and wonder when it would be my turn.'

'But you survived.'

'And, oh madam, I do wish I hadn't!'

It took some minutes before Peg's tears abated sufficiently for her to continue her story. 'Four weeks I was in that house on my own after they took the others away. Four weeks of just the rats scratching in the walls and remembering my brothers and sisters crying and moaning before they died. The watchmen threw me a bit of bread in through the window sometimes and told me to pray. But I'd prayed every day while my whole family died so what was the use of that?'

It was hard for Susannah to find any comfort for the poor girl and it quite took her mind off her troubles with Henry.

'After the quarantine was over the watchmen unlocked the door and I went outside.' Peg wiped her nose on the back of her hand. 'None of the neighbours would come near me and I sat on the step while they smoked the house to cleanse it. But where was I to go? I had no money for the rent and no family.'

'Is that when you met Mr Savage?'

'Not then. A fine lady came by and I told her

what had happened. She said she'd take me home to Cock Lane in Moor Fields to meet her daughters.'

'How kind of her!'

'That's what I thought at first but it wasn't, see! Mistress McGregor had six daughters and they made a fuss of me. Then she gave me a good dinner and a bath and put me in a new dress.' She held out her skirts to display her petticoat. 'Beautiful, isn't it?' she breathed.

'But too fancy for work, Peg. I'll find you something more suitable and you can save this one for best. And then what happened?'

'The next day she said I'd have to earn my keep. I said I'd scrub the floors or anything but she said her brother was coming to visit and I was to be nice to him.'

Susannah had an idea now of where the girl's story was leading. 'And did her brother come?'

Peg nodded. 'Mistress McGregor called me down to meet him. We had a glass of wine which made my head spin and then she said she had business to attend to and I was to stay and entertain the gentleman. She'd only been gone a minute when he put his hand up my petticoat. I screamed but no one came.'

'Oh Peg!'

'But I wasn't having no gentleman putting his hand on my honour and I snatched up the candlestick and whacked him over the head with it. He went straight to sleep I can tell you!' She smiled with grim satisfaction.

'So what did you do then?'

'Cleared off out the window. I jumped down and landed on Mr Savage who was walking by.'

'What fortune!'

'Wasn't it?' said a voice behind her.

Susannah's heart began to hammer and she spun round to see her husband standing in the kitchen doorway.

'I couldn't leave her there, could I?' he said.

Unable to meet his eyes, Susannah shook her head.

'And then I thought; my wife can train her to be our maid. And you've promised you'll work hard for us, haven't you, Peg?'

'Yes, indeed, sir!'

'Perhaps then we could start with some breakfast?'

Peg dropped a curtsy and set about collecting the plates and cutting the bread.

'What else was I to do?' asked Henry as they sat down at the dining-room table. 'She looked so forlorn I hadn't the heart to leave her in the gutter.'

He appeared his usual cheerful self and if it hadn't been for her lingering soreness, Susannah would have wondered if she'd imagined their unsatisfactory wedding night.

'You have a kind heart, Henry, but you must see that Peg has no experience of managing a house as large as this?'

'But I have every faith in *you*, Mistress Savage! And you can be sure she will be faithful to us since we saved her from a life of shame.'

Henry didn't appear to be bearing any grudges towards her and Susannah felt a sudden, surprising rush of affection for her new husband. 'Still, I hope you will be patient with us if your dinner is late or your shirts imperfectly ironed.'

'You will find that I am a patient man,

Susannah.'

'There is very little in the larder. Peg and I must visit the market after breakfast if we are to have any dinner. I shall need some housekeeping money.'

'Yes.' Henry pursed his lips and looked thoughtful. 'Let us have only a little bread and cheese for our dinner today. I could hardly eat another thing after all the delicacies at our wedding breakfast.'

Susannah raised her eyebrows since Henry had demolished most of the breakfast loaf single-handedly. She didn't, however, feel she knew him quite well enough yet to pass comment.

'Besides,' said Henry, 'your father is to call this morning and you will wish to see him. You can go to the market this afternoon and find something tasty for our supper.'

'Father didn't tell me he was coming.'

'It's a matter of business.'

After breakfast Henry retired to his study, leaving Susannah to acquaint herself with her new home.

She examined the tapestries which hung on the dining-room walls and wondered if the previous mistress of the house had worked them or if they had been ordered from the Low Countries. They fitted the walls so perfectly that she could only conclude they had been designed expressly for the room, even though the bloodthirsty depiction of a boar hunt was an unpleasant reminder of the origins of the roast pork that might be served there.

In the parlour Susannah ran her fingers over the large stone fireplace and the carved oak panel above it. There had been a fall of soot into the hearth and she made a mental note to ask Peg to clear it away. And although the girl had removed the sheets from the furniture everything was covered with a fine film of sea-coal dust.

Trying out a chair with velvet upholstery, Susannah leaned her head back to look up at the ceiling high above her. Intricate plasterwork formed a geometric pattern of squares and circles, some of which had paintings in the middle. It was an impressive building but somehow it didn't have the charm of her cramped old home over the apothecary shop. She couldn't help laughing aloud at the irony of it; Arabella would be green with envy when she saw this house.

The remainder of the morning was spent with Peg, instructing her in her duties. In the afternoons Susannah would teach her the rudiments of cooking. But really, she thought, if Henry could afford to buy this large and luxurious property, surely he could afford at least one other servant?

After Susannah and Henry had eaten their meagre dinner of bread and cheese, Susannah dusted the parlour and then sat by the window mending a tear in one of the cushions while she waited for her father to arrive. The tree-lined courtyard outside was peaceful and most unlike the hurly-burly of Fleet Street. But of course, even Fleet Street was quieter now since so many people had fled the city.

It wasn't long before Susannah spied her father. Ned accompanied him and they carried a strongbox between them. When Peg opened the door to their knock Susannah leaned over the banisters and called out to them.

The door to Henry's study opened and he ran down the stairs to relieve Cornelius of his burden.

'Good afternoon, sir, and welcome. Susannah, take your father into the parlour and I will join you in a moment.'

Susannah kissed Cornelius and drew him by the hand into the parlour.

'Well, this is all mighty fine, Susannah. You have done well for yourself.'

'The house is so large that it is a little daunting. I shall be kept very busy.'

'That's no bad thing, in my opinion.' He lifted her chin with his finger. 'But are you happy, Susannah?'

She dropped her eyelashes, her cheeks flaming under her father's enquiring gaze.

'As you can see, I will be very comfortable here.'

Cornelius kissed her forehead and released her. 'I am glad of it.'

Henry joined them and poured the wine that Susannah had drawn from the barrel she'd found in the cellar.

'Henry, shall we complete our business?' said Cornelius. 'I have some papers for you to sign.'

Later that afternoon, after her father had left, Susannah heard a chinking noise as she passed Henry's study. The door was ajar; inside she saw him sitting at his desk counting coins into little towers.

He glanced up at her, his eyes gleaming. 'Your dowry, my dear. Your father promised I should have it the day after the wedding and he has been as good as his word.' He picked up one of the piles of coins and held them out to her. 'Go to the market now and find something nice for our supper.' He lifted the lid of the strongbox and scooped the remaining coins into it.

Susannah caught her breath to see that it was almost full.

He locked the box and tucked the key inside his waistcoat. 'Off you go, then!'

Setting off to the market with Peg, Susannah kept thinking of the strongbox full of coins. She knew that Henry, her father and his lawyer had spent several hours closeted together before the wedding but she'd had no idea that her dowry was for so large a sum. She should have been pleased that her father considered her to be worth so much but she couldn't dispel the uneasy feeling that he had simply sold her to Henry to avoid discord with Arabella.

Chapter 7

Some weeks later Susannah was peering out of the window into the dark, wondering what had kept Henry out so late yet again, when she heard the chilling rumble of cartwheels rolling past and the bellman's cry of 'Bring out your dead! Bring out your dead!'

A scream came from upstairs, making her start and drop the curtain as she turned to see Peg running down the stairs in her nightgown.

'Oh madam, don't let them take me!'

'Of course they won't take you, Peg. You are quite well.'

'They tumbled my family onto the cart all anyhow, with my mam's skirt up over her knees,' she sobbed. 'She'd have died of shame if she'd a known.'

'But she didn't know and she's at peace now.'

There was no consoling the girl and at last Susannah led her back to her attic room and promised to stay with her until she went to sleep. 'Close your eyes now,' she said.

Peg's snuffling breaths eventually turned to small snores but she still gripped Susannah's hand when she tried to leave.

Susannah breathed deeply, counting her own breaths all the while, to control her own fears which threatened to blossom up in her chest and choke her if she allowed herself to think of them. Hard work was the best antidote to their dread of catching the plague and she had been sure to keep both herself and Peg busy. They went out most days to buy food but so many shops were shut up that the once-frenetic streets had become as quiet as on the Sabbath. The few remaining market stalls were half empty and Susannah was irritated at having to spend good money on wilting cabbages and wrinkled carrots. She took particular care to carry a small pot of vinegar with her and instructed the stallholders to drop her change into the pot to cleanse it, thereby reducing the risk of pestilential infection.

Married life was much lonelier than Susannah had anticipated. Each evening she changed into her best clothes and waited eagerly for Henry to return. Each day she saved up any interesting snippets of news, determined to have a lively conversation with the stranger who was her husband. Most evenings she was disappointed when he returned home too late to eat the supper she had prepared and went straight to bed. On the other evenings he was curiously distracted and barely responded to her overtures. Her promise to herself on her wedding day to learn to love Henry and to make him love her back was proving more difficult than she had imagined. The marriage still hadn't been consummated and she couldn't decide if she was relieved or disappointed.

The fear in the streets meant that Susannah had little opportunity to make the acquaintance of her neighbours. Those who had not already left town stayed indoors unless there was a pressing reason to go out. The fishmonger told her that one of her neighbours, a Dutch merchant and his family, had barricaded themselves inside with provisions sufficient to last until the emergency was over. In some of the main thoroughfares grass was growing amongst the cobbles, an unimaginable state of affairs.

The weather turned cool and russet leaves drifted down from the trees in the courtyard. In the afternoons Susannah taught Peg to make jellies, preserves and cordials from whatever fruit was available, in readiness for the winter ahead. It was essential, she found, to keep busy in order not to think too hard about both her disillusionment with the married state and the rising bills of mortality. In an effort to lift the malaise that had settled upon her, Susannah decided to invite her father and Arabella to dinner. As an afterthought she suggested that Henry ask his cousin and their aunt to join them. It would be a special occasion; their first party, and she was sure she could make Henry proud of her.

Peg helped Susannah to move all the furniture in the dining room so that they could clean the cobwebs off the tapestries. It was as they heaved

114

the great court cupboard aside that Susannah saw something glinting down behind it.

'Hold still a moment,' she said to Peg as she stretched down the narrow space against the wall. The object was just out of reach so she poked the besom into the gap and pushed it until she retrieved a small brooch, gold with a central ruby and seed pearls set around the edge.

'Oh, ma'am,' said Peg with round eyes. 'That looks valuable.'

'Too valuable to keep. I'll have to ask Henry to contact the previous owners of the house so that it can be returned. Meanwhile, I'll put it in my trunk for safekeeping.'

*   *   *

On the appointed day Susannah set off to the market at daybreak and managed to procure a fine leg of mutton, three rabbits and a chicken for a fricassee in the French fashion. Henry had particularly liked the last fricassee she had made for him.

Susannah listened out for the church bells and was dismayed that Henry hadn't arrived home by five. The guests would arrive in half an hour and he would have little time to change into the clean shirt and damask coat she had laid out for him.

William Ambrose, however, arrived exactly on time. He was accompanied by his aunt, leaning heavily upon her silver-topped cane. Henry was still out.

'You're honoured,' said Agnes Fygge as Peg took her cloak. 'I hardly ever venture out these days but I had a mind to see you since you've not seen fit to

115

call upon me. Was my wedding present not grand enough for you?'

'Indeed it was!' stuttered Susannah.

'I received your letter of thanks, very prettily written too, but you could have called.'

'I should have been glad to do so but Henry said you preferred to keep yourself cloistered at home for fear of the pestilence.'

'Did he, now?' She smoothed down her black silk skirt, old fashioned but of good quality and heavily encrusted with French lace. 'And where is my nephew?'

Susannah wondered that too. 'I'm sure he'll not be long.'

Cornelius and Arabella arrived shortly afterwards and Susannah was astonished to see how large Arabella had grown in the last month. In spite of that, pregnancy suited her. 'Are you keeping well, Arabella?' she asked.

'My condition is fatiguing,' she said, 'but Cornelius has insisted we have a nursemaid for the children so I am able to rest a little now.' She glanced around the drawing room. 'I need not ask how you are since I can see that you have fallen on good fortune. Who would have thought it?'

Susannah was secretly gratified that her stepmother's eyes were wide with envy.

The guests were on their second glass of wine and dusk was falling when Susannah glimpsed Peg making faces at her through the doorway. She excused herself and left the room.

'Oh, madam, the mutton's boiled dry! I tried to keep it warm at the edge of the fire until the master returns but it's caught and one side is all black. Whatever shall we do?'

116

Susannah sighed, her annoyance with Henry rising. She had particularly asked him to be home promptly to greet his guests. 'Lift it out of the pan onto a board and slice off the burned bit. Then carve it as neatly as you can into thick slices and arrange it on a platter. You can sprinkle it with chopped parsley and perhaps the burned flavour won't be too noticeable. And when you've done that we'll sit down to eat.'

'But what about the master?'

'We can't wait any longer. Mistress Leyton is becoming irritable and Dr Ambrose's stomach is growling with hunger.'

A short while later, reluctantly accepting that Henry wasn't going to arrive in time, Susannah led her guests into the dining room.

'Well, this is very fine!' said Agnes Fygge, her inquisitive black eyes raking over the dinner table. Susannah had polished the table with beeswax and it was set with the best glassware and the napkins folded into elaborate shapes in the latest fashion. The platter of boiled mutton sat beside the chicken and rabbit fricassee. There was an eel pie, a variety of salads and vegetables together with a treacle tart of generous proportions and a dish of roasted quinces. The centre of the table was adorned with a magnificent, double-branched silver candelabra, the candles already lit.

'As you can see, your wedding present stands in the place of honour,' said Susannah.

Gratified, Agnes Fygge settled herself onto her chair and William Ambrose placed her stick beside her where she could reach it. 'Don't fuss over me, Will!' she said.

'I never do, Aunt.'

'Hmm.' She frowned at him. 'You mean that you try not to let me know that you do.'

He smiled and rested his hand affectionately upon her shoulder. 'You understand me too well.'

'Susannah, where *is* Henry?' asked Arabella.

'I expect he has some pressing business to attend to.' Susannah smiled but it felt as if her face was cracking. She sat on the edge of her chair, listening all the time for his footsteps coming up the front steps. Wherever could he be?

'I find it most strange that you do not know your husband's whereabouts,' said Arabella. 'Did you not enquire of him when he left home? I should have thought you would show a *little* interest in his plans. Has he sent a message?'

'I'm sure he has a good reason for being late, Arabella,' said Susannah defensively.

'He shows little respect for your feelings if he has not the courtesy to let you know his whereabouts. And how very awkward it is for you, not to have a host for your dinner!' Arabella's eyes gleamed with spite.

Susannah's cheeks burned with humiliation but she couldn't think of a suitable riposte.

'Not awkward at all,' said William Ambrose. 'This is a family party, is it not? And my cousin's wife is a perfect hostess in her husband's unexpected absence.'

Susannah blinked, taken aback by his unlooked for support. 'Thank you,' she said. 'Perhaps I may call upon you to pour the wine as Henry isn't here yet?' She wondered for a moment about Henry's comment that his cousin had been disappointed in love. William Ambrose would be more than pleasant-looking if only he'd take that frequent scowl off his face.

The dinner passed off tolerably well and Susannah smiled and chatted with her guests, while all the time she felt as if she had swallowed a stone that threatened to choke her.

Henry had still not returned by the time her guests made ready to leave.

'You must be sure to send word tomorrow to tell us that Henry has returned safely,' said Arabella with false solicitude as Cornelius tenderly wrapped her cloak round her shoulders.

'I'm sure he must have sent a message which has gone astray,' said Susannah with equally false gaiety.

Dr Ambrose kissed her cheek. 'A very good dinner,' he said. 'Henry will be sorry to have missed it.'

'Bad manners, I call it,' said Mistress Fygge.

Susannah shut the front door behind the last guest and leaned against it with her eyes closed. Disappointment and humiliation made her want to crawl into bed and pull the blankets over her head.

Forcing herself to rally, she helped Peg to wash up the dishes and clean the kitchen, expecting to hear Henry's footsteps all the while.

By midnight, going upstairs alone, she really began to worry. What if some accident had befallen Henry? Or, God forbid, that he had become unwell? She undressed and paced around the bedchamber in her nightshift. Eventually she pulled a chair up to the window and sat with the curtain round her shoulders while she watched the moonlit courtyard below.

It was almost dawn when Henry returned. She saw him walking across the courtyard with slightly unsteady steps and ran down the stairs and out into the night.

'Henry, where have you been? Are you all right?' She caught hold of his arm, the tears running down her face. 'You cannot *imagine* how anxious I've been.'

'Susannah? What are you doing out here in your night shift?'

'I thought you must have been struck down by the plague or set upon by footpads.'

'Footpads? What nonsensical notion is this? There's hardly a person out on the streets. I merely stayed to play a game of cards with some friends.'

'Cards? But . . .' A spark of anger ignited. 'But you know we had guests this evening. I made you a rabbit and chicken fricassee especially and you stayed with friends playing cards? Henry how *could* you!'

'Did you tell me you were having a party?'

'Of course I did!'

'Oh. Well, did you save me some of the fricassee?'

'No, I did not! And I doubt I shall ever make it for you again.' She turned and ran back indoors.

*　　　*　　　*

Henry was often out past midnight. He was rarely home at all, except to accompany her to church on Sundays. This left Susannah long, lonely evenings to read her precious books but sometimes the ticking of the clock seemed so loud in the silent house that it unnerved her. She tried to stay awake for Henry's return but he often crept in so late that she would only open one eye as he slipped into bed beside her.

120

On these occasions his breath invariably smelled of the alehouse and the heavy odour of tobacco smoke clung to his hair. Sometimes he carried with him a faint perfume that reminded her of the orris root in her father's apothecary.

'Must you go so much into public places, Henry?' she asked one night when he came in after a late evening. She sat up in bed and wrapped her arms around her knees. 'You put yourself at risk of contagion.'

'All my business is conducted in the coffee shops and taverns,' he said as he pulled his shirt over his head. 'It's hard enough to drum up new business when so few people are abroad that I must take every opportunity, however late it is.'

'But I worry about you, Henry.'

Henry yawned and kissed her cheek. 'You are a dutiful wife, Susannah.'

Hesitantly she touched his arm. She so wanted him to notice her, to love her. 'I do try to be,' she said.

'I believe you do.' He climbed into bed beside her and kissed her perfunctorily on her cheek. 'Go to sleep now.' He turned on his side and before two minutes has passed he had fallen asleep.

Susannah lay staring into the dark while she listened to Henry's puffing breaths. What was the matter with her, she wondered? She had at first refused to marry him because she was so terrified of the risk of bearing a child but now that he showed no interest in his conjugal rights she was anxious that he found her ugly. As each day passed in waiting for Henry to come home, it seemed that she was still waiting for her marriage to begin. As things were, she and Henry might have been mere acquaintances who happened to live in the same house. What could she possibly do to change this?

*   *   *

Loneliness drove Susannah out of the safety of her home to brave the streets to visit Martha. The air was full of acrid smoke, which made her cough as she hurried along with a handkerchief held over her nose. Flames leaped from the bonfires that had been lit in the streets in an attempt to smoke out the pestilence. She couldn't help wondering if they would all die of an inflammation of the lungs before the plague was subdued.

Crowded so close together, the roofs of the houses appeared to lean inwards and, at eleven in the morning, the swirling smoke turned day into twilight. Ash drifted down, settling upon her head and shoulders. She broke out in goose pimples at the thought that the streets must resemble the landscape of hell. Passing the churchyard she was sure of it when she saw an open pit with the bodies of the dead exposed for all to see. The sickly stench of corruption made her gag and she hurried over to the other side of the street to escape it.

Martha, as neat as ever in a clean cap and starched collar, was nursing baby James when she arrived.

'How fast he's grown!' said Susannah.

'Mother's milk,' said Martha, her soft face glowing with contentment. She kissed the baby's fat little cheek and propped him up on her shoulder. 'I couldn't bear the thought of sending him to a wet nurse so I insisted he stay at home with us.' Her expression was dreamy as she rocked the baby

122

and patted his back. 'But he's grown so much he'll barely fit into his christening gown today, never mind next week.'

'You'll have to starve him until then,' joked Susannah.

'I'd hoped your new husband would have spared you for long enough to visit an old friend before now.'

'I've missed you, Martha.'

'Sit and tell me your news. How is married life?'

'I hardly know yet. Keeping such a large house takes up most of my time. It's rather more grand than necessary for two people.'

'And how is Henry?'

'Very well.'

'And?'

'And what?'

'For goodness' sake, Susannah! The Lord intended married love to be a comfort. How do you find him *as a husband*?'

'Oh, that. He is no trouble to me. What more can I say?'

Martha pursed her lips. 'Well, I hope he's a comfort to you. And you to him.'

'He works hard and I make sure there is always a good supper ready for him when he comes in.'

'So now you can order your own home and time.'

'Oh yes, I have plenty of time! Henry's importing business is built upon the acquaintances he makes in the coffee houses and the Exchange. He's often away from home and I find the evenings very long. There is nothing to do but listen to the passing bell and wonder if the person who has died is someone I know.'

'You need more company, Susannah. Perhaps

123

you'd like to come and take your supper with us sometimes?' The baby hiccuped and Martha wiped a dribble of milk from his mouth.

'May I hold him?'

Martha kissed his velvety forehead. 'Will you go to your godmother, James?' The baby gave a contented burp. 'And who knows,' said Martha as she handed him to Susannah, 'perhaps you'll have a baby of your own to keep you company before long.'

Susannah cradled the baby's little head in her hand and tried not to weep. Would it ever be possible for her to have a child?

*   *   *

Dusk was falling when the sound of the door knocker made Susannah start awake. She heard footsteps echoing across the hall floor below and, by the time she had straightened her shawl and picked up the book which rested on the arm of her chair, the drawing-room door was opening.

'Dr Ambrose for you, madam,' said Peg.

'Mistress Savage.' William Ambrose took her hand. 'I came to see my cousin but I understand he is not at home.'

'He is rarely home, I'm afraid,' said Susannah.

'I merely called to pass the time of day.'

'Then perhaps you will take some refreshment?' She placed her book upon the side table, glad to have someone to talk to. 'Peg, bring up a jug of wine and the best glasses.'

'Yes, madam,' said Peg, scurrying off to the kitchen.

'You need not impress me with the best glasses,'

said Ambrose.

'Indeed not,' said Susannah. 'But Peg is very young and inexperienced. She must be taught the correct way of doing things. Please, sit down.'

William Ambrose's mouth turned up, just a little, at the corners. 'I'm pleased you feel no need to stand on ceremony with me. So, where is Henry tonight?'

'Who can say? The Star coffee house, probably. Or the Stag or the Crown and Cushion, perhaps. He makes his rounds of them all, talking up business wherever he can.'

'I see. I'm pleased he's working hard to make a success of his new venture. It will be difficult for him as the sea trade is so curtailed at present.'

'He curses the war with the Dutch but tells me he is working on promises. Promises that when the ports are open to all he will be able to deliver the goods ordered. It seems that the Dutch are stealing our trade since the British aren't welcome everywhere in case they bring the pestilence.'

'Then we must live in the expectation that the present crisis will soon be over.'

'And you? You must be fully occupied with so many sick?'

'Many of my patients have died.' He rubbed his eyes and Susannah noticed how tired he looked. 'The plague presents in so many different ways: an ague, a burning fever, a headache or a fit of giddiness. These are all symptoms of other, lesser illnesses and throw people into a fit of the panics if they so much as cough. But then, if it is the plague, sometimes a whole family is carried off in a matter of hours. And then another, who is very ill, recovers just when you think he is past hoping for.'

'My maid lost her whole family. I wonder if she will ever be able to forget the shock of it.'

'She will not be alone in that.' He said no more then as Peg brought in the wine and placed it on the table.

'Poor child,' he said, after she had gone. 'I have observed that the sickness takes its strongest hold where many of the poorer sort are all crowded together. They live in squalor side by side with the rats and there is never enough food.'

'Are you not afraid?' asked Susannah.

Ambrose was silent for a moment. 'What thinking person would not be?'

'And yet you still tend to the sick?'

'Someone has to help them. And I wear my thick cloak and the beaked mask when I go to the houses that have been shut up and give my advice through the window. If I tended the sick directly I'd have to stay in quarantine and then I couldn't help the others.'

'I know that some of the sick pay a nurse to look after them.'

Ambrose made an expression of disgust. 'Often no more than a homeless old woman without medical knowledge seeking to make her fortune, I fear.'

'But I suppose that is more use than nothing?'

'Not if she murders her patients.'

'Murders them!'

'I have seen cases where the nurse waits for the sick to die and then steals their treasures. Who knows if she helps them to meet their Maker faster than He intended?'

Susannah shook her head in disbelief. 'The world is no longer the safe place I once thought it.'

'You only have to look in the streets to see that. But let us talk of more cheerful things. How is your father?'

'Busy. I fear his apprentice still has a great deal to learn.'

'He will notice your absence in the dispensary.'

'And I do so miss my work.'

'But your work now is to keep house for Henry.'

'Yes.' She restrained herself from saying that it seemed something of a waste of time keeping house for a man who was rarely there. She changed the subject. 'When he was young, Father wanted to be a doctor, like you.'

'I believe he would have made an excellent physician.'

'Sadly, it was not to be. After my grandfather died, Father was adopted by a wealthy cousin, who had no heir. This cousin intended to send him to Italy to study at the university in Siena but then his wife gave birth to a son. She was forty years old and had been childless during twenty years of marriage so it seemed like a miracle.'

'And your father did not go to Siena?'

'No. It was a great disappointment to him. The cousin decided to reserve his fortune for his new heir and it was much less expensive for Father to train as an apothecary.'

'And he is well respected in his profession by all who know him.' Ambrose glanced at Susannah's book on the table beside her. 'May I see what it is you are reading? A romantic novel, I suppose?'

She picked up the heavy tome and offered it to him.

'Oh!' Ambrose's eyebrows shot up. Hooke's *Micrographia*. What led you to read a work such as this?'

'Father and I went to one of Hooke's lectures at Gresham College. This book is a marvellous and fascinating thing. Do unfold the illustrations! Hooke used an instrument called a microscope which magnifies objects to many times their natural size and then he was able to capture them in the minutest detail. Just look at that drawing of a louse! Have you ever *seen* anything so remarkable?'

'Indeed I have. I, too, own a copy of this book. I suppose I shouldn't be surprised that a woman such as you would find it interesting.'

Susannah was unsure if this was a compliment or not. 'Father and I often went to the lectures at Gresham College.'

'Then it is my misfortune we never met there. I did meet your father there, once. We saw one of Boyle's experiments with an air pump. He demonstrated that a dog could be kept alive with its chest opened, provided air was pumped in and out of its lungs.'

'The poor dog!'

'I tried very hard not to think of the dog but only about what use the experiment could be put to in the saving of human life. Your father and I had a prolonged discussion on the subject.'

'Father loves a good argument of that kind, taking first one side and then the other.'

'And he has passed on his love of learning to you.'

'He always says knowledge is strength.'

Downstairs, the front door slammed and booted feet clattered across the hall and then up the stairs.

Susannah recognised Henry's footsteps and suppressed a pang of disappointment that he had arrived to interrupt such an interesting discussion.

The drawing-room door opened and Henry strode in to clap his cousin on the shoulder. 'Will! What brings you here?'

'I came to call on you and since you were not at home your wife has been entertaining me with a drawing of a louse.'

'Oh that! She showed it to me, too. Makes me itch just to look at it.'

'Curious, though, don't you think?'

'I've just come from a cock fight in Shoe Lane. That's much more my idea of entertainment!'

*   *   *

Susannah was in the garden folding the washing when she saw her father come running up the path towards her.

'This is a pleasant surprise!' she said.

'Oh, Susannah, a terrible thing . . .'

Cornelius's wig was awry and his face was wet with tears.

'Whatever is the matter?' she asked. She clasped her hand to her breast. 'Not Arabella?'

'No, no. Not that, thank the Lord. It's Richard.'

'Richard Berry?'

'My dear old friend . . .' His face crumpled and suddenly he looked every one of his fifty-six years. 'I went to call upon him this morning but as I drew near to his house I saw the cross on the door. I shouted up at the windows but they were tight shut. And then a woman in the house next door called out to me. They took Richard and Bridie away on the dead-cart last night!'

'Oh, no!'

'My oldest friend . . . gone! I can hardly believe it to be true. And poor Bridie, as true a wife as any man could wish for.'

He began to shake with the shock of it and she took him inside to warm him by the kitchen fire and make him a calming draught of camomile tea.

'It's a dreadful thing,' she said, hardly able to believe that it was true. 'Richard was always like an uncle to me, full of tricks and games. And Bridie was so kind after Mother died.'

Cornelius sipped the hot infusion. 'Your dear mother was fond of Richard and Bridie, too. We had some fine times together when we were all young.'

Later, when he had talked at length about his recollections of the youthful pranks they had played upon each other, he was calm again.

'I must go home. Arabella will be worried.' He sighed. 'But I confess I am enjoying the tranquil peace of your kitchen. There is nowhere to escape the constant clamour at home. I had not realised how much disturbance three small children can make. You and your brother were biddable children, always able to amuse yourselves.'

'Modern children are allowed more latitude, I think.'

'But is that a good thing?' asked Cornelius gloomily.

'I shall walk home with you,' said Susannah.

'I would be glad of your company.'

'Then you shall have it.' She tucked her father's hand into the crook of her arm and they set off.

Ned opened the shop door for them when he saw them coming.

'How are you, Ned?' asked Susannah.

'Well, thank you, miss.' He coloured beetroot and stuttered, 'Sorry ... madam.'

Susannah stopped inside the door, closed her eyes and inhaled deeply. How she had missed that aroma! Amongst the multitude of mingled scents she could recognise wintergreen and oil of cloves, sulphur and turpentine, lavender and liquorice. A fire flickered in the grate to dispel the autumn chill and the great pestle and mortar was in its usual place next to the jar of leeches. The apothecary shop was exactly as she remembered it.

'Let us find Arabella and tell her the sad news,' said Cornelius.

They found her upstairs in the parlour, sitting on a new chair with carved arms and a high back. Her hands were folded on the mound of her stomach and her feet rested on a footstool that Susannah had not seen before.

'Father has had a terrible shock,' said Susannah. 'So I brought him home.'

'Richard Berry, my old friend ...' said Cornelius, barely able to speak again.

'What about him?'

'He's dead!' said Cornelius in tragic tones. 'Visited by the plague. Carried Bridie off, too.'Arabella drew in her breath sharply. 'I trust you didn't go near them? I cannot have you in the house if you are infected. Thank goodness I told the nursemaid to take the children out for the afternoon!'

'Of course he isn't infected,' said Susannah. 'Richard and Bridie were taken away before Father even arrived at their house.'

'Still, I'll thank you not to come too close, sir! I will not risk my health.'

'There is no risk, Arabella,' said Cornelius, sitting down heavily.

'Are you quite sure?'

'Yes, my dear, I'm sure.'

Arabella sniffed. 'I never did like that Richard Berry. He played a terrible trick on us at our wedding with that pie full of birds. Most unseemly. He was a bad influence on you, Cornelius.'

He bowed his head and said nothing while Susannah gritted her teeth and resisted the impulse to slap her stepmother's face.

'Well, Susannah, what do you think of the changes I've made?' said Arabella.

Susannah glanced at her father who sat with his eyes closed. 'Changes?'

'Really, even you must have noticed the improvements I've made to this room!'

Susannah looked around her and her mouth fell open. She had been so concerned for her father that until then she hadn't noticed her surroundings. Everything was different. The old honey-coloured panelling that she used to polish lovingly with beeswax had been clumsily painted to resemble the now more fashionable walnut, a tapestry in crude shades of red and blue hung on one wall and every piece of furniture that she had grown up with had been banished. The new furniture was in the Chinese style, lacquered a bright red, and it sat awkwardly in the small parlour. 'What have you done?' she said at last.

'If I am to be forced to live over a shop in cramped conditions, I will at least have some new furnishings. Just because you live in an opulent new home don't think that other people are inferior to you.'

132

'I don't!'

'Arabella admired the tapestries in your dining room,' said Cornelius. 'And I promised her that she could choose new furnishings to her own taste.'

Susannah swallowed. 'Yes, I can see that. What happened to the cushion covers that my mother worked? And the samplers?'

'I let the maids have the samplers in the attics. The cushion covers were shabby and I threw them away.'

'I see.' She looked at her father who stared at her, beseeching her with his eyes not to make a scene. She took a deep breath. 'I can see that your new furnishings suit you perfectly and I hope they bring you joy.' She stood up. 'And now I think it's time I returned home.'

Home, she thought, as she walked along Fleet Street. The word conjured up all the images of her childhood and the memories of her mother and the scents of lavender and baking. Home certainly wasn't the new house she lived in with Henry and it would never again be the rooms over the shop that Arabella had made her own. Misery engulfed her. So where *is* my home? she wondered.

Into Darkness

November 1665

Chapter 8

Something started Susannah awake in the middle of the night. She sat up in bed and stared into the darkness, listening. Someone was sobbing. The door to the bedchamber was ajar and a candle still burned in the corridor, where she had left it to light Henry to bed. Pulling her wrap round her shoulders she went to investigate. The door to Henry's study was open and, following the sound of weeping, she looked inside.

Henry sat in the shadows, his head down on his arms.

'Henry! Whatever is the matter?'

He sat up and wiped his eyes on his cuff but didn't answer her.

'What is it?'

He looked at her, his bottom lip trembling.

She ran to him and took him in her arms. 'Tell me!'

'It's nothing!'

'Of course it is! You can tell me, I am your wife, after all.' She kissed his forehead and was overwhelmed with a sudden tenderness for him as she rocked him against her breast.

He began to weep again, his head on her shoulder as she stroked his hair. Hot tears soaked into her nightshift.

'I'm so homesick!' he sobbed.

'But you *are* home.'

'No, my *real* home in Barbados!'

'This is your home now,' Susannah soothed.

'This!' His voice was full of disgust. 'This

137

damnable country is so damp and plague-stricken and the house so quiet and cold that I cannot bear to spend time here.'

'I thought . . . I thought you stayed away because you have to seek new business?'

'This house chills me in spirit as well as body.'

Cut to the quick, Susannah defended herself. 'I do my very best to make it welcoming for you.'

'It's not your fault.' He rubbed his face dry with the back of his hand. 'It's just so different from what I'm used to. I wish I could take you to see the Savage Plantation so you could feel the heat soaking into your bones. It feels as if the very sun is inside you. Then', he drew a ragged breath, 'in the evenings the whistling frogs fill the air with their song, which sounds like the music of a thousand flutes. But most of all I miss hearing the slaves singing in the night. The men have deep voices as rich as the molasses they make from the sugar cane and the women join in with such sweet harmony. When I was a little child I used to sleep with my nursemaid and if I woke she would sing one of those plaintive melodies and rock me until I fell asleep, my head pillowed on her warm breast. I miss it all so much!'

'I had not realised you were so homesick.'

'It eats into my very soul that I can never return.'

'But why did you leave, if you loved it so?'

Henry hesitated. 'My father and I do not see eye to eye. He will never understand . . .'

He looked as sad and lost as a small boy and Susannah wanted nothing more than to kiss his troubles away.

'It's impossible for you to imagine how it is at home,' he sniffed. 'The plantation has made my family rich but at such a cost! At first my father used indentured servants from England but he soon discovered that if he used slaves they could work in the heat of the fields for much longer. And they were cheap.'

'I remember you said that they could be trained.'

'Are they not people just like us?'

'Like us? I don't know. I never imagined ...'

'Neither did my father. But the slaves have souls, just as we do. He buys and sells them like animals but I *know* them. Not the men in the fields, perhaps, but the house slaves. Yes, of course there are some stupid or dishonest slaves but you cannot tell me that there aren't Englishmen like that too?'

'Why, no, of course not.'

'Some of the house slaves were my childhood companions. Erasmus learned his lessons at my side and can write as fair a hand as my own. My father was angry when he found out, of course, and had him beaten. And his sister, Phoebe, sweet Phoebe, was always full of laughter and song. I begged Father to free them both but he only laughed. Poor Phoebe and Erasmus; it wasn't their fault they were born slaves. And, oh Susannah, how I miss them!' he whispered, his voice full of longing.

'Perhaps I can understand a little of your distress. I too have left a home I loved.'

'But that's quite different! You can go back and visit whenever you want to.'

Cold fingers ran down Susannah's spine as she remembered her stepmother's refurbished parlour. 'I cannot. The home I loved exists only in my memories now.'

'And mine.'

Henry's misery added to her own and Susannah

139

felt close to tears herself. But perhaps, in time, she and her husband would be able to comfort each other?

*   *   *

Henry's mood didn't improve as the weather turned foggy and frosty. The long nights and sunless days crushed his spirits and Susannah and Peg were kept fully occupied in tending the fires. The high ceilings, which had made the house so light and airy in the summer, seemed to suck the heat out of the rooms, leaving them all shivering.

In the dining room, Henry stirred the fire with the poker as it sulked in the grate.

'What the devil's the matter with this fire, Susannah?'

'The coal is wet. It's difficult to buy good fuel since our coal merchant went to the plague pit. The new man doesn't know us and isn't prepared to do us any favours.'

'We'll freeze to death if he isn't more obliging.'

'He might be more obliging if you settled his bill.'

Henry blew on his hands. 'I'd never have come to this wretched country if I'd known it was likely to turn a man's blood to ice in his veins.'

Peg, her face pinched with the cold, pushed open the door and carried in the soup tureen.

The draught from the open door caused Henry to shiver convulsively. 'God dammit, girl, close the door behind you, can't you?' He sneezed suddenly. 'I knew it!' he said. 'I'm sickening for something. My head aches and I'm shivering so much that I'm likely to shake my teeth out.' He sneezed violently again, four times in succession.

Peg stared at him in horror before letting out a wail and dropping the tureen with a crash to the floor. 'It's the pestilence! You've caught the pestilence like my mam and dad! We're all going to die!'

Susannah's heart missed a beat. 'Of course it's not the pestilence! Your master has merely taken a chill.' She picked up the broken pieces of the soup tureen and held them out to the girl. 'Go and fetch a cloth; there's soup halfway up the walls.'

Peg squealed and retreated to the corner of the room, her hands held up protectively in front of her face. 'Go away! Don't come near me! I don't want to die!'

'For goodness' sake, Peg! Calm down and do as you are bid.'

But there was no placating the girl and she fled to barricade herself in the kitchen.

After a while Susannah gave up pleading with her through the keyhole and returned to the dining room. She found Henry huddled up in a chair by the fire, his face ashen, and she felt the first stirrings of fear.

'Could she be right, Susannah? Have I got the plague?'

Hesitating only a moment, she lightly touched Henry's forehead. 'I don't think you're ill enough for that.'

'But it can worsen very quickly. My back aches and my head throbs.'

'I'm sure it's only a chill,' said Susannah with more confidence than she felt. She took a deep breath and repressed the urge to run far away from any potential sickness. 'But perhaps we should take some precautions. It wouldn't be fair to risk anyone

141

else's health, would it?'

* * *

For several days Henry was in a state of panic, spending hours examining himself for pestilential tokens and railing at the business that forced him to spend too much time in alehouses and coffee shops. Secretly Susannah was worried too and sent for Dr Ambrose. He came at once and Susannah made him stand on the front doorstep while she kept her distance from him in the hall. He listened gravely as she described Henry's symptoms.

'Time will tell,' he said. 'Keep a close eye on him but I suspect that if it is the plague there would have been more obvious manifestations of the disease by now. Call for me if you need to and I'll come at once.'

By the fifth day Susannah was confident that it was nothing more sinister than a tiresome cold and came out of her self-imposed isolation. Peg had been scared half to death by her master's illness and would only put the trays of food and medicine outside the door before scuttling back to the kitchen.

Susannah was heartily sick of nursing Henry, who had moved on from being weakly grateful for everything that she did for him to a state of bad-tempered misery. She tried reading to him but it gave him a headache. He couldn't concentrate well enough to play cards and then sulked when he lost. He didn't fancy the tansy custard she made especially for him and there was no subject on which he wished to converse. Nothing she could do lifted his spirits.

142

At last she came to a decision. 'I'm going to venture out,' she told him.

Henry sat hunched up in bed with a blanket over his head and a steaming basin of friar's balsam on his knees to ease his breathing. 'Damn this godforsaken country!' he coughed. 'Build up the fire, can't you? My very bones are frozen.'

'I shall visit Father and fetch some more cough linctus for you,' she said, heaping more coal on the fire.

'I hope it won't taste as filthy as the last lot!'

She took a deep breath, resisting the impulse to snap at him. 'I'll add some extra honey.'

He pulled the blanket off his head and sighed. 'I don't know why you put up with me.'

'Sometimes it's hard.'

His mouth twisted into something like a smile. 'Honest, too! I think I've done well to secure you as my wife. When I'm better, perhaps I'll be able to make it up to you. Buy you something pretty.'

'I have everything I could wish for Henry. Except . . .'

'What? A new shawl or a pair of kid gloves, maybe?'

'No, not that. We need something to lift us out of this fit of the megrims. There isn't much fun to be had at the moment, is there? The risk of infection is too great to make an unnecessary visit to a tavern and even the playhouses are shut. Perhaps we could have a little party? It would be something to look forward to.'

Henry lay back against the pillows and closed his eyes. 'Why not? It might bring this mausoleum of a house to life.'

'Then I'll leave you to have a nap while I visit

143

Father.'

The ground was slippery with ice as Susannah picked her way carefully through the streets, the wooden soles of her overshoes slipping on the cobbles. The frosty weather was a blessing in one respect. The bills of mortality had begun to fall, not enough for general rejoicing but sufficient for cautious optimism. The stench from the graveyards and the street drains that had been so overpowering in the summer heat was less noticeable now, replaced with the usual winter smell of sulphurous sea-coal smog.

Cornelius was out when Susannah arrived at the apothecary shop. Ned was sprawled over the counter, the tip of his tongue protruding while he laboured over the writing out of some new labels for the drawers. 'The master's gone to visit Mistress Franklin with the quinsy.'

Susannah held her hands out to the fire, wincing as the blood thawed in her tingling fingers. Chilled through, she turned her back to the fire and discreetly lifted her coat to feel the heat upon the back of her legs. She smiled briefly to herself at a sudden recollection of William Ambrose doing just the same thing in January that year while she spied on him from behind the dispensary curtains.

'I need some items from the dispensary,' she said to Ned.

He shrugged and continued with his task while Susannah filled her basket.

Cornelius arrived home and his face was lit by his smile when he saw his daughter. 'An unexpected pleasure!' he said, kissing her cheek.

'Henry is suffering miserably with a chill and I came to replenish my medicine cupboard.'

144

'Poor Henry! I dare say he's badly affected by the cold weather. London in winter must be very different from Barbados, especially with such a freeze as this.'

'Certainly he's out of temper with the world. May I take these herbs and a large bottle of our special cough linctus?'

'Help yourself. Ned made the last batch so you can let me know what you think of it. I'll tell Arabella you're here. She'll be glad of the company.'

Running footfalls and a scream came from upstairs, followed by childish voices raised in a heated altercation.

'That new nursemaid has no control over those children,' said Cornelius, his face set. 'I'm beginning to think you were right and I should hire a second nursemaid for when the baby arrives.'

Arabella reclined upon her new chinoiserie day bed. Her hair was perfectly curled and she wore a silk wrap in her favourite blue but nothing could conceal the size of her belly or the puffiness of her face.

'Are you quite well, Arabella?' asked Susannah as her father drew a chair forward for her. She was shocked by her stepmother's appearance.

'My condition is extremely tiresome,' said Arabella. 'The thought of another two months lying upon a chaise with nothing to divert me is hardly to be borne.' She plucked fretfully at one of her curls. 'Cornelius, ask Jennet to bring me a dish of curds and cream, will you? And some of those candied figs.'

'As you wish, my dear. Shall you take a glass of something, Susannah?'

145

Susannah shook her head. 'I must go. Henry needs me while he is ill.'

'Surely you have maids to nurse him?' asked Arabella.

'Only young Peg and she's no use as a nurse.'

Arabella frowned. 'I thought you'd have more servants in a house such as that.'

'There is only myself and Henry so we have no need of an army of servants. Besides, when he is well, Henry is hardly ever at home.'

'That leaves you free to gossip with your friends, I suppose. And I daresay it will not be long before you are in an interesting condition yourself.' Arabella's gaze dropped for a second to Susannah's stomach.

Not much chance of that, as things stood, thought Susannah.

They sat in silence until Arabella brightened as she thought of something. 'Horatia Thynne called upon me last week.'

'Horatia Thynne?'

'Surely you remember? Horatia caught Henry's eye before he married you.'

'I never met her.'

'She told me an interesting thing.' Arabella's eyes sparkled with malice.

'Really?'

'Apparently, she turned Henry down! I'd assumed he decided against her, in spite of her fortune, since she's not an attractive girl. Not so. Henry was determined to take her to the altar but in the end her father wouldn't allow it. Henry was quite put out.' She leaned forward. 'Horatia's father had heard rumours that Henry visited houses of ill repute.'

Susannah gasped. 'Then he was misinformed.' A movement in the doorway caught her attention. Her father stood there, an expression of shock on his face.

'I wouldn't be so sure of that!' continued Arabella with relish. 'He's a terrible flirt.' She smiled. 'He flirted with me all the time he was courting you.'

'It's time I went.' Susannah stood up, unable to bear spending a second longer in her stepmother's presence.

Cornelius accompanied her downstairs. 'I am sorry for what Arabella said to you about Henry. I'm sure it's simply idle gossip.'

'Of course it is! And I suppose Arabella has nothing else to amuse her at the moment.'

'The waiting makes her a little shrewish.'

'And you? How are you bearing the waiting?'

Cornelius grimaced. 'I'm looking forward to having my sweet Arabella back again. And, of course, I'm anxious that there should be a happy outcome. Birth is a dangerous passage.'

'I'll never forget what happened to Mama.' Susannah gripped the handle of her basket until her knuckles went white.

'I think of it, too.'

Susannah opened her mouth to say that Arabella seemed to be very big for seven months when she was struck by a thought. Perhaps her father had anticipated the wedding and the baby was actually almost at full term. Her face flooded scarlet at the thought; she gathered up her basket and went out into the fog.

*   *   *

147

When she reached home, Susannah found that Henry had fallen asleep. He looked curiously young and vulnerable as he lay with one hand outflung on the pillow and his fingers curled over his open palm. She laid her hand on his brow and, finding it to be cool, opened the window a crack to freshen the air.

Downstairs, she added some extra honey to Henry's cough linctus and then boiled up the rue, wormwood and other herbs to make a decoction. As she finished, Henry opened the kitchen door.

'There you are!' he said. 'I'm hungry. Where's Peg?'

'I sent her to the market. You must be feeling better if you're hungry. Shall I heat some soup or muddle you some eggs?'

'I could fancy some eggs.' He pulled a chair up to the kitchen fire and watched her as she broke eggs into a basin.

Henry's appetite had indeed returned and he demolished a plate of eggs and several slices of bread in no time at all. Since his humour appeared to have been restored along with his health, she suggested they stay cosily by the kitchen fire and play cards. The rest of the afternoon passed very pleasantly.

Later, as they undressed ready for bed, Henry put his arms round her and kissed her cheek. 'You're a good wife, Susannah.'

Lying next to him as he drifted off to sleep, she prayed that, in time, their marriage would become more than a convenience. If Henry thought she was a good wife perhaps he would, at last, grow to love her? Even if what Arabella had said was true and Henry had only married her as second best, at least it had saved her from a worse fate. After all, if it hadn't been for Henry, she might now be struggling to teach the pudding-faced Driscoll girls to dance the gavotte. As for Henry visiting houses of ill repute, she dismissed that as pure spite on Arabella's behalf. Besides, he appeared to have no strong need for a woman's attentions in the bedchamber. And if ever he did, he must know that she waited night after night for him to come to their bed.

Chapter 9

Christmas Day dawned fair and clear. Susannah scraped the ice off the inside of the bedchamber window to reveal the snow-covered courtyard below. Frost had touched the trees with wintry fingers and the pale sun sparked diamonds off the tracery of branches.

'Henry? Come and see! I hoped it would snow; the sky had that heavy, yellow look yesterday.'

Henry groaned and turned over. 'Too much wine last night.' He pulled the covers back over his head.

'Come on, we have lain in bed far too long already. I still have preparations to make for the dinner and we mustn't be late for church.'

'You're always busy,' Henry sighed. 'What you need is some more help with the housework.'

'I've been telling you that for weeks!'

'In fact,' suddenly his eyes were alight with enthusiasm. 'What you need is a house slave.'

'No doubt! Meanwhile, if you'd help to carry the coal upstairs once in a while I'd be happy.'

It took a great deal of chivvying to get Henry dressed but they arrived at the church in time to nod at faces they knew. The young parson gave a very dull sermon and Susannah's thoughts began to drift. She had looked forward to this day all month, polishing the house from cellar to attic and planning the feast. The jollity of the Christmas celebrations was exactly what was needed to dispel the winter gloom and it was to be quite a party. Cornelius, Arabella and the children had been invited, along with Henry's Aunt Agnes and William Ambrose as well as Martha and her family.

Henry's head began to nod as the sermon went on and on. Susannah prodded him every time his breathing threatened to turn into snores and he shook himself upright again while she ran over in her mind the list of things she had to do before their guests arrived. Peg had been left in charge of the spit and she hoped that she wouldn't let the leg of beef or the capons burn.

At last the congregation filed outside. Already the snow was touched with black smuts from the soot-laden air. It was too cold to linger more than a few minutes to wish the other churchgoers a merry Christmas before they returned home.

The house welcomed them with the smell of roasting beef and Susannah was relieved to find that Peg had managed to keep the meat basted and that the plum pudding was steaming merrily away.

'I've roasted the apples in ale just like you said and the jelly is setting outside on the windowsill,' said Peg. 'And before you ask, I remembered to cover it against smuts.'

'Well done, Peg! I can see that you have everything in hand.'

150

Upstairs, the great table in the dining room had been polished to a high shine and all the carved chairs would be used for the dinner that day. Susannah had decorated the table with bunches of rosemary and berried holly and the best glasses and linen. She had fixed beeswax candles into Agnes Fygge's candelabra and had festooned it with trailing ivy.

She looked around her with satisfaction. Fires burned in every room in the house and a bunch of mistletoe hung in the hall. The stairs were garlanded with greenery, which perfumed the air with a pleasant resinous scent. Everything was ready. Surely Henry would be proud of her achievements? She smiled, imagining him taking her in his arms and telling her that he loved her. She wanted that more than anything. At that moment the door knocker sounded, heralding the first guests.

*   *   *

After they had rolled away from the table full of plum pudding and sweetmeats, they played blind man's buff and then Martha's husband, Josiah, took out his fiddle and started to play a country dance tune. When Susannah's foot began to tap Henry took her by one hand and Martha by the other, calling to William to join them. Soon everyone, except Agnes who was too crippled and Arabella who was too pregnant, had joined in. The children whooped in excitement as they became so giddy with twirling around that they fell over into a tangled, screaming heap.

'There will be tears if they are allowed to run

wild,' said Susannah. 'I shall call for Peg to take them into another room to amuse them for a little while.'

Once the children had gone, Josiah played a slower and more refined French tune. The men faced the women in a line and each bowed, shook his dance partner by the hand and kissed her cheek before moving on to a new partner. Arabella allowed herself to be led onto the floor by Cornelius and in spite of her bulk she swept across the floor like a stately galleon. The clip and scrape of leather shoes upon the wooden floor and the swish of silk skirts was curiously soothing as the dancers concentrated upon their steps. Susannah found herself facing William Ambrose, who moved more gracefully than she would have expected, barely touching her fingertips as he shook her hand and turned her round.

'I haven't enjoyed a Christmas celebration as much as this since I was a child,' he murmured. 'And it was kind of you to ask Aunt Agnes. She does so love a party. There is little enough fun these days.'

'I miss going to the playhouse now that all the theatres are closed. My father took me to see Ben Jonson's *Volpone* at Drury Lane last year.'

'I saw it too! Most amusing.'

As he kissed her cheek before moving on Susannah noticed that he carried with him the sweet scent of rosemary and freshly ironed linen. She lost the measure of the steps for a moment and was relieved that her father was her next partner; he held her steady until she found the rhythm again.

Darkness was falling when the sound of singing

152

drifted up from below. The guests leaned out of the window to watch the carollers stamping their feet in the snow while they sang and when they had finished, threw down apples, nuts and coins for them. Susannah sent Peg outside to bid them come into the hall and warm themselves by the fire and take a glass of punch. Guests and carol singers sang a round of 'We Wish You a Merry Christmas' and 'I Saw Three Ships Come Sailing In' before the carollers continued on down the street.

'We must leave you too,' said Cornelius. 'The children are becoming fretful.'

One by one the guests left until finally only Susannah and Henry remained.

'I am to be congratulated on having a wife who is such an excellent hostess,' said Henry. 'Even dour old Will managed to smile a little and I didn't hear any of Aunt Agnes's sharp set-downs.'

'She certainly enjoyed her dinner.' Susannah swelled with happiness. 'Oh, Henry, this house is made for parties, isn't it?'

'I liked hearing the sound of children's voices.' Suddenly Henry's expression was almost unbearably sad.

'What is it, Henry?'

'I don't suppose I will ever have a Christmas at home again.'

She bit her lip. 'I have tried so very hard to make everything perfect for you; to make *this* your home.'

'I know.' His voice was flat. 'But this is another place entirely.'

She swallowed, her disappointment threatening to engulf her.

'I didn't mean to make you sad,' sighed Henry. 'I can't bear to have miserable faces around me.

Come, give me a kiss!'

Susannah turned her face up to his and he pecked her on the lips.

'Let me look at you!' He studied her face as if he'd never seen it before. 'You're very pretty tonight,' he said.

'A little gaiety puts me in better looks.'

'Then we shall have more of it.' He wound his fingers through her hair and kissed her again, more lingeringly this time.

Susannah returned his kiss, happy that, at long last, he was taking notice of her. She had imagined so often being enfolded in his arms that now it had happened, she felt as if she were in a dream. Henry's lips were upon her own but, although it was what she had longed for, it left her strangely unmoved.

Soon his kisses became more urgent and his hands roved over her hips and breasts. 'When I hold you like this I can almost imagine a happy future for us,' he whispered. 'I can and will bear this dismal country if you are by my side.'

Moved by this expression of sentiment for her, Susannah barely protested when he unlaced her bodice and laid her on the Persian carpet by the drawing-room fire. She watched his face in the warm reflected glow of the flames and returned his kisses with a passion that was almost real. She dared not speak, since that had caused him such a difficulty on their wedding night.

His mouth moved over her breasts, leaving little damp spots, which quickly turned cold. Shivering in spite of the fire, she wrapped her arms round him.

She tensed for a moment when he reached down

154

and slid his hand up inside her skirt, fumbling through her petticoats. He was more gentle this time and she parted her legs a little to receive him. She began to feel again the languor that had overtaken her before and she closed her eyes and allowed her thoughts to drift away.

Henry's face was buried in her neck and his breath quickened as he moved his hips against her leg. He suddenly withdrew his hand from Susannah's skirts and the abrupt movement caused her to open her eyes, jolting her back into the moment. Hurriedly unbuttoning his breeches, he threw her petticoats up over her waist and climbed on top of her.

His entry made her catch her breath. As he moved within her Susannah stared up at the ceiling; it was uncomfortable but not painful and not particularly pleasurable, she decided.

Henry pulled her arms above her head and held her wrists together as he began to thrust faster and faster. Susannah peeped at him through half closed lashes and saw that his eyes were screwed shut and his teeth clenched.

It was all over very quickly.

He let out his breath suddenly, arched his back and then collapsed heavily onto her.

They lay still for a few moments, while Susannah heaved a quiet sigh of relief. Now that she was truly Henry's wife their love would surely flower. She experienced a sudden rush of tenderness for him and tentatively stroked his hair, waiting for his words of love.

Then Henry glanced at her.

Susannah blinked, uncomprehending.

He disentangled himself from the sea of her

skirts, stood up and hastily buttoned his breeches. He didn't look at her again. 'I'm going to my study,' he said.

Susannah opened her mouth to speak but his grim face forbade it. He had looked at her as if she disgusted him.

Humiliation scalded her cheeks as she watched him stride away without giving her a backward glance or a kind word. The door slammed behind him.

Chapter 10

It was Twelfth Night and snowflakes drifted past the window from the leaden sky above. Susannah was taking down the Christmas greenery in the hall when someone hammered on the door knocker and made her start so much that she nearly fell off the ladder.

Peg opened the door and Ned stood there, heaving for breath. 'Miss Susannah, you must come at once!'

'What has happened?'

'It's the mistress.'

'The baby?'

He nodded.

'I knew it! It's early. Is all going well?'

Ned shrugged. 'She's screaming enough to turn your blood to ice. The children were so frightened Jennet's had to take them out, in spite of the snow.'

Susannah snatched up her cloak. 'I'll come straight away.'

Cornelius, unshaven and without his wig, was

waiting on the doorstep of the apothecary shop for her.

'How is she?' Susannah asked, shaking snowflakes off her hair.

'I can hardly bear it! She won't let me see her and I'm mad with worry. Arabella is such a delicate little thing but her belly is huge. How will she ever give birth to such a big baby? She's been labouring all night and she's crying out so much it frightens me. I've sent up raspberry leaf tea but nothing seems to ease her pains.'

A series of blood-curdling yells came from upstairs, arresting her father's torrent of words.

'She's strong enough to shout, at least,' said Susannah, her anxiety abating a little.

'But how long can she go on like this?' Cornelius drew a shuddering breath. 'What if it's like your mama? What if—'

'Don't!' Susannah said, more sharply than she meant. 'I'm sure all will be well. Have you tried dog mercury?'

He looked thoughtful. 'No, I haven't.'

'Then I suggest you make yourself busy in the dispensary while I go up and see her.'

Arabella lay back flat on her back, red-faced and with her hair damp and tangled upon the pillow. Her hands clutched convulsively over the mound of her belly. 'What do *you* want?' she asked. 'Come to gloat? Does it please you to see me in my death spasms?'

'I came to see if I can fetch you anything. Father is making you an infusion of dog mercury to ease the passage.'

'Another of his foul-tasting concoctions! This is all his fault. If he didn't keep pestering me for his

157

conjugal rights I wouldn't be close to death now. Nevermore! If I survive this I shall never allow him into my bedchamber again. Now go away and leave me to die in peace!'

Susannah's old fears made her hands shake and she clasped them tightly together.

The midwife came forward with a basin of water to wipe Arabella's face and Susannah was relieved to recognise Goody Joan.

'Now then, Mistress Leyton, your friend is only trying to help you,' she soothed.

'She's not my friend; she's my husband's daughter and I don't want her here. Ooooh! Another one! Get her out!' Arabella screwed her face up tight and groaned.

'Wait outside,' whispered Goody Joan to Susannah. 'I'll come and speak to you after this pain passes.'

Susannah waited on the landing, pleating the curtain with restless fingers and staring out of the window at Fleet Street to take her mind off what was happening.

The cry of the knife-grinder drifted up to her and she saw a chimney sweep with his bundle of rods and brushes carving his way through the passers-by, leaving sooty footsteps behind him in the snow.

Another high-pitched scream came from the bedchamber and Susannah's heart began to race again. What if Arabella did die? Perhaps then she would be able to return to her beloved home and resume her work in the dispensary. Everything could be just as it was and she would be happy again. Of course, there would be Arabella's children but without their mother's interference she was sure she could discipline them into becoming respectful little citizens. Her mind ran on in this way before coming to a sudden stop. Ashamed at her train of thought, she had entirely forgotten for a moment that she was married to Henry now. She could never return to her childhood home.

A noise behind her caused her to turn and she saw Goody Joan closing the bedchamber door behind her.

'I am concerned about Mistress Leyton,' she said, anxiety wrinkling her pink cheeks so that she resembled a rosy apple stored too long. 'The baby is coming feet first.'

'Oh, no!' Susannah bit her lip as guilt overwhelmed her. Much as she wished Arabella had never come into her life she didn't want any harm to come to her; her father would be devastated. 'Is she going to die?'

'I certainly hope not,' said Goody Joan briskly. 'However, I'm not too proud to accept a physician's assistance and I'd like you to send for Dr Ambrose. I trust him and we have worked together before in instances like this.'

'I know Dr Ambrose.'

'Send for him straight away, then. And tell him I said he was to bring his special instruments.'

Susannah gripped the windowsill, suddenly faint. 'You're not going to cut the baby out?'

Goody Joan shook her head. 'I'm not expecting to take such desperate measures. But Dr Ambrose has devised an instrument to pull the baby out of the birth passage if it's necessary. Then, will you go to the kitchen and heat some goose grease? Pour it through a clean muslin cloth, cool it in a basin and bring it to me. I'll use it to ease the passage.'

Dr Ambrose arrived in a flurry of snow.

'Thank you for coming so quickly,' said Cornelius. 'I'm half dead with worry.'

'Did you bring your instruments?' asked Susannah.

Ambrose nodded. 'Take me to your stepmother, if you will.' He briefly rested a hand on Cornelius's shoulder. 'I'll do my best for her.'

They followed the sounds of screeching and yelling up the stairs and Susannah stood in the doorway, dry-mouthed with fear. Dr Ambrose washed his hands in a basin before gently palpating Arabella's abdomen, all the while speaking calming words to her.

Susannah had never noticed his hands before. His fingers were long and his nails well shaped with paler half moons. He had rolled up his shirtsleeves and she observed the light covering of dark hair on his forearms. How gently he touched Arabella's pale skin and how very different it had been for poor mama with Dr Ogilby.

Dr Ambrose took the midwife aside for a whispered consultation. Then from his bag he took out an instrument shaped like two large skimming spoons with long handles. 'When you feel the next pain, Mistress Leyton, push down.'

Arabella groaned.

Susannah couldn't bear to watch. She put her hands over her ears to shut out the screams and went to look out of the landing window again.

A short while later she heard a baby's high-pitched wail and let out a whimper of relief. She ran to the bedchamber, where Goody Joan was wiping the infant's face while he protested vigorously.

'But he's so tiny!' said Susannah. 'I thought the

160

trouble was caused by a big baby?'

'Mistress Leyton hasn't finished yet. Here,' she held the baby out to Susannah, 'you wrap him up nice and warm while I assist Dr Ambrose. There's another one.'

'Twins?'

'I couldn't be sure but I did wonder. That's why I sent for the physician.'

Susannah stroked the baby's cheek, marvelling at his tiny perfection, and he turned towards her finger, seeking her with his mouth. She swaddled him in a cloth and held him to her chest, his little head nodding against her neck, while she blinked back tears of relief and envy. Would she ever live through childbirth to hold a babe of her own in her arms?

Soon the cry of the second baby wavered in the air and Cornelius stood in the doorway, stunned. Wordlessly, he handed a beaker of liquid to the midwife.

'An infusion of dog mercury,' said Susannah. 'It will release the afterbirth.'

Goody Joan nodded and supported Arabella while she drank it.

Susannah put more coal on the fire, closed the shutters against the darkness and lit the candles.

A short while later Arabella, her hair combed and wearing a clean nightshift, sat up against the pillows with her husband at her side and a swaddled baby on each arm.

'Two sons!' said Cornelius, shaking his head. 'These are God's riches indeed. But most of all you are safe, my sweet Arabella. I don't know what I would have done—'

'Shhh! All is well, Cornelius.' Arabella glowed

161

with maternal pride. 'I shall need special care for some time after my ordeal, of course. And another nursemaid will be essential now.'

'Anything you say, my dear. Anything at all.' Cornelius shook his head again. 'Two sons!'

Downstairs a door slammed. Thunderous footsteps clattered up the wooden stairs and Arabella's three older children burst into the room.

'Gently!' cautioned Cornelius.

'Mama!' Harriet flung herself at her mother and the two boys scrambled up onto the bed, exclaiming at their new brothers.

Susannah stood in the doorway watching the cosy domestic scene. A touch on her shoulder made her jump.

'It's dark and a blizzard is blowing up,' said Dr Ambrose. 'I shall walk you home.'

'There is no need!'

'I cannot imagine your husband would care for you to be out, alone, after dark.'

Susannah glanced again at the happy family scene, which no longer included her. Somewhere deep in her breast was an aching hollow so deep she thought she might fall in and never climb out. 'Perhaps not,' she said, wondering if Henry would even notice.

She fetched her cloak and Dr Ambrose took her arm and led her outside into the darkness.

Chapter 11

Later, Susannah wasn't quite sure what sparked off the argument. They'd never discussed what happened between them on Christmas Day but, strangely, Henry had been in a more cheerful frame of mind of late, going about his business humming to himself and talking about the future as if it was full of interesting possibilities again.

'In the spring, perhaps we'll find a little house in the country,' he said as he shaved that morning.

Susannah, sitting on the end of the bed, watched as he made circles on his cheek with the soapy shaving brush. 'I thought you needed to be near the docks and the coffee houses and the Exchange for your business?'

'I do but you could enjoy good country air while I'm working in the city.'

'I would love a garden,' said Susannah, getting up to put more coal on the fire. 'But Peg and I have enough to do trying to keep the dirt down in this house without another one in the country to manage.' Shivering in the chilly air, she hopped back into bed and pulled the blankets up to her chin again.

'What you need are house slaves.'

'What do you mean?'

'Don't you remember? At Christmas I said we needed some. I've thought it all through. You shall have a woman to do the washing and cleaning, a man to carry the coal and a boy to run your errands.'

Susannah laughed. 'But, Henry, simply another

housemaid will do.'

'Nonsense! The slaves can stay to look after me in the city, while you go to the country.' Henry smiled. 'The perfect solution!'

'I don't want to live in the country on my own and I don't want any slaves.'

Henry frowned. 'I've already said you shall have three house slaves. I'll not have any more turnip-faced little maids dragged in from the gutter.'

'Henry, that's no way to speak about Peg! She's learning fast and we manage very well.'

He shrugged. 'Well enough, I suppose. But my mind is made up.'

'But I don't *want* slaves in the house. I should feel outnumbered. Besides, I'm not sure I like the idea of people stolen from their homes and sold into slavery.'

'You like sugar, don't you?'

'Who doesn't?'

'Well, then! You can't have sugar without slaves. It simply isn't economically possible.'

'I still don't want any slaves here.'

'There is nothing more to discuss. Damnation! Now look what you've made me do.' He wiped blood from his face onto the clean white towel. 'Besides, I've already arranged for them to be sent from Barbados.'

'Henry! You might have consulted me.'

'I'm telling you now ...'

'Exactly!'

'And there is nothing more to be said on the matter. Why, even Aunt Agnes has a blackamoor to run her errands.'

'I have Peg to run mine. We certainly don't need

three extra servants.'

'I had not thought to find you so ungrateful. You're always bleating on about how hard it is to keep house with only one.'

'I am not!' said Susannah, stung by the injustice of his comment. She threw back the blankets and stood in front of him. 'I won't have them in my house!'

'*Your* house?' Henry's eyes glittered and he dropped his razor into the basin with a clatter. 'You forget yourself, madam. This is my house and you live here only by my grace. Perhaps you should cast your mind back to a time you were glad enough to accept my proposal as a happier alternative to working as a servant yourself?'

Susannah gasped. 'I think it most ungallant of you to throw that back in my face. I have made every effort to be a good wife to you.' Then, before she could bite her tongue, she said, 'And it isn't as if my father didn't pay you enough to take me off his hands. You had yourself a very good bargain in me.'

'Well,' he said, staring at her with sudden animosity, 'that's for me to judge, isn't it?'

Hurt and angry in equal measures, Susannah didn't trust herself to speak. She dressed in silence, all the while replaying the conversation in her mind and resentfully imagining the alternative responses she could have made. Meanwhile, Henry put on his coat and left the bedchamber without even looking at her.

Sighing, Susannah followed him downstairs, having come to the conclusion that it was obviously going to be up to her to make the peace. Perhaps she *had* been making a fuss about nothing. There was no doubt she had been so used to making her own decisions over household matters for so many years that it had brought her up short to have to bow to a husband's decree. Ah well, extra help in the house might be a good thing. Maybe now she'd have time to learn to play the virginals after all.

The decision to placate Henry was taken away from her, however, since she had gone no further than the top of the stairs when she heard his staccato footsteps across the hall, immediately followed by the slamming of the front door.

She stood in the silence of the hall, fury seething in her breast, then marched into the kitchen where she made Peg's life miserable for the rest of the day by commandeering her assistance in rolling up the rush matting throughout the house and scrubbing all the floorboards.

Unsurprisingly, Henry didn't come home for either dinner or supper. Susannah sat by herself in solitary splendour with the grand table laid with a fine linen cloth and the best beeswax candles burning in Agnes Fygge's grand candelabra. She was damned if Henry would return to find her weeping over a bowl of gruel by the kitchen fire.

The candles burned down into their sockets and still she sat at the table. At last, tired and irritable and with her hands raw from scrubbing floors, she went upstairs to bed.

The next morning Susannah woke to find that Henry's side of the bed was still empty. She glanced into the other bedchambers but he wasn't there. Running downstairs she searched everywhere for him, even looking into the coal cellar, before accepting that he had not returned. She dressed, cursing under her breath all the while at the selfish behaviour of men who thought they owed no consideration to their wives.

The morning passed slowly, so in the afternoon she set off to visit her father to distract herself from the nagging worry of Henry's whereabouts. The streets were teeming again. The hard frost had caused the bills of mortality to fall further; the plague didn't like the cold, and the cautious confidence of the populace was shown by the number of people in the street again. Life had to go on.

She made a detour to the Star coffee shop, a favourite haunt of Henry's. The small window panes were cloudy with condensation but as she stood there the door opened and two men came out drawing their cloaks close against the bitter wind. A blast of warm air laden with the rich smell of coffee followed them and Susannah contemplated poking her nose inside to look for Henry. However coffee shops were not for ladies. Instead, she called to the two men as they went off down the street.

'Excuse me, but have you seen my husband, Mr Henry Savage?'

They turned to look at her, eyebrows raised and she stared back boldly, all the while silently cursing Henry for putting her in the humiliating position of having to ask.

'Savage? I saw him last week but he's not in the Star this morning. You might try the Harte and Garter.'

'Thank you, sir, I will.'

Susannah hurried away to the Harte and Garter but it was the same story. Henry hadn't been seen there for several days. Tight-lipped with annoyance, she set off to her father's house.

167

Susannah heard the twins screaming even before she opened the door to the shop. The household was turned entirely upside down by the two tiny tyrants who lay head to foot in their cradle exercising their lungs at full volume. Arabella had retired to bed in hysterics, leaving the nursemaids attempting to placate the infants. Susannah took her new brothers in her arms and rocked them, kissing their angry little faces before handing them back.

Cornelius was mixing gripe water in the dispensary and hadn't the energy to do much more than kiss his daughter's cheek.

'I wondered if Henry had passed this way?' she said, dipping her finger into the simmering pan of gripe water and tasting it. 'More aniseed.'

'Who?' Cornelius tipped another spoonful of aniseeds into the pan.

'Henry.'

'Oh. Was he coming here? Haven't seen him. Do you think I should put more sugar in this?'

'No, it's fine.'

'Colic is a terrible thing. You had it, too. Makes everyone out of sorts. You'll come to the christening, won't you? Samuel and Joshua, we're calling them. I did want you to be godmother but I'm afraid Arabella . . .'

'It's all right, I understand.'

'I knew you would. You're a good girl, Susannah.' He scratched at his head under his wig. 'If only they'd sleep through the night. If it's not one it's the other.'

'Martha says the early weeks can be difficult.'

'I'd forgotten just how difficult.'

Susannah hugged him. 'Try to snatch some rest

when the babies sleep.'

'That's just it. They never do. Anyway, better get on. Send my best wishes to Henry.'

Susannah dawdled her way home in spite of the icy wind and threatening snow and stopped at the Exchange to buy some ribbons to pass the time. Darkness was falling by the time she opened her front door in the full expectation of finding Henry in his study. Peg, however, was just lighting the candles and told her that the master still wasn't at home.

Carrying a light up to the drawing room, Susannah began to feel anxious. Surely their disagreement hadn't been serious enough for him to stay away so long? Where could he be? Perhaps he'd gone to stay at his Aunt Agnes's house. That must be it! If he hadn't returned by the morning she'd go and find out for herself.

She sat by the fire and tried to read but she simply wasn't able to concentrate on the *Faerie Queene*. Staring into the flames, she rehearsed what she would say to Henry when he finally arrived. Resentfully, she decided she would probably be forced either to eat humble pie or to pretend nothing had happened in the interests of marital peace.

An hour or two later she heard the door knocker sound. Henry! She ran downstairs and saw Peg about to open the door. 'It's all right, Peg. You can go back to the kitchen,' she said, drawing back the bolts herself. 'Henry, where have you been? You really are the most inconsiderate . . .' She stopped. The man, swathed in a cloak and with his hat pulled down against the sleet, stepped out of the shadows. It was William Ambrose.

He took off his hat. 'I believe you expected my cousin?'

'Please, come in,' stammered Susannah. 'Forgive me. I was worried, you see and I thought you were Henry.'

'Where has he gone?'

'That's just it; I don't know.'

'Late for his supper?'

'If it were only that! He's late for *yesterday's* supper. Henry didn't come home last night and I have no idea where he is.'

'I see now why you called him inconsiderate.' Ambrose removed his hat. 'Is he in the habit of absenting himself like this?'

'I rarely know where he is and he's often late but he's never stayed away overnight before. Well, not quite all night, anyway.' She bit her lip. 'The thing is . . . we had a quarrel.'

'Ah, I see.'

'He's sent to Barbados for some slaves and I said I didn't want them.'

Ambrose's silver-headed cane slipped from his fingers and clattered to the floor. 'He did what?'

'He told me he'd sent for some slaves. I didn't like the idea and he was angry with me and stormed out of the house.'

Tight-lipped, Ambrose said, 'I saw him yesterday afternoon.'

'Where was he?'

Ambrose bent down to pick up his cane. 'I didn't speak to him. I was on my way to visit a patient at Bethlehem Hospital.'

'Bedlam?' Susannah repressed an expression of distaste. 'I hear people pay for the amusement of watching the lunatics raving in their cells.'

'Hardly amusing but it's true that the patients are treated with little compassion.'

'But what was Henry doing there?'

'I saw him elsewhere—at Moor Fields—when I was on my way to Bishopsgate to visit Bethlehem Hospital. Henry was . . .' He hesitated. 'He was going into a tavern.'

'Which one? I shall fetch my cloak and go there at once.'

'You will not!'

Susannah's mouth fell open.

'*I* shall go,' he said.

'But . . .'

'Henry is my cousin. Besides, it's not safe for you to go out on your own in the dark.'

'Then I shall come with you.'

'Out of the question! You will stay here and wait in case Henry returns. He will have left the tavern long ago but I can ask if anyone knows of his whereabouts.'

It irked her but Susannah knew that what Ambrose suggested made good sense.

'I'll come back to let you know what I find out.' Dr Ambrose put on his hat and gloves. 'Oh, I forgot the reason for my visit.' He pulled out a folio from underneath his cloak. 'I thought you might like to borrow this. It's Jonson's *Volpone*. I remembered that you said you enjoyed seeing the play in Drury Lane. Perhaps it will help you to pass the time until Henry and I return?'

Before she could answer, Ambrose had gone out into the night.

*   *   *

171

She had fallen asleep over *Volpone* and the drawing-room fire had crumbled into ashes when the door knocker sounded. Stiff-limbed from the cold, she stumbled to the door but when she opened it William Ambrose was alone. Her hopeful smile faded. 'You didn't find him, then?'

'May I come in? It's freezing.'

'Of course.' Susannah led the way back to the drawing room and stirred the embers with the poker, anxiety tightening its hold on her chest.

Ambrose poured coal from the scuttle into the grate, and then took the poker from her. 'Have you any brandy?' he asked, once the fire was burning brightly again.

'Only rum.'

'That'll do. Fetch some glasses.'

Susannah did as she was bid and they sat each side of the fire warming their toes. 'Did no one at the tavern know where he went?' she asked.

'Drink your rum,' he said.

She sipped the drink and it ran like liquid fire down her throat. '*Someone* must have seen him.'

'They did. Susannah, it's not good news.'

'What has happened?' She could hear the shrill note of anxiety in her voice.

'You must prepare yourself.'

'For what? *Where is Henry?*'

'Henry was taken ill.' Dr Ambrose's voice was gentle. 'The sickness came upon him very quickly. I am sorry to tell you he died early this morning.'

'Died?' Her heart began to flutter and she turned deathly cold. 'But . . . he can't have! He was here only two days ago. They must have made a mistake.'

'There is no mistake. I saw his body.'

172

The finality in Ambrose's voice made her gasp. She reared up and, as blackness clouded her vision, she clung, swaying, to the marble chimneypiece.

'I'm afraid it is true.'

'Not Henry! We didn't have the chance to make up our disagreement.' She gulped back her tears. 'I must go to him! We must bring him back here and prepare him for burial.'

'You cannot go out. Besides, he is already buried.'

'But who ...'

'In cases of the plague the authorities take the body away.'

She swayed again, her breath threatening to choke her. 'Sweet Lord, not that! He was so very frightened of the plague.'

Ambrose spoke gently to her. 'Susannah, you realise that it's possible you may be infected, too?'

Cold fingers of dread ran down her spine. 'I feel well. A little tired of late, perhaps, but nothing more.'

'Good. But you should still not go abroad until we are sure you are well.'

'No. I can see that. And you must keep away from me.' Suddenly she gasped. 'I visited Father yesterday. I kissed the babies!'

'Susannah, you show no signs of sickness so I doubt you are infected. Try not to worry too much and I will call every day.'

His kindness caused her tears to overflow. 'We argued. Oh, William, I wish Henry and I hadn't quarrelled before he died!'

Afterwards, she blushed to remember how she had clung to him and unconsciously used his Christian name.

Chapter 12

Once again Susannah confined herself to her bedchamber, while Peg retreated to the kitchen. Living in fear of plague symptoms appearing, she examined herself at frequent intervals for buboes or discoloration on her skin. Every tickle in her throat, each suspicion of a headache or hint of nausea sent her into a flutter of panic. She paced the bedchamber floor, twelve steps one way and ten the other, until she almost wore holes in the matting.

This time, Susannah would have been delighted to have Henry's company, however bad-tempered. Unbidden, a hideous vision of his body tipped unceremoniously into the pit rose up in her mind. She scrubbed her knuckles into her eyes to dispel the image of his handsome features bloated and distorted by death.

Alone and frightened, she stared out of the window for hours at a time, hoping that her father would visit, even if only for a moment, so that she could call down to him from her window. But he never came.

She put on her black mourning dress, even though she would see no one. Black suited her mood. Slipping off her wedding band, she tied it on a black ribbon and hung it round her neck as a sign of her widowhood. Deathly tired, she lay on her bed and pictured scenarios of Henry's lonely death, bitterly regretting that now there would never be an opportunity for their marriage to blossom. Her marriage had been a failure and she would never wed again. Sadness overwhelmed her and she wept.

Martha called by and handed a basket of bread, some eggs and an apple tart to Peg.

'She said to send her love,' Peg said through the keyhole. 'And that she'll be praying for you.'

Dr Ambrose, garbed in his heavy cloak and beaked mask, called briefly most days and spoke to her from behind the bedroom door. 'I visited your Father this morning,' he said on one of his visits. 'He sent you a bottle of his Plague Prevention Cordial, with his love. I shall put it here on the floor for you.'

'There is no sign of the sickness there?'

'None.'

'I'd never forgive myself ...'

'You are still well?'

'Yes. Only lonely and miserable. I cannot help my mind running on and I see ...' her breath caught on a sob, 'I see frightening pictures in my head of Henry's poor body thrown into the plague pit.'

There was silence for a moment from the other side of the door. 'I will return tomorrow,' he said. Then she heard his footsteps retreating down the stairs.

*   *   *

The following afternoon Doctor Ambrose called again.

'Open the door,' he said.

'But ...'

'It's been three weeks now. Are you still well?'

'Yes.'

'I shall come in, then.' He stood in the doorway with a bag in his hands, frowning at her. 'You're too

175

thin. Haven't you been eating?'

She shrugged. 'Peg has brought me food but I have no appetite. Everything turns my stomach. I can't help thinking about Henry.'

'Lift your hair so that I can see your neck.'

Obediently she held up her curls while he examined her neck. She trembled at his touch as he turned her to the light. His fingers were cool upon her skin and she was very conscious of his proximity. It had been a long while since she had been touched by anybody with such gentleness.

'And you have no plague spots on your body?'

She shook her head.

'No swellings?'

'None.'

'Good.' He opened his bag and took out a chessboard.'

'Chess! I used to play with my father. He said I was a better player than he is.'

'Then I shan't have to explain the rules to you.' He put the board on the small table in front of the fire and set out the pieces. 'Another week and we will declare your quarantine over. Meanwhile, I'll decide for myself how good you are.'

He played in silence, concentrating on the board and only occasionally lifting his gaze to see if her face gave away her strategy.

'Checkmate!' he said, at last.

Susannah sighed and stretched. 'Look, it's dark! I was trying so hard to beat you that I didn't realise how much time had passed.'

'I have patients to visit.' Dr Ambrose swept the chess pieces into his bag. 'Before I go I shall tell Peg to make you a nourishing broth. Be sure to drink it.'

'Yes, Doctor.'

He glanced at her to see if she was mocking him. 'I'm off to lay a poultice on one of my patients. I'm so late he'll probably either have died or recovered by himself. Either way my reputation is lost.' His dark eyes gleamed.

'I've been very glad of your company.' Depression and loneliness settled upon her again at the thought of his leaving.

'One more week and you'll be able to go out again.' He picked up his bag and left.

*   *   *

Six days later, Susannah was curled up on the window seat wrapped in a blanket and keeping an eye open for William Ambrose's dark-cloaked figure crossing the courtyard on his afternoon visit. He had come every day, setting up the chess pieces after enquiring about her health and then making his moves with silent absorption. At the end of each game, which he invariably won, he left with hardly a word except for reminding her to eat. On one occasion he brought her an orange, an unaccustomed luxury at that time of year. After he had gone she peeled it, sniffing at the sharply aromatic oils that were released as she dug her thumbnail into its waxy skin. She ate each segment slowly, catching up the last drops of the juice with the tip of her tongue.

A carriage swished through the slush in the courtyard below and drew up at the front of the house. Rubbing a circle in the frosted window pane, Susannah peered down and watched the portly figure of a man descend from the coach and hurry up the steps to her front door. She heard Peg's footsteps crossing the hall as she went to answer the knocker and then raised voices. Opening the bedchamber door a crack, she listened to the argument going on downstairs.

'No, you cannot!' said Peg. 'My mistress is resting.'

'Then we shall have to wake her, shan't we?'

'She is not to be disturbed!'

'We'll see about that!'

'Sir, I beg you ...!'

Heavy footfalls pounded up the stairs and Susannah closed the bedchamber door and leaned against it, her heart thumping. Almost immediately there was a peremptory knock and then the door was flung wide. A middle-aged man in a green travelling cloak with a feathered hat over his full-bottomed wig stood there, breathing heavily. Peg hovered behind him, wringing her hands.

'Sir, what do you mean by this?' asked Susannah, fear making her bold.

'Where is Mr Savage?'

Susannah stood her ground. 'And who might you be, to so rudely enter my house and accost me in my bedchamber?'

'*Your* bedchamber, is it? I am George Radlett, as you must know. I ask you again, madam, where is your husband?'

'What is that to you?'

'A pile of guineas, that's what! I want the money he owes me for the rent. And I didn't receive the case of rum he promised me, either.'

Susannah frowned, bewildered. 'What rent and what rum?'

'He promised me a case of rum once the *Mary*

178

Jane docked. As to the rent, he sweet-talked me into agreeing to let him rent my house at a preposterously low sum while I retired to the country, my wife having no mind to be struck down with the plague. Savage persuaded me that it would be preferable to have a tenant rather than leave it prey to looters in the emergency but I've never seen a penny of the rent we agreed.'

Susannah stared at him, anger and confusion churning in the pit of her stomach. Henry had lied to her!

'Well?' he demanded, bright spots of magenta burning in his florid cheeks. 'I will have my money and then you can both pack your bags and get out immediately. I ask you again: where is Mr Savage?'

'I know nothing of this,' she said. Her vision wavered and she leaned against the wall, suddenly faint. He spoke again but she couldn't hear him for the roaring in her ears. She took a deep breath. 'Sir, my husband is dead.'

'You need not think you can lie your way out of your difficulties, madam.' He took a step nearer, pushing his face threateningly close to hers so that she could smell his rank breath and see the white bristles on his chin. *'Where is he?'*

'In the plague pit.'

George Radlett froze, then backed away from her as if he'd been scalded. 'You're lying!' he said but the expression in his eyes was uneasy.

'Do you not see that I am in mourning? And did my maid not warn you that I am still in quarantine? Or did you force your way into my bedchamber without listening to her? You may wish that you hadn't.'

'Are you threatening me?'

179

'Not at all. But my husband has died from the plague and as I feel unwell it's fair to warn you that you may become infected too, if you remain.' Susannah almost felt sorry for George Radlett as she watched the colour drain away from his face.

'When did he die?'

'A few days since,' she lied.

He removed himself to the doorway, holding a handkerchief over his mouth. 'I shall return in a month,' he said, 'and I do not expect to find you here. The house is to be fumigated from the attics to the cellars.'

'I will be gone by then,' said Susannah, her mouth curving in a half-smile. 'One way or the other.'

George Radlett turned and sprinted down the stairs.

By the time Dr Ambrose arrived, Susannah had stopped pacing the floor but she still trembled.

'What has happened?' he asked.

'It's such a shock,' Susannah said, after she had explained. 'I thought the house belonged to Henry. He implied that it was his and he certainly never said anything to me about paying rent. Did you know about this?'

Ambrose shook his head. 'He was full of how well he was doing in business and he always had plenty of money to spend in the taverns and coffee houses.'

'One thing is clear,' said Susannah. 'I can't stay here.'

'Where will you go?'

'Thankfully, there's still my dowry. I shall settle the debt and rent a small house.'

'You would not return home to live with your

180

family?'

'I cannot. The house is too small, particularly since the twins were born, and Arabella would not like it. And to be truthful, neither should I.'

'No, I can understand that. Perhaps you'd like me to make enquiries about a suitable house?'

A little of Susannah's worry lifted. 'I must be gone in less than four weeks and I hardly know where to begin.'

Dr Ambrose frowned thoughtfully. 'Perhaps the first thing is to ascertain your exact financial position.'

'Would you . . .' she hesitated, 'I don't like to ask my father to help me. His life is so taken up with his new family now and he has no time. Would you help me to sort through Henry's papers? Apart from keeping the apothecary shop books, I know little about financial affairs.'

'I'll do what I can. As time is of the essence, shall we take a look in Henry's study now?'

*   *   *

Two hours later, Susannah said goodbye to William Ambrose. She returned to her bedchamber and poked the fire into flames. It was dark so she closed the shutters and went to light the candles but thought better of it. Chilled to the bone, she pulled a blanket round her shoulders, drew a chair up to the fire and stared into the flames. Something akin to hatred for Henry began to burn in her breast and she wrapped her arms tightly across her body in an attempt to stop herself shaking.

She hadn't understood at first. William Ambrose's expression had become even grimmer than usual as he picked up and read the heap of papers he'd found in the cupboard in Henry's study. 'If you don't mind me asking, how much was your dowry?' he asked.

'Father never told me but I saw Henry counting it just after we were married. It was a great deal more than I expected. It's in that strongbox.' Susannah went over to the box and tried to open it but there was a small padlock through the hasp. 'Perhaps there's a key in the cupboard?'

'I didn't see one. Perhaps Henry had it on his person when he . . .' He stopped. 'Let me.' Ambrose took a penknife from his pocket and carefully forced the lock. He lifted the lid and took out a pile of papers. Quickly, he sifted through them. 'More unpaid bills. A butcher's account, a brown velvet coat with gold lacing, an embroidered waistcoat, a dinner for four people at the Stag Tavern, two diamond shoe buckles, coal merchant's account, two dozen embroidered handkerchiefs, one wedding ring, a pair of pearl earrings . . .'

'Pearl earrings? He didn't buy me any pearl earrings!'

'. . . hire of a coach and two horses . . .'

'Give them to me. I'll settle them,' said Susannah. She lifted out a further handful of papers and then frowned as she inspected the bottom of the box. 'But this box was half full with golden guineas. Where are they?' Somewhere deep inside icy certainty was forming. 'Henry must have hidden them away somewhere safe.' She snatched open the cupboard doors and searched the shelves one by one.

'They're not there, Susannah.'

'They must be!' She swept the remaining papers

182

off the shelves and onto the floor, along with broken quills, bottles of ink, a mouldy piece of bread and an apple core and ran her hands over the space behind. 'Perhaps he's hidden them under the floorboards? That's where they'll be!' She scrabbled at the matting, dragging it back and breaking her fingernails in the cracks between the boards, searching for a secret hiding place.

'Help me, can't you!' Frantically, she continued her search.

William caught hold of her elbow and pulled her to her feet. 'Susannah, it's gone.'

'It can't be! It was here only a few months ago.'

'There are still enough unpaid bills here to swallow up a fortune. I should have guessed . . .'

'Guessed what?'

'He had so little when he arrived in this country and was so used to living a life of ease in Barbados; it must have been difficult for him to understand how to manage his money. As it was, Aunt Agnes and I lent him a sizeable sum to get him started.'

'But he worked hard at his new business! I hardly ever saw him because he was always out making new contacts.'

Ambrose sighed. 'I wonder how much of his time was spent in building his business and how much in hiding from the truth? He liked the company of those he met in the alehouses and taverns. He was endlessly charming and generous to his new friends. I often saw him offering his hospitality to all around town with little regard to the expense.'

'But he couldn't have drunk away my *entire* dowry!' Outrage made her cheeks flame.

'Where is it, then?'

Susannah swallowed, fear rising up in her

throat and threatening to choke her. 'But if I have no money and no home, what will I do now?' she whispered.

*   *   *

Susannah did not sleep at all that night. Earlier that evening she had counted out the handful of coins put aside for housekeeping and realised that, even if she was careful, there wasn't enough to last a fortnight. She walked the floor with her heartbeat hammering in her ears while she considered her options. In truth, there were few. She could go home, she could find work as a servant, or she could marry again. But who would have her, a maiden no longer and her dowry gone? An apothecary's daughter, a dead man's penniless widow; she, Susannah alone, was nothing.

At first light, she went down into the kitchen and ground some coffee, boiling it up with plenty of sugar, hoping to fortify herself. But after only two sips anxiety overcame her and she felt too sick to face any more. Fidgety, she sat down at the kitchen table and vigorously polished all the pewter plate, all the while her mind running round and round like a caged rat.

In the end she faced up to the unpalatable truth that there was nothing else to do but to go home and throw herself upon Arabella's mercy.

She had only just put all the plates back on the dresser when the door knocker sounded. It was Agnes Fygge and William Ambrose. Susannah glanced at Ambrose but he refused to meet her eye.

'You're wearing mourning then, even though my nephew left you destitute?' said Agnes, as she followed Susannah into the drawing room.

'I shall miss him,' said Susannah quietly. It was the truth, even though she would have murdered him if he stood before her now.

'William tells me you must leave this house.'

'I shall go home.'

'Hmm.' Agnes studied her with her sharp, black eyes. 'And what about your stepmother?'

Susannah shrugged.

'You'll regret it. She's not one to be accommodating, that one.'

'My father will not see me in difficult circumstances.'

'You think that? I credited you with more perception. Cornelius dances to his wife's tune now.' She turned to William Ambrose. 'Is she ill? She doesn't look strong.'

'It is hardly surprising if my cousin's widow needs a little time to recover from the shock.'

'She has no time! She cannot afford the luxury of wallowing in her grief.'

'I am not wallowing!' said Susannah, her cheeks burning with sudden rage. 'And I'll thank you not to discuss my future as if I am not present.'

'I might make use of you.'

'I beg your pardon?'

'I need a waiting woman. You might do. What do you say to that?'

Susannah realised her mouth was open and snapped it shut. 'Thank you, Mistress Fygge, but I have no need to be your servant.'

'Hoity-toity!'

William Ambrose raised one eyebrow but said nothing.

'Since your nephew has indeed left me destitute,

185

I shall return home to my father.'

'You'll not bear it for long, mark my words. I give it two days and then you'll be knocking on my door begging me to take you in.'

'I promise you, I shall not!'

Agnes Fygge glared at her and Susannah stared angrily back until the old woman dropped her gaze with a sigh. Leaning heavily upon her monkey-headed cane she turned to her nephew. 'Take me home, William. I'm wasting my time here with this obstinate girl. You've lost your best opportunity, miss. Good day to you.'

William Ambrose doffed his hat to her, took his aunt's arm and they left.

A short while later Susannah set off for the apothecary shop. Still simmering with suppressed anger, she knew that she had no other choice but to beg to be allowed to return home, in whatever lowly position Arabella decided she would allow her.

The shop door was locked and no amount of hammering brought anyone to open it. She could hear the babies wailing from an upstairs window and so she walked back along Fleet Street and turned into the alley which ran alongside the back yard. She stood on tiptoe and reached up to run her fingers along the rough top of the wall until she found the hidden key for the back gate.

Ned, standing on a stool, hung over the opposite wall making conversation with the neighbour's serving girl. He jumped when the yard gate creaked open, slid down and continued his task of scrubbing out the big copper still in the yard.

'I wondered where you were,' said Susannah 'There's no one attending to the shop.'

'Master's in the nursery.' He glanced skyward.

'Again.' He turned back to the still.

Jennet was in the scullery peeling potatoes for dinner and safely familiar in her usual brown dress and white collar. 'Miss Susannah, what a welcome sight!'

Susannah stood by the warmth of the fire, sniffing the air. 'You've been making jumbals,' she said.

Jennet sat her down with a mug of ale and a freshly baked sugar cake. 'You'd best have another when you've finished that one,' she said. 'You're as thin as a lath. I was sorry to hear about your husband. The master's been sick with worry for you.'

Susannah couldn't stop herself. 'Not worried enough to visit me though.'

'He wanted to,' said Jennet, heaving the pot of potatoes onto the fire, 'but the mistress wasn't having any of it. "You'll bring the infection back home", she said.'

'My quarantine is over now and I'm well.'

'You don't look it, if you don't mind my saying so, miss. Black circles under your eyes. Not sleeping, I suppose.' A baby started to cry upstairs, soon joined by his twin. 'Come to that, none of us are sleeping and the whole household is out of sorts.'

'I'll go up and see Father,' said Susannah, brushing crumbs off her skirt.

She found Cornelius in her old bedroom, walking back and forth with a howling baby over each shoulder.

His face lit up when he saw her and he hugged her tightly. 'I thank God you've been spared!'

'Where are the nursemaids?' shouted Susannah

as she relieved her father of one of the twins.

'The children were quarrelsome and I sent them all out for a walk.'

'And Arabella?'

'Lying down. She needs a lot of rest and nourishing food with two babies to feed. There, there, Joshua. Don't take on so!'

'I'm sure she does,' said Susannah wryly.

'I'm so very happy to see you and so sorry about poor Henry,' shouted Cornelius, struggling to make himself heard over the screaming infants. 'William Ambrose has called several times to tell me how you were going on.'

'It would have been an even longer and more difficult month without him.'

'I wanted to come to see you but I could only have stood outside and called up to the window. Still, now you can go out and about again.'

'Father ...'

'Shhh! Look!' Miraculously, little Joshua's angry cries were settling down into sobs. Cornelius took the baby's hand and pushed the tiny thumb into the infant's mouth.

Joshua closed his eyes and started to suck vigorously.

Susannah tried the same trick with Samuel and in a few moments they were able to put the twins side by side in their crib. The sudden silence roared in her ears.

Cornelius took her by the hand and they tiptoed from the room. 'Perhaps I'm getting the hang of it, at last,' he said. 'Some days I'm at my wits' end and think I cannot go on for all the upset and disturbance. Is it too much to expect a little peace at my age?'

188

'The shop is unattended,' said Susannah.

'Ned . . .'

'Is in the yard making sheep's eyes at our neighbour's maid.'

They went downstairs and Cornelius unlocked the shop door. 'Nothing is the same since you left,' he said.

'That's what I want to talk to you about, Father. Now that Henry's gone . . .'

Cornelius shook his head. 'Susannah, we both know it wouldn't work for you to come back here. Everything is different.'

Fear gnawed at her. 'But I have nowhere to go!'

'Whatever do you mean?'

'The house didn't belong to Henry after all. He merely rented it and the owners are coming back.'

'But . . .' An expression of outrage flitted across Cornelius's face. 'Henry assured me that it was his own!'

'Well, it wasn't.'

He shook his head. 'To think I was so deceived! Henry could be such a charmer. But that house is far too large for you on your own, Susannah. Now that you are a widow you must rent somewhere smaller.'

'I would have, if Henry hadn't spent my dowry.'

'Spent your dowry? What do you mean?'

'Just that.'

'But . . .' His face turned ashen. 'But I gave him nearly all my savings. He was intending to offer for Horatia Thynne and I wanted to secure him for you. I thought he'd make you happy. I wanted you to have a comfortable life and he *promised* me he'd look after you.' He paced up and down, his breathing suddenly erratic. 'What little money I have left I need for my new family. As it is, I shall have to work in the shop until the day I die.'

Susannah felt the panic begin to rise up in her again. 'But what can I do? Where can I go?'

Cornelius covered his face in his hands. 'However will we manage? The house is overflowing with children and serving maids; we're bursting at the seams. There isn't even room for you any more in the attics. And you and Arabella and her children will never live in harmony.' His shoulders began to heave. 'What have I done?' he sobbed. 'My love for Arabella clouded my judgement and now ...'

'Shhh!' Susannah held him and patted his back while she fought down the icy terror that threatened to suffocate her. Father was right, of course. The strain of living with Arabella again would be intolerable for all of them; if it had been unbearable before, how much worse would it be now with twin babies and extra nursemaids?

Cornelius wiped his eyes and drew a deep breath. 'We will have to find a way. Perhaps we could empty the dispensary and put you a bed behind the curtain?' He bit his lip. 'Ned sleeps close by under the counter in the shop but I can't think how else ...' Anxiety etched deep lines on his face.

He looks suddenly *old*, Susannah thought with a pang, too old to be so troubled by the discord of squabbling women. She came to a decision. 'It's all right, Father.' She was surprised how calm she sounded. 'I can see that my return would be an unendurable burden for us all. I will have to do what other destitute widows do and find employment as a servant.'

'My dearest child, I wish there was another way.'

The relief in his voice was tangible. 'But unless you catch the eye of a wealthy man I cannot see what other choice there is for you. Except,' he paused, 'perhaps you could sell your mother's pearl pendant and her miniature?'

'Never!

'Then I hope, for your sake, that you'll find employment soon.'

Trudging home through the frozen streets, tears of mingled fear and resentment blinded Susannah. A beggar woman, huddled in a ragged blanket in the gutter, reached out and touched her on the ankle as she passed. Recoiling, Susannah fumbled in her pocket and dropped a coin in the woman's hand.

'Lord bless ya,' said the beggar, glancing up, her desperate gaze meeting Susannah's for a second.

Susannah flinched. The woman would have been pretty once, before the French pox started to eat away at her nose. Who had this miserable wreck of humanity been before she fell on hard times and ended up living in tatters on the street? Had she, too, run out of choices?

Peg was scraping the steps free of ice when Susannah arrived back home. She looked up from her broom, searched Susannah's face then turned back to her task without a word. Poor Peg! Her future, too, relied upon Susannah's. It was no good moping about waiting for something to happen. She thawed herself out by the fire, pushed her curls back under her plainest hat and left the house again.

*　　　*　　　*

191

The following week passed in a daze. Susannah traipsed all over the city, calling upon all the richest people she knew, many of them her father's customers. One after the other, they shook their heads at her request for work. In desperation she took to knocking on the doors of any large house that she came across but no one wanted even a serving maid.

Sick with exhaustion and fear, she took to her bed and lay huddled under the covers, shutting out the world.

Peg brought her bowls of soup that she couldn't eat and brushed her hair until she slept again.

'You're so kind to me, Peg,' whispered Susannah, too exhausted to lift her head. 'I'm so tired I hardly know how to go on but I must! Time is running out and before we know it Mr Radlett will be hammering on the door ready to throw us out. There must be *someone* looking for a housekeeper and a maid.'

'No one wants servants now,' said Peg. 'I've asked everyone I know but there are hundreds of girls living on the streets since their masters left London to escape the pestilence.' Her lip trembled. 'I shall have to go back to Moor Fields and knock on Mrs McGregor's door in Cock Lane.'

'You cannot!'

'What else can I do? What else can *you* do?'

Susannah had no answer to that.

*   *   *

The long freeze continued but, nevetheless, fear for the future drove her to continue her quest for employment, however lowly the position. But still

192

no one would take her on and whether the refusals were indifferent, rude or apologetic, it was all the same to her.

Dusk was falling when she returned home. Snow had been drifting down all afternoon covering the frozen filth of the streets in a clean white blanket and muffling all sound. Now it began to fall in earnest, great flakes twisting to the ground. Very few people were about. Exhaustion slowed Susannah's steps and she found herself longing to lie down and let the snow enfold her in its pillowy embrace.

Her feet were numb with cold as they crunched through the snow and she was light-headed from lack of sustenance. She thought she was near home but everything looked different under the snow. Suddenly confused, she turned round but snowflakes whirled before her eyes and the light was fading fast. Panic set in and she began to run, desperate to find the house before dark fell completely. She slipped and fell headlong, the force of the fall crushing the breath out of her.

Once she had heaved the air into her lungs again she was too tired to do more than lie still, the cold seeping into the inmost recesses of her body. It was a blessed relief to close her eyes and surrender consciousness.

Something warm and wet washed her face. Opening her eyes she saw a large brown dog staring at her from a few inches away. There was a shout and a stone landed with a sound like a pistol shot on the frozen ground beside her; the dog yelped and ran away. A light appeared, bobbing up and down as it approached. Then hands pulled at her and she was hoisted upwards like a sack of potatoes. She hung, bent over double, with her arms and head dangling. Confused, she watched her hat fall off into the snow and disappear from view as she was carried away.

*   *   *

It was the burning of pins and needles in her extremities that awoke her. Fire flickered orange in the grate and the heat seeping into her fingers and toes made her cry out as they thawed. At the sound of her voice a figure on the other side of the fire stood up, casting a dark shadow up the walls. Susannah shrank back, her mouth dry.

'It's all right. You're safe.' William Ambrose took her hands and rubbed them between his own. His touch was gentle but his expression was remote.

'What happened?'

'I called upon you and your maid was anxious. A blizzard was blowing up so I went to look for you.'

'I couldn't find the house.'

'You were only on the other side of the courtyard. Wherever did you think you were going?'

'I didn't lose my way on purpose!' Susannah winced as Ambrose flexed her fingers. She'd have chilblains again.

He let go of her hand and sat back in the chair. 'Susannah, this has got to stop now. You can't spend day after day trudging around looking for work.'

'So what do you suggest?' Anger made her ball up her fists. 'A little walk down to Whitechapel or Wapping, perhaps? I understand the sailors are always looking for new girls. Why, they may even

194

overlook my age if the candle is held low.'

The shock on Ambrose's face gave Susannah some small satisfaction. How *dare* he pass judgement on her?

'I don't presume to pass judgement on you,' he said quietly, just as if he'd heard her thoughts.

'I have to do *something*. It would have put an intolerable strain upon my father if I had gone back to my old home. There is simply no room for me. And Henry has left me destitute and so I must find some other means of support.' A tear ran down her cheek and she buried her face in her hands.

'Susannah, you have to think of the future now.' He rested a hand on her arm but she shook it off.

'What do you *suppose* I've been doing? I can't eat or sleep for worrying about it. I've knocked on almost every door in the city begging for work. And there are still Henry's debts to settle. If you're so clever, tell me what more I can do?'

'My aunt is right; you are an obstinate girl. She made you a perfectly good offer.'

'Which I refused.' Susannah lifted her chin. That had been a bad mistake but she was damned if she'd let this insufferably interfering doctor know that she knew it.

'The time is past for false pride. You have another to consider.'

'Peg? Do you think I don't know that? Everywhere I've been I've asked for a position for her, too.'

'I'm not talking about Peg. Susannah, you must face facts.'

'What facts? That in a few days Peg and I will be living on the streets, or if we're really lucky we'll find a place in a workhouse? I think I'd rather visit

195

Mistress McGregor in Cock Lane and throw myself upon her charity.'

'Mistress McGregor? What do you know of her?' asked William, his tone sharp.

'She took Peg in then tried to put her to work in her brothel. Can you imagine? Peg's little more than a child! She scrambled out of a window and tumbled to the ground in front of Henry, who brought her home to be our maid.'

'I see.' Ambrose stared into the fire. 'Susannah, is it possible you haven't realised . . .' He stood up and paced the floor with his hands thrust deep into his pockets. 'Peg tells me that you aren't eating properly.'

Susannah shrugged. 'I'm so worried that I can't eat. Food makes me retch.'

'And you are tired?'

'Bone weary. Sleep eludes me.'

'And Peg also tells me . . .' He hesitated.

'What right have you to discuss me with my maid?'

'I will do whatever is necessary to ensure my patients' good health.'

'But I am not your patient.'

He raised one eyebrow and she had the grace to blush. 'Peg tells me that she has not washed your monthly rags this past two months.'

Susannah's mouth fell open. 'She talked to you about such intimate matters?'

'Reluctantly. But I am a doctor and she has your well-being at heart. As I do. She is worried about you. Susannah, you must know that you are carrying Henry's child?'

'Henry's child?'

'It's not such a surprising thing, is it?'

196

'No! Oh please, no!' Spots of light flickered at the edge of her vision and William Ambrose's voice calling her name faded away. As the blackness engulfed her she understood that, even though Henry was dead, he was still able to deal her another blow.

House of Shadows

March 1666

Chapter 13

The Thames was close enough for her to hear the raucous cries of the ferrymen and for the stink of the mud at low tide to permeate the air as Susannah picked her way through the frozen mire in Whyteladies Lane. Gulls wheeled overhead in a leaden sky. Jostled this way and that by the stream of people passing by, she kept her gaze upwards, searching for a particular signboard. At last she saw it, a faded sign painted with a ship's wheel which swung from the jettied first floor of a single-gabled house crowded in amongst similarly ancient dwellings.

Susannah lifted the dolphin's head knocker of the Captain's House and let it fall. As the sound echoed inside, she peered through the grille in the door but no light appeared to penetrate. This wasn't at all what she had expected. After a few moments no one had arrived and she deliberated upon whether she should knock again or wait a while longer. Agnes Fygge, crippled as she was, might need plenty of time to reach the door.

A cart trundled down the lane, throwing up a wake of slush onto Susannah's skirt; by the time she had shaken off the worst of it the door had clicked open. The entrance passage was empty and she stood shivering on the doorstep waiting for her eyes to adjust to the gloom. A small sound, a suppressed giggle she thought, made her take a step forward.

'Hello?'

Silence.

In front of her was a whisper of movement in the

shadows and then she heard it again. Definitely a giggle. ' Mistress Fygge?'

After a moment a flash of white appeared briefly in the gloom.

'Who's there?' She began to make out a black form in front of her. Unable to believe what she was seeing, she squinted into the dark at the two-headed monster taking shape before her eyes.

A deep, rich chuckle reverberated along the passage and then came a sudden piercing shriek as part of the monster flew free and launched itself at Susannah, landing on her shoulder with a thud.

Terror made her heart somersault as she screamed and flailed at the thing that had attached itself to her, pulling at her hair and pinching her cheeks.

'Emmanuel!' Agnes Fygge's voice called sharply from the back of the passageway. 'Take that spawn of Satan and get out of my sight!'

The monster loomed closer and snatched at the creature on Susannah's shoulder.

Blinking in shock, she saw that the 'monster' was a burly man, an African in a blue velvet coat. In his brawny arms he held a small monkey, dressed in a matching blue velvet coat and a little skullcap. Both wore silver collars round their necks. The black man smiled and his teeth flashed white in the darkness before he turned and carried the chattering monkey away.

'So you've come, then?' said Agnes Fygge. 'Follow me, unless your wits have been addled by that boy up to his tricks again?' She turned and hobbled away, leaving the quivering Susannah to follow or not, as she chose.

Susannah glanced behind her at the open door

202

and the busy lane outside. It was tempting. Sighing, she slipped off her clogs and closed the door behind her.

Mistress Fygge pulled aside a tapestry curtain to reveal a shadowy staircase and began to haul herself painfully up the winding stairs. There was a strong smell of smoking fires. At the top she pushed open the door with her stick and light flooded onto the landing. She turned to see if Susannah was following before limping through the doorway.

The first impression that Susannah had was of the light and space and then of the great heat. She stood open-mouthed and stared about her. The dark and draughty passageway had given no hint of what to expect in the chamber upstairs. The ceiling soared high above her, supported by beams like the ribcage of a whale. Daylight poured in through tall, narrow windows with tops shaped like clover leaves. In a vast stone fireplace which took up most of the end wall a fire in was roaring away, the flames leaping up the chimney and smoke spiralling up to the apex of the ceiling.

'It's a church!' breathed Susannah.

'A chapel, in fact. This was once a priory.' Mistress Fygge lowered herself carefully into the great chair beside the fireplace and motioned Susannah to take the smaller chair opposite. She waved the smoke away from her face and coughed. 'Wind's in the east again. So, Henry has left you a memento of himself?'

Susannah bowed her head, terror threatening to rise up and choke her. Even thinking about the baby growing inside her made her shake with fear.

'What are you looking so sick about?'

'I hadn't expected . . . It was a shock to realise

that I'm carrying a child. I've been so anxious about the future that the possibility of it didn't occur to me. And I don't know how I shall manage. Especially now. I had expected to return to my father's home but . . .'

'Your stepmother wouldn't have you?'

'There is no room since the twins arrived.' She took a deep breath and launched into her prepared speech. 'It was wrong of me to be so discourteous to you when you offered me a position as your waiting woman. I have come to ask you if you would forgive me and to promise that, should your offer still be open, I would endeavour to serve you well.'

'You have some humility then? Not easy to find employment, especially with a baby in your belly.'

'No.'

'Good.' Agnes Fygge gave a wolfish smile. 'Can't have my nephew's pregnant widow scurrying around the streets looking for work as a kitchen maid. Whatever would people think of me? So you will stop all the nonsense and come and live here.'

'Dr Ambrose said . . .'

'Why do you persist in calling him that when his name is William?'

Susannah heard a movement in the doorway and turned her head to see Dr Ambrose. She looked down at her shoes, not wanting him to see her having to beg his aunt for a home.

'Like it or not, you're part of this family now,' said Mistress Fygge, 'and this family takes care of its own. Isn't that right, William?'

'Indeed it is,' said William Ambrose from the doorway.

'Time you saw some sense, miss. Gallivanting all over the city offering yourself up at kitchen doors;

204

it's a disgrace! Why didn't you come to me in the first place? Pride is a sin, as you well know.'

'Yes, madam. And I'm very grateful.' It galled her to say it, but it was true. At least when she died in childbed there would be a roof over her head.

'I expect you'll earn your keep.'

'Yes, madam.'

'Enough, then! Emmanuel will accompany you home and fetch your boxes. I'll expect you back here this afternoon. You can read to me. William will show you out.' She leaned back and closed her eyes. The interview was over.

*   *   *

Emmanuel, pulling a handcart, remained three paces behind Susannah as she returned to her house. She felt his stare upon her back and held her head high, refusing to look behind her, just as if she was a lady of quality out shopping with her blackamoor.

Peg's eyes opened wide when she saw her mistress's companion.

'Take Emmanuel round to the kitchen door, Peg and put the handcart in the garden. I don't want the neighbours to see us leaving.'

'Leaving? You've found somewhere?'

'We're moving to the house of my husband's aunt.'

She became very still. 'Both of us?'

'I said I wouldn't abandon you, didn't I?'

Peg closed her eyes and let out a sigh of relief and Susannah bit her lip. She would have to deal with Agnes Fygge's protests later. Meanwhile, there was packing to do.

205

It didn't take long. She folded her clothes into her trunk, along with her mother's miniature and her precious pearl pendant and added the candelabra that Agnes Fygge had given to her as a wedding present. Her books she placed on top of Henry's bills in her father's strongbox. Perhaps one day she would be able to pay off her husband's creditors, including the unpleasant Mr Radlett. That reminded her of the little brooch she had found in the dining room and she slid her hand into the lining of her trunk to extract it. She would place it on the drawing-room chimney piece with a note for when he returned.

She took a last look round the bedchamber she had shared with Henry. At their wedding she had been so full of hope for their future but here she was, poised yet again, to begin a different life. But this time she had the terrifying addition of a child growing inside her.

Hearing the sound of carriage wheels stopping outside, she peered out of the window and gasped. Scooping up her skirts, she ran downstairs to the kitchen.

'Quick!' she said. 'Mr Radlett and his family are here! Emmanuel, put the boxes on the handcart. Now!'

'Yes'm.'

'Peg, help him!'

They wrestled the trunks onto the cart, and Emmanuel shoved it along the path to the end of the garden with Peg scurrying along behind.

Susannah hesitated. Dammit, she refused to sneak away like a thieving servant. 'Go on,' she said. 'Wait for me at the end of the road.'

'But ma'am!' Peg's face was pinched with fright.

'He'll skin you alive!'

'Don't worry about me. Now go!' Susannah latched the back gate behind them, then braced her shoulders and went back inside.

Mr Radlett was striding about in the hall making a great deal of noise opening all the doors. 'Still here! I'm surprised you have the gall, madam.' He scowled. 'I told you to be gone!'

'I shall leave in a few moments but I have something to return to you.'

'Get out of my house! Now!' Mr Radlett's jowls became dangerously suffused with scarlet.

Footsteps pattered down the passage and a fashionably dressed lady of middle years appeared and looked over Mr Radlett's shoulder. 'George, what is it?'

'Mistress Radlett?' Susannah came forward and proffered the brooch. 'Might this be yours?'

'Oh!' The lady pushed her husband aside. 'Wherever did you find it?'

'It was behind the court cupboard in the dining room when I moved it to polish the floor.'

'George, look! I never thought to see this again.' She pressed it to her lips. 'My husband gave this to me when our first son was born. It's so very precious to me.'

The colour in George Radlett's face subsided from beetroot to rose. 'Be gone with you, madam! This is my house and I'll not have you within half a mile of it.'

'George! How can you!' Mistress Radlett took her husband's arm. 'Take no notice of him, my dear! His bark is definitely worse than his bite.'

'But she's been living in *our* house, *rent free* ...'

'At a time we had no need of the house. And

look about you, George! Can you see signs of neglect or damage? On the contrary, this lady even polished behind that great cupboard of your mother's that I certainly never bothered to move. Our house has been well cared for while we have been absent. And I'm grateful to you for it, madam.'

'But the *rent* ...'

'There is no rent for this lady to pay. Now be a dear, George and come with me to oversee the unloading of our boxes.'

'I do intend to pay you the rent my husband agreed to,' said Susannah. 'It may take me some time ...'

'Nonsense! There is no debt and I have my brooch returned safely to me,' said Mistress Radlett, a smile on her pretty face. 'Now, let me show you out.'

Susannah held her head high and swept down the front steps for the last time.

*   *   *

'I have brought Peg, my maid,' said Susannah looking Mistress Fygge firmly in the eye.

'Oh, you have, have you? And who is going to feed and clothe her do you suppose?'

'She works hard and is honest. And she doesn't eat very much.' Susannah held her breath.

Mistress Fygge stared back at her and all at once there was laughter in her eyes. 'I think if Henry had survived, he would have met his match in you, miss. Ah well, we can always use another pair of hands to carry coal up to the fires and we can't have you doing that in your condition, can we? You can

208

go down into the kitchen presently and see my housekeeper, Mistress Oliver. She'll put Peg to work soon enough.'

'Thank you, madam.' Susannah had the grace to blush.

'And what do you think your duties might be?'

'Whatever you wish them to be,' said Susannah as meekly as she was able.

'Quite right! You shall read to me, be my secretary, make intelligent conversation when required and be silent when not.'

'Yes, madam.'

'William tells me you play chess?'

'He is a better player than I.'

'And I. So perhaps we will be well matched.' She sighed. 'I'm tired. I'm always tired these days and I wish to rest. Put another piece of coal on the fire and then you can ask Mistress Oliver to show you to your bedchamber.'

Susannah, braving the shroud of smoke hanging over the fire, did as she was told before returning to find Peg.

Mistress Oliver was a big woman and the cavernous kitchen underneath the chapel was her kingdom. Her sleeves were rolled up to expose arms as solid and fleshy as hams and wisps of coarse black hair escaped from her cap as she stirred a vat of simmering cow's head on the fire.

'So you're Master Henry's wife?' she said. 'He always had such a merry twinkle in his eye. A sad day when he passed away. And especially so for you, since you're thrown on the mistress's charity.'

Susannah gently pushed Peg forward. 'I have brought my maid, Peg, to assist you.'

Mistress Oliver looked her up and down. 'A bit

small, isn't she? Better feed her up if I'm going to get any useful work out of her.'

'Peg is a good worker.'

'She'd better be or she'll feel my hazel switch across her back.' She winked at Susannah, to belie her harsh words. 'I'll have no slackers in my kitchen. You can start by peeling those turnips, girl.'

Peg took off her shawl and set to work without a word.

'Mistress Fygge said you would show me my bedchamber.'

'You'll probably want to dust it again yourself. It's been waiting for you this past month. Can't keep the smuts down in the winter,' said Mistress Oliver as she led the way up the stairs.

On the landing she opened the door opposite the chapel and Susannah found herself in a long, panelled corridor with rooms leading off along one side. Beyond a right-angled turn in the corridor Mistress Oliver opened a door near the end.

'Come down to the kitchen if you could eat a bit of bread and cheese. Do you have strange fancies? My cousin used to eat coal when she was expecting.'

'Coal? No, nothing like that.'

'Best get on.' The door slammed shut and Mistress Oliver's clogs clattered away down the corridor.

The bedchamber was panelled in oak with a faded Turkey rug on the floor beside the four-poster bed. A fire had been lit to take the chill away. The real joy of the room, however, was the pair of tall windows which admitted a stream of light, even though the day was dull. Susannah went over to the window seat and wiped the dusty

210

bloom off one of the panes of glass with her finger. Expecting to find a view of higgledy-piggledy rooflines and dilapidated dwellings all crowded together, she caught her breath.

Down below was a garden. Cloisters ran round the three sides of it that she could see and the stone walls of the chapel rose up opposite her. Although the garden was drifted in snow she could make out the topiary shapes of yew trees and low box hedges containing a rose garden. The sheer, unexpected delight of such an open, tranquil space set within the surrounding maze of twisting alleys, tenements and courtyards made her spirits lift.

In the middle of the garden the snow had been heaped into a snowman with two pieces of coal for his eyes and a carrot for his nose. A hat with a jaunty feather topped him off. Susannah smiled. There was something about this rambling home that felt welcoming, a stark contrast to the chilly, newly built perfection of the house she had shared with Henry.

A shuffling sound came from the corridor and then a scratching at the door. She opened it to find the monkey in the blue coat sitting in the doorway with its long tail curled round its feet. Susannah hastily backed away but it seemed quite calm. The little creature, its face and chest a pretty cream in contrast to its dark brown fur, stared at her with soulful eyes. Chattering at her, it held out its arms and then leaped up onto her shoulder. More prepared this time, she managed not to scream and stood very still while it lifted her hair and inspected her ear with a leathery little finger.

Suddenly it cocked its head, jumped off her shoulder and bounded back along the corridor. A few seconds later it reappeared with Emmanuel, who had dragged Susannah's boxes upstairs.

'You gave me a nasty fright earlier on,' said Susannah severely. 'I hope you are sorry for it?'

Emmanuel's white teeth flashed again and he chuckled. 'Very sorry, missus.'

'I should hope so too! How long have you had the monkey?'

'Aphra here when I came. She belong the captain.'

'The captain?'

'Missus Agnes's husband. Missus Oliver says you unpack and then come down to kitchen. Double quick.' He rolled his eyes. 'When she say "double quick" she *mean* double quick.'

'I shall come as soon as I'm ready.'

Emmanuel laughed, his shoulders heaving at the joke. He held out his hand to Aphra, who ran up his arm and settled herself into her accustomed place on his shoulder.

It didn't take long for Susannah to stow her few clothes into the linen press. Her books found a home on the window seat and her comb on the washstand. Finally she placed the candelabra on the small table beside the bed. With one last glance at the garden below, she made her way down to the kitchen.

*   *   *

Later, Agnes Fygge woke up tetchy. 'Where have you been?' she asked.

'Mistress Oliver found some jobs for me to do in the pantry.'

Agnes craned her neck. 'Where's that dratted

212

boy Emmanuel?'

'Hardly a boy.'

'He's just turned fourteen.'

Susannah raised her eyebrows. 'He's well grown for fourteen. Is that usual for Africans?'

'Good food and bad blood have made him big. He was only a tot of five or so when he came here. My brother ought to take him back and put him to work on the plantation. Heaven knows, he's too big to have around here any more. Keep tripping over him. Open the door and shout for him, will you?'

Emmanuel and his simian companion scurried up the stairs at the sound of Susannah's voice.

'You've kept me waiting, Emmanuel,' said Agnes Fygge. 'You know I don't like to be kept waiting.'

'Sorry, missus.' He went to an elaborately carved cupboard and took out a clay pipe and a bag of tobacco. Lighting a taper in the fire, he handed the pipe to Mistress Fygge and held the taper while she sucked at the pipe.

The old woman closed her eyes and sighed. 'That's better. I always like tobacco in the afternoon. You can read to me for a while, Susannah. *The Merchant of Venice*, I think.'

Emmanuel drew a footstool up to the fire and stared into the flames while Aphra searched his woolly hair.

Reading aloud, Susannah recalled the times she had sat beside the fire reading it with her father, taking turns to play the different characters.

Gradually the light faded and Peg crept in to light the candles and prepare the table for supper.

Susannah noticed that the companion to her candelabra was placed upon the table. She slipped away to bring her own down from her bedchamber

213

and arranged the two of them, one at each end. 'Back in its rightful place,' she said and saw a small smile pass over Agnes's face.

William returned from visiting his patients in time to take supper with Susannah and his aunt. He ate in silence, listening to his aunt's comments and only replying when it was absolutely necessary. At the end of the meal he rinsed his fingers and wiped them on a napkin.

'I'll bid you both goodnight,' he said. 'I shall be in the study and expect you will have retired by the time I have finished my reading.'

'I had hoped you'd join us for a game of cards, Will.'

'Not tonight, Aunt.' He kissed her cheek, nodded at Susannah and left the room.

Agnes sighed. 'He used to be such a happy boy. My husband doted on him. You see, Will was the son we never had.'

'Was he very young when his parents died?'

'Ten years old. He had a baby sister too but she perished from the same typhoid outbreak that killed their father.'

'And their mother?'

An expression of pain passed across her face. 'My sister Constance died of a broken heart.'

'And so you raised him as your own?'

'My husband was captain of the *The Adventurer* and took him to sea with him. Plucky little lad he was. Happy to climb up to the top of the rigging but never got his sea legs. Sick as a dog every time they sailed. Eventually Richard had to give up the idea of keeping the boy by his side. In any case, Will was always determined to be a doctor.'

'He seems to be a good one.'

214

'The best.'

'I wondered if you have any errands you'd like me to run tomorrow? I'd like to visit my father and let him know where I am living now, if I may?'

'Of course you may!' said Agnes crossly. 'And you can bring me back a bottle of rosewater. Just because I'm old and wrinkled doesn't mean I don't like to look after myself.'

*　　　*　　　*

After Susannah had helped Agnes to bed that evening she went down to the kitchen to find Peg sitting at the table next to Emmanuel, both of them eating bread and dripping. Mistress Oliver sat beside them with a glass of ale.

'Going to eat us out of hearth and home,' she said gloomily. 'Like that plague of locusts in the Bible.'

'I came to see how Peg has settled in.'

'Doing all right by herself, as you can see.'

Emmanuel nudged Peg and then looked innocently at his supper when she giggled.

Susannah smiled; it seemed she had made a friend already.

'Goodnight, then.'

'Take a candle with you. This old house is full of shadows.'

The fire in Susannah's bedchamber had died down. She stirred the embers until they glowed before climbing into bed. Dust showered down onto the counterpane as she drew the bed curtains around her. It must have been very much longer than the month that Mistress Oliver mentioned since the room had had anything more than a cursory dust and she determined to clean the room to her own standards the following day.

The strange bed was lumpy and Susannah could not sleep. She stared into the dark, listening to the old house creak as the timbers settled and thinking about the chilling prospect of the child growing within her, like a maggot in an oak apple. Part of her still expected, and hoped, to find blood between her thighs.

All at once fright erupted and she leaped out of bed and paced backwards and forwards in front of the dying fire while she tried to catch her breath. Gripped by terror, she was haunted by memories of her mother's terrible death and she knew that this child, Henry's, would kill her, too. She had to do something! The night was long but at the end of it she had come to a decision.

*   *   *

The following day Susannah began to learn her duties and wrote several letters for Agnes since her poor crippled hands could no longer hold a quill. She read a little more of *The Merchant of Venice* and cut up her meat for her at dinner. In the afternoon, once Agnes had settled down for a rest, she set off for the apothecary shop.

When she arrived she was relieved that her father was out visiting a customer and Ned was minding the shop. She drew the dispensary curtain behind her and hastily took down Culpeper's *Complete Herbal and English Physician* from the shelf. She flicked through the pages until she found what she was looking for and then measured out two ounces of grains of paradise with trembling

216

hands. She spilled the iron filings as she weighed them out and had to sweep them up and start again. Hurriedly she gathered together an ounce of turmeric and the same of long pepper and some pennyroyal. She twisted each one into a scrap of brown paper, all the while listening for her father's return. Just as she put the items in the bottom of her basket she heard the shop bell and then her father's voice. Hastily, she covered the basket with a cloth and waited until she heard Cornelius's steps upon the stairs before hurriedly lifting down the storage jars that contained the remaining herbs she sought. She measured out dog mercury gathered from the village of Brookland in Romney Marsh and a generous handful of wormwood, some garden rue, horehound and powdered nettles. A bottle of rosewater followed the other items into the basket, which she placed under the counter before going upstairs to greet her father.

Later she returned to the Captain's House and looked round the kitchen door. It was deserted; presumably Mistress Oliver was off duty until it was time to prepare the supper. Relieved, Susannah put her basket on the table and hurried to the pantry. She took out the pot of honey she'd seen at breakfast and scooped a spoonful into a small basin. Then she unwrapped the ingredients from her basket and mixed them together. Rolling the resulting electuary into sticky little balls the size of a walnut, she placed them upon a small plate before quickly washing up the basin and putting it away. One each night and morning should have the desired result. Picking up one of the balls, she was about to pop it in her mouth when she heard Mistress Oliver's heavy footfalls approaching along

217

the passage.

Glancing wildly around for a hiding place, she shoved the plate of medicine onto the top shelf of the larder, pushing it right to the back.

The kitchen door opened.

'You're back, then?' Mistress Oliver said.

Susannah palmed the medicine ball, her stomach clenching in guilt. 'Is Mistress Fygge awake yet?'

'She's calling for you. You can take her a glass of ale.'

The medicine ball in Susannah's hand had disintegrated into a sticky mess and she surreptitiously wiped it onto a cloth before taking the ale upstairs to her mistress. It would have to wait until later.

The rest of the afternoon passed pleasantly enough but she couldn't concentrate for thinking of the medicine balls hidden in the larder.

After supper, Susannah waited until she judged that the dishes would be washed and put away before she poked her nose into the kitchen.

Mistress Oliver sat at the table regaling Peg and Emmanuel with amusing stories of her youth and Susannah retreated.

At last, Agnes went to bed. Susannah stood at the top of the stairs but she could still hear voices and laughter in the kitchen below. Nearly crying with frustration, she took herself off to her bedchamber.

She read for a while but couldn't concentrate and lay thinking about her mother and the baby that had died.

After what seemed like an aeon, the house became quiet.

Susannah slipped from her warm bed. Shivering

with more than the cold, she crept down to the kitchen where she lit a candle with a taper from the fire, then climbed up on a stool to reach the top shelf of the larder. She took the plate and looked at the little medicine balls glistening in the flickering light. Picking one up, she stared at it in the palm of her hand. She had never made such a powerful medicine before and would have refused to do so if asked by any of the customers in the shop. Slowly she opened her mouth and put it on her tongue. Her heart began to beat very fast. This terrible medicine could change the course of her life. And take that of the child she carried. *Yes, and damn your soul!* Susannah started; it was as if she could hear Martha's voice in her head.

The honey in her mouth began to melt and she scrambled down from the stool in a sudden panic. She spat the medicine into the kitchen fire from where it spat back at her with a little shower of sparks.

Chapter 14

The long freeze finally broke at the end of March and soon the gutters and drains were running with melted snow. April came, bringing the sun, but one fine spring morning was disturbed by a banging on the front door.

'He's very angry, ma'am,' said Peg. 'He says he won't leave until you've paid him off.'

Susannah, with sinking heart, went to talk to the caller, a shoemaker, who claimed that he was owed for a pair of shoes with silver buckles.

'It's all very well you claiming you can't pay me what your husband owes but that doesn't put food in my children's bellies, does it?' He stood with his hands on his hips, waiting.

'I have said I will pay you a little each month until the debt is discharged,' said Susannah, wrong-footed because she knew he had every right to expect to be paid. 'Truly, I can do no more.'

'I'll wager *you'll* eat dinner tonight but my Bess and Jem must starve until next month!'

'If I could pay you now, I would.' She could feel the pulse beating in her throat as he glowered at her.

'I'll have my money now and I'm not moving until I get it!'

Agnes heard the raised voices and came to see what was causing the commotion. She banged her stick on the floor with such authority that both Susannah and the shoemaker fell silent.

'You may render my nephew's account to me,' she said.

She counted out the requisite number of coins into the shoemaker's outstretched hand and then called for Emmanuel and instructed him to accompany the tradesman to the door. 'I shall rest in my room for a while,' she said, in response to Susannah's heartfelt thanks. 'You may attend me at dinner.'

'Thank you so much, Agnes.'

'But where will it end?' muttered Agnes as she hobbled away.

Susannah was glad to escape into the garden.

Pacing up and down in the spring sunshine, she wondered if the rest of Henry's creditors would find her and cause more unpleasant scenes. She had devoted a great deal of her waking thoughts over the past weeks to dreaming up ways of paying them off.

After a while she felt calmer and sat on the bench in the arbour of clipped yew. Drifting over the rooftops were the sounds of wheels on cobbles and the cry of the oyster seller but they were far enough away not to intrude upon the peace as she contemplated her new life.

She had found a rhythm to her days and discovered that she liked Agnes Fygge, despite the old woman's acid tongue; she determined to do all she could to make herself indispensable. During the nights, however, Susannah tossed and turned while she worried about the burden of debt she carried and how she would provide for a child, assuming she survived the birth. Exhausted from restless nights and lulled by the drowsy cooing of the pigeons in the loft, she turned her face up to the warmth of the pale sunshine and fell into a doze.

A little later, quick footsteps on the path woke her and she saw Peg trotting towards her, wiping her hands upon her apron. 'There's a messenger here,' she said. 'He came looking for Mr Savage.'

'Oh no, not another one! What does he want?'

'He's a sailor. Quite a rough sort of person.'

By the time they reached the kitchen Mistress Oliver had settled the messenger by the kitchen fire and the two of them were enjoying a spot of flirtation over a glass of ale.

'I believe you are looking for my husband?' said Susannah.

The sailor wiped his mouth on the back of his hand. 'Aye. Is he here?'

'No. My husband passed away.'

He sucked his teeth. 'The *Mary Jane* is in. Mr Savage's goods are waiting to be collected.'

'Oh!' It had never occurred to Susannah that Henry's business interests would continue even though he was dead. 'I shall have to make arrangements,' she said. A glimmer of hope lifted her spirits.

'Best not leave it too long or the consignment will walk right off the quay by itself.'

'Very good. I shall see to it.' She tipped him a halfpenny and then went and knocked on the study door.

William Ambrose sat at his desk making notes.

'I've had a visitor,' she said. 'The *Mary Jane* has docked and Henry's consignment of rum and sugar is sitting on the quayside.'

William frowned but then his face cleared. 'But this is good news.'

'I've been so anxious about Henry's debts.' Relief made her forget her usual reserve with him. 'I had no idea how I'd ever be able to pay off all Henry's creditors but now I'm hoping this might be the answer. I wondered if you might accompany me to the docks?'

They took a hackney carriage although, as William said, it would have been as quick to walk since the volume of traffic was so great. An endless stream of carts and drays, carriages and horses, all with business at the wharves and warehouses, threaded their way along Thames Street. The noise was tremendous; shouting and banging, the creaking of the ropes as crates and barrels were thumped to the ground, running footsteps and voices raised in a myriad of tongues.

The *Mary Jane* towered above them as sailors

and merchants flowed across the gangplank. There was a strong smell of decaying fish in the air, which made Susannah wrinkle her nose. William took her arm and led her aboard. They found the captain's cabin and explained to him that Susannah was Henry's widow. After some discussion, Susannah signed a sheaf of documents and took ownership of the consignment.

'I shall send a cart to collect the goods tomorrow,' said William.

'I'd as soon you took the black cargo away now,' said the captain. 'They don't travel well and I'll not be responsible for any more wastage. You can come back for the barrels and crates later.'

Susannah watched William's expression turn thunderous.

'What is it?' she asked.

'How many?' William asked the captain, ignoring Susannah entirely.

'Two remaining.'

'Where are they?'

'I'll have 'em brought up from the hold. I'll do you a favour and ask my men to put a bucket of water over 'em first, shall I? Several weeks at sea doesn't make 'em smell of roses.' The captain laughed raucously, mightily pleased with his joke.

'William?' Susannah put a hand on his arm. 'What is it?'

'My dear cousin seems to have left us with a problem. There are two slaves to be collected.'

'Slaves? But . . .'

'I believe you said you argued with Henry when he told you he'd sent to Barbados for some slaves?'

'I did. I completely forgot about it until now. You don't mean . . .?'

'I'm afraid so.'

Susannah turned cold. 'Can't he take them back again?'

'I doubt they'd survive a second journey straight after this one. One of them has already died.'

'William, what are we to do? I can't possibly keep them!'

Susannah and William waited on deck until the captain came up through the hatch from below. One of his men followed, dragging a chain behind him. On the end of the chain stumbled a black woman, her thin cotton dress soaked and clinging to her skin. A scrawny child of about five and clad only in filthy rags clutched her hand but in any case he wouldn't have been easily separated from his mother since their ankles were chained together. Shivering violently, they stood bowed and blinking in the daylight.

Susannah gagged at the reek that emanated from the couple and lifted a corner of her cloak to cover her nose.

'Phoebe?' William advanced to more closely examine the woman. 'Phoebe, is it you?' His face was taut with shock.

Slowly she turned and looked at him, a tiny flame of hope in her dull eyes. When she opened her mouth to speak William gave a barely imperceptible shake of his head.

'Phoebe, this is Mistress Savage, my cousin's wife and your new mistress,' he said.

Phoebe licked her lips, cracked and bleeding. 'Massa Savage wife?'

'And I am very sorry to tell you that Mr Savage is dead.'

She began to sway, her eyelids fluttering, and the

child let out a small cry of distress.

William hurried to catch her before she fell to the ground and supported her until the fainting fit passed.

Susannah watched, made uneasy by his close attention to the slave woman.

After a moment or two Phoebe's eyes flickered open and William released her. She looked wildly about her until she saw the boy. Clutching for his hand, she whispered, 'Erasmus dead, too.'

'I'm truly sorry to hear it. And is this little Joseph?'

Phoebe nodded and pushed him forward.

William tipped up the child's tear-stained little face and studied it for some moments. Then he ruffled the child's curly hair and said, 'You will be safe now, Joseph.'

'You know these people?' asked Susannah, drawing William away. Nose wrinkling, she noticed that the front of his cloak was soiled from the filth caked over the woman's clothing.

'Phoebe and her brother, Erasmus, were the children of Henry's nursemaid and just before I returned to England I assisted at Joseph's birth. I came to know Phoebe and Erasmus very well during my year on Uncle's plantation. But I hardly recognised Phoebe since she has grown so thin and sickly.'

'And Phoebe's brother died on the journey?'

William's mouth tightened. 'Conditions in the hold of a ship are barely fit for animals, never mind a child.'

'What about her husband?'

'She has no husband,' said William shortly.

Susannah glanced at the woman again to find

225

that she was looking intently back at her. The boy, lighter-skinned than his mother, clung to her hand and stared at the ground, as if he had given up expecting anything at all from life. Something about his skinny legs and knobbly knees suddenly made Susannah want to cry. 'The boy will catch a chill,' she said. 'It's inhuman to keep them outside in this cold wind when they're soaked through. And they have no shoes.'

The driver of the hackney carriage refused to allow the woman and her child in his carriage. 'I'd never be able to pick up another fare until I'd scrubbed the stink away,' he said, not unreasonably.

'We'll walk home,' said William. He unlocked the slaves from their chains with the key the captain had given him.

'Won't they run away?' asked Susannah.

'Where do you think they'd run to?'

Susannah was close enough to smell sweat, vomit and worse upon them. Nevertheless, she took off her shawl and wrapped it round the boy's shoulders, tying it in a knot at the front. Feeling rather pleased with her selfless act of charity, she said, 'There, that's better, isn't it?'

Phoebe glanced up at her with a hostile stare then dropped her gaze to the ground.

Susannah took a hasty step back. Had she imagined it, or did the other woman's eyes burn with something that looked like hatred? Flustered, she turned and bumped into William.

'Let's get on,' he said.

*   *   *

Mistress Oliver wasn't happy about the new

members of the household. 'What use will they be? Look at them! More mouths to feed, that's all.'

William soon put a stop to her complaining with a few sharp words and sent her off to seek out some cast-off shoes and clothing for them.

Peg was instructed to carry jugs of water out to the scullery to fill the washtub.

Avoiding looking directly at Phoebe, Susannah gave her a piece of soap and a scrubbing brush and stood over her while she stripped and scrubbed herself and her child clean.

Susannah couldn't help looking at the woman's naked body, so strangely different from her own. She was so thin that her dark skin was wrinkled and her breasts lay like empty purses against her ribcage. The boy had skin the colour of milky coffee; he was neither black nor white and she wondered if this variety in colour was normal. She knew so little about Africans but perhaps he would turn darker as he grew older?

Once the slaves had dried themselves, Susannah held out a small shirt, breeches and coat to Joseph. Still trembling, he kept his gaze fixed firmly on the floor. Susannah looked at Phoebe.

Slowly she reached out her hand and took the clothes from her. She dressed the boy, who stood like a dummy while his mother stuffed his arms into the coat sleeves. Then she turned and waited, eyes downcast, until Susannah gave her a patched old gown and a shawl for herself.

Susannah herded the couple back into the kitchen and braved Mistress Oliver's temper by asking her to feed the new arrivals. The cook banged down a loaf of bread and a bowl of dripping, together with a jug of ale, and went off to

227

the pantry, muttering under her breath.

Susannah watched the boy look at the bread and then at his mother with enormous brown eyes.

Phoebe nodded almost imperceptibly at him and he fell upon his dinner, cramming it into his mouth so that his cheeks bulged, while tears rolled down his face. She reached out and gently lifted a tear away with her thumb, a muscle trembling in her jaw.

Susannah noticed that she didn't eat herself until the boy had finished. All at once Susannah felt ashamed to be watching them and quietly withdrew. As she went upstairs she passed the chapel and heard Agnes's angry voice coming from within.

'I'm not taking in any *more* waifs and strays, Will. Of *course* you must get rid of them!'

'I cannot!'

Susannah's cheeks burned and she stopped with her hand on the latch. Her father always said that eavesdroppers never heard any good of themselves and although she knew she should have declared her presence, she stayed motionless behind the half-open door.

'What do you mean by that, William?

Careful not to move her feet and make a floorboard creak, Susannah leaned forward a little and peered through the crack between the door and the frame.

'I knew Phoebe and Erasmus from my time in Barbados. Poor Erasmus didn't survive the journey, chained up in the hold of the *Mary Jane*, and Phoebe is brought very low. When I last saw her she was not the sorry creature she is today.'

'That's all very well, but . . .'

'Phoebe has her child with her.'

228

'They are Susannah's slaves. She can free them and let them seek employment elsewhere.'

'You know they wouldn't last a minute out on the streets of London!'

'I said, I'm not having them here!' Agnes thumped her hand on the arm of her chair.

Through the gap between the door and the door frame, Susannah saw the stubborn set of her jaw and how William's hands were clenched into fists behind his back.

There was silence for a moment then William spoke again. 'Aunt . . . you don't understand.' His voice was quiet and Susannah had to strain to hear. 'I lived on the plantation for a year and in that time I came to know Phoebe well. Very well.' He turned to gaze out of the window. 'She was a trusted house slave, full of life and laughter. She sang to herself as she went about her work and even my uncle, bad-tempered as he was, rarely failed to respond to her smile.'

'I've told you that I don't want any more slaves, William. Emmanuel is becoming too big to keep as it is.'

'Aunt, I was there when Phoebe's son Joseph was born. You haven't seen the boy yet. The child is . . . well, he's a mulatto.'

'A what?'

'He's half white.'

There was a long pause in which Susannah heard the faint sound of the rag and bone man's call drifting over the rooftops.

'What are you telling me?' said Agnes at last.

'We must find a home for them here. Joseph is . . . family.'

'God in heaven! Your child?'

Susannah pressed her hand over her mouth to stifle her gasp. She stumbled away from the door and ran down the corridor to her bedchamber where she closed the door behind her and pressed her back against it, her chest heaving. She couldn't explain why she was so disturbed by the knowledge of the slave child's paternity but she felt like weeping.

*   *   *

The following morning Susannah gained permission from Agnes to call on all those people who had placed orders with Henry for sugar and rum.

'The sooner you discharge Henry's debts, the better,' said Agnes. 'I do not care to be disturbed by his creditors banging on my door.'

'No, indeed!' said Susannah. 'I shall waste no time.'

'And speak to Mistress Oliver. She has a brother who is a carter; he can make the deliveries for you and you can be sure he's reasonably honest.'

It took Susannah several days to visit all Henry's customers to discuss the delivery of the goods. Some had changed their minds or were out of town and a few produced papers to show that they had already paid half the cost in advance. In the evenings, after Agnes had retired, she sat with paper and pen calculating how much was due to her and attempted to match up the sums with piles of bills and the scribbled notes Henry had left behind.

At last she believed she had it all worked out. The candle had burned down in its socket and she rubbed her eyes, strained with exhaustion.

'Have you found homes for all the goods?'

William's voice came from behind her and she started. Hand clutching at her breast, she turned to face him but could not meet his eyes. She was still shocked by the revelation that Joseph was his child. And that, therefore, William and Phoebe . . .

'Did I startle you?'

'A little.' Her face was hot as she forced her thoughts away from a shocking vision of a naked William clasping Phoebe in a passionate embrace and firmly back to the matter in hand. 'I still have two barrels of rum that are surplus to requirements. I was wondering if I should visit one of the alehouses and ask . . .'

'Certainly not!' William's face was grim. 'But I shall ask on your behalf.'

'Thank you, William.' Her gratitude that he would take this task away from her made her sigh in relief. 'Then I believe I can pay almost all the money Henry owed. I may have to throw myself on the mercy of his creditors and plead with them to let me pay a little less than they expect but I hope to have repaid the majority in the next seven days. Perhaps, in time, I can pay the remainder. Unfortunately the wages of a waiting woman are small and it will be hard to save at all when I have a child to support.'

'You must let me have an account of the remaining debts and I shall settle them.'

'No! I beg your pardon. It is a generous offer but this is something I must do myself. I should not wish to be beholden . . .'

'Beholden!' The glint of fury in his eyes made Susannah blink. 'If my cousin had not spent your dowry on fripperies you would not now be . . .' The candle flickered and went out.

Susannah heard him sigh. His outgoing breath disturbed the air in the sudden intimacy of the darkness and made her uncomfortably conscious of how close he was.

'Let us wait and see what price I can achieve for your barrels of rum,' he said. 'Then we can talk about settling the debts. It's late and you should rest. I don't like to see you looking so tired and anxious.'

'I thank you for your kindness,' she said, 'but I cannot rest until I have discharged my husband's obligations.'

*   *   *

Agnes had fallen asleep again, the pain in her swollen joints eased by the heat of the fire. Susannah stopped reading aloud and rested the book on her knee. Emmanuel sat in his usual place on the footstool at Agnes's feet with the little ape curled up in his arms.

Emmanuel glanced up at Susannah, his eyes full of mischief. He took the still-smoking pipe from Agnes's limp hand and shook the contents into the hearth. Then he stretched up and broke off a twig of rosemary from the little vase of greenery that Susannah had collected from the garden that morning, packed the leaves into the pipe and placed it on the table beside Agnes.

'You are very naughty,' whispered Susannah with mock severity.

Emmanuel giggled behind his hand. 'You stay with Missus? Please? I go kitchen and see Phoebe.'

She felt sorry for him and it was hard to resist the appeal in his eyes. 'Don't be long, then. You know

232

your mistress likes you to be on hand in case she needs anything.'

He shrugged. 'You are here. I stay beside her all day and she have to think hard for errands for me.'

'She's a good mistress.'

'Yes. But everything is the same every day. I sit by her feet for all my life,' he said gloomily.

'Can you remember what it was like on the plantation before you came here?'

'I remember Mammy singing me.'

'What happened to her?'

'She get sick and die and I cry and cry.'

Sudden sympathy for the orphaned child made Susannah reach out for his hand. 'My mother died, too. You never forget the sadness, do you?'

Emmanuel shook his head, his brown eyes mournful. 'But Phoebe came.' His face broke into a wide grin. 'She like my big sister. She make me eat again and she sing to me. I never think I see her again.'

Susannah recollected for a moment Phoebe's protective tenderness with her son. William's son. 'Wouldn't you like to go back to the plantation?'

'No!' He rolled his eyes. 'In the fields men die. They work hard under hot sun and overseer beat them. Flies eat the broken skin. My father, he die after a beating. I *never* want to go back.'

'How very dreadful!'

Emmanuel leaned forward. 'If I am bad Missus say she will send me to the fields. Please, you will tell her I must not go?'

'Then you must be good, Emmanuel and give her no cause to be angry with you.'

'But *every* day I sit here by Missus. I want to go outside, to see . . .' He stretched his arms wide,

233

'Everything!'

'I'll stay here with your mistress.' She smiled at him. 'You go and see Phoebe for a while.'

He snatched up her hand and pressed it to his lips, then raced down the stairs making small whoops of glee with the chattering monkey running after him.

Susannah glanced at Agnes who was undisturbed by the boy's noisy exit and continued to sleep in her chair.

It was true what Emmanuel said, reflected Susannah. The days were all alike in the Captain's House. Agnes's poor old bones were too rheumaticky for her to want to go out and the outings to church twice each Sunday were occasions to be anticipated with pleasure as a break in the usual routine. The most exciting things that had happened lately were the pedlar's visit and a neighbour practising a new tune on his viol by the open window.

William's return each day after visiting his patients might bring news of the outside world but in the weeks since they had brought Phoebe and Joseph home Susannah could hardly bear to look at him. What could have possessed him? It wasn't the fact that she was an African and so unlike a white woman that upset her but that Phoebe was so surly. She stared at the ground most of the time, refusing to meet Susannah's eyes or to return her smiles. But then, sometimes, she would stare at Susannah in a way that made her go hot. The woman was perfectly civil to William, so at least Susannah had quashed her fears that perhaps he had taken her by force. But surely his liaison with Phoebe, even though it had resulted in a child, could not

234

have been what Henry had referred to as a great disappointment in love?

An excited babble of voices drifted up from outside and Susannah went to the window to look down at the garden. Emmanuel was running, zigzagging backwards and forwards, chased by Joseph. The little boy was breathless with laughter, his hands held out in front of him reaching for the older boy who ducked behind a clipped yew. Emmanuel jumped out from behind the bush and snatched the child up into the air, making him scream with excitement.

Restlessness overcame Susannah again. All at once she longed to be away from the claustrophobic heat of the chapel, outside in the sunshine, skipping and playing without a care as she had when she was a child.

Phoebe came into view and called to Joseph who ran and clasped his arms round her knees. She lifted him onto her hip and nuzzled him. Emmanuel followed and Susannah watched Phoebe reach up and pull his ear affectionately.

Then William walked into the garden. He saw the others and went to speak with them. He ruffled Joseph's hair as he spoke to Phoebe.

Susannah studied the four of them intently as they chatted easily amongst themselves. Something made her feel uncomfortable. It surprised her to discover it was jealousy. Then, almost as if Phoebe sensed she was being watched, she lifted her head and stared straight back at her.

'What are you looking at, Susannah?' Agnes was awake again.

Susannah moved away from the window. 'I was watching Emmanuel playing in the garden with

Joseph.'

'Emmanuel's job isn't to play with that child!' Agnes sighed. 'My intention is for him to instruct Joseph in his duties as my new page. I still have Emmanuel's outgrown blue coats put by in a trunk somewhere. You can look them out for me later on and find one to fit the child.'

'If Joseph is to be your new page, you will still keep Emmanuel here with you, won't you?'

'How many pages do we need? Emmanuel is too cumbersome to have underfoot any more. And he's become irritatingly fidgety.'

'But you won't send him back to the plantation?' Fear for Emmanuel made her anxious.

'I use the threat of it as a stick to beat him when he misbehaves. I expect he can work in the kitchens for now. The boy is strong, but too mischievous for his own good and for my comfort.' She eased herself in the chair. 'Susannah, make one of your poultices for my knee will you? It pains me more than I can bear today.'

Phoebe was sweeping the floor when Susannah went down to the kitchen. She turned away without acknowledging Susannah's nod and carried on with her task so slowly that it appeared insolent.

Peg was at the sink scouring the pots with sand and singing a strange little melody to herself.

'You sound happy, Peg,' said Susannah.

She gave Susannah a smile which lit up her pinched little face. 'Oh yes, ma'am. Emmanuel taught me a new song. His mother used to sing it to him.'

'I'm to make Mistress Fygge a poultice but first I wondered if you could find me a crust of bread? My stomach is growling with hunger again.'

236

Peg nodded wisely. 'It'll be the baby. Mam was always taken by hunger when the baby began to grow.'

'Is that what it is?'

Phoebe dropped her broom with a clatter. She picked it up with a stony face and then began to vigorously sweep the pile of dirt towards the kitchen door.

Susannah sat at the table to eat her bread. It was true that she hardly ever resorted to the ginger cordial any more to settle the nausea of her early pregnancy and mealtimes never seemed to come early enough. And the baby *was* growing. She'd tried to ignore it but she'd had to loosen her bodices already and would need to let out her skirts before long. As usual, every time her thoughts touched upon the baby and the impending birth she spiralled into panic. Suddenly dry-mouthed with dread again, she crumbled the remaining bread between her fingers and once more forced herself to suppress all thoughts of the coming child's existence.

Chapter 15

Susannah had lit the candles and almost finished her supper by the time William arrived home. Her spirits rose unaccountably as she heard his boots coming up the stairs but when he pushed open the door she saw that he was in one of his morose moods.

'I didn't wait for you,' she said, passing him a platter of cold meat and cheese. 'And Agnes's joints were paining her so I helped her to bed earlier on.'

William pulled up a chair and sat down without saying a word. Hunched over the table he began to pick at the piece of cheese on his trencher.

Susannah waited for him to break the silence. 'Did you visit the apothecary shop?' she asked at last.

He glanced up. 'What?'

'I asked if you would visit my father's shop and bring me some herbs to make a poultice for Agnes.'

'I don't remember that.'

'William! It was only this morning, just as you were going out!'

He picked up an apple and began to peel it in silence.

Susannah watched candlelight glinting on the knife as the skin fell into a long red ribbon on his plate. Had he even heard her? 'Agnes is in a great deal of pain.'

William looked up at her and she was shocked to see how drawn and white he was. 'I lost a patient in Long Acre today,' he said. 'The plague again.'

Susannah tensed, suddenly fearful for him. For all of them. 'Were you exposed to it?'

He shook his head. 'I could do nothing but stand helplessly by while the watchman shut up the rest of the family. It's an almost certain death sentence for them.'

'I hoped the long freeze would end the infection. I can hardly bear the thought of the coming summer, being trapped in the city, never knowing which one of our friends and neighbours might succumb next.' For a moment she remembered how fractious Arabella had been during her pregnancy the previous summer and almost felt sympathy for

238

her.

'All my knowledge and training counts for nothing,' said William, slicing his apple into pieces with brutal precision. 'I can do no more than make the sick comfortable until they die. I've tried cutting the buboes to allow the putrefaction to escape, fumigating the sickroom and administering every combination of herbs known to man but in the end it's still God's will as to whether a patient survives.'

Pushing her plate away, Susannah stood up so abruptly that her chair tipped over. 'I thought you didn't expose yourself to infection?'

'Most doctors and apothecaries have decamped and the sick need me.'

'But you might bring the sickness home with you! William, you must be careful. What would Agnes do if you sickened? It would break her heart. Aren't you afraid?'

'Of course I'm afraid! I lie awake in a cold sweat worrying about it but what else can I do? Not one of us is safe.'

'Don't say that!' Her breath was tight in her throat. 'I dream of escaping to the country before something dreadful happens to us all. I want to breathe clean air and know that the pestilence is far away.' She could hear the rising hysteria in her voice.

William stared at her, his face expressionless. 'It's hard for you, being tied to Agnes's apron strings, isn't it?'

She shrugged, wondering at his sudden change of subject. 'When I was working in the dispensary I was useful. Father allowed me more freedom than most women dream of but everything is different now and I'm hardly in a position to complain.

Agnes threw me a lifeline and I shall never be able to repay her for that. I don't know what would have happened to me if . . .'

'Agnes is lucky to have found you. You are a worthy companion for her.' William stood up. 'I'm going to my study.'

Susannah stared after him, a flush of delight and astonishment warming her throat. A compliment from William was as rare and precious as sunshine at midnight.

*   *   *

Two days later a messenger arrived bringing a note for Agnes.

'It's from my old friend, Mary Westacott,' she said, her wrinkled old face wreathed in smiles. 'She's travelling up from Devon to visit her son in Hatfield and will come and break her journey with me for a few days.'

Mary Westacott arrived in time for dinner the next day and she and Agnes chattered away together like a pair of magpies. Emmanuel and Joseph crouched in a huddle at the other end of the chapel teasing Aphra with a pigeon's feather and planning mischief. Susannah sat on the window seat darning a worn Flemish-work cushion while the two old ladies appeared to forget her existence as they caught up on all the gossip of the previous ten years. When they had run out of reputations to ruin they turned to reminiscing.

After a while, lulled by the sound of their voices, Susannah leaned her head back against the wall and dozed.

She awoke with a start when the latch clicked

240

and felt a rush of pleasure when William pushed open the door.

'You remember Mary Westacott, don't you, Will?' said Agnes.

'Certainly I do,' said William, bowing over Mary's hand. 'I'm happy to see you again. Aunt Agnes will be pleased to have your company.'

'We have a great deal to talk about. So many of my friends are dead that it's good to be with someone of my own age for a change.'

'Since you are both so well occupied, Aunt, I wonder if you could spare Susannah tomorrow?'

'Spare her? What did you have in mind?'

'I prescribe some country air to bring the colour back into her cheeks. I have business at Merryfields and shall be making a visit there.'

Agnes raised her eyebrows. 'Would you like to accompany William on a visit to Richmond, Susannah?'

'If you have no need of me, I should be glad to do so,' said Susannah, her heart lifting at the very thought. She held her breath while Agnes pursed her lips and thought about it.

'It would not be seemly for you to travel alone with William,' said Agnes at last.

'Joseph can accompany us,' said William. 'The child would enjoy a boat trip.'

Susannah glanced at him, wondering if he was seeking an opportunity to know his son better. The thought troubled her.

Emmanuel, sitting by Agnes's feet, stirred and stared at her with desperation in his eyes. 'Perhaps I might take Emmanuel with me?' She was rewarded with the sight of Emmanuel's face breaking into a wide grin.

241

Agnes nodded. 'That is a better idea. I will spare him for the day but Joseph shall remain by my side in his place.'

Susannah tried to read William's expression, to see if he minded not taking his small son with him; but his face remained impassive.

'Very good,' said William. 'Susannah, you had better be prepared to leave early in the morning as we shall be rowing against the stream. You will excuse me from the dinner table today, ladies? I have several patients to see this evening as I shall be out of town tomorrow.' He bowed and left.

'Well,' said Mary, 'your nephew has grown into a fine gentleman, Agnes.'

'He'll do well enough,' said Agnes, unable to conceal the love she felt for him in her proud smile.

'I am surprised he doesn't take a wife.'

'William has never been one to flatter the ladies and it would take an exceptional girl to capture his heart.'

'He was perfectly charming to me.'

Agnes cackled. 'Perhaps you'd better propose to him yourself, then!'

Mary laughed so much that she developed a fit of the hiccups and Susannah had to send Joseph to the kitchen to fetch a glass of ale to wash them away.

*   *   *

Susannah was so excited at the prospect of the day's excursion that she rose before first light. Outside her bedchamber window the sun was peeking through pink clouds and she hummed to herself as she pinned up her hair. She wished

242

she had something pretty to wear rather than her usual mourning dress and then was overcome with guilt that the thought was disrespectful to Henry's memory.

William was already seated at the dining table in the chapel when she arrived.

'I hope I haven't kept you waiting?' she said.

'Not at all. Make a good breakfast; it may be difficult to find any dinner while we're travelling.'

Phoebe carried in a tray and laid the table with the remains of the previous night's pie, a loaf of bread, some apples and a jug of ale.

Susannah followed Phoebe's movements closely, wondering if anything in her behaviour would hint at the special relationship she had with William. Her expression, however, was as insolent as ever when she glanced up to see Susannah watching her.

Eyes lowered again, Phoebe asked, 'Anything else, sir?'

'That will be all.'

Susannah noticed that she was filling out with regular food and her skin now had the glow of good health. Phoebe left the room, her hips swaying, leaving Susannah feeling vaguely irritated. William cut a large piece of the pie and placed it on Susannah's plate. 'Eat up! You're too thin.'

'I'm hungry all the time.'

'A good sign that everything is as it ought to be.'

William was in better spirits, Susannah thought. Perhaps the prospect of a jaunt to the country had put him in a holiday mood too. 'Where is it we are going to today?' she asked.

'I must visit my old family home. When my parents died I came to live with Aunt Agnes but I could never bear to sell Merryfields. I have business

243

there today with my tenant.'

'Shall you ever return?'

He tore off a chunk of yesterday's bread and dunked it into his ale. 'There is much for me to do in London. Especially now that the plague is gaining strength again. I consider it my duty as a physician to stay here.' He drank his ale. 'By the way, I wanted you to know that I have agreed a good price for your rum. You should be able to settle some more of Henry's debts.'

'What a relief! I'm so grateful to you.'

'Think nothing of it.' William delved into his coat pocket and pulled out a leather purse. 'I couldn't have the family name besmirched, could I? And Aunt Agnes has suggested that, since she's so pleased with you, she will increase your salary a little. I hope you will soon be debt free.'

Susannah took the proffered purse. 'I cannot thank you enough.'

Emmanuel pushed open the door, carrying a basket and a folded rug.

'We're ready to leave whenever you wish,' said Susannah.

William had arranged for a boat to wait for them at the public stairs at Whitefriars. He held Susannah's arm firmly as they went down the steps, worn and slippery with green slime, and settled her in the boat with the blanket tucked over her knees. The river eddied around them in a froth of oily scum and Susannah saw a drowned rat, bloated to twice its normal size, swirl past. She held a handkerchief soaked in lavender water to her nose to mask the stink.

The boatman pulled away, the sun warm enough already to raise beads of sweat on his brow as he

244

rowed upstream. The river was congested with ferry boats and barges loaded with coal or timber and the boatman had to keep his wits about him to prevent a collision.

Susannah found plenty to interest her as they passed Somerset House and the New Exchange and then Whitehall and Westminster. Soon she was able to forget the stench of the river, becoming mesmerised by the sun making diamonds of the drips falling from the oars. The regular *squeak-thunk* as the boatman strained at the rowlocks was curiously soothing as they surged through the water.

Before long they left behind the busy stretch of river and the air became fresher. Trees, newly clothed in green, dipped their branches into the turgid depths of the water and ducks paddled alongside, quacking raucously. Emmanuel lay face down at the back of the boat, trailing his fingers and snatching at floating leaves. Every so often he turned to give Susannah a broad smile over his shoulder.

William intercepted one of the boy's smiles and his own lips twitched in amusement. 'It would appear I have unwittingly given two inmates of the Captain's House a free pass out of gaol for the day.'

'For all his size, Emmanuel is no more than a boy,' said Susannah. 'He chafes at being confined.'

'My aunt has kept him by her side for too long. It's time he was put to work where he can use his strength.'

Susannah wondered if William planned to send Emmanuel away, having persuaded Agnes that Joseph could take his place. No doubt he would wish to keep his son by his side. 'But what else

245

could Emmanuel do?' she asked.

'He should be sent back to the plantation.'

Impulsively Susannah reached out and clutched at William's sleeve. 'Please, don't do that! He's terrified of being sent to work in the fields. His father died horribly after the overseer beat him.'

William raised his eyebrows. 'I should have thought he would be happiest back in Barbados but it is true that life as a field hand is hard for those who do not obey.' He looked at her curiously. 'You take an interest in the boy?'

'I have come to know him well after all the hours we spend together in Agnes's company. I had not imagined I would ever become friends with an African but in many ways he is no different from how I remember my brother, Tom.'

'And now Joseph is to take Emmanuel's place. Will you take an interest in him, too?'

'Why, yes, I suppose I will.' How could she *not* be interested in a child who was the product of such an unusual union?

'Perhaps you will teach him his lessons?'

Susannah opened her mouth to speak, then shut it again. She had been about to ask if an African child, or half-African anyway, was capable of learning to read but it seemed an impolite question since Joseph was William's son.

'Do I surmise that you were about to ask if Joseph is intelligent enough to learn his lessons?'

'I have little experience by which to judge him,' said Susannah in as cool a voice as she could manage. Damn him! How did he so often know what she was thinking?

'I believe him entirely capable of learning to read and I believe you are entirely capable of teaching him.'

'I'm honoured,' she said drily.

'Think nothing of it.'

Susannah was surprised to see an impish gleam in his eye.

'It would be a challenge for you and help to pass the time when my aunt is dozing by the fire. Besides, it would please me to see the boy educated. Perhaps, in time, it will allow him to have a better life. Like Emmanuel, he cannot remain a page for ever.'

'No, I can see that. But what else could he do?'

'He might find work as a superior servant. But, of course, he is your slave to do with as you see fit.'

'Not while I am dependent upon Agnes to keep him. Besides, I don't like the idea of owning another human being. I hadn't thought about it until I came to know Emmanuel. Surely it cannot be right that men and women are stolen from their homes to be sold into slavery, can it?'

'I agree with you but others would not. Whole fortunes are built upon slavery.'

'Joseph is only a child and if I sold him his new master might not be kind to him.'

'You could free him.'

'But not until he has grown up and has some means of supporting himself.'

'Exactly! So we come back to education.'

'Yes, I see,' said Susannah thoughtfully. 'I will do the best I can to help him.'

It was noon when they arrived at their destination. The boatman tied up at a landing stage nestling in amongst bulrushes and Susannah and her companions climbed out. There was little to see apart from trees and fields on the opposite bank.

William took her arm. 'Take care!' At the end of the landing stage was a door set into the wall. He took a key from his pocket and opened it.

Susannah stepped through the gate into a large orchard. The trees were clouded with blossom whose fragrant perfume scented the air. The grass was long and the hem of her skirt was soon sodden but she barely noticed as she exclaimed in delight at the wildflowers that grew so prolifically amongst the grass. A beehive stood a little way off and the sound of the bees hummed all around.

'When I was a boy I spent many a happy hour sitting in the branches of this old apple tree,' said William, smiling. 'And I learned to my cost not to be greedy with unripe plums from that tree over there. But come, we will go up to the house.'

Susannah marvelled that William was suddenly so approachable and at ease with himself. Perhaps this was the effect Merryfields had upon him?

They left the orchard and walked arm in arm along an avenue of clipped yew trees standing like sentries on either side of the gravel path. Facing them at the end of the avenue was a large house built of brick the colour of faded damask roses, with high gables and tall, twisted chimneys

'Merryfields,' said William.

Susannah smiled. 'It's beautiful!'

'Isn't it? Emmanuel, run up to the house and tell Mr Somerford that we have arrived.'

'If this was my house I should want to live here,' said Susannah.

'Merryfields deserves a family to bring it to life. And I am needed in London.'

'Could you not also be of use as a country doctor?'

'Are you trying to be rid of me?'

'No, of course not!' She stopped, seeing that he was smiling. He was teasing her. *Teasing* her! She had come to respect him, to like him, but she never expected him to unbend to this extent.

Roger Somerford, William's tenant, a jocular middle-aged man with a warm smile, came to greet them.

'May I introduce my kinswoman,' said William. 'Mistress Savage accompanied me today to escape from the noxious air of the city for a few hours.'

'My wife and daughters are away from home at present,' said Roger Somerford, a worried frown on his forehead, 'and, therefore, unable to entertain you while Dr Ambrose and I conclude our business.'

'Please, do not concern yourself,' said Susannah. 'If I may, I'll take a turn around the garden and sit quietly in the sunshine.'

'Your blackamoor may go to the kitchen for some refreshment and I will have my servants set up a table in the knot garden and bring you some cakes and ale.'

'I should like that very much.'

The two men, followed by Emmanuel, walked towards the house and disappeared inside.

Susannah wandered along the paths, stopping to inhale the scent of an early flowering honeysuckle and to examine an urn planted with exotic flowering bulbs from Holland.

After a while Emmanuel came running to tell her that refreshments were waiting for her and she followed him to the knot garden where a small table had been set up on the gravel amongst the clipped box hedges. A young maid waited to offer her a finger bowl and a fresh napkin and to pour her some ale and press her to eat a cake or two. After the girl had returned to the kitchens, Susannah ate two of the delicious little cakes, which were sprinkled with walnuts and sugar, licking her fingertip and collecting up the last crumbs.

Emmanuel watched her with hungry brown eyes and she teased him a little as her hand hovered over the last cake. Then she relented and handed it to Emmanuel. 'Stay here and enjoy it. I want to walk a little on my own.'

'Yes, missus,' he said, beaming. 'Thank you, missus.'

She dropped her napkin and bent down to retrieve it. As she sat up again she was aware of Emmanuel's gaze fixed upon the low neckline of her gown and flushed, conscious that pregnancy had magnified her usually modest décolletage. She supposed Emmanuel had reached an age when such things were of interest to him.

Rising from her chair without catching his eye, she went to explore a shady alley of pleached limes, which led to a pool with a splashing fountain in the centre. She let the cool water run through her fingers and then spied a stone bench in the sunshine by the garden wall. She sat down, revelling in the peace and quiet, so different from London where the sounds of the city were always present. It was a secret and special place that no one outside these garden walls would even know existed. How was it possible for William to own Merryfields and bear not to live there, she wondered?

She reached out to pinch the needle-like leaves of a lavender bush and sniffed at the sharp, clean scent upon her fingers. Behind the lavender bush grew tall stems of wormwood; she stood up to stroke their feathery fronds. As she looked more closely she saw mint and thyme thrusting new shoots through the blanket of weeds. A physic garden! Unable to resist, she pulled up a handful of chickweed and used a stick to pry loose a dandelion root. The soil was sun-warmed in her fingers and she was possessed with a wonderful sense of well-being.

It was as she tugged at a plantain that it happened. Nothing more than a flutter at first and then a more insistent tapping. She dropped the weed and pressed her hands to her stomach. There it was again!

'Oh!' she exclaimed. She sat down on the bench, her knees suddenly weak. She closed her eyes against the sun, waiting quietly; stars appeared on the inside of her eyelids and then she felt the tiny movement again.

She blinked away tears, her arms wrapped tightly round her waist. Her child was letting her know that it was alive and kicking! The wonder of the moment took her by complete surprise and she was overcome with shame that she had tried for so long to deny the infant's very existence. This was a real person in the making, as real as herself, with a soul of its own. 'I'm sorry,' she whispered. 'Forgive me!'

She pulled from her bodice the black ribbon with Henry's wedding ring threaded upon it. It was too late for Henry to know his child but she vowed then to give their baby enough love for both of them.

Footsteps crunched on gravel and she looked up to see William walking briskly along the path. She longed to share her sense of wonder with him but emotion made her face crumple.

'Susannah, you're crying!' He gripped her shoulder and kneeled down on the path to look into her face.

He was close enough for her to see flecks of gold in his dark eyes. It felt natural to her to lean her head so that her cheek rested upon his hand. She closed her eyes as she luxuriated in the warmth of his skin against her own.

'Susannah, my dear, what is it?'

She took a deep breath and wiped away her tears. 'Do not concern yourself, I am quite well. But the most marvellous thing has happened! My baby has quickened.' She smiled tremulously at him, anxious to share with him the gift of this perfect moment.

He saw the ribbon clasped in her fist and pulled it free. He stared down at her wedding ring. 'Do you miss him?' he asked, his face curiously expressionless.

How could she answer that with the truth? To say that she barely thought about Henry would appear callous in the extreme. 'I am sorry that my child will not know his father,' she said at last. 'But I am not afraid any more. I cannot explain it but now I'm sure my baby and I will both survive.'

'There is no reason at all why you should not.' William stood up and roughly brushed gravel from his breeches.

'My mother died in childbed,' she said. All at once it seemed imperative that she should confide in him, to make him understand. 'It was a brutal death and the baby died in the most horrible way imaginable.' She paused to take a steadying breath. 'I have always been deathly afraid that I should suffer the same fate.'

'Medical care is much better now than in your mother's time.'

His brusque tone made her uncomfortable. 'Look!' she said in an effort to recapture his former relaxed mood. 'I've found a herb garden. It's overgrown but I've pulled up some of the weeds.'

He leaned over to look at the ground and his expression softened. 'My mother planted this when I was no more than eight years old. I remember helping her to gather herbs for the still room.'

'How lucky she was to have such a delightful garden!'

'But not lucky enough to survive to enjoy it.'

They stood in silence for a while, each alone with their melancholy thoughts while Susannah's happy mood evaporated like morning mist.

'It's time to go,' said William shading his eyes against the sun. 'Where has that damned boy got to?'

Chapter 16

'Ninety-eight, ninety-nine, one hundred!'

She was laughing and running through a dark tunnel of trees, towards the light. At the end of the tunnel she stopped, blinking in the sunshine while she scanned the garden. A drift of mist lifted from the damp ground and, stretched across a branch, a spider's web was threaded with diamonds of dew. The door to the orchard was ajar and she slipped through it, walking barefoot through the long grass, the hem of her skirt heavy with moisture. A blackbird, sitting on a branch above her, uttered a warning cry and flitted off to a safer perch, silent now but still watching her with beady eyes.

Susannah stilled her breath and listened. The air vibrated with the humming of bees as they worked their way from clover to buttercups. A duck quacked on the other side of the high brick wall but still she couldn't hear the sound she was listening for. Then, on the other side of the orchard the long grass swayed and a small child with red-gold curls broke cover.

'I can see you!' called Susannah. She ran towards the child who darted behind an apple tree. 'Where are you?' She made a great play of searching behind each tree in the orchard, her expressions of dismay becoming more exaggerated as the child's giggles become louder. 'You naughty creature, hiding from your mama!' Creeping closer to the apple tree, she suddenly pounced.

Laughing, she snatched up the child and smothered it with kisses.

Warm little arms encircled her neck and she buried her face in the red-gold curls, overcome with love.

A sudden noise made her start and the world turned dark.

Susannah sat up in bed, her heart thumping. She could still remember the feel of the warm body of her child clasped to her breast but the vision of the idyllic scene in the golden sunshine had gone. Her child! Now that she was awake its absence was like an amputation. But then, as if to remind her of his existence, the baby within her gave a sharp kick and she hugged her arms tightly across her belly.

'It's all right, little one. Did I wake you when I started up?' she whispered. What was it that had woken her? She listened again in the darkness and was about to lie down again and try to recapture her dream when she heard a small noise.

Curious, she slipped out of bed and padded across the floor to lift the latch. She peered into the shadowy corridor but there was no movement and she held her breath, listening. Nothing. It was as she turned to go back into her bedchamber that something moved in her peripheral vision. She turned her head but it was gone. She stood still, breathing shallowly with every nerve tingling. There was no one there and yet she felt a stirring in the air as if someone had just passed by. Shivering, she crept along the corridor and glanced into Agnes's room but the old woman lay unmoving while she slept. Further along the corridor was William's room and she stood outside for a moment but there was no sound from within and she had no wish for him to discover her hovering outside his door in her nightgown.

* * *

The pestilence took hold again as the summer arrived. Many of those who had returned to the city during the winter fled to the country again. Those who remained were tense and watchful, ready to shun neighbours and friends at the slightest suspicion of ill health. Agnes ceased to attend Sunday services and Susannah buried her head under the blankets at night each time she heard the dead cart, followed by the wailing and sobbing of the bereaved.

Agnes was anxious about how they would manage if food supplies became short and she insisted that Susannah and Mistress Oliver arrange to fill one of the empty storerooms with vast quantities of dried beans, flour, sugar and other goods.

'We shall all be heartily sick of beans by the time we've worked our way through that little lot,' said Mistress Oliver.

William returned home very late, terse and uncommunicative and picked at his supper by candlelight.

'Can I fetch you something you'd rather eat?' asked Susannah, watching him push away a plate of cold chicken.

'What?' He looked up at her as if he had no idea who she was.

'Would you like a posset perhaps? Something easy to digest when you're tired.'

'Tired!' His laugh was humourless. 'It would take more than a posset to cure what ails me.' He balled up his fists and ground them into his eyes. 'I've seen such sights today, Susannah. Birth and death all within the space of half an hour. A mother, already sickening with the pestilence, and her babe born minutes before she passed.'

'Did the baby live?' The familiar anxiety made her cross her arms protectively over her stomach.

'He did. But who knows for how long? Mother and father already dead and a toothless old grandmother the only person left to take the child. What kind of life will he have? Better for him if he joins his mother.'

'Don't say that!'

'This is no time for sentiment, Susannah.'

'It isn't . . .'

'And this evening I was called to Bedlam.'

256

'The plague?'

'The flux. I wonder if I'll ever get the stench out of my nostrils. You have no idea of the horrors in that place. Old women jabbering away to themselves while they pull out their hair, men naked and smeared with excrement rolling on filthy straw, just as if they were animals. Their unholy screams and moans will haunt my dreams.'

Horrified, as much by the pain in William's eyes as by his words, she rested her hand briefly on his shoulder.

'If I'm having difficulty stomaching even the *idea* of having to return, can you begin to imagine what it must be like for one of the inmates?' he said. 'Their families have imprisoned them in hell and their only realistic hope of escape is death. Am I cheating them of that hope by trying to cure them of their ailments?'

Susannah wished she could take him in her arms and rock him against her breast to comfort him but she had no helpful answer to his question.

*　　　*　　　*

The cloister garden became Susannah's solace from the difficulties of the real world. Inspired by the herb garden at Merryfields she obtained permission from Agnes to take over a sunny patch of ground and set about freeing it of weeds. She begged some cuttings of rosemary and mint from Martha and hummed to herself as she planted and watered seeds.

Over the following weeks she watched with delight as the first green fingers of chives, parsley, feverfew and fennel scrabbled their way through the earth towards the light. There was intense pleasure for her in tending the tiny garden; the warm earth running through her fingers made her feel as if she was working in harness with Nature and as if anything was possible.

*   *   *

Susannah visited her father but he was tired and distracted since Arabella had fallen out with one of the nursemaids and sent her packing.

'She needn't think I'm going to take over the nursemaid's duties,' said Jennet as she pounded the washing in the tub with as much violence as if it were her mistress's head. 'I've more than enough to do with her ladyship taking no interest in the housekeeping except to complain. I don't mind telling you, Miss Susannah, that this house has gone to rack and ruin since you left. Squabbling children running in and out with muddy boots on, leaving doors open and dropping crusts and apple cores everywhere they go. It's not surprising we're overrun by rats.'

Susannah shuddered in disgust. 'Poor Tibby, she'd never have allowed that.'

'They've been in the pantry, bold as brass. And it's *her* fault that Tibby isn't here to put a stop to it,' said Jennet, her face grim.

Returning to the Captain's House that afternoon, Susannah stopped outside the front door, fumbling in her pocket for the key. She was just fitting it into the lock when the door opposite opened and a small boy tumbled out and landed on his hands and knees on the street. He began to roar in indignation.

Susannah hurried to pick him up and planted him squarely on his feet while he continued to bellow his displeasure. 'For goodness' sake!' said Susannah, pulling out a handkerchief and scrubbing at his hands. 'What a racket about nothing! Look, it's only a bit of horse dropping!' She extracted the piece of bread he was clutching in his grimy fist and threw it onto a nearby heap of refuse, causing his screams to rise to a crescendo.

'You can't eat that now; it's covered in filth from the drain.'

A young woman in a blue dress appeared in the open doorway. 'Edwin! What are you doing, you naughty boy!' Her voice was shrill with fear. 'You know I told you that you mustn't go outside. There might be sick people.'

'He fell over but he's quite all right,' said Susannah. 'I'm afraid he smells a bit. A horse must have passed this way only a few minutes ago.'

'That child will be the death of me,' said his mother, raising her eyes to heaven. 'Always in some kind of mischief.' Her round face creased into a smile as little Edwin clung to her knees, his screams subsiding. 'I should probably beat him but somehow I haven't the heart for it. Perhaps next time I will have a girl, a gentle soul who will sit at my knee working on her sampler or learning her psalms.'

'In my experience girls can be quite as naughty as boys,' said Susannah.

The young woman glanced at Susannah's bodice, now stretched tightly over her abdomen. 'Ah well! It looks as if it won't be long before you have your own little bundle of joy?'

'The end of September.'

'Your first?'

259

Susannah nodded.

'Your husband will be pleased if you give him a son.'

'My husband died some months ago.'

'Mercy! Was he an old man?'

'Not at all. The pestilence took him.'

The young woman gasped and shrank back, pushing Edwin behind her.

'Please, it's all right!' said Susannah. 'It was months ago and I'm quite well.'

'I thought an old woman and her son, a physician, lived in the Captain's House? I don't remember seeing a red cross on the door.'

'There wasn't one. My husband died in quite a different part of the city.'

Some of the anxiety left the young woman's face. 'However do you manage?'

'I live as a companion to my husband's aunt.'

'It's a terrible business, this pestilence.' Her grey eyes were shadowed. 'I'm too frightened to go out.' She gathered her child up into her arms and hugged him to her plump breast so tightly that he squawked. 'But once the streets are free from infection again, come and call on me.' She smiled. 'I should like to see your new baby when he arrives.'

'I'm Susannah Savage.'

'Jane Quick. Let's hope the streets are safe again soon.'

Susannah watched her new friend go inside and bolt the door behind her. She entered the Captain's House and went upstairs to take off her hat. Walking along the corridor she noticed that the door to one of the rooms normally closed up was ajar and she heard low voices coming from within. Curious, she looked inside. Emmanuel was leaning over Peg, imprisoning her against the wall.

'Emmanuel! What are you doing? Peg, be off to the kitchen at once!'

Peg, very pink about the face and with her cap awry, shot her a frightened look and scuttled off.

'Well, Emmanuel, what have you to say for yourself?'

His eyes opened very wide. 'Didn't mean nothing, missus.'

'Don't you ever let me catch you trying to steal a kiss from Peg again, or it'll be the worse for you!'

'Don't tell Missus Agnes; she'll send me back.'

The terror in his eyes made Susannah relent. 'You can find Joseph and bring him to me in the chapel.'

'Yes, missus.' His head nodded solemnly up and down.

'You will sit in silence beside me while I teach him his letters. And no naughty tricks!'

He shook his head vigorously from side to side.

'Go on then!'

Joseph had proved to be a willing scholar, even though his enthusiasm was greater than his skill. Susannah watched him concentrating hard on his slate, with a drift of chalk across his brown cheek and the tip of his tongue protruding as he shaped his letters. She studied his profile yet again, still seeking some resemblance to William but apart from his paler skin and narrower lips than his mother's, he appeared to carry a likeness only to his African forebears. She was pleased about that. It was disturbing enough to know that William was the child's father without the likeness being obvious.

Curiosity made Susannah reach out to touch

his woolly hair, surprisingly springy to her touch, and he glanced up at her with an enchanting smile. 'You are doing very well, Joseph,' she said. 'I think that's enough for today but next time I shall show you how to write your name.' She watched him go skipping off to play with Aphra and looked forward to telling William how well he was doing.

Emmanuel stirred the ashes in the hearth with the poker and then looked at Susannah out of the corner of his eye.

It wasn't until he had gone to coax Aphra down from the beams high up in the apex of the roof that Susannah realised he had drawn the shapes of his ABC in the ashes.

*   *   *

William began to come home later and later and looked more and more exhausted on those few occasions Susannah did see him. One evening she waited up in the chapel until after midnight, listening for him to come in. Holding up a candle to light the way, she watched him as he slowly climbed the stairs.

'William? I have some supper ready for you in the chapel.'

'Supper?' He rubbed a hand over his face. 'I can't remember the last time I ate.'

'Then it's important that you have something now.' She held her ground, refusing to allow him to pass. 'You cannot go on like this without becoming ill yourself. And then where would your patients be?'

'Susannah, I'm too tired . . .'

'Come and eat!' After a brief hesitation, he

followed her.

He ate with total concentration, swiftly demolishing a slice of beef pie then dismembering a chicken leg and sucking at the bone as if he hadn't eaten for days, which might indeed have been the case.

Susannah watched him as he ate; she had to stop herself from smoothing a lock of dark hair off his forehead. Lines of exhaustion were etched round his mouth and she worried for him.

At last he wiped his fingers on a napkin and eased back with a sigh.

'Better?' she asked.

The candles on the table between them cast shadows up onto his face, forming dark hollows under his cheekbones. He nodded and she waited.

'I've been to Bedlam again.'

Enclosed within the intimate circle of candlelight the rest of the world seemed far away. 'Was it very terrible?' she asked.

'It's impossible to describe the horror of it. The inmates are lost souls. Their terror eats into my mind and I cannot sleep.'

'But you have tended their ailments and eased their pain.'

'It's not enough. No one cares what happens to them; their families have cast them into hell.' He buried his face in his hands.

Uncertain, embarrassed, Susannah reached out and touched his arm. 'Someone must care about them or you would not have been sent for.'

'A mother with a guilty conscience asked me to visit her son. Seventeen years old and confined for stammering and the falling sickness! Most of the time he is as well as you or I. He should never have been sent to such a place.' His voice broke and he swallowed. 'But he died of the bloody flux and will no longer be an embarrassment to his family.'

'Can nothing be done to help the other inmates?'

'There are too many of them.'

'But you comforted that poor boy as he was dying.'

'To save one minnow from a raging torrent doesn't help the rest.'

'Yet you made a difference to *him*.'

William took his hands away from his face and stared at her. 'Yes, I suppose I did.'

Susannah picked up the candlesticks. 'It's late.' He followed her from the chapel as she lit the way along the corridor. She stopped outside the door of her bedchamber and handed him one of the candles, curiously reluctant to say goodnight. 'I think you will sleep now,' she said.

He smothered a yawn. 'Perhaps I will. God knows, I'm tired enough. Goodnight, Susannah. And thank you.'

Before she had time to realise what was happening he had pulled her to him and dropped a kiss on her forehead. Without a word, he made his way off along the corridor.

She watched him disappear round the turn while her heartbeat skipped and a sudden warmth climbed up her throat. She stood still for a moment in happy amazement, unwilling to break the spell, and then went into her room.

*   *   *

The next morning Susannah was combing Agnes's hair when William knocked on the bedchamber door.

'I came to speak with you, Aunt,' he said.

'Could it not have waited until I'm dressed?'

'I beg your pardon.'

'What is so important that it cannot wait?'

'Susannah is too pale from being so much shut up.' He sat on the edge of the bed and took Agnes's hand. 'She should take a walk in the fresh air and put the roses back in her cheeks for the sake of the child, don't you think? And I will sit beside you this morning. It is a long time since we have had a cosy chat, isn't it, Aunt?'

The old woman's face broke into a happy smile. 'It will be like the old days, before you became so serious. Put on my cap, Susannah, and you may leave us.'

Outside in the sunshine, Susannah almost skipped down the street. She breathed in deeply, not caring for the moment that the air carried the stink of putrefaction from the plague pit in the churchyard two streets away. She was free! As if in tune with her high spirits, the baby danced within her and she pressed her fingers to her stomach, laughing at the wonder of it.

An old man, hobbling by, looked at her strangely and crossed over to the other side of the street.

Before long she had come to Martha's house and was knocking on the door.

'What a lovely surprise! It's been weeks since I saw you,' exclaimed Martha as she kissed her cheek. 'Come into the garden and tell me all your news.'

In the dappled shade of the apple tree Martha's eldest child, Patience, rocked a cradle, draped with muslin to keep out the flies.

265

Inside Susannah saw her godson dozing peacefully with his thumb in his mouth. His cheeks, flushed with sleep, were as perfect as a ripe peach. Her heart turned over with sudden love for him. 'Isn't he beautiful?' she breathed.

'Especially when he's asleep,' said his mother with a proud smile.

'I can hardly believe that by the end of the summer I will have my own baby to rock in his cradle.' *If I don't die in childbed.* She pushed away the thought and forced herself to smile at her friend.

'Sit on the bench and try some of the gingerbread Patience made today,' said Martha, picking up a small shirt from the pile of mending beside her and threading her needle.

'You look very well,' she said a moment later, glancing at Susannah's stomach.

'Growing fatter by the minute, you mean! And I'll be even fatter if I eat too many of these delicious gingerbread men.'

'Not fatter, but the baby is growing and your bodice is too small.'

'I feel like a sausage that's too large for its skin. I have let out my skirts twice already and I fear there is no more material left in the seams.'

'I can lend you some looser gowns, if you like. I hope I shall not need them again for a while.'

Susannah put her hand to her side, unable to contain her smile. 'My baby is moving all the time now. It's so strange to think of him like a little fish swimming around in a bowl.'

'It is one of God's many miracles.'

'Martha, you cannot imagine how much I want this baby now! Since Father married Arabella I

266

have felt so alone but this child will be my very own to love. He gives me a whole new reason for being.'

Martha took Susannah's hands, her hazel eyes shining. 'I am happy to see that you are not afraid any more.'

'Of course I'm afraid! But I'm trying very hard not to be. In some ways I'm more terrified than ever. Now I am frightened not only for myself but for my baby too. I never imagined I should have a child and I cannot bear the thought that something dreadful might happen to him.'

'You must put your trust in God's hands, Susannah.'

'Were you *never* anxious about dying in childbed?'

Martha glanced at her brood of children playing with their hoops and spinning tops at the end of the garden. 'Of course! Usually it was in the depths of the night when the Devil tries to worm his way into your dreams. My deepest fear is always the thought of leaving my babies with no mother to care for them. But as you can see, it is God's will to keep me in good health.'

'Then I beg you to pray for me and my baby.'

'I already do,' said Martha. 'Now tell me your news. How does life go on in the Captain's House? Do you find William less stern as you come to know him?'

'I think . . .' Susannah hesitated. 'I think he is kinder than you might imagine from his manner. He rarely smiles but is selfless in helping those less fortunate than himself.'

'And your days are not too onerous in Mistress Fygge's employ?'

'I never forget my good fortune. She is a

considerate employer, even though a little crabby at times since she is always in pain.' Susannah sighed. 'But sometimes the days seem overlong. Reading aloud and helping an old lady to decide what to wear each day are trivial pursuits. I have skills which are now wasted and there is a lack of freedom, which irks me. Sometimes I think I am no more free than Henry's slaves.'

'But Mistress Fygge has allowed you to keep them?'

'William persuaded her.' Susannah paused. 'He takes a special interest in them since he knew Phoebe and her son from the time when he worked for his uncle in Barbados. He asked me to teach little Joseph his letters. He is an engaging child and I cannot help but become fond of him.'

'He is capable of learning then?'

'Indeed he is! Although I fear he would prefer to be running around in the garden with Emmanuel, seeking out mischief.'

Martha smiled. 'Like all boys.'

'But his mother doesn't like me teaching him.'

'Tell me about her.'

'Her appearance is curious to my eyes but there is something strangely attractive about her. Her eyes are sleepy and she moves with a languorous grace. Still, I don't like her. She watches me all the time and it makes the skin on the back of my neck prickle. To everyone else in the household she appears to know her place but she looks at me as if she hates me.'

'Why would she?'

'I'm not sure but she took against me from the minute she saw me. Then, last week, the silversmith delivered two silver collars, which Agnes had commissioned to match the one Emmanuel wears. It was the most extraordinary thing, Phoebe didn't even lift her gaze from the floor as I fastened the collar in place round her neck and she said nothing but I could feel waves of loathing emanating from her as strongly as the stench arising from a plague pit.'

'Why should she dislike such a costly gift? Surely you must have imagined it!'

'I assure you, I did not.' Susannah stopped, wondering if she should share her secret with Martha. She so longed to talk about it to someone. 'There is something else,' she said.

'What is that?'

'I overheard something which troubles me.'

'Oh?'

'It was when the slaves arrived. You see, Joseph was born while William was working on his uncle's plantation. I heard William tell Agnes that Joseph is his son.'

'No!' Martha's hands flew up to cover her mouth. 'But she's an African! Surely he couldn't . . .'

'He must have,' said Susannah. 'Did I say that Joseph's skin is an unusual light brown, neither dark nor white? I can't bear to think of it but each time I look at her, and then at Joseph, I am reminded of what must have occurred and it throws me into turmoil.'

'Then you must not think of it!' said Martha firmly.

'I cannot help it. And then, at our wedding, Henry and William argued. I didn't understand at the time but now, when I think about it . . .'

'What?' Martha's eyes were very wide and she leaned forward in her chair, her mending forgotten.

269

'I'd heard them quarrelling, you see. William said to Henry, "I don't want you to bring them here!" and Henry poked William in the chest and said that he'd *promised*.'

'I don't understand.'

'Henry had grown up with Phoebe and Erasmus and was fond of them. I believe he thought he could persuade William to do right by them once they were in England. After all, Joseph is William's son.'

'You do not think he and Phoebe still ...'

'No! No, I'm sure he doesn't.' Susannah stood up and paced about. '*Of course* not. It must have happened only once. Perhaps he had taken too much rum and his baser instincts got the better of him.'

'It upsets you to think of it, doesn't it? Perhaps you are jealous?'

'Jealous? Of Phoebe?'

'Of any woman who attracts William's attention.'

'What nonsense!'

'Is it?'

'Of course it is!' Then she remembered the way William had pulled her close and kissed her forehead the other night and all at once became uncomfortably warm.

James stirred in his cradle and began to whimper.

Susannah picked him up and paced briskly around the garden, patting his back to soothe his cries, but she saw Martha looking at her with a knowing smile on her lips.

Ghosts and Shadows

June 1666

Chapter 17

It was a combination of Mistress Oliver's heavy hand with the boiled mutton pudding and the warmth of the June night that kept Susannah awake. Moonlight bathed the room in a silvery luminosity far too bright for sleep. She kept her eyes tight closed and attempted to recapture the delightful dream she'd had of the child in the orchard but it remained elusive. The baby within her sensed her restlessness and performed a somersault, causing another wave of heartburn which forced her to rise. The floorboards creaked under her bare feet, echoing into the stillness of the night as she paced restlessly up and down. She pushed the window open wider and leaned out, the stone sill pressing into the hard swell of her belly. Lifting her hair off her neck, she allowed the soft breeze to cool her skin.

The sound of the watchman calling the hour drifted over the rooftops and cartwheels rattled across cobbles, making her shiver as she wondered if it was a dead cart making for the plague pit. Whatever was to become of them all? There was no sign that the plague was abating. Apprehension for the future, never far away, gripped her again.

A bat flitted across her line of vision and she watched as another joined it, weaving in and out of each other's flight path in a swooping ballet. Then her gaze was caught by a movement down in the garden.

Straining her eyes, she saw a figure walking slowly along the cloisters. The bright moon illuminated it briefly before it disappeared into the deep shadows of the arcading to reappear again a second later in the silvery light.

Then she heard the sound, a low keening of despair rising on the breeze that made her heart clench at the sheer desolation of it.

The figure emerged again from the shadows, head bowed and hands clasped.

Susannah caught her breath.

It was Phoebe who stood in the little patch of light, sobbing as if her heart was broken.

Confusion gripped Susannah. She stared down at the other woman. Her usual instinct would be to run to aid any soul in such terrible torment but their mutual dislike made her hesitate.

Then Phoebe disappeared.

Susannah peered again into the darkness, waiting, but not a soul stirred.

*   *   *

Susannah hurried along Fleet Street with her head down, picking her way through the muddy puddles left by the recent summer thunderstorm. Several of the shops in Fleet Street had the shutters up and the usual cheerful bustle was absent but then, most streets in the city were the same. A beggar, slumped against the wall, stirred and hopefully offered his stumps to her for inspection. She fumbled in her pocket and threw a few coins into his hat, wrinkling her nose at the smell of him, even though she kept her distance. No one in their right mind would risk sickness by approaching any stranger, never mind a beggar, in such times.

A dead rat, monstrously swollen and heaving

274

with maggots, lay in her path and she fought down a wave of nausea as she stepped over it. Even the rats were dying! Not far to go now. A few yards away the sign depicting the Unicorn and the Dragon creaked back and forth in the breeze. She pushed open the shop door and went inside.

Her father glanced up from the counter, his face breaking into a smile of welcome. 'Susannah, my dearest!'

His chin was rough against her cheek and she breathed in his familiar and comforting scent. She noticed that he no longer wore the splendid black wig in the shop but had retreated into the old brown one while he worked.

Holding her at arm's length, he studied her face. 'Are you well? You look blooming, though perhaps a little tired?'

'I'm finding it difficult to sleep. The baby kicks me awake and I have heartburn. Peppermint and fennel seed are what I need to soothe my stomach.'

'Infuse it in a pint of boiling water and . . .' He stopped. 'Sorry! Habit. You know as well as anyone how to prepare peppermint tea. It's such a shame that you can no longer . . .'

'Yes, isn't it? Still, I was able to feel useful by rubbing some oil of cloves onto Peg's gums the other day to relieve her toothache.'

Cornelius sighed. 'I miss you more than I can say. Not only for your assistance in the dispensary but for all the discussions we had,' he smiled, 'arguments even, about the latest plays and books. Arabella, for all her virtues, doesn't read or take an interest in current affairs. Sometimes I wish . . .'

'Me, too.'

Sudden tears glinted in his eyes. 'I'm a

275

sentimental old fool. Take no notice of me.' He took down one of the gallypots, shook out some dried peppermint, twisted it up in a piece of paper and handed it to her. 'Will you go upstairs and see the twins? Arabella is in the parlour and I'm sure she would be glad of some feminine company. She finds it lonely here.'

The last thing Susannah wanted was to pay a duty visit to Arabella but the pleading look in her father's eyes made her nod. 'Samuel and Joshua will have grown since I saw them last.'

'Indeed they have and their lung power has increased with them.'

'Do they still keep you awake in the night?'

'Not so much, thankfully. Although they are teething now and often fractious.'

'Shall you come up to sit with us?'

'In a little while. I have some urgent prescriptions to prepare. Yet another family struck down by the plague in Thames Street.'

'Then let me help you. I will visit Arabella afterwards.'

Susannah found her old, stained brown apron still hanging on the hook in the dispensary and wrapped it round herself like an old friend before she set to work.

'There seems to be no way to control the pestilence,' Susannah said. 'William is out at all times of the day and night tending to the sick. He cannot go on like this without becoming ill himself.' She gripped the edge of the counter until her knuckles were white, overcome by her fears again.

'He often comes to see me for his prescriptions,' said Cornelius. 'He has become the closest thing to a best friend to me since poor Richard was taken. Those physicians and apothecaries that are left in the city are stretched beyond all normal capabilities. Yet what else can we do but help those who need us?'

Once the medicines were made up and poured into bottles, Susannah took off her apron and reluctantly hung it up on the hook again.

'Since Ned has not yet returned I must deliver these straight away,' said Cornelius.

'Take no risks, I beg you! Leave the bottles on the doorstep.'

'I always do.' Cornelius hugged her, kissing the top of her head. 'Come and see me again soon.' He snatched up his hat from the counter and left.

Susannah washed the pestle and mortar and returned the gallypots to their rightful places. She noticed that some now had new labels in Ned's untidy hand but apart from that everything was just the same. There was still that familiar and well-loved aroma in the air and she breathed in deeply to savour it. Here, in the shop, she could imagine that nothing had ever changed. Sighing, she closed the door behind her and went into the passage.

There was a thunder of small feet clumping down the stairs and Arabella's three older children pushed past her, shrieking and bickering as they went.

Harriet stopped with her hands on her hips. 'Oh, it's you! What are you here for?'

'I've come to visit. How are the twins?'

Harriet pulled a face. 'Noisy and smelly.' She ran off after her brothers without a second glance.

Jennet was busy making a pudding in the kitchen and jumped when Susannah touched her arm. 'Miss

277

Susannah! You startled me!' She wiped floury hands on her apron. 'It's so good to see you at home.' Pleasure lit her homely features.

'Alas, not my home any more. I'm to go up and visit my stepmother but thought I'd come to see you first.'

'That's mighty kind of you, miss.'

'And I wondered if you might spare me a little bread and cheese? I am almost fainting with hunger.'

'Will you stay for dinner? I can put some extra onions in the pudding.'

'I've stayed too long already. Shall I help myself from the pantry?'

'Cover the cheese again when you've finished with it or those dratted rats will be in there gnawing at the master's Stilton. I asked the mistress if I couldn't have a kitchen cat again to keep the little pests down but she says cats in the kitchen are dirty.'

'So are rats. Still, I do remember poor old Tibby helping herself on more than one occasion to a nice piece of fish from the table or a custard put to cool.'

'Cats are thieves and no mistake but much better than traps at keeping down the rats. Now why don't you sit at the end of the table while I'm busy and tell me what you've been doing with yourself?'

Twenty minutes later Susannah shook the crumbs from her skirt into the hearth. 'I can't put it off any longer, Jennet; I must go upstairs. I daresay Arabella will enjoy ramming home the fact that I've lost my smart house and am now a servant.'

Arabella reclined upon her daybed looking out of the parlour window with a piece of embroidery lying ignored upon her knee.

Susannah stood in the doorway and repressed a shudder of distaste at her stepmother's Chinese furniture. How could she! But there was no changing the situation now so she had better put a good face on it.

Arabella turned and smiled. 'Susannah! I confess I am bored nearly to death so I am very pleased to see you. Come and sit by me and tell me your news.'

Surprised by the warmth of her reception, Susannah concluded that Arabella must indeed be extremely bored. 'I haven't a great deal of news,' she said. 'My days are largely spent with Mistress Fygge and she hardly ever goes out these days.'

'Very wise. The city is not safe but your father still refuses to decamp to the country. I cannot believe the pestilence is still with us after so long. I dare not go to the Exchange to buy so much as a ribbon or a pair of gloves without endangering my life and my friends rarely visit any more. Even our butcher has died and we cannot get a decent bit of mutton. It's all dreadfully fatiguing.'

'You have Father's books to help you pass the time.'

'Books!' She opened her blue eyes wide in amazement. 'What good are they? I want to go to a party and see a play or take dinner at an inn! My life is passing me by and there is no enjoyment.'

'You have your children and your house.'

'And a very poor house it is.'

'I always loved it here.'

'You had never known any better.'

Susannah forbore to make any comment on that. 'How are the children?'

'Mercifully quiet at the moment.'

'I saw Harriet and the boys on their way outside

but I should like to see the twins before I go.'

'They're asleep at present but you can look in on them if you wish.' Arabella stared at Susannah's expanding waistline. 'When is your baby expected to make an appearance? Another two or three months by the look of you?'

'The end of September.'

'And what plans have you made? Presumably you have some idea of where you will go and how you will manage after the child is born?'

'I shan't go anywhere. My husband's aunt has offered me and my baby a home.'

'Susannah, don't tell me you haven't even *thought* about this?' Arabella sat bolt upright, pushing her embroidery to the floor. 'Mistress Fygge is an old woman. What will you do when she dies?'

'She is quite well and has no intention of dying!'

'I don't suppose she has but nevertheless, she will. And then what?'

'Well,' Susannah hesitated, 'I assume William will inherit her property.'

'*He* will have no need of a waiting woman, will he? And it would not be seemly for you to stay on in the house with him. Alone.'

Susannah bit her lip as the precariousness of her situation came home to her. She felt an icy quiver of unease run down her back. Had she become too complacent? 'He would not turn me out,' she said.

'Don't you think you had better make sure of it?'

'That isn't something I could discuss with him!'

'Don't be obtuse, Susannah. I'm not suggesting you *talk* about what will happen after Agnes has gone to meet her Maker but that you *take steps* to ensure that you still have a future living in her house. With William.'

280

Susannah felt the heat creep up her cheeks as she understood Arabella's meaning.

'He won't be interested in you now, of course, not while you are bloated and ugly with his cousin's child in your belly, but you will need to move quickly once the baby is born. It's a shame you will be encumbered by Henry's child but you *must* find another husband as soon as possible. You could do worse you know. I grant you William always wears a sour expression but if you like your men with dark looks and can ignore his moods, he is really rather fine-looking.'

Susannah stared down at her hands folded in her lap, horrified by Arabella's suggestion. Her heart began to thud against her chest and sweat prickled under her arms. The very idea of making up to William in order to entrap him into marriage sickened her. And his expression wasn't sour, only unhappy. She pictured his face, closed in distress when he returned home after losing a patient. All at once she wanted to cry.

'I cannot . . .' She could hardly speak for the wild thoughts suddenly crowding into her head. And then, like a candle in the darkness, she understood the cause of her confusion.

Arabella sighed. 'Well, if you really *cannot* think of William as a suitable husband you will have to look elsewhere. But I urge you not to waste any time. You must look around you now and make your choice so that you can move swiftly after the baby is born. Time is not on your side and before you know it the first white hairs will arrive and another tooth will loosen and it will be too late. You will be doomed to spend the rest of your life as a servant to others and subject to their whims and fancies. You will have no security in your old age.'

'I think perhaps I will go and take a look at the twins.'

'Susannah, have you been listening at all to what I've been saying?'

'Yes, Arabella.'

'There's no need to look so shocked. Mistress Fygge has been useful to you but you *must* be prepared to make your own opportunities in life. There's no pleasure in being alone in the world with a child to support. Believe me, I know.'

'I suppose you do.'

'You must be prepared to make compromises. As I did. And, as far as I can see, William is your best opportunity at the moment, even if he isn't your ideal choice of husband.' She leaned forward. 'Look, I know we haven't always found each other congenial but now that you have left this house, I can, and do, offer you this advice in the true spirit of friendship. Life can be very frightening for a penniless widow with children.'

'Yes, I'm sure it is. And now I'll go up to the nursery, if I may.'

Arabella clicked her tongue in disgust. 'Be off with you, then! But don't come running back to me for help in five years' time when Agnes is dead, William is married to someone else and you have crow's feet and no man will look at you.'

*   *   *

Susannah found the nursemaids only too pleased to allow her to entertain her baby brothers for a while. Somehow the babies seemed to sense her reflective mood and sat quietly on her knee, batting at her curls with their tiny fists, an expression of intense concentration on their faces.

The trouble was, Susannah thought as she rocked Joshua and Samuel in her arms, the blinding revelation which had come to her while Arabella prattled on was so disturbing that it had rendered her speechless. Since she had never encountered a similar situation before she'd had no way of recognising the restlessness that had overtaken her of late and only now that did she understand its meaning. All at once it had become quite clear to her that, with close acquaintance and the passing of time, she had fallen hopelessly in love with William.

Chapter 18

Agnes had retired to her chamber for a nap. Dismissed, Susannah rested on her own bed for a while but she couldn't sleep for all the thoughts whirling round in her head. Lying with her hands clasped over her stomach so that she could feel every little movement within, she wondered how she could not have realised before how significantly her feelings for William had changed.

Of course he was still the same stern-faced, austere man he had always been but over the months she'd seen something, just a glimmer, of humour and vulnerability that had made her warm to him. No, a great deal more than that, she admitted to herself. But somehow it felt wrong to be falling in love with William while she was pregnant with his cousin's child. And then there was the distasteful fact of his past association with

Phoebe. Even forgetting that, it had taken Arabella to point out that, after Agnes had been released from her earthly cares, it would be impossible for Susannah to continue to live in the same house as William. The thought of him disappearing from her life had made her freeze in terror.

At last, finding it impossible to doze off, she decided to go down to the kitchen and make some ginger biscuits to tempt Agnes's appetite.

The kitchen was as busy as a beehive. Phoebe was scrubbing pots with Joseph at her side. Peg was sitting at one end of the kitchen table peeling a heap of vegetables and swatting Aphra's paw away as she tried to steal a carrot, while Emmanuel chuckled at the little ape's antics.

Mistress Oliver had her sleeves rolled up and was pummelling the bread dough as if she held a personal grudge against it, which, indeed, she did.

'Will I be in your way if I make some biscuits?' asked Susannah.

'You'd better hurry up. The fire will soon be too hot. That's the third baker we've lost to the pestilence this year. As if I didn't have enough to do without having to make all the bread too!'

'Can you not find another baker?' asked Susannah.

'I haven't time to be traipsing all over the city fetching the bread. Peg!'

Peg tapped Aphra on the muzzle and extracted a carrot from the monkey's paw. 'Yes, Mistress Oliver?'

'More coal! And look sharp about it! Make the fire good and hot or the bread will be as hard as a stone.'

Without a word Peg picked up the coal scuttle

284

from beside the fire and hurried off to the coal store.

'I'll help her,' said Emmanuel.

'Be quick or I'll come looking for you both. And don't you be dirtying that velvet coat of yours or you'll make the mistress angry.'

Aphra seized her chance and snatched a carrot before retreating to the top of the dresser, chattering with excitement at her prize. Joseph jumped about, throwing turnips at the monkey and shouting at her to come down while Phoebe clattered the pots as she put them away.

'Sometimes I think this kitchen is worse than Bedlam,' sighed the cook, pushing a stringy lock of hair off her face with a floury hand. 'I need to keep my eye on that pair. I caught 'em canoodling in the pantry the other day.'

Susannah pounded the lumps out of the sugar, wondering if she ought to be worried about Peg but then remembered the girl's account of how she had cracked Mistress McGregor's 'brother' over the head with a candlestick and jumped out of the window at the house in Cock Lane. She decided that Peg could look after herself. Nevertheless, she was relieved when Emmanuel appeared a few minutes later carrying the coal scuttle.

As she sieved the husks out of the flour, Susannah covertly watched Phoebe. She had found a length of blue cotton fabric and tied it round her head in a turban. It gave her a curiously dignified air as she moved slowly about her duties. There was no apparent sign of her distress of the previous night and she met Susannah's glance with such an impertinent look that it made Susannah gasp.

285

The sun was warm on Susannah's back and she hummed to herself while she watered the herb garden. The parsley had grown large enough now that she would be able to pick a few sprigs for the table. Perhaps she would make an omelette sprinkled with chopped herbs for William when he returned home. He'd seen such terrible suffering over the past few months and he looked so careworn that she longed to cosset him.

Kneeling down on the moist earth to pick the parsley, she imagined how they would sit alone by candlelight, talking together while he ate the omelette. She pictured him smiling at her and then he would take her hand and lift it to his lips. She would lean towards him, just a little, and then he'd . . . The toe of a man's boot appeared in her line of vision. She glanced up and saw the object of her daydream looking down at her with a half-smile that convinced her he must be able to read her thoughts. She felt the colour flood her cheeks and attempted to scramble to her feet but became so entangled in her damp skirt that she was obliged to accept his proffered hand, dropping the little bunch of parsley in the process.

'Your garden is proving successful,' William said, picking it up. Brushing earth and bits of weed off her skirt, Susannah prayed he could not see how her heart thudded in her breast. 'I have always wanted a garden,' she said, slightly out of breath. 'Have you seen how tightly the parsley curls? And it is such a beautiful shade of green.' He raised an eyebrow and she felt herself blush again. 'I'm babbling, aren't I? You shouldn't have crept up on me and caught me by surprise.'

'I had no intention of startling you but I admit that I was watching you while you worked. You seemed so content, humming away to yourself, that I didn't want to disturb you.'

'When I'm tending the garden I can't seem to worry about what else is going on in the world. All cares and concerns seem to be very far away. Close contact with the earth is very healing, don't you think?'

He looked at her for a long moment, his face expressionless, almost as if his thoughts were somewhere else. 'My mother used to say that,' he said at last. He blinked, as if breaking a spell. 'And you're right about the parsley.' He held the little bunch out to her. 'Its shade is very nearly as beautiful as the green of your eyes.'

Slowly she reached out her hand to take it from him and as their fingers met she heard his sharp intake of breath, just as if he'd been burned by her touch.

They remained frozen for a fragment of time that seemed to stretch into for ever while she stared at his hand against hers. Transfixed, she studied his long fingers and the tracery of veins shadowing through the lightly tanned skin on the back of his hands. She had a sudden and overwhelming desire to kiss the vulnerable-looking skin on the underside of his wrist where it disappeared under the lace at his cuffs.

Then his hand curled round hers in a grip so tight it made her gasp. 'Susannah?' His face was serious, no trace of humour now. 'I must talk to you.'

'Yes, William?' Surely he must see the pulse

287

beating in her throat? Was he going to admit to her his relationship to Joseph? Or dared she to hope ...

He swallowed and looked at their hands, fingers still intertwined. 'Perhaps you've become conscious that—'

A sudden shout made them both start and they let go of each other as if they were glowing embers. They turned to see Joseph chasing Emmanuel across the courtyard with a broom. The little boy shrieked with glee as Emmanuel twisted and turned, never quite letting Joseph catch him. They raced through the cloisters, their laughter echoing under the arcading, disappearing as quickly as they had arrived, leaving the garden quiet once more.

As Susannah turned to face William again she felt her baby kick and placed a hand against the tiny foot pressing inside her.

William's gaze dropped to the swell of her belly and he stepped back.

'William?'

'I must go to see my aunt,' he said. Abruptly he turned, strode across the garden and disappeared inside.

Tears blurred Susannah's vision. The parsley lay scattered upon the ground, and she bent to gather it up. The fresh green sprigs were bruised and flattened, crushed under William's foot as he had hurried to escape from her.

*   *   *

Susannah combed Agnes's hair and braided it into a thin plait, tying the end with a ribbon, all the while reliving her meeting in the garden with William.

Her pulse fluttered at the memory. 'Will you wear your nightcap?' she asked.

'It's too hot. I never have liked the heat of summer in the city. The stench breeds fevers and the plague is never far away. We've been lucky.'

'Except for Henry.'

Agnes shrugged. 'He should have known better than to go to taverns and alehouses; it was tempting the Devil to visit him with some vile sickness.'

'What else could he have done? He had to meet people to seek new business.'

'And look where it got him! And now Will is out day after day visiting the sick and putting himself at risk.' Agnes picked fretfully at the cuff of her nightgown.

Susannah gripped the comb so tightly that the ivory teeth bit into her palm. It was her constant fear that William would sicken.

'I never cared very much for Henry,' continued Agnes. 'He was too like his mother, seeking only pleasant diversions and unable to bear life's disappointments. Will, however is altogether different from his cousin.'

'He takes very great care of his patients.'

Agnes sighed. 'Close the curtains, will you? Help me into bed and read me something soothing.'

Susannah slowly pulled the curtains across the tightly closed window, reluctant to shut out the beauty of the fiery sunset. The bedchamber was claustrophobic from the warmth of the day but Agnes feared the noxious humours rising from the city even more than she disliked an overheated bedchamber.

Picking up a book from the bedside table, Susannah pulled the stool close to the candle. She forced her turbulent thoughts to the back of her mind as she began to read.

'Come live with me and be my love,
And we will all the pleasures prove,
That valleys, groves, hills and fields,
Woods or steepy mountains yields.'

She glanced at Agnes and saw that her eyes were closed. Just for a moment she let her thoughts drift to William and her visit to Merryfields. How peaceful it was there and how free from the cares of the world he had seemed then!

'And we will sit upon the rocks
Seeing the shepherds feed their flocks
By shallow rivers, to whose falls
Melodious birds sing madrigals.'

Agnes's mouth had fallen open and her breathing was even but Christopher Marlowe's words had no power to quieten Susannah's own confused frame of mind today.

In the garden that morning, how could she have imagined, even for a moment, that William cared for her? Her pregnancy revolted him and, as Arabella had pointed out, he could not possibly find her attractive while she was bloated and ugly with another man's child.

Taking care not to disturb her mistress, Susannah placed the book back on the bedside table and left the room.

Her thoughts were still so caught up with William that she didn't hear Joseph as he ran along the corridor behind her until he raced past. She put

290

out her hand and caught him. 'Where are you off to in such a hurry, little man?'

'Doan want to go to bed!'

'But it's late.' She looked up as she heard footsteps and saw Phoebe. 'There's your mama. Be a good boy and do as she bids you.'

Phoebe took the child's hand. 'Come, Joseph!'

'I'm not tired!'

'But you will be tired tomorrow if you don't rest now,' said Susannah. 'I don't want to see you falling asleep while I'm teaching you your letters. Your mama will be very proud of you when you can read and write, won't you, Phoebe?'

The black woman stuck out her bottom lip. 'A slave don't need letters,' she said. 'A slave needs freedom.'

'Perhaps . . .' Susannah hesitated, trying to ignore her antagonism, 'perhaps when Joseph is grown up, if he can read and learn how to make his own way in the world, perhaps then he might be free.'

'If *you* say he can be free? Why do *you* have the power for his life, or mine? What makes *you* better than Joseph and me?' Phoebe almost spat the words out and her eyes glittered with a dangerous light.

Susannah took a step back. 'I would like to see Joseph have opportunities but for that he needs education.'

'Education? Ha! A white man's word. You think my son need education because he is white man's son?'

'It's not just because Joseph is Dr Ambrose's son!'

Phoebe stared at her. Then a slow smile spread

291

across her face. 'You know Joseph is doctor's son? And you want help Joseph?'

'Dr Ambrose has asked me to teach Joseph his letters.'

Slowly Phoebe nodded. 'I seen you looking at Dr Ambrose. You think if you teach Joseph, the doctor love you.'

'How dare you!'

'Joseph is *my* son. And the doctor his father. Don't *you* forget it! Your husband die only a few months ago and already you look for a new man, even before baby come. My people have a name for women like dat.' Phoebe took a firm grip on Joseph's hand and pulled him away.

Susannah watched them disappear round the corner, her fingers twitching as she itched to slap the triumphant smile off the other woman's face. *How dare she!* She went into the chapel, slamming the door behind her to give vent to her feelings.

The dying sunset had painted the chapel walls a rich gold and Susannah curled up on the window seat to watch the orange disc of the sun drop behind the rooftops. After a while, the beauty of the sunset began to ease the agitation of her mind. The street below was already cast in shadow and a few people hurried by on their way home. A rat streaked along the ground, stopping to investigate a mound of kitchen waste, and then sat there, as bold as brass, gnawing a bone. One by one, candles appeared in the windows of the houses opposite as the light faded.

A familiar figure strode along the street, deftly sidestepping the rubbish.

William was early tonight, thought Susannah, her heart thudding. She smoothed her curls and

292

pinched her cheeks, desperately hoping he would seek her out and continue their interrupted conversation.

The front door clanged shut and footsteps mounted the stairs and echoed along the corridor, stopping outside the door to the chapel.

Susannah held her breath.

After a moment the footsteps continued.

Involuntarily, she called his name. 'William!'

The door creaked open and William's head appeared.

'Susannah, what are you doing here, sitting all alone in the gloom?'

'Agnes went early to bed and I've been watching the sunset.'

'Did you want something?'

Her blossoming hope died. 'No, I merely wondered if you'd had a good day.'

'In so far as there were no deaths, I suppose you could say I'd had a good day. And your health? It remains good?'

'Apart from a little backache and some bad dreams I am well, thank you.'

'I am pleased to hear it.'

'I saw Goody Joan the other day. She told me that vivid dreams are quite normal for a woman in my condition.'

'She is a fine midwife with a good record of successful births.' He stopped, as if he'd run out of commonplace conversation at last. 'I'll bid you goodnight, then.'

'Goodnight.'

Susannah turned her gaze back to the darkening street below, disappointment making her eyes smart. Had she imagined it then, that William had looked upon her with affection, no, *more* than affection in his eyes? Or was her present condition inflaming her imagination? But she had been so sure that he had been about to tell her that he cared for her.

It was no good sitting in the half-dark mooning like a lovesick calf over a man who simply thought of her as a patient. And a charity case, at that. As she uncurled herself from the window seat she saw the door of the house opposite flung wide. A young woman tumbled out whom Susannah recognised as Jane Quick. Her fair hair was uncovered and loose upon her shoulders. She ran across the street, heedless of the mire as she splashed through the stinking drain.

A second or so later Susannah started at the sound of hammering upon the knocker. By the time she had made her way down the stairs Peg had opened the door and Jane stood there wringing her hands and sobbing.

'The physician! Is he here? Please, he must come now! It's Edwin. He's been sniffing and sneezing with a summer cold but this evening he fell into a swoon and I can't wake him. He's burning with fever and I don't know what to do!'

Peg flattened herself against the wall. 'The plague? Go away! We don't want the plague here!'

'Peg!' said Susannah sharply. 'You forget yourself! Go upstairs and call Dr Ambrose. At once!'

'Yes, miss.' Peg scurried up the stairs.

Susannah swallowed back her own fear at the terror in Jane Quick's eyes. 'Go and sit with Edwin now,' she said. 'Dr Ambrose will come over to you. And I'll send you a bottle of a very good medicine that I have in the still room.'

Jane Quick had only been gone a moment when William hastened down the stairs, his beaked mask in his hand.

Susannah caught at his sleeve. 'William, be careful, won't you? What if it is the plague?'

'Then it is in the hands of God and there is little I can do except ease the child's suffering and wait.'

'But what if he sneezes over you?'

William gave a half-smile. 'I have long learned to dodge a sneeze. And in any case I have a theory that the plague isn't spread by sneezes and noxious air at all.'

'A theory! What good is that?'

'The best hope I have at present.'

'Wait, just a moment! I promised Mistress Quick a bottle of my Plague Prevention Syrup.' She rushed off to the still room and returned to thrust the bottle into William's hand. 'Take a dose yourself, too.'

He nodded and closed the door behind him.

*   *   *

It was dawn when Susannah was jolted awake. She had kept vigil on the chapel window seat, waiting for William to emerge from the house opposite, and finally dozed off just before dawn until the spine-chilling scream reverberated through the houses.

In the street below Jane Quick fought and twisted in her husband's arms as he attempted to quieten her shrieks. A horse and cart had stopped outside their house, its grim cargo of corpses half-covered with sacking. The driver jumped down

295

and held the horse's head as it whinnied and kicked up its heels, frightened by the commotion.

The small crowd fell back like the waters of the Red Sea as one of the buriers came out of the house carrying the body of a small boy.

Gasping in horror, Susannah hastened down the stairs in time to see William running out of the door in front of her.

'I didn't hear you come home!'

'I returned an hour ago, after I alerted the watchers that the boy was gravely ill.'

As the burier covered the boy with the sacking, Jane Quick began to thrash and scream again. 'Francis! Francis, don't let them take our baby! Can't you see? He's only sleeping. Just a little summer cold, that's all it is!'

'Jane, he's gone! Edwin has gone.' Francis Quick held his wife tightly to his chest, his face buried in her loosened hair.

All at once Jane gave up the fight and collapsed against him, weeping piteously.

The driver climbed back onto the cart, flicked the horse with his whip and trundled away.

Susannah bit her knuckles at the sight of Jane's distress, tears of pity on her face.

'You must go into your house now,' said William to the weeping couple. 'Do you have family who can feed you?'

'Feed us? Do you think we can eat while our son is on his way to the plague pit?' said Francis Quick.

Jane moaned and buried her face in her husband's shoulder.

'Do you have family nearby?' persisted William. 'Is there someone I can fetch for you?'

Quick shook his head. 'Our family is all in

Leicestershire. We only came to London a year back.'

'I must go with Edwin,' wailed Jane. 'I must know where they are taking him.'

She pulled away from her husband and made to run off after the cart but a heavily built man carrying a halberd stepped forward from the dissipating crowd and barred her way. 'Back in the house, mistress,' he said. 'You've to be quarantined.'

'But I must go ...'

'You cannot.' He grasped her with beefy hands and pushed her towards the open front door. 'And you, sir. Now.'

Defeated, the Quicks went inside.

White-faced, William moved to take hold of Susannah's arm but thought better of it. 'I must cleanse myself for fear of infection. Let me take you home.'

'William, I know them! I met Jane Quick and little Edwin a few weeks ago,' wept Susannah. 'Edwin fell over in a puddle and Jane scolded him. One minute he was a mischievous little boy and now he's about to be thrown into the pit and covered in quicklime like a piece of rotten horse meat!'

'Don't think of that. Remember he's gone to a better place.'

'Look! Oh, William, must they?'

The watchman had begun to nail shut the door to Jane Quick's house, each hammer blow making Susannah wince.

Inside the house Jane Quick began to scream again.

297

Chapter 19

Black depression settled over the household like a sea-coal fog. Susannah sat on the chapel window seat for hour after hour watching the house on the other side of the street, haunted by the memory of poor little Edwin's body. There was a red cross painted on the door now and passers-by gave it a wide margin. The watchman slouched on the doorstep picking his teeth with a knife and in the evenings he was replaced by another guard for the night shift.

William visited the Quicks every day, calling up to them through the upstairs window. He reported that the couple remained free of plague symptoms but suffered greatly from a sickness of the spirits.

A great pall of smoke rose up over the rooftops as Edwin's bed and all the household blankets and linen were thrown onto a bonfire in the back yard. Once it was apparent that his parents had not been immediately stricken down, Agnes gave Susannah leave to turn out the linen closet and to take a set of sheets and a blanket to the house over the street. Susannah fetched cleansing herbs from her father's shop for the Quicks to smoke away the pestilence and made up a basket of provisions for them.

Francis Quick lowered a rope from the window to haul up the basket. 'Thank you, Mistress Savage. The food we had has all spoiled and a month is a long time to go without.'

'I'll come by again,' said Susannah. 'How is poor Jane?'

'She lies on her bed weeping and is grown very

298

thin.'

'Tell her I am thinking of her.'

That evening William sighed and put down his knife. 'Don't keep watching me like that, Susannah! It puts me off my supper.'

'I want to be sure you haven't caught the infection from the Quicks.'

'Do you think I would stay here to endanger you all if I thought I was sickening? Eat your dinner and try not to worry.'

'But we do! What if—'

Agnes held up her hand to Susannah. 'William is a great deal more sensible than Henry,' she said.

'Good God, I should hope so!' said William, his expression aghast.

In the silence that followed Susannah found herself thinking that, however sensible William appeared, he was the one who had fathered a child by a slave woman.

William cut himself another slice of bread. 'It is interesting, and maybe I shall write a paper on it later on, but I can't help noticing that where there is overcrowding and poverty and filth, that's where the worst of the sickness lies. In the richer sort of households it's common for there to be only one or two victims, however much the patient sneezes. And not everyone who sickens dies.'

'So . . .' Susannah hesitated while she considered this new idea. 'So you don't think the pestilence is spread by sneezes and evil humours from the smog or the river?'

'I believe that either the good Lord is watching over me or that the infection cannot be spread by the means you describe. There may even be different sorts of the pestilence.' He leaned forward. 'If only we could rid the city of the rat-infested tenements and clean the filth from the alleys and drains I'm sure we could bring the plague under control.'

'There is always plague in the city,' said Agnes. 'It's been there for as long as I can remember, gathering strength every now and again and lying in wait for us.'

'There must be more we can do!' said Susannah. 'If only I'd been born a man I could have been an apothecary. Or even a doctor.'

William gave a tight little smile. 'But the world is a richer place for your feminine graces.'

Agnes cackled. 'It's a long time since I've heard you pay a woman a pretty compliment, William.'

'I am merely stating a truth,' he said.

Susannah was gratified to note that the tips of his ears had turned as pink as her cheeks. 'That's all very well,' she replied, 'but I serve no useful purpose any more and it irks me.'

'You *are* fulfilling a useful purpose in giving lessons to young Joseph. And I understand you are teaching Emmanuel too. I found him spelling out the words from my newspaper the other day.'

Agnes pushed her plate away. 'What purpose is there in teaching a slave to read and write, especially if he is strong and could be put to better use in the fields?'

'Every reason,' said William. 'A slave, a woman or a child from the poorest hovel, *everyone* should have the opportunity of an education. Who knows what treasures are hidden behind the most unlikely façades?'

'And what happens when you have educated every last serving wench?' Agnes banged her fist on the table. 'Who then will empty the slops?'

*   *   *

Susannah's sleep continued to be disturbed by nightmares and she woke early one morning all tangled up in the sheet and with her heart racing. She'd dreamed again of her mother's terrible struggle to give birth and of the baby's barbaric death. Her mother's anguish seemed so real that every time she dreamed of it, Susannah carried the pain in her breast the following day: an aching, empty feeling that made her fear afresh for the loss of her own child.

Heavy-hearted, she dressed and went downstairs.

Peg was busy banking up the fire, while Phoebe shined the pewter.

'You're up early,' said Mistress Oliver as she slid the bread into the oven and banged the door shut behind it. 'Couldn't you sleep?'

'Bad dreams again.'

'Perhaps you'd better keep off the cheese at supper?'

Phoebe gave her a long, hard-eyed stare and turned back to the polishing.

Susannah glanced back over her shoulder as she left and could have sworn she saw a smile on the other woman's lips.

Agnes woke up in a disagreeable mood.

Susannah attempted to cajole her out of it, only to have her head nearly bitten off for her pains. She helped her to dress but the old woman was tetchy and difficult to please, changing her clothes twice.

'Bring me my looking-glass,' Agnes said. She scrutinised her reflection for some time. Then she

301

sighed. 'I never was a beauty, like my sister, but old age has cruelly stolen away what looks I had.'

'What you lack in youth is made up for in strength of character,' said Susannah.

'Why don't you simply say you think I am a cantankerous old biddy?'

'Because it isn't true. Not always, anyway,' she muttered, only half under her breath.

Agnes hooted with laughter. 'Fetch my rouge pot, miss, and I'll have no more of your impudence!'

Agnes eventually decided she was ready to face the world and, leaning heavily upon her stick, hobbled her way to the chapel.

Nothing pleased her that morning. Susannah offered to read to her but Agnes was in no mind to listen. They set up the chessboard but Agnes lost interest almost immediately. Emmanuel and Joseph's chatter gave her a headache and she sent them down to the kitchen. Peg brought in her dinner on a tray but Agnes barely tasted the rabbit fricassee or the salad of herbs.

Susannah, quite out of temper with it all, passed a miserable day undertaking her duties with less than usual care. Agnes drove her to distraction with her constant ruminating upon their probable fate if the plague drifted on the air towards the Captain's House. Added to this, Susannah had sharp pains in her hips and although she knew this was only because the ligaments were loosening to help the baby's passage, the discomfort made her quite as bad-tempered as Agnes.

*   *   *

Once they had finished supper, Susannah escaped into the cloisters where William discovered her weeping into her handkerchief. He carried a large parcel which he hastily put on the ground before sitting down on the bench beside her. 'Susannah, what is it?'

'Everything!' She sniffed and dabbed at her eyes.

'Why don't you tell me about it?' He touched her hand, stroking it softly with his forefinger in a way that made her want to lean her head against his broad chest.

'Agnes was cross with me all day and I lost my patience with her.'

He gave a wry smile. 'She's very difficult to please when the mood is on her.'

'And I've been having such frighteningly vivid dreams. I see my mother on her childbed, crying out for help while the doctor looms over her, laughing and sharpening his knife. '

'That's very unpleasant but it was only a dream, Susannah.'

'William, I'm so scared about the future!' Anxiety tightened her chest. 'I can't stay in this house for ever. Where will my baby and I go?' Tears began to flow again and she blew her nose noisily into her handkerchief.

'There's no question of you having to go anywhere else.'

'And I have heartburn all the time and my back aches and I've begun to waddle like a duck.'

William stared at her and then gave a shout of laughter. 'Come here!' He put his arm round her and pulled her against his chest. 'It's true that pregnant women are subject to peculiar dreams and strange fancies . . .'

303

'But I . . .'

'Shh!' He put his finger over her mouth. 'But this is the strangest fancy I ever heard.'

'What, worrying about what will become of me?' She closed her eyes, breathing in the smell of him, clean linen and warm skin, and revelling in the strength of his encircling arm, wishing the moment could last for ever.

'No. The duck. You could never, by any stretch of the imagination, be considered to move as gracelessly as a duck.' William took the soggy handkerchief from her and with infinite care wiped her tears away.

His face was so close to hers that Susannah could see the flecking of dark stubble on his jaw.

She moistened her lips and her heart began to do somersaults.

Slowly, William cupped her chin in both his hands and studied her face in minute detail. 'You are so very lovely,' he whispered.

'William?' she breathed.

He groaned and his mouth came down on hers.

Susannah slid her arms round his neck and drowned in the warmth of his kiss. Gentle and yet passionate, she could feel that he held himself back, which made her all the more eager for him. Loose-limbed and yielding, she wanted the moment never to end. She knew she would never forget that kiss, not if she lived to be seventy.

At last he released her and tipped her chin so that he could look deep into her eyes.

She felt a blush creep up her cheeks. 'The other day, in the garden . . .'

'I nearly kissed you then.'

'I thought so. But . . .'

'But what?'

'I wondered if I repulsed you.'

'How could you?'

'I saw you looking at me.' She touched a hand to her belly.

'Of course you don't repulse me! You're blooming like a glorious rose . . .'

'That waddles like a duck.'

'A glorious rose. But I thought you would find it indelicate of me to declare my feelings when you are carrying my cousin's child. And so soon into your widowhood.'

She looked away from his searching gaze. 'I didn't love Henry,' she said at last. 'I tried to. I wanted to. But I couldn't.'

He let out a slow sigh and stroked her cheek with his thumb. 'I can't say I'm sorry for that.'

'I was so shocked when I discovered I was to have his child.' Embarrassed, she looked down at the ground. 'The marriage wasn't . . . it wasn't consummated for some months. And then it was only the one time and I never imagined it would result in a child. Particularly as both Henry and I found it so . . . unsatisfactory.' Momentarily, she relived the humiliation she had suffered when Henry walked away from her. Defiantly, she looked William full in the face. 'I know it isn't seemly to talk of such things but I wanted you to know.'

His eyes met hers for a long moment. 'I'm very glad you told me. Too often I have imagined you and Henry . . .' He looked away from her, his jaw clenching. 'Jealousy is a terrible thing.'

'Yes,' said Susannah, thinking of Phoebe. She didn't want William to have secrets from her. Was this the right moment to tell him that she knew he had been Phoebe's lover and Joseph was his son?

William bent down to pick up the parcel from the ground. 'I have a present for you.'

The moment was lost. 'For me?' She took it from him, the weight of it heavy on her knee. Curious, she slipped the string off the parcel and pulled back the brown paper to expose the contents. She gasped with pleasure. Inside was an apothecary box made of willow wood and when she lifted up the hinged lid by the little brass handle she saw inside a miniature set of scales, a sharp knife, a pestle and mortar, a funnel and mixing bowl. All rested upon a tray, which lifted up to reveal phials of sulphur, mercury, salts and oils, together with little boxes of dried herbs. She picked up a silver measuring spoon and examined it. 'Oh William,' she breathed, 'it's the most beautiful thing I've ever seen!'

He threw his head back and laughed. 'Most women would reserve that kind of praise for rubies or pearls. But I thought you would like it.'

'I do!' She hugged him.

The door to the kitchen flew open and Phoebe ran out. She hesitated when she saw William and Susannah entwined together.

Susannah slowly disentangled her arms from William's neck.

Phoebe looked at Susannah with accusing eyes and then turned to William wringing her hands. 'Master, come quick!'

'What is it, Phoebe?'

'The missus. She beating Emmanuel! Come now!'

William gave Susannah a wry glance and they set off for the house.

Agnes was incandescent with rage and

Emmanuel cowered in the corner of the chapel as she laid about him with her stick. Joseph ran to his mother and buried his head in her apron while he cried with great gulping sobs. Aphra leaped up and down, her agitated screams adding to the confusion.

William prised the stick from Agnes's hand and made her sit down.

'I simply will not have it!' Her chin trembled. 'In my own house that . . . that . . . *slave* dares to molest my serving maid!'

'What serving maid?'

'Peg, of course! I came to find Susannah since she had chosen to neglect her duties even though she *knows* I need assistance to unlace my bodice.'

'Agnes, I'm sorry . . .'

The old woman ignored her. 'And what did I find? Emmanuel forcing the girl against the wall, tearing at her clothing while she cried out and struggled against him. I've had the care of that boy since he was five years old and now he betrays my trust. Take him out of my sight! Tomorrow you will go to the docks to find out when the next boat sails for Barbados. My brother shall have him back to work his fields. The overseer will make sure he has no time for ravishing the servants then!'

'No!' Susannah couldn't stop herself. 'Agnes, you can't!'

'Who gave you leave to speak, miss?'

Emmanuel let out a low moan and threw himself at Agnes's feet but she kicked herself free of his clutching hands. 'Shut him up in the cellar, William. Come, Susannah!'

Casting a pleading look at William, Susannah had no choice but to follow her.

Once Agnes had been unlaced and put to bed, still simmering with anger, Susannah ran up to the attics and knocked on Peg's door. Hearing no answer she lifted the latch to find Peg lying face down on her bed.

'Did he hurt you, Peg?'

She turned over, her eyelids red and swollen, and shook her head. 'Oh, miss, the mistress will turn me off without a reference!'

'No, she won't. It's Emmanuel she's angry with. She's locked him in the cellar.' Susannah patted the girl's shoulder but she continued to cry as if her heart would break. 'Did he force you?'

Peg shook her head again, choking back the sobs. 'The mistress is going to send him back to Barbados.'

Peg burst into noisy tears again.

At least Agnes had arrived in time to save Peg from dishonour, thought Susannah as she patted the girl's heaving shoulders and made comforting noises. Poor, motherless little scrap, her short life had been full of fears and she had been fond of Emmanuel, who made her laugh. Susannah sat down on the edge of the bed stroking Peg's hair until her sobs subsided and she fell asleep.

Watching the light begin to fade through the attic window, Susannah's thoughts were in a whirl. She needed time to assimilate what had happened with William and over and over again she relived the moment when he kissed her.

As darkness fell, she stood up and crept towards the door.

'Miss?'

'Yes, Peg?'

'Emmanuel was my friend. Why does God take

308

away everyone I love?'

'I can't answer that. He must have His reasons.'

'I wish my mother hadn't died,' Peg whispered.

Susannah paused in the doorway, remembering her own mother. 'So do I.'

Downstairs the atmosphere in the kitchen was sombre. Phoebe wept silently as she went about her duties and even Mistress Oliver's chins trembled as she scrubbed fiercely at the kitchen table. 'I should have realised and stopped it,' she said. 'Big as he is, Emmanuel is little more than a child. I knew he had his eye on Peg but I never thought ...'

'We're all guilty of that. He's fond of Peg and I suppose he was carried away by his feelings for her. But what he did was very wrong. I'm going to talk to him.'

'The master has him locked up tight in the cellar and we've instructions not to go near.'

'I shall go anyway.'

She went down, holding her nose as she passed the overflowing slops drain. The coal-cellar door was closed and padlocked and the key nowhere to be seen. 'Emmanuel?'

Somewhere behind the door she thought she heard a movement. She called his name again but there was no reply. 'Emmanuel, don't be afraid, I shall speak to Dr Ambrose.'

She found William in his study, twirling one of the captain's globes on its stand, lost in thought.

Susannah watched him for a moment, studying the shadows and planes of his face in the dying light.

He glanced up and his frown disappeared. 'Susannah! I wondered where you were. I looked everywhere for you.'

309

'I helped Agnes to bed and then went to sit with Peg. She's very upset.'

'What did she say about Emmanuel? *Did* he ravish her?'

'She says not, though I suspect they let their feelings for each other run away with them. Shall I light the candle?'

William reached out a hand to her and pulled her onto his knee. 'No, I like the gloaming.' He picked up a lock of her hair and pulled it through his fingers, watching the curl spring back into place. 'Your hair is the colour of the chestnuts I used to collect as a boy. At Christmas, we always roasted them on the fire at Merryfields.'

Susannah rested against William's chest and hoped she wasn't too heavy on his knee. It was odd how very comfortable she felt with him, as if she had come home after a long journey. There was no trace of severity in his face at all when such a smile lit his eyes. She spun the globe, searching for the Americas, where her brother Tom lived. 'William, you won't really send Emmanuel back to Barbados, will you? He may have done wrong but I'm sure he's learned his lesson.'

'Agnes will not allow him to stay here.'

'But she must!'

'Where else can he go?'

'He could . . .' She floundered. 'He could go and work for another mistress.'

'Who will employ an overgrown black page? The streets are awash with servants abandoned by masters who have fled to escape the plague. You know yourself how very hard it is to find a placement. And Emmanuel would come without a reference.'

310

'He's strong. Perhaps he could work on a farm in the country?'

'Country people will be suspicious of a black face. They're not as used to such sights as we are in London and I doubt he'd find work there. In any case, he is Agnes's slave. Unless she chooses to free him she can do whatsoever she wills with him. And she is determined he will go back to the plantation.'

'Then we must change her mind! He didn't really hurt poor Peg.'

'I don't agree. He is a young man, overstrong and with the sap rising in him. He must leave the Captain's House and be put to hard physical work so that he has no time or energy left to make such mischief.'

Susannah pushed herself off William's knee. 'Emmanuel is terrified of being sent back to the plantation. You must not allow that to happen! He's been a part of this household for nearly all his life; everything he knows is within these walls.'

'Not any more.'

'I cannot believe you are so hard-hearted!'

'Trust me to know best how to deal with this, Susannah.'

'Don't patronise me!' Rage boiled up in her breast. What was the matter with him that he couldn't understand what a terrible thing banishment back to the plantation would be for Emmanuel? 'I'm disappointed in you, William. I thought you had more compassion.'

'And I had hoped that by now you would trust me.'

They glared at each other.

Stunned, Susannah couldn't believe how quickly matters had changed between them and a hollow ache of misery blossomed under her ribs. If he'd made even a small movement towards her she would have fallen into his arms.

After a long moment she turned and left the room without looking back.

Chapter 20

William had already taken Emmanuel away with him by the time Susannah went down to the kitchen early the following morning. Peg crept about her duties hunched over like a little old woman. Phoebe, her eyes still swollen with weeping, pushed roughly past Susannah with a bucket of night-slops on her way to the cellar, while Joseph trailed after her asking again and again when Emmanuel was coming back.

'And you can wipe that sour expression off your face, miss,' said Agnes later on as Susannah laced her into her bodice.

'I am not sour, Agnes, only sad.'

'I thought you were fond of Peg and I'm surprised you take such a lenient view of Emmanuel's conduct.'

'Of course I'm fond of Peg! But Emmanuel *didn't* ravish her.'

'It was only a matter of time. You must have noticed the lascivious looks he gave her?'

'But even so . . . to get rid of him like a puppy you have grown tired of . . .'

'I forbid you to speak of it again! You shall train Joseph to take up Emmanuel's place. You can start by teaching him how to deliver a message and the correct way to address his betters.'

'Yes, Agnes.'

Susannah moved about her duties in stubborn silence, pinning Agnes's hair up under her cap, pulling back the bedlinen to air and folding away her nightshift.

After she was dressed, Agnes dismissed her and continued to sit before her dressing table, lost in thought.

*   *   *

Two days later, preoccupied by anxieties, Susannah was sewing clothes for her baby in the garden. Agnes had given her a fine linen sheet, washed over the years into silky softness, and told her to sit outside and make herself busy. Only too happy to escape from the claustrophobia of her mistress's bedchamber, she had collected her sewing box and settled herself in the dappled shade of a honeysuckle bush. William hadn't spoken to her since their argument. Pride forbade her from chasing after him and, in any case, she still believed he was in the wrong.

Fashioning the tiny garments made her realise that in a very few weeks she would, please God, hold her baby safely in her arms. But what then? What if the baby cried as much as Samuel and Joshua? Would she be able to fulfil her duties as Agnes's waiting woman? Would Agnes find an excuse to send her away? Relations between them had been strained since Emmanuel's banishment.

It was while she was mulling over these worrying thoughts that she heard a footstep upon the flags and looked up to see William approaching. Still

313

angry with him, she bent her head over her sewing without greeting him.

He stood before her, waiting.

'You're back, then,' said Susannah at last.

'As you see. Have you forgiven me yet?'

She stabbed the needle into the tiny shirt she was sewing and pricked her finger. Drawing in her breath in irritation, she watched a drop of blood spread across the linen.

'It's not *my* forgiveness you should seek. I hope you can sleep at night when you think about how Emmanuel is suffering.'

'I dealt with Emmanuel in the way I thought best.'

'I wonder what gives you the right to believe you know what is best for him?'

He opened his mouth as if to speak, then snapped it shut again. 'Susannah, I ask you to trust me on this. I have done nothing to bring any harm to Emmanuel. Now let us speak no more of it. Besides, I have brought something for you.'

'Another present? I do hope you're not trying to bribe me with some trinket?'

'Susannah! Will you never let it go? In any case, this present isn't for you.'

'Oh!' Disappointment made her put down her sewing.

'Wait here a moment.' William went inside and reappeared a moment later carrying a large parcel wrapped up in hessian. 'Open it!' he said, depositing the heavy bundle by her feet.

She pulled aside the sacking and revealed an oak cradle, carved with a twisting pattern of oak leaves and acorns. She stared at it, at a loss for words. How could she possibly show her pleasure in this

314

wonderful gift when she was so angry with him? At last, running her finger over one of the carved acorns, she said quietly, 'William, it's exquisite! I had thought that my baby would spend his first months in a rush basket but this will give him a splendid start in life.'

'I hoped you'd like it. I collected it from the attics at Merryfields. I spent my first months tucked up in this cradle, while my mother rocked it with her foot and sang to me.'

'It was yours?'

'And my sister's and my father's.' He looked down at his feet. 'Once I thought that I might have a son to sleep in it but it was not to be.'

Susannah waited, wondering if he would tell her the truth now about Joseph, but he only said, 'It seems fitting that Henry's child should use it.'

'Thank you, William,' she said, touched by his thoughtful act.

'And now I'd better brave my aunt's temper and go to see how she does.' Swiftly he bent down and kissed the curve of her neck before returning to the house.

Touching her neck, where she could still feel the imprint of his kiss, she watched him stride away. She bit her lip, wondering if, by accepting the gift of cradle, she had condoned Emmanuel's banishment.

*　　　*　　　*

That night, Susannah dreamed again that she was sitting beside her mother in the birthing chamber, waiting. It was dark, save a candle flickering on the washstand and the fire glowing orange in the grate. The overheated air was so thick and still that she could taste it and the sound of her mother's laboured breathing filled her ears. Goody Tresswell stirred the fire and sprinkled bitter herbs onto the embers. The resinous twigs caught alight and spat bright sparks up the chimney. Acrid smoke drifted in a cloud across the room, making Susannah's eyes water.

She started as the front door slammed. Voices. Heavy footsteps on the stairs. The door rattled open and Dr Ogilby's shadow loomed up to cover the wall.

'Soon have it out!' he said. He held up a boning knife so that it glinted in the firelight while he tested the blade with his finger.

Mama struggled to sit, her fear as sharp as broken glass. 'Don't let him hurt my baby!'

Smiling, Dr Ogilby turned to her.

Sobbing, Susannah pinioned her mother's arms.

'Don't let him hurt my baby!'

Her mother's screams reverberated all around. Ogilby's hot, rum-laden breath was moist on her cheek as he leaned over them.

Susannah awoke on a sob, her hand to her cheek. She had felt breath on her face. Hadn't she? She lay with her eyes wide open, staring into the threatening dark. Echoes of her mother's screams ebbed and flowed in her head, filling her with terror. And then she heard a regular, insistent creaking and shook off the last remnant of sleep.

Throwing back the sheet in fright, she sat up. Once her eyes had accustomed themselves to the dark she noticed the cradle. It moved gently from side to side as if rocked by an unseen hand.

She blundered her way to the door and out into the passage. Leaning against the wall until her

316

racing heartbeat had slowed a little, she persuaded herself that she was only suffering from a night terror. She put her hand to her cheek again. Yet it had felt so real.

She stood for some moments outside her bedchamber, too fearful to go back inside. At last she lifted the latch.

The first grey light of dawn filtered through the window onto the motionless cradle at the foot of her bed. She rested her hand upon it, tracing the carved oak leaves with her fingertips. Had she only imagined that the cradle had rocked?

*   *   *

The week ended with a heavy thunderstorm which cleared the air for a few days before the humidity began to build up again. The oppressive night air seemed almost to throb with heat, threatening to suffocate Susannah and, her belly as tight as a drum at the end of her seventh month, she was only able to sleep fitfully. The most pleasant part of the day was just after dawn; she treasured her early-morning walks in the garden before she was obliged to wait on Agnes.

Before breakfast she went outside where the air was still cool and the reek of the Thames was almost drowned by the sweet scent of roses and honeysuckle. She knelt awkwardly on the ground to tend the herb garden but the baby kicked her sharply in the ribs as if protesting at its confinement. Then a movement in the cloisters caught her eye and she looked up but whoever it was had disappeared. Pushing her garden knife into the ground to remove a dandelion she paused, feeling the back of her neck prickle. She shot a glance behind her and caught a glimpse of Phoebe peering at her from the arcading. There was such malevolence in her look that, all at once, Susannah gathered up her skirts and hurried from the garden as fast as her belly would allow her.

*   *   *

The chapel windows were tightly closed and the trapped air, heavy with smoke from Agnes's pipe, pressed down upon Susannah, making her shift uncomfortably on her chair. Perspiration beaded her brow. Discreetly she eased her shift away from her underarms and sat up straighter so that the bones of her bodice didn't dig into her flesh more than necessary.

Where was William, she wondered? There had been a coolness between them over Emmanuel's banishment but then he had given her the cradle and kissed her neck. A sudden tremor ran through her groin as she remembered the feeling of his lips and the slight roughness of his beard prickling her skin. He still seemed to care for her, even though she remained aloof, waiting for him to apologise. But what if she was reading more into his interest in her than he really felt? He'd kissed her but it had hardly been a declaration of undying love. Damn the man! Why did he have to be so elusive?

She stood up and walked to the window to look outside. If it became any hotter she felt she'd explode, like an overfilled kettle on the fire. She sighed. A wasp buzzed against the glass, seemingly as desperate as herself to escape.

'Why don't you go and visit that friend of yours?'

asked Agnes. 'You're as fidgety as a rat caught in a drain.'

Susannah's spirits revived at once. She'd be able to talk to Martha about William. 'If you're sure you don't need me ...?'

'Need you? How d'you think I managed before you came? Run along with you, miss! And don't go near any strangers; you never know where the sickness lurks.'

Outside in the street the air was a little cooler, although there was a peculiar stillness everywhere. On the spur of the moment, Susannah knocked on Jane Quick's door, thinking to ask if she would like to go with her to Martha's house. The sound of the knocker echoed inside the hall.

An upstairs window scraped open in the house next door and an elderly woman leaned out. 'She's gone. Her husband sent for her yesterday from Surrey.' The window banged shut again.

Susannah stared at the door for a moment, saddened that Jane hadn't come to say goodbye. But these were exceptional times.

Agnes needn't have worried about strangers coming too close. The streets were quiet and anyone Susannah met hurried past with their faces averted, just as keen to avoid contact as she was.

Entering the court where Martha lived, Susannah was greeted by the sight of two men piling furniture onto a cart. Baskets of household possessions stood on the dusty ground. The front door of Martha's house was open and another man came out carrying a chair with Martha's familiar sewing box resting on the seat.

'Where are you taking that?' asked Susannah, anxiety suddenly twisting her insides.

'Following the missus' orders,' he said.

'Where is she?'

He nodded his head at the door and Susannah ran inside. She found Martha with her hair tied up in a duster, standing before the dresser and handing down the plates to Patience. The smaller children ran in and out of the room and James gurgled in his cradle.

Susannah sank down onto a chair and fanned herself with her hand, suddenly faint with heat and unease. 'Thank the Lord that you are well,' she said. 'When I saw your furniture being taken away I thought . . .'

Martha came and poured a glass of ale for Susannah. 'You've saved me a visit. I was planning to see you before we go.'

'Go? Where?' asked Susannah, bewildered.

'Kent. Josiah's brother sent his cart for us and we'll live with him until we find work and a place of our own.' She tucked away a loose strand of hair that had freed itself from the duster and stuck to the perspiration beading her brow. 'Though how we'll all fit into his cottage I can't imagine.'

'But why?'

'You of all people should know that! We'll not stay here any longer to risk our children's lives. Andrew Baker and all his family on the other side of the court were stricken and passed away last week. I've known them ever since Josiah and I first walked out together.' Martha lifted a corner of her apron and wiped her eyes.

'I thought you put your trust in the Lord?'

'The Lord looks after those who look after themselves.'

'Everyone is dying or leaving!' Susannah heard

the desolation in her voice. 'What shall I do without you, Martha?'

'You shall visit me when your baby is born and you have recovered strength enough to travel.'

'If Agnes can spare me. And I'll write and tell you all the London news.'

Martha smiled, just a little. 'You forget, my dear. I cannot read.'

Susannah made her way back to the Captain's House with a heavy heart. She had never thought that her childhood friend would leave the city and the prospect of giving birth and tending her baby without Martha's patient guidance left her bereft. Overheated from the walk, Susannah went straight to the kitchen in search of a drink.

Peg sat at the kitchen table, looking pale and wan while she picked slugs out of a bowl of salad greens.

Mistress Oliver had loosened her bodice and sat overflowing on a stool, wriggling her toes in a basin of cold water. She made no attempt to stand up when she saw Susannah, merely saying, 'You might like to try this. Very soothing for swollen ankles.'

'Perhaps I will,' replied Susannah. 'Next time you could put in some mint leaves to increase the cooling effect. Meanwhile, may I have a glass of ale?'

'Peg, fetch it, will you? And you might as well bring the pike for dinner. It's gone a bit ripe in the heat and I need to soak it in vinegar.'

Susannah followed the kitchen maid down the corridor to the storerooms.

'You're very pale, Peg. Are you not sleeping well?'

'It's too hot to sleep.'

321

In the pantry Peg handed Susannah a jug of ale. 'Mistress Oliver will take a glass, too, I expect. I'll fetch the fish.' She picked up a platter covered in a muslin cloth and pulled back the covering to look at the pike.

A strong smell of ammonia rose from it, making Susannah cover her nose with her hand. Peg turned as green as a new leaf and burst into noisy sobs.

'What is it, Peg?'

'I'm so unhappy, ma'am! I don't want to be in the city no more! Everything smells bad and I'm frightened of the plague and it's too hot and, oh, I do miss Emmanuel so much that I think my heart will break.'

'What Emmanuel did was wrong, Peg.'

'He didn't do nothing wrong! I never let him, even though I wanted him to. And now I don't sleep for thinking about him on that boat, kept below decks in the dark and the heat, soaked in his own filth, just like Phoebe and Joseph. And if he doesn't die on the journey, they'll beat him to death him on the plantation.'

'Not if he behaves himself.'

'I might as well throw myself in the river.' She looked up at Susannah, her eyes drowned in tears. 'I'll never be happy again.'

'Don't say such a wicked thing!'

'But ma'am, it's true. And everywhere I look I see something to remind me of Emmanuel. I hate London! Especially I hate this house; I'd rather be in Cock Alley. All the bad things happened here. I want to go back to the country.' Her voice ended on a wail.

Susannah handed her a clean handkerchief to dry her eyes. 'I'll see if I can think of something.'

322

'Oh, please, madam! I knew you could help me.'

*　　　*　　　*

Peg's faith in her was completely unfounded, thought Susannah a few days later. She'd racked her brains trying to think of someone who might take the girl in and give her a home in the country but in the end she put aside her pride and went to find William in his study.

'I don't know what to do for the best but I don't want it on my conscience if the poor child throws herself into the river. She's grown so thin and she's still pining for Emmanuel.'

'It's a predicament, isn't it?' said William. 'Peg and Emmanuel are barely more than children but they do seem to have formed a deep attachment for each other. I'll make enquiries to see if I can find her another situation in the country.'

'I'll miss her if she goes.' Sadly she said, 'Everyone is deserting me.'

William nodded and turned his attention back to his books.

Susannah waited for a moment but he appeared to have forgotten her. Did she mean nothing to him? Or had he changed his mind and decided to avoid her? At last, heavy with despair, she left the room, closing the door quietly behind her.

Chapter 21

Susannah was woken early by footsteps in the corridor. She recognised the sound of William's boots as they clipped along the oak boards and thought that it must be Joseph's feet she could hear skittering along behind him. She experienced a twinge of jealousy that William had found time to spend with his son while she was ignored. The baby stirred in her belly, stretching and putting an intolerable strain on her bladder. Time to get up.

Once dressed, she went down to the kitchen for an early breakfast.

'Peg's overslept again,' grumbled Mistress Oliver. 'In my day Cook would have given me a good thrashing if I was late. I wanted her to go to the market early; it's hard enough to find what you need these days without leaving it too late. I'd use the butcher's on the other side of the street but the meat's always covered in flies and that wife of his is a slattern and never washes the blood off the floors.'

'Couldn't Phoebe go instead?'

'She's no use, neither. No idea how to choose a decent bit of mutton.'

'Perhaps they didn't have mutton in Barbados?' said Susannah. 'Shall I wake Peg? Or shall I set off to the market? By the time Peg is dressed I could already be there.'

'That's true enough. Fetch me some salad greens too if you can get them. And a block of salt and whatever vegetables you can find.'

The market was even smaller than the last time

Susannah had been, and the prices higher, but she was able to secure a leg of mutton, a dozen eggs, a few withered carrots and a bunch of overpriced greens. At the last stall she found a box of sugar plums and, on an impulse, bought them for Agnes. She knew her mistress had a sweet tooth and thought they might lift her spirits.

The scent of new-baked bread wafted from the kitchen as she returned home and Susannah's stomach growled in anticipation. She put the basket on the table and cut herself a spongy chunk from the warm loaf.

Mistress Oliver rummaged through the contents of the basket. 'Where's the salt?'

'There wasn't any,' mumbled Susannah through a mouthful of bread.

'No salt? What's the world coming to? Carrots aren't much good neither but that's a fine leg of mutton. What's this? Did I ask you to buy sugar plums?'

'No, you didn't. I paid for them myself. They're for Mistress Fygge.'

Mistress Oliver sniffed. 'You'll get heartburn if you eat that bread while it's fresh.'

Agnes was pleased with her sugar plums and quickly forgave Susannah for going off without asking permission. 'But I'll not condone laziness in the servants. Is Peg back at her duties now?'

'I'm sure Mistress Oliver will have punished her by making her do the worst jobs she can find,' said Susannah.

Later, after Agnes was dressed and sitting in the chapel with a pipe in her hand, a book of poetry on her knee and Joseph at her feet, Susannah slipped away to the kitchen again.

Mistress Oliver and Phoebe were heaving a vast pan of stock off the fire. Phoebe burned her hand and started, causing some of the stock to fall on the flames. A cloud of hissing steam enveloped both of them in its vapour.

'Get out of my kitchen, you useless lump!' shouted Mistress Oliver. 'Go and scrub the cellar floor; the drain's overflowed again.'

Phoebe cast a resentful glance at Susannah and fled.

'Is Peg here?' asked Susannah.

'No, she isn't!' Mistress Oliver wiped steam off her scarlet face with the back of her hand. 'She's only done a runner, hasn't she? No good will come of it, I can tell you.'

'But where would she go?'

'If I knew that I'd drag her back, kicking and screaming. For all her faults she's the best kitchen maid I've had in years. Ungrateful little madam! After all I've done for her ...'

Susannah hurried upstairs to Peg's attic room under the eaves. What if she had taken off and thrown herself in the river? Heart thudding, she flung open the door. The bed had been stripped bare and the worn blanket folded. The hook on the back of the door was empty and there was nothing at all on the chair or under the bed. It was as if Peg had never existed.

Susannah slumped down on the thin mattress, her knees weak with relief. Peg wouldn't have bothered to leave everything neat and tidy if she was going to drown herself. Silly, silly Peg! Why had she run away without even saying goodbye? But where could she have gone?

During the afternoon, as she settled Agnes for

an afternoon doze, she gasped as the answer to that question popped into her head. Instead of retiring to her own bedchamber for an hour or two she picked a bunch of rosemary and sweet herbs from the garden and twisted them into a nosegay. Holding this to her nose to ward off evil humours, she slipped out of the street door and set off. Walking was becoming increasingly tiring for her and it was impossible to see all the potholes in the road due to the bulge of her stomach. After she'd slipped twice, she hailed a hansom cab. 'Cock Alley in Moor Fields,' she said, ignoring the driver's raised eyebrows.

The driver stopped at the end of Cock Alley, it being too narrow for the cab to enter. She paid him off and lifted her skirts out of the dust. Two men lounging in an alehouse doorway whistled at her and then nudged each other, laughing coarsely as she drew closer and they noticed the swell of her belly. 'Someone got there first by the look of it!'

She put her nose in the air and stepped carefully around a dog scavenging amongst potato peelings.

A girl sat on the sill of an open window, listlessly swinging her bare legs. A sailor walking from the other end of the alley stopped to talk to her and she nodded at the open door of the house and he disappeared inside.

Susannah stopped and looked about her. Which house? There was no help for it; she'd have to ask for directions. She banged her fist on the nearest door and waited.

After a few moments it opened a crack and a pair of eyes peered at her from the shadows. 'What d'you want?'

'Please will you direct me to Mistress

McGregor's house?'

The door opened a little more to reveal a woman of uncertain age dressed in a loose wrap, in spite of the time of day. 'Mistress McGregor? Not looking for a job, are you?' The woman burst into gales of laughter, exposing a mouthful of bad teeth. 'Bit late for that, dearie, if you don't mind my saying so. You look as if you're fit to drop it any day.'

'Please tell me, which is Mistress McGregor's house?' Susannah persisted.

'Up the other end of the alley, dearie. The house with the red door.'

Susannah picked her way along the alley until she found a scarlet door with a brass knocker in the shape of a heart. She banged it down a couple of times. The door opened almost immediately.

A strikingly handsome girl with black hair and her breasts almost exposed by her low-cut bodice stood in the doorway. 'Yes?'

'I'm looking for Mistress McGregor,' said Susannah.

'Not at home.'

'May I come in?'

'Not sure about that . . .'

'Please?' Susannah rested her hand on her stomach. 'I need to rest for a moment.'

'Suppose it can't do no harm.'

Susannah followed the girl into the parlour and sat down on a comfortably padded sofa piled with plump cushions.

'What's your business with Mistress McGregor?'

'I wanted to ask her if she has seen Peg, my serving girl, today.'

'Peg? There's no Peg here.'

'Are you quite sure?'

'I've only just risen from my bed but there's been no one here today.'

'Have you lived here long?'

'Six months, near enough.'

Susannah's hopes were dashed. 'Then you won't remember Peg. She came here last September.'

'Peg? Not little Peg?' The girl put her hand over her mouth, her eyes alive with mirth. 'I've heard about her! She bashed a customer over the head with a candlestick and legged it out the window. Mother McGregor was that angry! She'd been paid a hefty fee to find a young maid for the customer and instead she had to pay him to keep his mouth shut. Cracking bruise he had.'

'I thought you weren't here then?'

'Topaz told me.' The girl called out of the door. 'Tope! Tope, come on down. There's a lady looking for that Peg.'

Topaz had black skin, handsomely set off by her ochre silk wrap. Her hair was wrapped in an exotic gold turban and she carried with her a heavy, spicy perfume.

'You lookin' for Peg?' Her voice was rich and melodious.

'She's my serving maid. I wondered if she might have come here.'

Topaz shook her head, the pearl drops she wore quivering from the lobes of her ears. 'Are you Mistress Savage?'

Astonished, Susannah said, 'How did you know?'

'Henry spoke about you. He took Peg home with him after she ran away from Mother McGregor. Said you'd grown fond of her.'

'Henry? I don't understand.'

'I was with him when he died. Thought I was for

the pit, too, thanks to him! And then his cousin, the doctor, came and told the authorities there'd been a death in the house and we were all shut up. Cost Dorcas and Abigail their lives. Cost us all a month's wages.'

Susannah's face flamed. 'Henry was one of your clients?'

'Certainly he was. Became uncommon fond of me.'

Susannah swallowed down the bitter bile that rose in her throat but before she could speak the front door slammed and footsteps clattered down the hall.

'Girls! Mother's home!'

Mistress McGregor's plump body was stuffed into a crimson taffeta dress with a great deal of black lace and knots of silk ribbons. Her elaborately curled hair was an unlikely shade of red and matched her improbably rouged cheeks. 'And who have we here?' she asked.

'This is Henry's missus,' said Topaz. 'Come to see if Peg has been back to visit us.'

Susannah stood up. 'Have you seen her, madam?'

'Peg? Why, that conniving little piece of dirt! Cost me a fortune, she did. If she had been here I'd have whipped her to the other end of the city.' Mistress McGregor looked more closely at Susannah. 'Henry Savage's wife? You're better-looking than I'd have expected. Is that his brat you're carrying? Henry brought nothing but trouble on us, even though we was so accommodating. Topaz never had no time for other clients while Henry were around. Couldn't get enough of her.'

330

Topaz laughed. 'That's the truth! If the plague hadn't carried him off I'd have been worn out by now.'

Susannah couldn't stop herself. 'I don't want to hear it!'

'If a wife doesn't do her duty by her husband, she's only herself to blame when he looks elsewhere for his comforts,' Mistress McGregor cackled.

Gripping her hands together to stop herself from slapping the painted face, Susannah only said, 'If Peg should come here, will you tell her that she's to come back to me?'

'I'm not listening to any more about that girl. Your husband and that doctor cousin of his, between them they nearly put me out of business. Now get out of my house!' Mistress McGregor prodded Susannah in the chest. 'Go on. There's no call for your sort here.'

Susannah lifted her chin and walked slowly towards the front door, hoping the three sniggering women wouldn't see how she was shaking. Once she was over the threshold she picked up her skirts and scuttled away, their mocking laughter ringing in her ears.

*   *   *

That evening, still seething with shame and indignation, Susannah lay in wait for William. She hovered in the open doorway of the Captain's House, peering up and down the narrow street into the setting sun. At last she saw his tall silhouette, the long black cloak flapping around his ankles and the beaked plague mask under his wide-brimmed hat. He held his staff up high and passers-by melted away as if by magic.

'There's something of the actor about you,' Susannah said as he stepped inside. 'Does it make you feel powerful to be cutting a swathe through the terrified crowd everywhere you go?'

'Good evening, Susannah.' His voice was muffled under the pointed mask and he struggled to untie the strings that held it in place.

'For goodness' sake! Let me!' Susannah yanked at the knots until the mask came free.

William rubbed his face where the mask had left red weals on his cheekbones. 'Sometimes I think I'll die of asphyxia under that thing,' he said, hanging it up together with his cloak on the hook.

'I've got a bone to pick with you.'

'Before or during supper?'

'I'm in no mood for jesting, William!'

'So I can see.'

'Come into one of the storerooms. What I have to say to you can't be said in front of Agnes.'

'How intriguing! Do, please, lead the way.'

He followed her along the passage and into the flour and dry goods store and waited politely while she closed the door firmly behind them.

'You lied to me!' she said.

He raised one eyebrow but his face was wary.

'Why didn't you *tell* me?'

'About what?'

'About how Henry died, of course! I've been to Mistress McGregor's house.'

'God's teeth, Susannah! You went to Cock Alley?'

'Obviously, since that is where Mistress McGregor lives.'

'Cock Alley is no place for a decent woman. You

should never . . .'

'And that is where I found out, in the most humiliating way possible, about Henry's . . .' she waved her hand in the air while she sought a suitable way to phrase it, 'about Henry's *excursions* to the house with the red door.'

'I didn't lie to you, Susannah.'

'You hid the truth from me! You let me be humiliated by Mistress McGregor.' The memory of it brought the heat to her face again.

A muscle flickered in William's jaw. 'And in your distress, when I told you of Henry's death, do you consider it would have helped you to know that he died in the arms of a common whore?'

She bit her lip in an attempt to stop it trembling. 'I met Topaz, Henry's . . . paramour,' she said. 'Mistress McGregor told me it was my fault that Henry visited such a place. She said that I wasn't a good wife . . .' Swallowing, she attempted to regain her composure. 'I tried so hard to be the wife Henry wanted but, whatever I did, it was never enough.'

'Damn his eyes!' William moved so swiftly Susannah had no chance of escape. He snatched her into his arms and covered her face with fierce kisses. 'He had a pearl beyond price and couldn't see it. My cousin was a wastrel and a scoundrel and he didn't deserve even your little finger. I *burned* when I saw the way he treated you and I wish now that I'd given him the thrashing he deserved for the pain he caused you.'

Almost against her will, Susannah found herself allowing William to kiss her. Her anger melted like snow in sun as she lost herself in his hard embrace. He pushed her back against the wall so that she

333

couldn't escape, even if she had wanted to. At last he released her, leaving her shaky and melting with desire. She made a small movement towards him again but he held her at arm's length, his breath uneven. Susannah made a conscious effort to slow her own breathing. 'I suppose it would not do for Mistress Oliver or Phoebe to find us shut away alone in here.'

'No, it would not.'

'What really makes me angry', said Susannah, 'is that all the time Henry said he was working to increase his fortune, he was spending mine. And on another woman at that.'

'I know. I'm ashamed he shared my blood.'

'Did you ever meet Topaz?'

'I did. She was in a state of sobbing hysteria when I arrived at Mistress McGregor's house that time. Henry had sent for me when he fell ill but he was dead by the time I arrived. The house was in an uproar and I had to drag some of the girls back inside as they tried to leave.'

'But why did Henry choose Topaz?'

William was silent. Then he said, 'Perhaps she reminded him of home. He grew up with black people all around him and they didn't seem strange to him. Why, even his nurse was more of a mother to him than his own.'

'I suppose so.'

'When I lived at the plantation for that year, I came to know the house slaves well. Ignorant people assume that they are little better than animals but it isn't so. They all had their own different ways, likes and dislikes, a sense of humour or a choleric disposition; they feel happiness and sorrow, just as we do.'

'And you found it possible to be friends with them?'

'I did.'

More than friends, in Phoebe's case, she thought, a sudden hot knife of jealously spearing her heart.

'Whatever made you visit Mistress McGregor's house in the first place, Susannah?'

'I was looking for Peg. She's disappeared.'

'Peg? Oh dear.' William sighed. 'If I'd only thought . . .'

'Thought what?'

'I was going to tell you as soon as I came home but you were lying in wait for me with murderous intent and I didn't have the chance.'

'What are you talking about?'

'The opportunity arose and I had to move quickly. I took Peg away early this morning.'

'Took her where?'

'To Merryfields. Roger Somerford, my tenant, was prepared to give her a position. We couldn't have Peg throwing herself in the river, could we?'

Susannah's heart lifted. So Peg had been saved, after all.

'Come,' said William, holding out his hand. 'We'd better leave this storeroom now. If you smile at me like that I'll have to kiss you again.' His expression became sombre. 'But perhaps next time you'll trust me?'

Chapter 22

The oppressive weather continued and Susannah spent her days reading to Agnes or sewing clothes for the baby. Forced by circumstances to sit still for long periods of time, claustrophobia often overwhelmed her. The sensation of marking time grew stronger even as her stomach grew rounder. Day after day, she sat daydreaming, with her stitching forgotten on her lap, staring out of the tightly closed window while Agnes snored in the chair beside her.

The future held so many unknowns. Would her baby be born safely and would she survive to look after him? Did William truly love her or was she a mere passing fancy? What, if any, were his intentions? And what would happen if Agnes passed away? These anxieties made her head hurt and even oil of lavender rubbed on to her temples didn't alleviate the ache.

'Take the boy outside and let him have a run around,' said Agnes, one afternoon. 'I can't stand to have him fidgeting near me.'

Joseph let out a cry of glee as they went out into the garden. 'You shall play with the whip and hoop for a while,' Susannah said, 'and then we will continue with your lessons.'

She walked round the garden while the boy raced along the cloisters, bowling his hoop in front of him and laughing with delight. Perhaps, she thought, when her baby was a little older he would be a playmate for young Joseph.

Once Joseph had run off some of his energy

Susannah made him sit at her feet. He didn't really take to learning but was a charming child with a ready smile and was quite happy to humour her by attempting to copy the letters she drew on his slate.

'This is an "O",' she said. 'An "O" for orange. Make it nice and round like a ball.'

He bent his head over the slate, his pink tongue protruding between his lips as he copied the letter.

Susannah had spent a great deal of time studying the length of the boy's fingers and his earlobes and the set of his shoulders in the hours he had sat beside her. She wondered if she could detect some likeness to William in the shape of his eyes but whereas Joseph's eyes were merry and quick, his father's were usually sombre. Sometimes though, when William looked at her, he was unable to conceal the spark of humour in his eyes, and it was then that she thought she perceived some similarity. She couldn't dislike Joseph but she suffered torments of jealousy whenever she allowed herself to think about Phoebe, naked, lying in William's arms.

Footsteps along the cloister caused her to turn and a sudden burst of happiness made her smile. 'William! We don't usually see you at this time of day.'

'I was on the way to see my next patient and thought I'd call in.'

Pleasure coloured her cheeks as she made room for him to sit beside her.

He smiled, his brown eyes warm in the sunlight. 'I see you are working at your lessons, Joseph.'

The boy looked up and flashed a gap-toothed smile. 'It's an orange,' he said. 'One day I'll have an orange. And I'll get one for Mammy, too.'

'Very creditable!' William nodded approvingly. 'And how are you today, Susannah?'

'Hot and uncomfortable.'

'These last weeks before a baby comes can be very trying.'

'I'm filled with anxious thoughts as the time draws nearer. My days are taken up with trivial tasks and there is little to distract me. And I do so miss working with Father.'

William squeezed her hand. 'Before long you will have your child to keep you busy.'

'But once he is grown, what then? As a woman and a mother, am I no use for anything else? Surely I could offer valuable assistance in these difficult times? So many of the apothecaries have gone and I could take a small part in filling that void.'

'Working in your father's dispensary was really important to you, wasn't it?'

Susannah nodded, the loss of it lodged sharply in her chest.

'Perhaps . . .' He paused, his gaze fixed on the ground while he thought. 'Perhaps your father would welcome some help in the shop for a day or two each week once the baby is weaned?'

'Possibly. If Arabella allowed it. But Agnes has given me a home and she could hardly be expected to approve if I'm not here to wait upon her.'

One after the other the church bells began to toll the hour and William stood up. 'I must continue my rounds. I have a patient waiting for me with a scurvy in his gums.'

'Cloves boiled in rosewater, dried and then ground to a powder and rubbed on the gums is effective.'

'And the strained rosewater can be drunk in the

338

morning on an empty stomach.' William smiled. 'I have been to see your father and he provided me with the very same powder and decoction you mention.'

'Everything I know I have learned from him.'

'And you were an excellent student. But now I must be on my way. I shall return in time for supper today.' He patted the boy's springy curls. 'Joseph, I look forward to seeing what progress you have made in a few days' time.'

That evening Susannah made a special effort to dress her hair becomingly. She could do nothing to conceal her bulk except to wear a lace shawl round her shoulders. She put on her mother's pearl pendant, which nestled between the fullness of her breasts and drew the eye away from her swollen abdomen. Thankfully, her arms were still slender.

Agnes had been resting in her room and Susannah went to help her rise and to straighten her cap.

'William will join us for supper tonight,' she said.

'Is that why you're looking so fine?' The old woman's eyes gleamed with amusement at Susannah's blush. 'Don't think I haven't noticed the way you look at each other. But don't set your hopes too high, miss. William is a hard nut to crack for any female with designs upon him. And in your condition . . .'

'I assure you . . .'

Agnes held up her hand. 'You're not the first to be interested. But I warn you that he had his fingers burned once and is unlikely to commit himself to any woman again.'

'Again?' Susannah bit her lip.

Agnes cackled in amusement. 'You're dying to

339

ask me, aren't you? Well, I shall put you out of your misery. His wife betrayed him.'

William had a wife! She sank down onto a chair, suddenly ice-cold.

'Don't look like that!' said Agnes. 'The silly girl ran away with William's so-called best friend. She fell off the horse as they galloped away into the night, broke her neck and killed herself. And the babe she was carrying. William never was sure if the child Catherine carried was his.'

'How very dreadful for him!' Susannah was deeply ashamed at the relief she felt.

'Said he'd never trust a woman again. The experience made him dour. After that he went off to Barbados to forget her betrayal and there's not been a woman since who's caught his fancy. So don't think that putting on a pretty gown is sufficient to encourage him to make a proposal.'

Susannah handed Agnes the hand mirror, while she wondered if the death of William's traitorous wife was what had made him seek solace in Phoebe's accommodating arms.

Still downcast by Agnes's comments when William arrived home, Susannah found it impossible to meet his eyes. Unusually good-humoured, he sat beside his aunt and engaged her in a lively discussion on the Dutch trade routes.

Phoebe, carrying a tray loaded with the supper dishes, pushed the door open with her hip and set the table in her usual unhurried fashion.

Susannah watched her, imagining her dressed in ochre silk with her head wrapped in an exotic gold turban and with gold bracelets upon her wrist instead of a silver collar round her neck. The woman moved with an easy grace, her figure

340

attractively curved now that she wasn't half-starved. It wasn't hard any more to imagine that William could find her alluring.

She shot a sideways glance at William, who smiled at Phoebe as she filled his glass and placed a clean napkin beside him. Jealousy bored into her like a sharp spike.

William continued arguing companionably with Agnes, but he barely looked at Susannah at all.

Susannah pushed cold mutton and pickle around her plate, too despondent to swallow a morsel. She had so looked forward to an opportunity to enjoy William's company and he scarcely spoke to her except to ask her to pass the salt.

Once they had finished supper William excused himself with a bland smile and went to his study.

Agnes decided to retire early.

Dejected, Susannah accompanied Agnes to her bedchamber and helped her to undress. Folding her mistress's gown and putting it away in the linen press, she had to suppress a smile when she found the box of sugar plums almost empty. The old lady certainly had a sweet tooth.

'You're very quiet this evening. I've upset you, haven't I?' said Agnes. 'There's no cause to sulk because I speak my mind. It's not that I would be entirely against such a match, you understand . . .'

'There has been no mention of such a thing!'

'I have the eyes to see and I know where your heart is leading you, miss. As I was saying, it's not that I'd be against such a match, but I believe it to be unlikely William will ever make such a commitment again.'

Susannah took her time in folding the rest of Agnes's clothes and avoided meeting her inquisitive gaze. 'I do not look for such a commitment from my husband's cousin,' she lied.

Agnes cackled with laughter. 'But it would be mighty convenient, wouldn't it?'

'My most pressing concern now is to be safely delivered of Henry's child,' Susannah said with all the dignity she could muster.

'Ah, well. It is true that childbirth is a dangerous time for a woman and I shall pray for you.'

'Thank you.' Outwardly calm, Susannah trembled inside, reminded again of her old fears.

'Good night, Susannah.'

'Sleep well, Agnes.'

Susannah closed the bedchamber door behind her with a sigh of relief. As she went along the passage the door to William's study opened. He stood in front of her, his eyes glittering like jet in the candlelight.

'What is it?' she asked.

'I wanted to tell you how lovely you look tonight.'

Her spirits lifted in an instant. 'I thought you didn't care to notice me this evening?'

'I know my aunt and she was watching us. But there are some things best hidden from interfering old busybodies, don't you think?' He took the candlestick from her and placed it carefully on the hall chest. Turning to face her again, he lightly brushed her cheek with his knuckles.

His touch shot an arrow of longing deep into Susannah's pelvis. Warmth rose up her body, leaving every nerve tingling and yearning for him. Slowly she turned her face to kiss his fingers, watching his eyes grow heavy-lidded with desire.

He let out a small sigh and drew her to him.

Stumbling against his chest, her knees suddenly

342

liquescent, she felt the drumbeat of his heart against her breast as he put his arms round her.

William rested his chin on her forehead and they swayed together in the shadowy corridor for a moment as long as eternity.

A quiet happiness settled upon Susannah, a deep certainty that she was where she was destined to be.

Entwining his hands in her hair, he tipped her face up to his. His mouth was hot and Susannah trembled as she felt the hardness of his body pressed against her own. Aching for him, she returned his kisses with fervour, not caring if he thought her wanton.

At last, he drew a shuddering breath and cupped her face in his hands. 'My lovely, sweet Susannah,' he whispered. 'You must know that I have grown to love you?'

Joy erupted within her and she turned her face up to his again.

But he gently removed her arms from his neck and kissed her fingers. 'It's no good,' he said. 'You're too lovely to resist. I must go now, before I forget my manners entirely.'

Before she had time to recover her breath he'd retreated into his study and closed the door.

Heart singing, she sank against the wall, her fingers touching her bruised mouth where she could still feel the burning heat of his kisses. *He had said he loved her!*

*   *   *

Sleep was a long time coming that night. Susannah paced around her bedchamber and then leaned against the window watching the bats swoop and

343

flitter over the garden by the light of the moon. The night air was sultry and she was suffocated by her long linen nightgown. Pulling at the neck ties, she dragged it over her head and let it fall to the ground. She opened the window wide and let the air play over her naked body while she relived William's kisses. Hot with longing, she wished that he *had* forgotten his manners.

She smiled to herself in the darkness, imagining his hands on her naked back, her breasts . . . Their wedding night would be so different from the mortification she had experienced with Henry. She knew with every fibre of her being that there were heights of pleasure to be found with William that she had never experienced. But then a little worm of unease began to gnaw at her. Was Agnes right? Although he'd said he loved her, did he intend marriage or simply to make her his mistress? Could she capture his heart and hope for marriage where others had failed? And if he wouldn't marry her could she, or would she, settle for a life as his kept woman? These fretful thoughts rolled round and round in her mind like a suckling pig on a spit.

When at last exhaustion overcame her she lay down on the bed and fell into a deep sleep.

*   *   *

A current of air dragged Susannah back to semi-consciousness. She sighed and turned over, still half asleep. Beginning to drift off again, the click of the latch made her jerk awake and she started up, clutching at the sheet to cover her nakedness. A breeze had risen and stirred the curtains at the window. Then the bedchamber door moved a little

344

in the draught. She distinctly remembered closing it. Someone must have lifted the latch and failed to close it properly. Had William visited her room and watched her, naked, while she slept? Such a thought made her burn with shame and excitement. It was some time before she fell asleep again.

Later, she was awoken again by muted voices. Holding her breath, she strained her ears. A mere whisper of sound, bare feet on boards, made her sit up. She snatched up her nightshift and threw it over her head before stealing into the corridor. It was silent and deserted in the pale dawn light but the tapestry that hung at the turn of the corridor stirred slightly, as if someone had passed by in haste. She crept along the passage and looked round the corner but all she could see were closed doors.

She opened each door in turn but every room was empty save for dust-sheeted furniture. Standing stock-still, she listened into the silence but only heard the singing in her ears. Then there came the distinct sound of a woman's cough and the floorboards above her creaked.

Hurrying to the attic staircase, she climbed the stairs. Perhaps Peg had been unhappy with her new master and had secretly returned? But Peg's garret was as she had seen it last, silent and devoid of all possessions except for the thin blanket folded at the foot of the bed.

It was then that she heard the scrape of a door opening. Holding her breath, she looked through the crack in Peg's doorway. Surely it was too early even for Phoebe to be starting her duties?

Whispering voices made her catch her breath. What she saw then made her press her knuckles to her mouth to stop herself from crying out.

345

William, with bare feet and dressed in no more than his nightgown, came out of Phoebe's room.

Phoebe was silhouetted in the lighted doorway, the swell of her full breasts and the curve of her hips clearly discernible under her thin shift.

William put his hands on her shoulders and murmured something to her. She nodded, her liquid brown eyes gazing up at his. He touched her cheek and she covered his hand with her own as he whispered something to her that Susannah could not hear.

Phoebe smiled tremulously back at him.

Susannah felt as if she had been gutted with a red-hot filleting knife. *How could he?* She wrapped her arms round her belly and held back a cry of anguish.

William padded across the corridor and went silently down the stairs.

Susannah began to shake so violently that her teeth chattered and she moved blindly away from the door. As she turned, she caught the latch with her sleeve and froze as the sound reverberated into the silence.

Phoebe crossed the landing and pushed the door wide open.'

She stood there for a moment, her face impassive.

Susannah could not speak; her distress at what she had witnessed was too agonising to bear.

Then Phoebe went back into her room. She closed the door softly but not before Susannah had seen the look of triumph on her face.

The Valley of the Shadow of Death

July 1666

Chapter 23

Bedlinen washed early that morning and draped over a line in the garden had already dried stiff in the sizzling noonday sun. Clouds floated across the sky but in the shelter of the cloisters the breeze barely stirred the heavy air.

Despair lodged like a stone under Susannah's breastbone and her baby kicked and stretched against her diaphragm so that she could hardly breathe. The humiliating encounter with Phoebe replayed itself again and again in her mind's eye. She tormented herself with the thought that if she had followed William into his study earlier that evening, if she had offered herself to him, he would have had no need to seek his pleasures in Phoebe's bed.

Joseph, sitting with Aphra beside Susannah's feet, pushed his slate away and sprawled on the ground. 'Finished,' he said.

Susannah picked up the slate and looked at the row of carelessly formed letters. 'No, not like that, Joseph.' She snatched the chalk from his hand. 'Sit up properly and think about what you're doing!'

'Doan want to!'

His petulance made her anger flare. 'You will do as you are bid!'

Aphra shrieked and scrambled up to the top of the rose arch.

Joseph glanced up at Susannah, his eyes wide and frightened.

It was wrong to take out her wretchedness on the child but it was impossible not to see him as

349

a permanent and painful reminder of William's liaison with Phoebe. The liaison which had begun again. And last night she had seen with her own eyes the tender way in which William had touched Phoebe after he had risen from her bed. Apparently, their affair was much more than a casual coupling and Joseph, the product of that love, must surely bind them together? She sighed. 'Come, Joseph. Sit beside me and I'll help you.'

He perched on the edge of the bench, his fingers clenched in his lap. 'You goin' to beat me, miss?'

'No Joseph, I am not. But you must learn to sit still and do your lessons.'

'Why?'

She studied his face but it showed no hint of insolence. He looked as tired as she felt and his eyes lacked their usual sparkle. 'Because it's a great gift to be able to read and write. It will open new worlds for you.' Joseph didn't look convinced and she was too dispirited to insist they continue. 'We'll leave it there for today. Mistress Oliver bought a basket of plums from the market and she needs some help to prepare them.' She held out her hand to him.

The kitchen simmered in the heat from the fire and Mistress Oliver's face glistened, her cheeks as magenta as the plums in the basket.

Phoebe listlessly turned a row of chickens on the spit and greasy smoke hung in a foul-smelling cloud under the ceiling.

Joseph let go of Susannah's hand and ran to his mother. Her face sparked into life as she bent to touch his upturned face. When she saw Susannah watching she pulled the child to her side.

Susannah avoided meeting Phoebe's bold stare

by turning her back. She was damned if she'd let the other woman see the dark circles of misery under her eyes but she couldn't prevent a picture of William lying in Phoebe's arms flashing through her mind. She shook her head to free herself of the image. 'Mistress Oliver, shall Joseph and I stone the plums?'

'I'd be glad of it,' said the cook, wiping her dripping face on her forearm. 'Though, Lord knows, the pastry for the pie will be heavy in this heat.'

Susannah held her hand out to Joseph, avoiding Phoebe's hostile glare. 'Come, Joseph, you can help me to carry the basket.'

The boy looked at his mother and after a brief hesitation she gave him a small nod before turning back to the spit.

They sat on the garden bench with the basket between them; Susannah picked up the first plum and cut through the purple skin to expose the juicy yellow flesh. A worm had eaten a tunnel through to the stone, leaving a gritty brown trail, so she carved out the spoiled flesh and threw it in the rose bed. She sliced through the next plum and twisted it apart. Perfect. She handed it to Joseph. 'You can eat one, if you like.'

The boy turned down the corners of his mouth. 'I never goin' to eat plums. Mammy say plums gives you a pain in the belly.'

'Only if you eat too many.' She gritted her teeth to prevent herself saying something she'd probably regret about Joseph's mammy.

'Mammy says . . .'

'Never *mind* what Mammy says!' Susannah wiped perspiration off her top lip with the back of her hand.

The sheets on the line stirred a little and she glanced up as a shadow passed over the sun. A great black cloud was looming up over the rooftops. There was an almost unbearable tension in the humid air. Closing her eyes, she imagined cooling rain pouring down upon her upturned face and washing away her misery.

'Miss?'

She opened her eyes. 'Yes, Joseph?'

'You sad?'

She swallowed, the child's unexpected sympathy made her want to weep. 'A little,' she said.

'Because I'm bad?'

'You're not bad, Joseph.' He was an endearing child and she had no desire to make him fearful. 'I'm hot and out of sorts. I do so wish I could escape this house.'

'Why doan you go then?'

'I can't.'

'Why not? You not a slave. Mammy say *you* can go where you like.'

'It's not so simple.'

Joseph shrugged and turned back to stoning the plums.

Susannah gazed at the nape of the boy's neck, his soft skin the colour of a walnut kernel. The silver collar which encircled his slender neck was finely crafted but must be hot and heavy to wear in this weather. It suddenly occurred to her to wonder if Phoebe saw the collars, expensive as they were, not as an adornment but as a symbol of their slavery. But if she and Joseph had not been found a home in the Captain's House what would have become of them? Come to that, if Agnes had not taken her in she also would have died of starvation. Did that make her a slave too?

A breeze lifted the hair on the back of her neck and the drying sheets suddenly billowed out like the sail of a ship. The sun still burned down but in the past few minutes the sky had turned an ominous shade of slate. Intent on the gathering clouds, she sliced the last plum in half and nicked her finger. A bead of blood grew on her fingertip and she sucked it away, the metallic taste mixed with the sweetness of plum juice.

'It's going to rain, Joseph. Fetch your mother to take in the washing.'

He trotted back to the kitchen door and she wondered yet again what she would say to William when she saw him. It was unbelievable to her that he could have kissed her with such passion last evening and then have gone, so soon afterwards, to Phoebe's bed. She would never have believed him so fickle and it undermined her very foundations that she had misjudged his character so badly. She toyed with the notion of confronting him but what good would that do? Even if he begged her forgiveness, she would never rid herself of the vision of that moment of intimacy when he had touched Phoebe's cheek so tenderly.

The rose bushes rocked in a sudden gust of wind, scattering petals on the gravel, while the sheets on the line flapped and snapped. A drop of rain fell with a *plop* onto Susannah's knee, forming a dark circle on her skirt. Overhead a black cloud hovered, edged with brilliant light as dazzling as a hundred thousand candles. Another raindrop landed on her upturned face. All at once the wind dropped, the sun disappeared and the garden became deathly

353

still. She held her breath, waiting.

Then the rain came. It fell from the darkening sky just as if a giant hand had poured it through a sieve. Hissing straight down it bounced off the ground, soaking Susannah's shoulders and splashing the hem of her skirt in seconds. She hurried to gather up the sheets. Fighting the bulky weight of the damp linen, she began to drag the sheets off the line and bundle them up into her arms.

Phoebe, followed by Joseph, ran from the kitchen and snatched the rest of the sheets off the line.

'Joseph, hurry! Fetch your slate and chalk before it's ruined,' said Susannah.

'Leave it!' Phoebe grasped the boy's hand. 'You doan need waste your time with letters.'

Joseph looked uncertainly first at his mother then at Susannah.

Susannah fixed Phoebe with a baleful stare, determined that in this, at least, she would have mastery. 'Do as I tell you, Joseph!'

All three stood for an endless moment while the rain cascaded over them and swirled around their feet on the sun-baked ground.

Then, one by one, Joseph pulled free his mother's fingers from his hand and set off, head bowed, to the bench where he had abandoned his slate.

The desolation in Phoebe's face made Susannah bite her lip. But after a moment the other woman turned and sprinted back to the house.

Susannah followed more slowly, taking care not to slip on the thin mud that was forming on the ground.

'Mercy! You're soaked,' exclaimed Mistress Oliver. 'Phoebe, go and hang the sheets in the loft to dry. That's a proper storm brewing, I do believe.'

Susannah wiped the rain from her face with the corner of a sheet. 'Perhaps it will clear the air. Joseph, take off your coat and Phoebe can put it to dry.'

Joseph pulled off the blue velvet jacket and handed it to his mother, who took it without looking at him. She gathered up the wet linen and left the room.

'What's the matter with her?' asked Mistress Oliver. 'Face as thunderous as the weather.'

'She disapproves of me giving Joseph lessons.'

'Who can blame her? What will a slave do with learning? In my opinion . . .'

The front-door knocker sounded, once, twice and then in a great tattoo.

'Mercy me!' Mistress Oliver wiped her hands upon her apron and set off down the passage. 'It must be someone for the doctor.'

Susannah wrung the water out of her hair and was on the point of going upstairs to change into dry clothes when she heard raised voices in the hall. Surely she recognised that voice? She hurried along the passage.

'Oh, Miss Susannah! I've come straight away. It's terrible . . .'

'Jennet, what is it?' Alarm made Susannah's voice sharp with foreboding.

'It's Mr Leyton, Miss.' Jennet was trembling uncontrollably, the rain dripping off her sodden skirt and making a puddle on the Persian rug.

'What happened?'

'The master woke up a-coughing and a-sneezing

355

and now he's burning with the fever and the mistress is having a screaming fit.' She dropped her voice to a whisper. 'He's got the black boils.'

A shard of terror pierced Susannah's insides. 'Sweet Lord, not the plague!'

Mistress Oliver shrieked and scuttled back to the kitchen.

Susannah sank onto the hall chair. When the faintness had passed she struggled to her feet. 'I must go to Father at once!'

'You can't, miss! You'll catch it yourself.'

Heedless, Susannah pulled open the front door and stood for a moment in the doorway before plunging out into the teeming rain.

Whyteladies Lane was swirling with water from the overflowing drain, the cobbles slippery underfoot. Susannah hurried along as fast as she could, the mud ankle-deep in places. Almost blinded by the hammering rain, she skidded on something unpleasantly soft, tripped, righted herself and then lost her balance again. Gasping, she braced her hands forward to protect her unborn child as she began the inevitable tumble to the ground.

Strong hands grasped her from behind and pulled her up. 'Slow down, Miss Susannah! It won't help your father if you miscarry.'

Susannah found herself in Jennet's broad arms. She let out one sob and then took a deep breath while she willed her racing heart to steady. 'I'm all right now. Come on!'

Jennet linked arms with her and they stumbled up Whyteladies Lane together, slip-sliding through the mire.

The first slow rumble of thunder began, rolling

around the sky like a wagon wheel on the loose. Lightning flickered. A coach splashed past, throwing water up high in its wake.

The two women flattened themselves against a wall to avoid the spray just as the thunder cracked. Hands clasped, they stepped over the swirling torrent of rainwater that ran across the top of the alley and turned onto the main thoroughfare. A stream of carriages, on their way to the Bolt and Tun, swished past, splashing pedestrians and buildings alike.

At last they reached the sign of the Unicorn and the Dragon. A small crowd had gathered, taking shelter from the rain in the doorway of the glovemaker's shop opposite. A watchman stood on the step of the apothecary shop and Susannah gasped in horror when she saw that already a painted red cross glistened on the door. She pressed her face against the window. Inside all was as usual; the pestle and mortar sat on the counter next to the jar of leeches and the cone of sugar, in comfortable familiarity. Except that her father and Ned weren't in the shop.

'Let me in!' she called to the watchman.

He shook his head. 'No one's to go in or out.'

'But my father and his wife are in there and my baby brothers!'

'You can't go in.' He folded his arms and scowled at her.

'Have you no pity?' she asked.

'Have *you* no pity for the child you carry?'

Jennet took hold of her arm. 'Come away, Miss Susannah.'

Susannah let Jennet lead her away and then stood in the road looking up at the windows. 'Let's try the kitchen door,' she said. 'I must see Father. What if he dies, Jennet, and I haven't said goodbye to him?' She set off down the road to the familiar passage between the buildings which led to the back of the yard. The rain fell harder still and the hem of her skirt was caked and heavy with mud. The key was in its usual hiding place; she unlocked the gate and splashed through the yard to the kitchen door. She turned the handle but then saw the shiny new nails hammered into the timber. Banging on the door, she screamed and shouted her father's name, her voice drowned out by the thunder rumbling overhead and the water gushing from the roof onto the ground.

Jennet pulled her arm. 'It's no use, Miss Susannah.'

Defeated, Susannah sank against the yard wall, her face in her hands.

Lightning fractured the sky and she looked up. Her father's white face was at the bedroom window.

'Father!'

He looked down at her and mouthed something she couldn't hear.

Hope surged in her heart. 'I'm coming, Father! I'll bribe the watchman to let me in.'

He shook his head and pressed his hands flat against the streaming window pane. Faltering then, he collapsed against the window, his palms sliding down the glass until he disappeared from view.

Susannah stared upwards, willing him to reappear. She stifled a sob; if she gave in to tears she thought she might not be able to stop and there were still decisions to make. She turned to Jennet. 'Were Arabella and the children well when you left?'

358

'They were screaming and crying something terrible when I slipped out of the back door. You could hear the hullabaloo half way up Fleet Street. Either they've gone or they've fallen ill all of a sudden.'

'What about Ned?'

'He took to his bed with a rattling cough this morning.'

'So Father and Ned may be on their own with no one to nurse them?'

Jennet nodded, her face stricken.

Susannah lifted her skirts out of the mud and started back to Fleet Street with Jennet trailing behind her.

The watchman leaned on his halberd, his coat collar pulled up against the hammering rain.

'Let me pass,' said Susannah.

'You want to die, do you? You and your babe?' Water ran down his cheeks and dripped off his chin in a continual stream.

Susannah hesitated, torn between risking her baby's life and the yearning to comfort her father.

'Pray to the good Lord and hope he will be merciful. Go along home now, madam, before you drown.'

How *could* she abandon her father? She made up her mind. 'I'll pay you to let me in!'

'Trying to bribe me now, is it?' Lightning flashed again and a second later thunder cracked and echoed around the sky. 'How much?' shouted the watchman over the clamour of the drumming rain.

Susannah looked into his greedy eyes. Would it be so terrible to die and leave behind all her fears? William and Henry had both betrayed her. Who

359

else loved her now but her father?

'How much?' shouted the watchman, again.

She took a deep breath and tried to still her shaking hands. 'Everything I have,' she said.

Another gigantic clap of thunder made her gasp.

'Let's see your money, then,' said the watchman.

'I'll have to fetch it.'

'Well, I'm not going anywhere.' He folded his arms.

Susannah had gone only a few steps when she saw a tall man hurrying towards the shop. His cloak flapped wetly around his knees and water funnelled off his hat onto the beaked mask below. Her heart began to race again. William. Only the day before she would have run to him but now she simply stood with legs as heavy as lead and watched him approach.

'Susannah. I came as soon as I heard.'

'Father has the pestilence,' she said, unable to meet his eyes. 'And Ned is sickening.'

'Arabella and the children?'

She shrugged, dashing the streaming water off her face with the back of her hand. 'She ran away before the house was shut up. I saw Father . . .' She broke down then, the memory of his white face at the window too much to bear.

William caught her by the shoulders. 'How bad is he?'

'Very weak.'

'My poor master has the black boils and a fever, sir,' said Jennet, through chattering teeth.

Susannah shook herself free of William's hands. 'I must help him!'

'You cannot.' His black eyes flashed above the white mask.

360

'I can and I will. But first I have to go home and collect my savings.'

'Your savings?'

'I haven't much but the watchman will let me in if—'

'Susannah! What are you thinking of?' He pulled off his mask. 'You cannot put yourself at such risk!'

'What does that matter any more?' She was too exhausted to argue about it. 'All I want is to be with Father.' Rain thudded down on Susannah's head and her hair, escaped from its pins, clung like seaweed to her shoulders.

Lightning forked across the sky, illuminating the street with brilliant intensity.

'And you are prepared to risk your baby's life, too?' William's voice was cold. 'I had not thought you so selfish.'

A sudden flash of anger made her hold her head up high and stare him down. 'And I suppose you are a model of perfection?'

Thunder exploded and reverberated around the rooftops, louder than a thousand cannons.

'Your father would not wish you and his grandchild to die in vain,' shouted William as the heavens tore apart above them. '*I* shall go into the house.'

'No!'

'Who better?'

'Sir?' Jennet caught hold of his sleeve, her chin trembling and her eyes wide with terror. 'Let me come with you.'

'You? Why would you want to return to a house of sickness?'

'Where else can I go?' Her voice quavered. 'I have no family and this has been my home for more

361

years than I can remember. Mr Leyton has always been so good to me and I can help to nurse him.'

'You may sicken.'

'Perhaps I am already infected.' She stood up and braced her shoulders. 'God will decide what becomes of me.

'Then so be it. I shall be glad of your assistance. We must put a poultice on the boils and draw out the evil humours. Let us waste no more time.'

'You cannot, William!' cried Susannah, clutching at his sleeve.

Ignoring her, he strode back to the watchman. 'Stand aside!'

The watchman barred the door with his halberd. 'No one comes out. No one goes in. Those are my orders.'

'And do your orders include taking bribes to allow people to leave the premises?' William caught the watchman by his collar and roughly pushed him back against the wall. 'Where is the lady of the house and her children? If they have been allowed to escape, possibly carrying infection with them, I can assure you the authorities will take such a matter very seriously.'

The watchman shuffled his feet. 'I can't help it if madam escaped out of a bedroom window and across the rooftops, can I?'

'This maid came from the house. She may already carry the sickness and I am sure you will agree that it is better for her to be confined inside? And as a doctor, I shall tend to the sick myself.'

'If you go in and you don't come out on the dead-cart, you'll be quarantined,' warned the watchman.

William released him.

362

'And I won't take no bribes to let you out earlier, seeing as the authorities are so strict.' The watchman grinned, showing the black stumps of his teeth.

Susannah caught hold of Jennet's arm, her sleeve sodden under her hand. 'Are you sure you want to do this?'

'I'm afraid of dying but I'm more afraid of being alone in the world.' The maid struggled to find a smile. 'Look after yourself and your babe, Miss Susannah, and I will help the doctor to tend your dear father.'

Speechless, Susannah gathered Jennet into her arms and hugged her fiercely.

'We have no time to waste,' said William.

The watchman unlocked the door. 'Go on with you, then.'

As lightning fizzled and spat, ripping across the leaden sky, Jennet bolted through the doorway glancing back white-faced over her shoulder before she disappeared.

William wiped his dripping face. 'I'll do my very best for your father,' he said. 'Come at noon tomorrow and I'll let you know how he fares.'

Susannah fought to find the words to express her tumultuous thoughts. In the end, she only said, 'You will do this, risk your life, for him?'

'I will do this for you, Susannah.' He looked at her for a long moment before he, too, went into the house.

The watchman slammed the door shut and turned the key in the lock.

Thunder cracked again, the violence of the storm only matched by the desolation in Susannah's heart. Soaked to the skin, she stared at the red cross on the door and then at the words painted below. *Lord have mercy on us,* she read.

Chapter 24

'Dammit, Susannah!' Agnes dropped her pipe upon her lap, heedless of the tobacco stains upon her skirt. 'He's all I have left. How could you let him?'

'You know better than I that William will always do as he pleases,' she said bitterly.

'I thought you had more influence over him.'

'As you can see, I have not,' said Susannah. But guilt and dread pricked her. Agnes was right; she should have tried harder to dissuade William from entering the house. But Father had been so alone and frightened.

Agnes's dark eyes glittered with unshed tears. 'How will we manage without him, Susannah?' she whispered. 'I had not thought he would leave the world before me.'

'Don't!' Sudden panic made Susannah shout, her voice echoing round the chapel's high ceiling. She clasped her hands together to still their trembling. 'All is not yet lost. He has worked amongst the sick and remained well during this past terrible year.'

'But never before shut up in a house with the dying.' Agnes's bent and knobbled hands twisted around the head of her cane. 'William is the son I never had.'

'I know.'

They sat in silence for the rest of the afternoon, each absorbed in their own fearful thoughts, while outside the rain cascaded down the windows.

At suppertime Phoebe brought in a tray of cold gammon and bread. She avoided looking at Susannah and left the chapel as quietly as she had entered it.

Susannah could barely swallow since nausea brought on by fright made her stomach heave at the sight of the thick pink and white slabs of meat.

Agnes ate little and retired to her bedchamber shortly afterwards.

The downpour stopped at last and Susannah slipped outside to take the evening air. The flowers were rain-drenched and her herbs had been flattened. She walked through the cloisters, perfumed with honeysuckle mixed with the warm, woody scent of moist earth.

Sitting on the bench while the light faded, she watched the bats flitter in the gloaming. She tortured herself by imagining her father's agonies as William laid on steaming poultices to draw out the evil humours from the buboes. Unable to cry, she rocked herself backwards and forwards, her pain and loneliness as sharp as if she had swallowed broken glass. Each minute seemed like an hour and she still had to endure the night before she could discover her father's fate. Her baby stirred inside her and she hugged her stomach, wondering if her father would survive to see his grandchild.

Despair descended then and at last she gave herself up to a storm of weeping. The events of the past few days had tossed her from sublime happiness to the utmost misery. She cried for what might have been: the death of her child's father and her disappointing marriage, the love she thought had grown between herself and William that had turned out to be so hollow, her father's love that she had taken for granted until he snatched it away and gave it to Arabella. Most of all she cried out from the fear of living in a world without either her father or William there to love her.

The morning was a long time coming. At dawn Susannah gave up trying to sleep. She dressed and went down to the kitchen where Mistress Oliver was putting the bread into the oven.

'Needn't ask what kind of a night you've had,' said the cook. 'And I don't suppose the mistress fared much better.'

'It's the waiting and the wondering that's so dreadful.'

'I'll make you a pot of coffee to take up to the mistress. No doubt she's been lying awake and a-wondering, too.'

The sound of the pestle grinding coffee beans in the mortar raised a vision in Susannah's mind of her father standing behind the counter in the apothecary shop mixing medicines over the years. She swallowed back the lump in her throat. It was too terrible to contemplate that he might not continue his work for years to come. She stared into the fire, willing herself to empty her mind of such thoughts.

Before long the scent of freshly baked bread began to vie with the aroma of the coffee simmering on the fire. Mistress Oliver strained the coffee through a piece of muslin, sawed some slices off the new loaf and slapped them down on the table.

Susannah, suddenly overwhelmed by hunger, bit into the warm bread and washed it down with a gulp of hot coffee. 'I'll put the rest on a tray and take it up to Mistress Fygge,' she said, brushing crumbs off her skirt.

A wall of heat and smoke hit her as she opened the bedchamber door. Agnes was already sitting up in bed and Phoebe was kneeling in front of the grate sweeping up the ashes.

'Shall I open the window?' asked Susannah. She took care not to acknowledge Phoebe's presence.

'No!' Agnes shuddered. 'The very air is dangerous. We can't know what sickness is carried on the breeze.'

Surreptitiously, Susannah wiped the perspiration off her forehead.

Dwarfed by the four-poster, Agnes looked somehow shrunken, with her hands clasped to her chest and her thin plait lying over her shoulder. 'I shall stay in bed today,' she said.

'Would you like me to read to you, to help pass the time?'

'Maybe later. But come and give me the news as soon as you return.'

Susannah attempted to make herself busy but she couldn't settle and all the while the weight of dread pressed down upon her like a flat iron. She finished sewing another tiny vest for her baby and placed it in the chest in her bedchamber along with the others. Watching the sun climb higher in the sky, she listened out for the church bells, counting the hours as they passed.

Eventually it was time to go. Mistress Oliver packed a basket with provisions and Susannah put it over her arm. At the last moment she decided to pick some herbs; the fresh rosemary would make a soothing infusion to ease Ned's cough.

Water still swirled in the drains and detritus washed up against the walls had been left high and dry by the previous day's torrents. The gulls from the river wheeled and cried overhead, swooping down to snatch at the debris. Susannah's advanced state of pregnancy made her balance unsteady and she had to take care not to lose her footing on the cobbles.

She was hot and out of breath by the time she arrived at the sign of the Unicorn and the Dragon. The watchman lounged on the step, barring the door.

'What news?' she asked.

He stood up straighter but his eyes slid away from hers, causing cold fingers of apprehension to run down her back. 'Best call your friends,' he said. He banged on the door with his fist. 'Oi! Come to the window!'

The casement opened and Jennet looked out, her face swollen with weeping.

'Oh, Jennet!' Susannah clutched her hands together over her breast in fear.

The maid choked back a sob. 'They took him away last night!'

Susannah, suddenly faint, leaned her hand against the wall to steady herself. 'Not Father! Please say it isn't so.'

'Oh no, miss, not your father but poor Ned.'

'Ned? But I've brought rosemary to make an infusion for his cough!'

'Too late, Miss Susannah. The sickness came over him very sudden and he went into convulsions. All blotchy and burning up with the fever he was and crying out for his mother.'

Susannah pictured the apprentice's eager young face, his life so cruelly cut short, but she couldn't help the unchristian thought that she was glad it

368

was Ned and not her father who had perished.

'The cart came for him before light this morning,' wept Jennet. 'When the doctor and I carried him down the stairs I slipped and nearly dropped him. His head banged against the wall with a terrible thump and I can still hear the echo in my ears, over and over again. And the dead-cart was already overflowing with corpses and I keep remembering him being carried off.'

'You've been very brave, Jennet.'

'Now I'm praying for the master. He wouldn't like the dead-cart at all.'

'Does he suffer greatly?'

William's face appeared at the window behind Jennet. She moved away and he leaned out over the sill. 'Your father is very ill, Susannah. We have bathed him in cool water to bring down his body heat and placed poultices on the buboes to draw the poison to the surface. Some of the boils have burst, which is encouraging. I can do no more now than to make him comfortable.'

'Will he live?'

'I cannot tell and will not make you false promises, Susannah.'

False promises! She studied his face, his expression so concerned for her, yet he had led her to believe that he cared deeply for her and still he had betrayed her with Phoebe. She hardly knew what to believe any more. 'Can I fetch anything to ease his suffering?' she said, at last.

'We have all the medicines we could need, here in the shop. All we can do now is to put our trust in the Lord.'

Susannah nodded, unable to speak for the fear that tears would overwhelm her.

'I see you have been kind enough to bring us some provisions,' said William. He disappeared inside for a moment and then lowered a bed sheet out of the window.

Susannah tied a corner of the linen round the handle of the basket and watched as he pulled it up.

'Come and see us again tomorrow,' he said. 'Susannah?'

'Yes?' She met his eyes, hope flaring in her breast again. Perhaps he would beg her forgiveness.

But all he said was, 'Send my love to Aunt Agnes. And try to keep calm. The Lord will decide what is to happen and anxiety will not help either you or your babe.'

Disappointment felled her hopes. She turned and stumbled away.

*   *   *

There was a sense of unreality about the next twenty-four hours. The routine of the day continued on almost as normal, while terror gripped at Susannah's insides with razor-sharp claws.

She moved slowly about her duties, hardly speaking unless Agnes addressed her directly, focusing only upon the moment when it would be the time to go to her father's shop for news.

Agnes's fear for William showed in her temper and she brushed aside with irritation Susannah's suggestion that she rest in bed for the morning.

'Don't fuss over me, miss!'

Biting her lip, Susannah did as she was bid. Once the lacing of the bodices and the dressing of the hair had been accomplished, she helped Agnes to the chair by the window with her book of poems by her side.

'You are dismissed but be sure to come and tell me the news when you return.'

'Yes, Agnes.'

'And Susannah? Tell Will I am proud of him. I may think he has made a foolish decision but I would not have expected less of him.'

Chapter 25

Mistress Oliver tucked a jar of plum preserve into the basket. 'The master's favourite,' she said. 'And there's the last of the gammon for him. Phoebe will carry the basket to the end of Whyteladies Lane for you. I can tell your back is aching again.'

'It does pain me and I'm tired of looking and feeling like an overinflated pig's bladder.'

'Ah well, not long to go now till you'll have that sweet babe in your arms and then you'll know what tiredness is all about! Phoebe, you can leave the pans to soak for now and carry the basket.'

'Yes'm.' Phoebe dried her hands on her apron and slid the basket handle over her arm.

The heat of the sun had turned the mud in the lane to dust again and two dogs fought over a bone unearthed from the refuse. The swirling torrent in the central drain had subsided and Susannah found the way easier going than on the previous day.

At the end of the lane she took the basket from Phoebe. Her hand brushed accidentally against the other woman's and as she glanced up their eyes met.

Phoebe stared back, her brown-sugar eyes giving

nothing away. She walked away without looking back.

Susannah had half expected her to send a message to William and was astonished at the other woman's passivity while her lover was locked up in a plague house. She lodged the basket into the crook of her elbow and set off towards Fleet Street. Unaccountably her spirits lifted. The air was a little fresher than in previous days and some of Father's boils had burst, which was good news indeed. Some said that if the poisons were drained from the pestilential risings, a patient might recover. Father was still vigorous for his age and his health had always been good so surely the outlook was promising? No doubt he would continue to improve a little, day by day.

It was in this spirit of hope that Susannah arrived at the apothecary shop. The watchman saw her coming and tipped his hat to her before banging on the door. 'Oi,' he shouted. 'To the window! The lady's here.'

The casement opened wider and William leaned out. 'Susannah.'

The tone of his voice, kind, gentle, stopped her in her tracks. Carefully she placed the basket on the ground. She knew with dreadful certainty what he had to tell her, even before he uttered another word. All at once she was deathly cold. Everything faded away, except for William's face.

'When,' she asked.

'Not an hour since. I sat up with him all night and we talked a little but he grew weaker and weaker until he drew his last breath.'

How strange, she thought, she was calm and rational even though inside her head someone was screaming. 'Was his passing gentle?'

'My dear, I cannot say he did not suffer but I made him as comfortable as possible.'

'I am grateful to you for that.'

'Some of the time he thought that I was your brother, Tom. He took my hand and asked me to find you. Your name was the last word on his lips.'

Susannah faltered then. She uttered a cry of desolation, the sky above began to spin and her vision darkened. From a great distance she heard William shout her name.

The watchman caught her as she slipped to the ground. 'Upsadaisy, missus!' He supported her until the faintness passed. 'Better now?'

'My father is dead!'

'Yes, missus, I know. Gorn to a better place, I should say.'

'Susannah! Susannah?'

Releasing herself from the watchman's brawny arms, she looked up to where William was framed in the open window.

'Susannah, are you all right?'

Her lips were numb and she had begun to shiver uncontrollably and couldn't stop her teeth chattering together. 'Merely a little faint,' she said. 'It has passed now. You see, I had persuaded myself that Father would have improved today.'

William slammed his hand against the window frame. 'Goddamnit, Susannah! I can do nothing to help you while I'm incarcerated here.'

'You did everything you could to help Father. Nothing else matters now. What of you and Jennet? Are you still well?'

He nodded. 'But Jennet is in low spirits. She loved her master and is conscious that now there are many uncertainties for her future.'

'And there is nothing I can say to bring her comfort,' said Susannah bitterly. 'There is no certainty for any woman's future without a man to support her.'

'We have to stay here until the quarantine is lifted.'

'What will happen to Father now?'

'The cart will come for him this evening.'

Susannah put her hand over her mouth. 'I must see him one last time.'

'No, you must not! Susannah, I beg you, do not do this. You will distress yourself and may cause ill to your baby. It is far better for you to remember him in happier times than to see him as he is now.'

'But don't you understand? If I cannot say goodbye to him I shall never really believe he has gone.'

'I advise against it.'

'Is he such a terrible sight?'

'It's not that . . .'

'What then?'

'The buriers will come for him.' William rubbed his eyes, his exhaustion clear to see. 'They have become so used to collecting corpses that they do not always treat the dead with proper respect and it will be distressing for you.'

'Nonetheless, I will be here.'

He stared at her for a moment and then said, 'I can see your mind is made up and I haven't the will to argue with you.'

'I have brought you provisions. Pull up the basket and I shall return later.'

After the basket had been emptied Susannah set off towards The Captain's House again.

Agnes knew what had happened as soon as she saw Susannah's face. 'I am truly sorry, my dear. Your father was a fine man, even if he did let that flibberty-gibbet wife of his lead him a merry dance. The world will be a poorer place without him.'

Susannah nodded, her eyes brimming. 'Arabella ought to know that she is a widow and the twins fatherless. I can only think that she must have gone to her brother's house in Shoreditch. May I send Phoebe with a note for her?'

'Do as you think fit, though I hardly see her as a grieving widow.'

'I want to be sure Joshua and Samuel are safe. And then I shall go again to the house this evening. I must be there when the cart comes.'

'I shan't ask you if that is a sensible notion. I expect you wish to catch a last glimpse of him?'

'I *must* see where he is buried. How else can I know where to show my child his grandfather's grave?'

'Then you shall take Phoebe with you.'

'No! I mean, thank you for your concern but I prefer to go alone.'

'I will worry if you are alone in the streets after dark. Go and rest now since you will be late to bed.'

Susannah lay down but could not sleep. Screwing her eyes tight shut, she sought comfort in imagining herself back in the time when her life had been so safe and carefree. She pictured her mother bent over the counter in the apothecary shop, straining lavender steeped in sweet almond oil through muslin. Mama had applied a drop of the perfumed oil to her wrist and she could still summon up the soothing, flowery scent of it, which had accompanied her all day.

Her father had been happy then. Later, after Mama's tragic death, he and Susannah had taken solace in the apothecary shop. He'd taught her everything he knew and trusted her to experiment with even the most expensive ingredients.

She curled up into a tight little ball while she remembered the contented hours she had spent in his company. Never again would she be able to argue with him the merits of spirits of scurvy grass over fresh lemon juice for the loosening of the teeth or delight in their mutual interest at one of the lectures at Gresham College or simply enjoy sitting by the fireside in peaceful harmony. She tormented herself with these reminiscences until the light began to fade.

At last she sat up and rubbed the feeling back into her limbs. She felt as hollow and light as thistledown as she went to find Agnes. The chapel was overheated and hazy with smoke from the rosemary burning in the hearth.

'Agnes, I'm leaving now.'

'Keep the door closed! I am determined to fume away any contagion that dares to enter my house,' said Agnes. 'You still insist on going tonight?'

Susannah nodded.

'Then be sure to cover your face when the buriers come. Sprinkle vinegar on a handkerchief and hold it to your nose. Touch nothing and I will pray that you are kept safe from infection.'

'Thank you.'

Agnes's lips curled in a grim smile. 'I believe you are as stubborn as I am. Go then! Phoebe is waiting for you.'

'She need not accompany me.'

'You will not vex me by arguing.'

It was very nearly dark and Phoebe carried a lantern to light the way. They walked side by side in silence, avoiding the beggars that snatched at the hems of their skirts and crossing the street into the shadows without a word spoken as they passed the open door of a noisy tavern. Warm, foetid air and the sound of drunken laughter drifted after them.

When they arrived at the apothecary shop, candles burned in every window.

'Go home, madam,' the watchman said. 'No good will come of your presence here.'

'Will the dead-cart come soon?' she asked.

'Soon enough.'

William threw open the casement and leaned out. 'You came then?'

'As you see.'

'I have used the best linen I could find to make a winding cloth for your father and Jennet and I have carried him down and rested him on the counter in the shop.'

'He would have liked that,' said Susannah, a quiver in her voice.

In the distance she heard a bell ringing. Her insides lurched and she began to tremble.

'The cart is coming,' said William.

The bell rang again and now she could hear the mournful cry of the bellman.

'Bring out your dead! Bring out your dead!'

The bell became louder and the people hurrying along Fleet Street flattened themselves against the walls to give the bellman a wide berth. The horse-drawn cart, lit by lamps, lurched out of the darkness, trundling over the cobbles with its sorry load. Two buriers, dressed in high boots and shrouded in long capes, followed with lamps swaying in their hands. A number of weeping men and women walked behind.

The watchman held his lamp high and stepped into the dead-cart's path. Then he motioned Susannah and Phoebe to stand well back and took the door key from his pocket.

William waited inside with Jennet behind him.

Her heart thumping against her ribcage, Susannah watched William speak a few words to one of the buriers as he came forward. She heard the chink of coins changing hands. Then the buriers went inside the shop and she waited, her eyes fixed on the open door, while she clenched her fists so hard that her nails drew blood on her palms.

The men reappeared a few moments later, carrying Cornelius's linen-wrapped body between them. A corner of his winding sheet had come loose and trailed in the dust. They carried him with as much ceremony as if he were a rolled-up carpet, no longer wanted and about to be put into storage.

Susannah pressed her hands to her mouth, suppressing an involuntary cry. Was this cumbersome parcel all that remained of her beloved father? She tilted forward, in a despairing need to throw herself upon his body and pull away the winding sheet to see his face one last time.

The watchman grasped her tightly by the arm and dragged her back. 'No you don't, missus!'

One burier held up a lantern and threw aside the sacking on top of the cart.

Susannah gasped and reeled back. Corpses, some wrapped in rags, some naked, were stacked in an untidy heap. A young woman dressed only in her night shift lay spread-eagled on her back, her golden hair falling in a waterfall over the edge of the cart and her swollen neck black and suppurating.

In the doorway, Jennet let out a screech and covered her face with her apron.

Susannah stared at the cart in horror, revulsion making her stomach churn. 'You can't put my father in there!' She fumbled for the vinegar-soaked handkerchief in her pocket and clasped it over her nose, retching at the stench of the dead. Even by the wavering light of the lantern she could see, and smell, the terrible pestilential tokens on the corpses.

'Death is the great leveller,' said the burier who held Cornelius's legs. He nodded at the other, carrying the shoulders. 'On three,' he said. 'One, two, three!'

They swung the body up between them and dumped it upon the cart. It landed with a thud on top of the young woman with the blond hair.

One of the buriers cackled and nudged his assistant. 'That's one old man gone happy to the grave!'

'Tuck 'em up nice and warm together for all eternity, shall we?' Still chuckling, they threw the sacking back over the top, took hold of the horse's head again and the cart rolled on its way.

Susannah, frozen with horror, stared at William, framed in the doorway.

'I wish you hadn't come here tonight,' he said. 'No daughter should have to see such a sight.'

The watchman came forward. 'Inside with you, sir. Now!'

'May I not offer this lady a few words of comfort?'

'Not if you don't want to pass on the contagion.

Go on, inside with you!'

'Susannah . . .' The door slammed in William's face.

Susannah watched the tail end of the dead-cart disappearing down Fleet Street, the lantern bobbing up and down. She heaved a great sigh. She knew what she had to do now. She *must* see where they were taking her father.

'Missus!' Phoebe hastened behind her.

Susannah waited impatiently for her to catch up before following the cart.

Presently the cart stopped outside a milliner's shop. A knot of people waited outside, talking in hushed tones. Screaming and crying came from an upstairs window as the buriers brought out the tiny corpses of three children. Their father stood nearby in shocked silence as they were thrown onto the cart.

An old woman fainted and her husband began to shout, tearing at his hair and railing at God for forsaking his grandchildren.

Susannah looked away, unable to bear the weight of their grief added to her own.

The cart moved on again, the horse's hooves clip-clopping over the cobbles. The children's father followed and then the other grieving relatives in a ragged procession.

At last they reached the high fence which surrounded the plague pit. Susannah gagged into her handkerchief at the sickly stench of corruption which filled the air, saturating it in despair.

Phoebe turned aside with a groan and vomited onto the ground.

The bellman rang his bell vigorously and called out, 'Open the gate!'

After a moment the palisade quivered and then a section opened inwards and admitted the cart.

The procession attempted to follow but the watchmen barred the way. The father of the dead children, overcome by grief, began roaring and shouting and in only a few moments a fist fight had broken out between the relatives and the watchmen as the mourners were denied access.

Susannah took her chance. 'Stay here!' she hissed to Phoebe. She slipped through the gate while the watchmen were occupied and hovered in the shadows while she took in the scene before her. Numb with horror, she gazed at the burial trench. No preacher could have described a vision of hell as terrible as this.

Lanterns hung on poles, casting flickering light into the pit, some forty feet by twelve. The bottom was only eight feet or so below the surface now and she caught glimpses of half-buried bodies, a grinning skull, an out-thrust hand. The sweet reek of rotting flesh was overpowering, a hundred times worse than the overflowing sewers in August or the stench of simmering fish bones from the gluemaker's vat.

Susannah started as the gate slammed shut behind her. The screaming and wailing continued outside the palisade.

The horse and cart were backed up to the pit with a great deal of shouting and the buriers, like some hellish demons, began to drag the corpses off the cart and hurl them into the hole.

The children went first, spinning towards the centre of the pit with their arms and legs flying out like little rag dolls. Susannah's father was next to be dragged off the cart. She suppressed a moan as the loose end of the winding sheet unravelled and she caught a glimpse of his bare foot swinging free. The sight of his naked toes was almost her undoing. She lurched forward, desperate to snatch up his foot and press it to her cheek, to touch her father's skin for one last time, but she stumbled and fell to her knees. By this time the buriers had heaved his body into the pit. The other corpses followed, tumbled on top of each other with no thought given to any respect for the dead.

Shaking with distress, Susannah watched the buriers sprinkle quicklime over the bodies and then set to with their shovels, spreading a thin layer of earth over the lot. She kept her eyes fixed upon her father's last resting place until the men had finished. Once they were leaning on their shovels, slaking their thirst with a jar of beer, she gathered up a handful of earth and crept towards the edge of the trench. She scattered the earth onto the spot where she had last seen her father's body. 'Ashes to ashes, dust to dust,' she murmured.

She stared into the pit, remembering her last sight of her father at the window. Now she would never know what his final words to her were. She wept then, hot tears coursing down her cheeks until, at last, all her emotions were deadened.

The bell rang again and the gates opened to admit another cart. Keeping to the shadows, Susannah stole through the gate and out into the street again.

Chapter 26

The following week passed in a haze for Susannah. She slept a little but only to be haunted by terrifying dreams of her father's corpse rising from the plague pit, trailing earth and putrefying skin behind him as he wandered the streets searching for Arabella and the children.

She wrote a letter to her brother, Tom, the ink blotched and tear-stained, to tell him of their father's terrible death. He was all the family she had left now and she wished with all her heart that she could be with him so that they might mourn together.

She took the letter to the docks to find a sailor to carry it to Virginia. He snatched her money and then stuffed the letter carelessly into his jacket and she turned away in despair with no idea if it would ever reach her brother's hands.

Each day she dragged herself to the apothecary shop with leaden feet, terrified as to what she might find. Each day her grief was renewed as she stood outside the window to be reminded of the last time she had seen her father. Sorrow made her so weary that she longed to be able to go inside and climb the stairs to her old bedchamber, where she could curl up and fall asleep, never to wake again.

But William and Jennet showed no signs of sickness so far.

Jennet made it her business to scrub the house from top to bottom; William fumigated each room in turn while they hung out of the windows coughing until the smoke had dissipated.

'I am passing the time in discovering your father's library,' said William, wiping the smoke-induced tears from his eyes, 'and have been reading his treatises on the merits of Galen versus Hippocrates. Your father was a learned man as well as one of the best apothecaries I knew.'

'He would have been so pleased you thought that.' Susannah found it helped her to talk of her father, to remember the good things rather than the sad times that followed.

'If you had been his son, you would have been an excellent apothecary, too.' William drummed his fingers on the windowsill. 'It's making me fretful to be so confined and I've had a great deal of time to ponder on certain matters.'

'Now you know as well as I how arduous it is to be in enforced idleness when you are used to being industrious,' said Susannah.

A small frown appeared on William's forehead. 'I was thinking that, perhaps when I am released from here . . .'

'Perhaps what?'

He shook his head. 'I've been making plans but if I'm spared, there will be enough time for that later. You are grieving for your father and should not be troubled by fanciful ideas and I have kept you talking too long.'

'I'll bring you more provisions tomorrow.' But she made no move to go, reluctant to leave him in case he sickened and died while she was away. Even though he had betrayed her so cruelly, the very thought of him dying made her feel as if there was a tight band crushing her chest.

'Send Aunt Agnes my love, won't you?'

She hesitated but the Devil made her say it.

384

'And shall I send your special love to Phoebe and Joseph?'

'Phoebe and Joseph?' His brow wrinkled.

She waited, trying to find the right words to tell him that she knew about his treachery, but failed.

'Susannah?' William's expression was concerned. 'You look exhausted. Go home and rest.'

If she hadn't seen him with her own eyes leaving Phoebe's room that night, she would never have guessed that he could be so duplicitous. 'I'll come tomorrow with more provisions,' she said.

*   *   *

On the walk home Susannah admitted to herself that she still loved William, in spite of the shameful way he had behaved. Nevertheless, he had been extraordinarily brave and selfless in nursing her father and Ned and he had shown every concern for her well-being since Father had died. Part of her wished that she had never gone up to the attics that night and then she might never have known about his betrayal.

Turning into Whyteladies Lane, she wondered again where her stepmother could be. A note had come back from Arabella's brother to say that she and the children were not with him and he had no idea of her present whereabouts. Susannah was anxious about the twins and sad at losing touch with her baby brothers. They were her only remaining family in the country and it was of great importance to her that they knew what sort of a man their father had been. She knew she couldn't rely upon Arabella to keep his memory alive for them and was still pondering on how to find them as she neared the Captain's House.

Three small boys ran out of the butcher's shop, shrieking as they chased each other down the lane. They darted from side to side, dashing in front of Susannah and nearly sending her flying. One of the boys was Joseph.

'Joseph!'

He glanced back, stopped and then came towards her, dragging his feet. 'Yes, miss?'

'Joseph, you know you're not to play in the street.'

'But . . .'

'Come inside now!'

The boy stuck out his bottom lip but followed her into the house.

Susannah returned the basket to the kitchen, where Mistress Oliver was standing at the table dismembering a couple of capons with a cleaver.

'All still well?' asked the cook, with a sharply enquiring look.

Susannah nodded.

'Thank the Lord for that!' She pushed aside a mess of entrails and a dish of lardy cake to make more room before she chopped off the capons' heads.

Joseph eyed the lardy cake and, unable to resist such temptation, shot out a hand and stole a slice.

Mistress Oliver grabbed his wrist and threatened him with the cleaver. 'Where've you been, you young scallywag?'

'I found him running out of that dirty butcher's shop with those raggedy boys of theirs,' said Susannah.

'Didn't your mother tell you you're not to play outside, Joseph? And especially not with the butcher's boys. Lead you into trouble they will. Now sit down at the table and eat that lardy cake. Don't want you dropping crumbs all over the place and encouraging the rats.'

*   *   *

Agnes was relieved to hear that William and Jennet remained well. 'But I shall keep vigil in my chamber until William is returned safely to me,' she said. 'You must continue to visit the apothecary shop every day to bring back news. Now tell me; is there any sign of Arabella?'

'None at all. I shan't be sorry if I never see her again but I would dearly like to know the whereabouts of my little brothers.'

'She's bound to turn up in due course. And I shouldn't worry too much about the twins. Their mother will fall on her feet; her kind always does.'

Susannah read to Agnes for much of the afternoon, though she often slipped and stumbled over the words as her mind drifted away on waves of anxiety and sadness.

Phoebe carried in a supper tray. Susannah attempted to take it from her but Phoebe, her expression sullen, pushed past her and set it down on the table by the window.

Susannah gave a mental shrug. She was too unhappy to be bothered with the woman's continuing hostility. Phoebe had unaccountably disliked her from the day they met and she couldn't imagine anything that would ever change that now.

Later that evening Susannah returned Agnes's empty tray to the kitchen.

Phoebe was scouring the pots while Mistress

Oliver sat on a stool soaking her feet in a basin.

'The mistress ate her dinner, then?' she asked.

Joseph ran into the kitchen and buried his face in his mother's skirts.

'Most of it.'

Susannah turned her head as Phoebe clattered the pots and then began to scold Joseph. The boy was whimpering and scratching at his arms while his mother shook him. 'I done tole you not to go outside, you bad boy!'

'What's the matter?' asked Susannah.

Phoebe pulled up the boy's shirt to expose his chest, presently scattered with angry purple pimples.

'Fleas,' said Susannah peering at the spots. 'It's only flea bites.' She breathed a sigh of relief.

'That'll teach you to play with the butcher's ragamuffins,' said Mistress Oliver.

'Joseph, run upstairs to my bedchamber and fetch my apothecary's box,' said Susannah. 'I'll rub some marigold salve on the bites to ease the itching.'

Phoebe glanced up at her from lowered lashes and turned back to her son. 'Next time, you listen to *me*, boy!'

'Yes'm, Mammy.'

The child looked so chastened that Susannah had to suppress a small smile.

*   *   *

After Agnes had been settled down for the night, Susannah sat on the window seat in the chapel watching the sunset until the last streaks of gold faded into darkness. Perhaps William was watching the sunset, too, she thought. She pictured him pacing up and down the sitting room above the apothecary shop, frustration at his confinement in every step. Idly she wondered what the plans were that he had been making. He was so used to ordering his own life that he would find this time of quarantine very difficult. If she had been with him, if only things had been different, they could have sat together in quiet companionship reading her father's books or playing chess.

She daydreamed for a while, imagining the two of them growing closer. But it *was* only a daydream and would never come true since it had turned out to be Phoebe that he wanted after all. There had only been such a short time of happiness until her hopes had been shattered.

She wiped away a tear on the back of her hand. Whether or not William loved her, she was still fearful that he would sicken and die. And now Father was dead and the twins, Martha and Henry, Jane Quick, Peg and Emmanuel had all gone. In a strange way she even missed Arabella and her children.

Her belly moved as the child within stirred and she cupped the pointed little heel with her palm as it pushed against her skin. Sorrow and unrequited love made miserable companions; if it hadn't been for the baby she might have turned her face to the wall and never opened her eyes again. Her head drooped with exhaustion. One by one she took the pins out of her hair and let it fall around her shoulders. She sat quietly for a while, then undressed and went to bed.

*   *   *

389

The long, shrill cry pierced the night, shocking Susannah awake. She was out of bed and in the corridor with her heart racing before she realised where she was.

The terrible wail of desolation came again, making the hairs stand up on the back of her neck. She followed the sound, running up the stairs to the attic as fast as her bulk would allow her.

Phoebe stood at the top of the stairs with Joseph clutched to her breast. Wild-eyed, she couldn't speak but shrieked and ran towards Susannah.

'Phoebe, what is it?' She caught hold of the woman's arm and shook her. 'Tell me!'

Gasping for breath, Phoebe held Joseph out towards her with shaking hands.

The child's face and chest were blotched purplish-red around the flea bites and his breathing laboured. Susannah could feel the heat radiating from his little body. 'He has a fever,' she said.

Wailing all the while, Phoebe turned Joseph's head.

Susannah became very still. A large swelling on the side of his neck was already blackening. 'Sweet Lord!' she whispered. 'It's the plague.'

Phoebe shrieked again and ran back into her attic room.

Cold with shock, Susannah stood in the corridor, her mind unable to grasp this terrible turn of events. It was Agnes's voice, sharp with anxiety, calling from the foot of the stairs which shook her out of her stupor.

'What is it, Susannah?'

'Don't come up! It's Joseph. He's been stricken.'

Agnes let out a small mew of terror.

'Listen to me, Agnes!'

The old woman nodded her head, leaning heavily upon her stick for support.

All at once Susannah became icy calm. She pressed her knuckles against her mouth while she ordered her thoughts. It was obvious what she had to do. William had been prepared to sacrifice himself for her father's sake and now she, too, must be prepared to risk her own life in doing what she could for William's son.

'I shall remain here in the attics with Phoebe and Joseph,' she said. 'You must stay in your part of the house and you may avoid the infection. Mistress Oliver shall leave us water and provisions at the foot of the stairs every day but no one is to come up. Do you understand?'

Agnes nodded again.

'We will need a bottle of my Plague Prevention Syrup from the still room, bitter herbs to fumigate the rooms and enough coal to keep the fire burning. Oh, and a small pan, a skimming spoon and some muslin. And will you fetch my apothecary's box?'

'Whatever you need! We must inform the watchmen. I shall call out of the window.' Purposeful now, Agnes turned and hobbled away.

Phoebe hunched on the edge of the bed, keening as she rocked Joseph in her arms.

'Phoebe?' Susannah sat down beside her. 'All is not lost yet. Let me look at him.' She gently prised Phoebe's fingers loose, took Joseph from her and laid him on the bed. Carefully, she removed Joseph's nightshirt, leaving him naked except for his silver collar, and examined the bubo on his neck. Then, her heart sinking, she discovered that there was another one forming under his arm. He

391

moaned when she pressed it, his eyelids fluttering.

'He will die,' whispered Phoebe. 'My son will die.'

'I'm not giving up on him yet and you mustn't either. He may be able to hear you and you must encourage him to fight this pestilence. But now we need to bring his temperature down or the heat will cause an inflammation of the brain and he'll have fits. Fetch me a basin of water and a cloth.'

Phoebe looked at her with dull, brown eyes but didn't move.

'Do it! Now!'

Startled, Phoebe stood up.

Susannah opened the attic window to let out some of the oppressive August heat and set Phoebe to bathe the small body on the bed. After a while she touched Joseph's forehead with the back of her hand but he was still dangerously hot. She made Phoebe help her to drag the bed closer to the window so that the breeze could play upon his damp skin.

Agnes called up and Susannah went to the top of the stairs.

'We have brought all that you asked for and I will leave this little bell for you. Ring it if you need anything.'

'Will you let me have the key for Joseph's silver collar? It constricts his neck and increases his body heat.'

Agnes thrust a gnarled hand into the placket of her skirt and pulled out her pocket. Painstakingly she pulled apart the drawstrings and took out the key. 'I will put it here for you.' She placed it upon the lid of the apothecary's box.

'Now leave us.'

'I shall pray for you.'

'Let us hope that the Lord is listening, then.'

After Agnes had gone, Susannah made several journeys up and down the stairs to carry up all the items she had requested. Out of breath, she sat for a moment on the top step, holding her belly and rubbing at the ache in her back.

To avoid overheating the sick child she made a small fire in the grate of what had been Peg's room. She tipped the coal out of the bucket onto the floor beside the hearth and then lifted some of the glowing coals from the grate and put them in the coal bucket. From her apothecary's box she took out several packets of dried herbs and sprinkled them over the coals. Holding the smoking bucket at arm's length she carried it into the sickroom.

'This will purify the air,' she said. 'How is he now?'

'Hot. Very hot,' whispered Phoebe.

Coughing, Joseph twitched and muttered, his breathing harsh and uneven.

Susannah took the key from her pocket and unlocked the silver collar. Carefully she unhinged it and pulled it away from the thin little neck, exposing the dreadful purple swelling. Weighing the collar in her hand, she was shocked at how heavy it was.

'You must keep bathing him, Phoebe. And I will make him some medicine.' Taking a phial, she shook out a small quantity of willow bark into a pan. This she heated upon the fire until the liquid seethed and then she strained it through muslin and carried it back to the sickbed.

Phoebe propped the child up in her arms while Susannah dripped the willow tea into his mouth from a spoon.

All day they sat beside Joseph, taking it in turns to sponge him. The buboes grew larger, the skin around them blotched and angry. Susannah laid on hot cloths and poultices in an attempt to draw the poison to the surface.

Barely conscious, Joseph coughed and struggled for breath.

Susannah listened out for the church bells and every four hours spooned a little more of the willow bark tea into the child's mouth.

The light began to fade and Phoebe fell asleep with her head on the pillow beside her son.

Susannah lit the candles and sat watching Joseph's chest rise and fall. She could feel the heat radiating off him. She bathed him again, wiping the sweat off his face and neck. By now she knew every curve of his face and body; the usually smooth coffee-coloured skin so horribly blotched and empurpled. Propping him up on the pillow to ease his breathing, she went to fetch more hot cloths to lay on the buboes. He moaned and stirred as she pressed the linen down but the fever continued to rage.

Phoebe slept and Susannah let her be. She would wake soon enough if Joseph took a sudden turn for the worse.

There was nothing in the world that mattered any more outside this room lit only by flickering candles; not her dead father or her lost hopes of finding love, only this child, William's child, fighting to live.

Shortly after three in the morning, over the harsh sound of Joseph's coughing, Susannah heard the bellman in the distance and then the dead-cart's wheels rolling over the cobbles. She shivered and gathered the boy into her arms, resting his hot little head against her chest, willing him to breathe.

*   *   *

As the first rosy light of dawn filtered through the attic window Susannah opened her eyes and lifted her chin off the top of Joseph's woolly head to find Phoebe staring at her. Stretching her legs, Susannah grimaced as pins and needles pricked at her feet. The room was cooler now; at least until the merciless heat of the midday sun began to beat down upon the roof again.

Phoebe took the child from her, kissing his face and rocking him. Susannah brewed more willow tea and tore the crust off the loaf that Agnes had left for them. 'You must eat,' she said, handing a piece to Phoebe.

The corners of Phoebe's mouth turned down and she turned her head away.

'If you don't eat you'll not be strong enough to fight the infection.'

'Why d'you care? Why you help us? We are only your slaves.'

Susannah pushed her hair off her face. 'Why are you always so hostile to me?' she said, too exhausted to be polite. 'You are never so rude to any of the others in this household.'

Phoebe shrugged, her bottom lip pushed out. 'You think you're better than me.'

'I don't know what you're talking about.'

'Joseph and me are your slaves. We have no life.' Phoebe smiled slyly. 'But William love me. You jealous of me?'

395

All at once Susannah's patience snapped. Of course she was jealous that William had gone to Phoebe's bed but she was not prepared to be taunted about it. 'I'm not jealous,' she lied, 'just not prepared to accept your impertinence. You've been sullen and ungrateful ever since you came here. Well, I'm sick of it and I'm sick of you! I don't want you to be my slave; I never asked for you to be sent here and you should be thankful that you weren't thrown out into the streets to fend for yourself. I don't *care* that Joseph is Dr Ambrose's son. All I'm trying to do is to help him and I have no intention of wasting my time discussing your insolence. Now move out of my way and let me give the child his medicine!'

Phoebe stared at her for a moment, amazement on her face.

That's shaken her, thought Susannah with some satisfaction.

Phoebe slowly retreated and stood in the corner, watching Susannah administer the willow tea.

'If you want to do something useful, go and heat up the poultice mixture in the pan and bring it to me,' she instructed. She breathed out slowly, letting the tension drain away. Surprisingly, succumbing to bad manners and saying exactly what she felt made her feel a great deal better.

The remainder of that day passed with no more than a few essential words exchanged between them but Susannah was conscious of Phoebe's covert glances all day long.

That night it was Susannah's turn to fall into a doze. Her back ached and she curled up on the end of the bed and closed her eyes.

Phoebe shook her awake, snatching at her arm.

396

'Missus! Missus!'

'Joseph?' Susannah sat up so suddenly that she went dizzy. After all her efforts she couldn't bear to lose him now!

'See!' said Phoebe. She peeled up a corner of the poultice on Joseph's neck.

Susannah hastily put a hand over her mouth and nose. The bubo had burst and foul-smelling matter had erupted through the poultice cloth and oozed down the child's neck.

Holding her breath, she peered at the crater left behind. 'We must clean this wound straight away. Fetch me some water and a cloth.' She moved the candle closer and examined the boy's chest. Some of the blotching had faded from his skin and his struggle for breath was less tortured.

The wound continued to suppurate through the night and by first light the swelling under his arm had grown.

'He's still very hot,' said Susannah, feeling his forehead. 'I wonder . . .'

Phoebe looked at her, a question in her eyes.

'Yes.' Decisively, Susannah opened the apothecary box and took out a sharp little knife. She tested the blade on her finger and Phoebe made a small sound under her breath. 'Hold him still!' said Susannah.

The bubo was the size of a gull's egg. Susannah studied it for a moment, then pushed the point of the blade into the swelling and stepped back as the poison spurted from the wound.

Joseph's eyes opened wide and he let out a cry.

Phoebe murmured to him as Susannah made a cut an inch long and watched as the remaining poison seeped out. She bathed the wound and set

397

a fresh poultice upon it. 'All we can do now is to wait,' she said.

They sat together watching the sleeping child while Susannah fretted about William and Jennet. They would be anxious because she hadn't come to bring them provisions. She worried about this all afternoon until eventually she went to the top of the stairs and rang the little bell Agnes had given her.

When Agnes came to the landing below, fear and expectation written upon her face, Susannah quickly brought her up to date with Joseph's progress. 'But I haven't taken food to William and Jennet,' she said.

'I sent one of the street children to pass on the news and take them some of our beans,' said Agnes. 'Our storeroom is still full of emergency rations. Plain food, maybe, but we won't starve. So who's laughing now, miss?'

'We're lucky that you're a woman of such sound sense, Agnes.'

'We're short of meat, though. Our watchman tells me the butcher's shop is shut up. Two of their children carried off on the cart, already.'

'So Joseph must have caught the infection from the butcher's boys. Let us pray he is stronger than they were.'

By six o'clock that evening Joseph's temperature had dropped a little. He still had a rattling cough but his breathing had eased. He turned from side to side and cried; pitiful weak cries but he was at least conscious of his surroundings.

Phoebe and Susannah drank the bean soup which Mistress Oliver left for them, sitting in silence on each side of the sickbed.

Joseph whimpered quietly and Phoebe put down her bowl and stroked his forehead. She began to sing to him, her husky voice crooning a strange little song so full of suppressed emotion that Susannah felt the tears spring to her eyes. In her weariness she put her head down on her arms lest the slave see her cry. Then Phoebe began to sing something that sounded like a lullaby and after a while Joseph quietened.

Susannah listened to the child's steady breathing and the rise and fall of Phoebe's singing and, try as she might, was unable to open her eyes.

Chapter 27

Susannah stood by the attic window watching the seagulls swooping and wheeling over the river. It was hard to breathe in the heat of the attic so it made her feel easier when she could look outside. She rubbed her aching back and envied the gulls their freedom of movement, longing to feel light and energetic again herself. But, of course, it wasn't only pregnancy that weighed her down but the burden of grief and fear.

She spread her hands out over her ripe belly, pressing her fingers into the taut skin and feeling the shape of her baby. He had little room to move now and when she was naked she would watch his elbows and heels pushing up peaks of skin as he stretched. In a month, God willing, he would be here. She smiled a little and tried hard not to think of her labours to come. At least they would all be out of quarantine by then, assuming none of them

399

sickened.

'Missus?' Phoebe stood in the doorway.

'Joseph?' Susannah's mouth went dry.

'Come!'

The boy lay back on the pillow, his eyes closed.

Susannah felt his forehead and his eyes opened. 'The fever has broken!' she said. She lifted up the wrappings to examine the wounds on his neck and in his armpit. 'Look, Phoebe! I do believe this is weeping less than before.'

Phoebe nodded, her brown eyes round with hope.

'Mammy?'

'Yes, baby?' Phoebe stroked his cheek.

'Mammy, I'm hungry.'

Susannah and Phoebe looked at each other in wonder.

'I'll ask Mistress Oliver to send up some of her bean soup,' said Susannah.

Phoebe fed Joseph the soup little by little from a spoon until the bowl was empty. He rubbed his tummy and rolled his eyes, making his audience laugh.

Phoebe's too-loud laughter turned into tears of relief, great gulping sobs that were unstoppable.

Susannah took her in her arms and patted her back, murmuring soothing words while Joseph watched his mother with frightened eyes.

*　　　*　　　*

Something had shifted in the way Phoebe behaved towards Susannah. Reprieved from her terror that Joseph would die, euphoria made her animated. In the long, hot hours that they sat by the child's

400

bedside over the following days while he gradually recovered, Phoebe talked about the plantation where she had spent most of her life.

'My mammy came to the plantation when it still new but Massa Savage, Massa Henry's father that is, picked Mammy out of the fields and made her a house slave. My brother Erasmus was newborn then and Mammy was nurse to Massa Henry, too.'

'Henry told me that his nurse was like a mother to him.'

'The missus,' Phoebe pursed her lips and shook her head, 'the missus was a cold lady.'

'So was Henry like his father, then?'

'No! Henry was . . .' Phoebe licked her lips and Susannah stared at them, fascinated by how different they were to her own. They resembled plump pink cushions on her chocolate-coloured face and she could begin to see what might have made Phoebe attractive to William.

'Massa Savage is a bad man. Henry and Erasmus like brothers. They always in trouble and the massa beat Erasmus if Henry do a bad thing and say he will send him to work in the fields.'

'How unfair!' Susannah thought again about Emmanuel, banished to the plantation. 'Phoebe, what about Emmanuel? Will Henry's father have put him to work in the fields?'

'Emmanuel is mos' likely still house slave. I know this in here.' She clasped her hand to her heart. 'He too valuable to work in fields. He die in the sun.'

'I hope you're right. I felt so bad that he was sent away, I pleaded with William but I couldn't stop it happening.' Susannah sighed. 'Poor Henry! He was so homesick for Barbados. He hated it here but he said he'd argued with his father and couldn't

401

return.'

'Bad, bad words between Massa Henry and Massa Savage.'

Susannah shifted on her chair and rubbed her abdomen. The skin was so tight that it itched all the time.

'When your baby coming?' asked Phoebe.

'Another month.'

'Henry's child. You call baby Henry, too?'

'Maybe. Or perhaps Harry. And Cornelius for my father.'

'Not William?'

'No,' said Susannah shortly. 'Of course not.'

Phoebe looked at her sideways. 'But you love the doctor.'

Susannah didn't answer, desolation sweeping over her again.

'He a good man.'

'But weak,' said Susannah. 'As you should know.' She stood up and walked to the window, stretching out the ache in her lower back. The sun was setting over the river, brushing the water with highlights of molten gold. She watched a boat sailing into the sunset and longed to be on it, with the wind in her hair. 'I'm so tired of being shut up in here,' she said. 'I want to be outside, somewhere away from the city where the air is clean and cool.'

On the bed Joseph stirred and coughed and Phoebe wiped the sweat off his face, singing to him all the while until he fell asleep again.

*   *   *

Since Joseph was on his way to recovery, Susannah retreated to Peg's old room to sleep. Exhausted by the afternoon heat, she rested on the thin straw mattress, turning from side to side seeking a comfortable position. Her back ached and the skin on her belly itched until she thought she'd go mad. The baby, as if sensing his mother's irritable mood, kicked her sharply under the diaphragm.

Giving up the idea of sleep, Susannah sat up and lowered her legs over the side of the bed. As she did so she heard a distinct 'pop' and felt a warm liquid gush from between her thighs. She stared in horror at the floor as a puddle formed around her feet.

'Phoebe!' she called, her voice thin with fear.

Phoebe came, terror written on her face. 'You sick?'

'No. It's not the pestilence. My waters have broken.'

'The baby is coming?'

'It can't! Not till next month.' But then a pain blossomed deep in her pelvis and Susannah gripped the edge of the bed in terror. 'It's too early. I can't have the baby now! Besides, I shall need Goody Joan.'

'Midwife can't come now.'

'Then I can't have the baby!'

Phoebe smiled. 'Baby don't wait for no midwife.'

'But . . .'

'Don't you worry! I birth many babies.'

Susannah nodded, fear spiralling up and threatening to choke her. 'What must I do?' she asked.

'Plenty of time. First baby take long time.'

'How long?' How would she manage without Goody Joan to help her? Would she die a painful death? What if the baby was feet first? What would become of her son, here in a plague house, if she died?'

'Missus?'

'Yes, Phoebe?'

'I take care of you. Rest now, ready for birthing dat baby. Come, sit with us!' She held out her hand and, slowly, Susannah reached out and took it.

They sat at Joseph's bedside and Phoebe told stories of her childhood while Joseph dozed, awoke and dozed again.

Susannah's hands twisted in her lap as she fought down her dread of the impending birth and felt the ache in her pelvis grow and fade, grow and fade. Anger gripped her. Where was her mother now, at this of all times, when she most needed her? But then her sense of abandonment was overtaken by shame as she relived the horror of her mother's death. A nightmare vision rose up before her of Dr Ogilby's monstrous shadow thrown up onto the walls as he performed his atrocities upon her mother's helpless form. Her breath began to quicken in panic and she stood up and stumbled over to the window.

She leaned out over the sill as far as she could, gulping in the overheated air, tasting the dust and the stale exhaled breath of a thousand citizens mixed with the stench of the river mud at low tide. The sun was beginning to lower itself behind the cathedral, leaching the colour out of the city. The night would come soon and drop its blanket of stifling darkness over them all and, perhaps, by the morning . . . Pressing her knuckles to her mouth, she wondered if she would ever see the sun rise again.

Forcing herself to breathe steadily, she glanced

404

back at Joseph on the bed, his mother stroking his forehead as she told him her stories. The sound of Phoebe's voice was hypnotic and Susannah began to listen to the words, visualising the warm wind in her hair and the sand between her toes as she listened to the stories of a carefree young Henry, Phoebe and Erasmus running into the sea to bathe, playing hide and seek amongst the sugar cane and stealing shoo fly pie from under the cook's nose.

After a while Susannah began to feel less agitated and she returned to sit beside Joseph's bed. She had no choice now but to trust in Phoebe's knowledge. The pains were becoming stronger. Each time she was gripped, she squirmed and rocked in her chair, watching with amazement how her belly pushed forward as it hardened.

'Missus?'

'Yes, Joseph?'

'You sick? You been eating sugar plums?'

'No. Not one.'

'Your belly hurting. *Sure* you haven't eaten too many sugar plums?'

'None, I promise you.'

'Missus is goin' have a baby,' said Phoebe.

'Oh!' Joseph's eyes widened. 'When?'

'Soon. Time you went to sleep now. Maybe in the morning the baby is here.' She sang to Joseph until his eyes drooped and finally closed. Then she pulled Susannah to her feet. 'We walk.'

'Walk?'

'Come! Make it easy for you.' She guided Susannah back to Peg's room.

Arm in arm they walked round and round the small room, resting only when Susannah had a pain. The pains became stronger and more regular and every time her rising terror threatened to overwhelm her, Phoebe massaged her back or sang to her until it had passed.

After a few hours Susannah was drooping with exhaustion but her panic had abated under Phoebe's calm care. 'I think I must rest a little,' she said.

'That's good,' said Phoebe. 'You sleep and I tell Missus Agnes 'bout the baby.'

Susannah lifted the lid of her apothecary's box and took out a small bottle. 'I will take a spoonful of syrup of poppies,' she said, 'to help me rest.'

Phoebe helped her into bed and left a candle burning. 'Call me and I will come.' She smoothed her hand over Susannah's forehead and down over her eyes. 'Sleep now.'

The syrup of poppies, combined with Susannah's exhaustion, had already begun to take effect and her eyelids were as heavy as stones when there was a movement of air beside her; her eyes flickered open in sudden alarm. The candle guttered on the washstand as Phoebe looked in at her from in the doorway but then the poppy syrup claimed her again and she drifted away into a slumber full of uneasy dreams.

She was on a small boat in a high sea. It had no sail and no oars and Susannah clutched at the sides as it bobbed about on the water. A wave was approaching fast, a great wall of green water racing towards her. She opened her mouth to scream but there was no sound. The wave snatched the boat and it climbed up on the swell, higher and higher, while the pain in her belly rose to a peak. She hung motionless at the crest of the wave for a few moments and then tipped over the edge and plunged down into the deep, dark depths below. Black water seethed and slapped at the sides of the boat and she tightened her hold until another wave gathered in the void. She opened her mouth to scream.

Water splashed onto her face and, gasping, she shook her head.

'Missus?'

She blinked her eyes open. The candle had burned down in its socket and she could see the window as a square of grey light in the darkness.

'You dreamin', missus.' Phoebe wiped her face.

There was a terrible pain deep in her belly. 'I hurt,' Susannah croaked. Her mouth was dry from the poppy syrup.

'Nothing good come without pain.'

The agony continued, each contraction coming faster now, barely leaving Susannah time to catch her breath before the next one. Accepting the pain rather than fighting against it made it a little easier, she found.

Suddenly there was a great downward pressure within her and she heard herself groan. The sound of it took her straight back to her mother's labours and she rolled her head from side to side on the pillow to shake the memory away.

Phoebe lifted Susannah's nightshift and parted her legs but by now Susannah was beyond embarrassment. Someone grunted and she was mildly surprised to realise that it was herself.

Then, as the pressure eased, she began to panic again. 'Phoebe, I can't do this!' She gripped Phoebe's wrist as if it were a lifeline. 'I don't want to die! I've changed my mind. Make it stop!'

Phoebe smiled and smoothed the damp curls

off Susannah's forehead. 'Nothing stop baby now. Come, sing with me!' She began to croon one of her strange songs, full of pain and yearning. Susannah tried to pick out the words and understood something about picking up the burden and pulling hard on the rope. She joined in a little with the chorus to distract herself from the shaking which chattered her teeth together.

Then, with a dreadful inevitability, the terrible pressure within her began again. She took a deep breath and did what her body told her to do.

'Soon, now,' said Phoebe.

The iron band round her belly eased and she closed her eyes, gathering strength. Then it began again.

'Push down!' urged Phoebe.

Susannah took a deep breath and pushed.

'Again!'

She felt as if she was splitting apart but the downward force only became stronger and she groaned as she felt Phoebe's fingers pressing against her private parts.

'One more,' said Phoebe.

'I can't; I'm too tired!'

'Push!'

Susannah gathered all her forces and pushed.

Something moved within her and Susannah screamed, as much in surprise as in pain.

'Again!'

'Aaagh!' There was a sudden slither of warm wetness between her thighs. The pressure had gone. Susannah pushed herself up on her elbows.

Phoebe bent over the baby, who lay limp and unmoving on the bloodstained sheets. It was a strange mauvey-grey colour.

'Shouldn't he cry?' said Susannah, waiting.

Curiosity suddenly gave way to blinding panic. 'Phoebe?' She watched Phoebe hurriedly put a finger in the baby's mouth and clear it of fluid then pick the infant up by its ankles and smack its bottom.

Silence.

'My baby!' cried Susannah. 'Please, Phoebe, do something!'

Snatching up the basin of water from the bedside, Phoebe dashed it over the babe.

It gave a gasp and then began a reedy wail.

Susannah let out her breath on a shuddering sob and stretched out her arms.

Phoebe wrapped the baby, screaming now, in a cloth and handed it to Susannah.

'Shush, shush, my sweeting!' She covered the angry infant in kisses mingled with tears, rocking it in her arms until it quietened. 'I nearly lost you, my precious. I nearly lost you!'

Phoebe sat down on the edge of the bed beside her, with her hands shaking violently in her lap.

Susannah leaned against her and then, slowly, she pulled aside the baby's wrappings. 'Oh!' she exclaimed. 'It's a girl!'

The baby peered back at her through eyelashes spiky with damp, her eyes dark blue and knowing.

Susannah could only stare back in wonder, tears streaming down her cheeks.

*   *   *

Later that day Susannah sat up in bed, nursing the baby.

Phoebe helped her at first, pinching her nipple

and pushing it into the baby's mouth until she sucked.

'It hurts,' said Susannah, curling up her toes.

'Not for long,' said Phoebe, sitting on the edge of the bed. 'And it stop the bleeding.' Smiling, she stroked the baby's forehead. 'She small but strong.'

The baby fed well, her tiny hand clutching at Susannah's breast. Every now and again she stopped sucking to open her eyes.

'Her eyes are so very blue!' exclaimed Susannah. 'They remind me so much of my mother. I shall name my baby Elizabeth, in her memory. But I will call her Beth.'

Chapter 28

During the weeks of Susannah's lying-in she was able, for the most part, to distance herself from the outside world and spent long hours simply looking at her baby, studying each tiny finger and examining every pore and crease of her soft skin. Beth was small, since she had arrived sooner than expected, but she was bright-eyed and lusty. In spite of her growing love for Beth, Susannah suffered an ever-present ache below her breastbone because her father was unable to share in her joy. And she missed William, wondering if she could ever repair the damage between them.

The days fell into a rhythm. Beth would cry fiercely for a while until she latched greedily onto her mother's breast. Then as the frantic sucking slowed she made small sounds of pleasure and both mother and baby would slip into a languid doze.

After they woke, Susannah would bathe and wrap the baby in her swaddling clothes before putting her back into William's cradle until she awoke again.

But, as the days passed, Arabella's words echoed in Susannah's mind. She *must* make plans for the future. Agnes would not live for ever and then what would she do? Arabella had been right; it would not be seemly for Susannah to remain in William's house unless they were married. And while, once, she had harboured secret hopes, that time had long gone.

The idea, when it came to her, was so blindingly obvious she couldn't imagine why it hadn't occurred to her before.

She would become an apothecary in her own right!

The more she thought about it the more certain she became. Widows took over their husbands' businesses, didn't they? Well, Arabella had gone without a trace but the shop was still there and she had the knowledge to run the business herself. Perhaps it would have been impossible even last year but the plague had turned the world upside down. There were few enough apothecaries and physicians left, so surely she would be able to overcome general disapproval by the sheer fact that apothecaries would be so badly needed?

This idea excited her and gave her the strength to look ahead. Physically she grew stronger too and chafed at her confinement in the attic. She lay propped up in bed for hour after hour with Beth on her knees planning the future.

'You shall learn how to weigh out the herbs and to use the big pestle and mortar. And I will teach you Latin and take you to see the latest plays and we will be servants to no one.'

411

All the while, Beth studied her mother's face just as if she understood every word.

Joseph, too, was making a good recovery.

'Bean soup again!' he said, making a face. 'I hate it!'

'There is nothing else, 'said Susannah. 'Better eat it and be grateful.' But, secretly, Susannah agreed with him. She began to dream of apple pie and roasted lamb and tansy custard.

At the end of her lying-in, Susannah took her first tentative steps out of bed. She felt light as a husk and was relieved to find that by pulling harder than usual at the laces, she fitted back into her bodice. The slight thickening of her waist was compensated for by the extra fullness of her breasts and she was secretly pleased to have more womanly curves than before.

She paced the floor with Beth in her arms, desperate to leave the stuffy attic. Standing by the window nearly all day, she yearned to be outside. 'And that, little Beth, is the great River Thames on its way out to sea. One day I will take you on a boat journey to the Tower and show you the lions in the royal menagerie. And over that way are Fleet Street and your grandfather's shop. As soon as we can leave this house I will take you there. You'll love it! It has a special scent all of its own: lavender and sulphur, rosewater and turpentine.'

Beth yawned widely, and closed her blue eyes, lulled by her mother's voice.

Susannah kissed the red-gold down on the top of her head, breathing deeply of her milky-sweet skin. Surely this was the most perfect child ever born since the beginning of time?

Phoebe put her head round the door and came

to stroke Beth's cheek.

'She's so beautiful, isn't she?' said Susannah. 'But I expect Henry would have wanted a son.'

Phoebe bit her lip. 'Henry *had* a son. My son.'

Susannah's mouth dropped open. 'Joseph? But Joseph is William's son.'

Phoebe shook her head. 'I *know* who is my child's father!'

'But . . . I don't understand.'

'Why you think Henry send for us? He want to marry me. He fight with his father who send him away.'

'To *marry* you?'

'He loved me and he was going to free me!' Phoebe stared defiantly at Susannah.

Susannah stared back. The truth dawned on her with all the force of a bucket of icy water thrown in her face. All at once many things began to fall into place: Henry's homesickness and his desire to send her away to the country while he stayed in the city with his slaves. She understood now why he had not wanted her in his bed and it explained his assignations with Topaz; seeking comfort in one who so resembled Phoebe. And, of course, his sudden interest in her after he discovered she would have a substantial dowry, which had enabled him to send for his son and the woman he loved.

'You angry?'

Susannah thought about it as she carefully laid the drowsy baby down on the bed beside her. 'No,' she said at last. Surprisingly, it was true. Sad, perhaps, at the misery and loneliness she had suffered but not angry. Because the most marvellous thing of all, the thing that made her heart sing until it nearly burst, was that Joseph was *not* William's son. Laughter bubbled up inside her. 'No, I'm not angry,' she said, grasping Phoebe's hands and pulling her into an embrace. 'I thought I was a bad wife but none of it was my fault after all!'

Phoebe frowned and shook herself free. 'I saw you, with your white skin, and I hated you. You took my man.'

'But you must know that I didn't marry him to hurt you? And I see clearly now that Henry only married me to take my money so that he could send for you. He never loved me.'

'You have Henry's child; a child that should have been mine.' Phoebe stuck out her jaw and her eyes glittered with unshed tears. 'You make me jealous. You had everything. And I had nothing, except my son. Then you teach Joseph the white man's ways so he can leave me. You took my man *and* you were free. And I . . . I am your slave.' Racked with sobs, she rocked herself backwards and forwards, hands twisting together in her lap.

Susannah knew, from bitter experience, how the heart-wrenching pain of jealousy could eat away at a person. She decided that the time was past for modesty. After all, without Phoebe's help, she and little Beth might have died. 'Phoebe, listen to me! Henry only lay with me once in all the time we married. It wasn't a happy experience and afterwards he was angry with himself and with me. I wanted to be a good wife to Henry but he never loved me, however hard I tried to please him. Believe me, I did try, but now I know why it was an impossible task. *It was because he loved you.*'

Phoebe's eyes glittered with bitterness. 'I had nothing, except my son. And you tried to take Joseph away from me, to make him love you. I

414

wanted you to suffer. And I wanted you to know how it feel when your man is with another woman.' She lifted her chin defiantly. 'So I tole you I took your man.'

'You're talking about William?'

Phoebe nodded. 'You love him? Tell me true.'

Susannah was too tired to dissemble and in any case she had been through so much with this woman by now that it seemed pointless to lie. She looked at her sleeping baby's face. 'I cannot help myself,' she said. 'Even though you took him into your bed I still love him.'

Phoebe sighed. 'You save my baby's life. I save your baby's life. Now we are sisters and I will tell you true. That night, the doctor came to my room only to see Joseph.' Phoebe took Susannah's hands. 'Look at me, missus! The doctor *never* come to my bed. Not here in the Captain's House or in the plantation. Never!'

'But I saw you together . . . in your night clothes.' Susannah gripped Phoebe's hands until her knuckles were white, a glimmer of hope growing in her heart. 'Do you *promise* me this is the truth?'

Phoebe nodded her head. 'He very kind. I very frightened. Joseph very sick. Doctor tole me Joseph had . . .' her brow furrowed while she sought the right phrase, 'He tole me Joseph had *surfeit of sugar plums*.' She smiled triumphantly.

Susannah frowned. Then she made the connection. 'Not Agnes's sugar plums? I *thought* she had been particularly greedy!'

'Joseph greedy. He so sick I thought he die. I not tell Agnes or she beat him.'

Susannah laughed a little too wildly, as she fought down tears. 'I doubt if Joseph will ever steal

415

sugar plums again.'

'This is true.'

Susannah glanced out of the window. She had to escape from the Captain's House, to run and run as fast as she could to the apothecary shop, to tell William *at once* that she loved him.

Phoebe glanced at Susannah out of the side of her eyes. 'I hate you so much for taking my Henry I think I will die. After dark, when everyone sleep, I walk through the house and cry for Henry. I came here to marry him and he is dead and you, his wife, are my new owner.' She swallowed back a sob. 'Sometimes I come in the night and look at you when you sleep. I *never* understand why Henry want you. You so thin, so pale; I look and look at you and wonder *why* my Henry marry you. I never understand.'

'Oh, Phoebe! There has been such terrible unhappiness and misunderstanding! Poor Henry, trapped in a marriage he didn't want so that he could afford to bring you here and you and I both so miserable.'

Phoebe nodded.

'But we must start afresh. Will you fetch me my pocket from the hook behind the door?'

Phoebe handed it to her and Susannah took out a key. 'Come closer,' she said. 'One day I promise I will free you and Joseph. I cannot do this while we depend upon Agnes to keep us. But for now . . .' She inserted the key into Phoebe's silver collar and unlocked it. 'Throw it out of the window,' she said.

Phoebe rubbed at the red marks round her neck. 'It cost a lot of money. Missus Agnes . . .'

'I'll deal with Agnes later.'

Hesitantly Phoebe picked up the collar and went

416

to the window. She glanced back at Susannah.

'Go on!'

Phoebe unlatched the casement. She turned back to look at Susannah again, who nodded encouragingly. Taking a deep breath, she let out a great cry of jubilation as she hurled the collar out. It flew up into the air and then span away across the rooftops.

Chapter 29

'I cannot believe', Susannah said to Phoebe, 'that we will sicken now. Joseph is almost well again and there is not the slightest sign that we have the infection.'

Phoebe nodded. 'The missus want to see you.'

Susannah wrapped Beth in her best shawl and carried her to the top of the stairs. She rang the bell and waited until she could hear Agnes's shuffling steps approaching.

'So you have risen from your childbed,' Agnes said. 'And are you to introduce me to my great niece?'

Susannah held the baby up so Agnes could see the infant's face. 'This is Elizabeth,' she said.

Agnes pursed her lips. 'She'll be a beauty,' she said. 'Like her mother. If we survive I shall stand as godmother to her.'

Eyes widening at the unexpected compliment, Susannah said, 'I would be honoured, ma'am.'

'And Joseph continues to recover?'

'He's beginning to resent our incarceration and becoming naughty.' Susannah smiled. 'I believe that signifies well.'

'And William and the maid will be freed from your father's house tomorrow. He sent a message to say that they are both well. I dare to hope that it is only the matter of a few hours now before he is returned safely to me and that soon it will be his turn to bring us baskets of provisions. I have become extremely tired of bean soup.'

'Still, we have been fortunate in your foresight, Agnes; without the beans we might have starved. But once we are free of quarantine, I shall not care a bean if a bean never passes my lips again.'

*   *   *

In the middle of the night Susannah dreamed that her mother stood beside her bed rocking the cradle and singing to the baby.

'Lullay my liking, my dear, my sweeting . . .'

Beth whimpered and Susannah stirred and awoke.

The wind had risen and rattled at the casement. The candle on the sill flickered in the draught.

Something made her uneasy. She scooped the baby out of the cradle and hugged her tightly to her chest then went quietly to look in the other attic room. But Phoebe was fast asleep with Joseph curled up in the curve of her body.

At the top of the stairs Susannah stood motionless, listening to the silence of the night until the baby began to cry.

After she had fed Beth, Susannah carried her to the rattling window and gazed out into

418

the darkness. The air smelled different; the ever-present odour of river mud was overlaid by the tang of woodsmoke, she thought. A sudden gust of wind snatched at the casement so that she had to haul on it and secure the latch before it smashed back against the wall.

In the east the sky was lit by a pink glow and she was surprised that it must already be near to sunrise. She kissed the baby's head. 'You have had a long sleep this time, my sweet.'

It was as she turned to put Beth back into her cradle that she saw the pink glow suddenly expand to light up the sky. She returned to the window. An explosion at one of the river-front warehouses, perhaps? A fire would be hard to control if the warehouse held brandy or timber. Some poor soul is likely to lose his livelihood tonight, she thought, as she climbed back into bed.

*   *   *

The following morning Susannah woke to hear the Sabbath Day church bells. At the window she frowned to see a pall of smoke upriver at London Bridge. The warehouse fire must have been a bad one. She was still watching the drifting smoke when she heard Agnes calling out to her.

'Are you well?' This was the question Agnes asked every morning.

'Never better!'

'Then come downstairs. The risk of you falling ill after all this time seems unlikely.'

'I agree.'

'And William will come today.' Agnes gave her a sly little smile. 'I expect you would like to come to

419

the window to speak with him?'

After the oppressive heat of the attics the chapel was spacious and airy and, filled with the spirit of liberation, Susannah skipped across the room, revelling in her new lightness. 'You cannot know how good it is to be able to take more than five steps in one direction,' she said, 'and to be able to look down onto the street at the people going about their everyday business.' She walked across the chapel to the window which faced the garden. 'How I have missed the garden! In fact, I think I'll go outside now and give Beth her first taste of the open air.'

'I shall come with you,' said Agnes.

The sun on Susannah's face made her heart sing and a brisk east wind whipped the colour into her cheeks.

The two women walked slowly around the cloisters and Susannah thought how very much she would miss the garden when she moved back to live in the apothecary shop again. But, of course, she would visit Agnes often.

'Can you smell smoke?' asked Agnes.

'There's always smoke, isn't there? But you're right. During the night I looked out and saw an explosion down by the river. A warehouse, I expect, and this morning I see the fire has spread to London Bridge. I was so excited at coming down from the attics that I forgot to mention it.'

'Perhaps Will may bring news of it. I shall go inside now and speak to John Fuller, our watchman. Quite a decent sort of person. Lost his brother to the plague so he's sympathetic to our plight. I'll ask him to keep a lookout for Will.'

Susannah followed Agnes back up to the chapel

and stood beside her as she called down to the watchman.

'There's a big fire in the city,' he said, his heavy eyebrows bristling with the importance of the news. 'Stupid baker in Pudding Lane didn't damp the fire under the ovens properly before he went to bed. The fire's spread right down to the river . . .'

'So it *was* a warehouse catching fire that I saw?'

'Indeed ma'am! More'n three hundred houses gone and the fire burning down Fish Hill and catching on the bridge. 'Tis a calamity and no mistake.'

Susannah's hands trembled as she dressed her hair carefully, put on her mother's pearl pendant and laced her bodice so tight she could barely breathe. Then she sat on the chapel window seat all morning, mending Agnes's chemise and wondering how long it would be before William would come.

John Fuller kept calling up to the window to give her the latest news. 'They say now that it was the French who started it. Damned Papists! The churches in the east of the city are ablaze,' he said, 'and in those that aren't burning, the congregation are hearing some pretty warm sermons warning sinners to repent or be consumed by hellfire.' But he didn't say he could see William coming along the street.

William didn't arrive in time for dinner.

Susannah returned to the attics to look out at the river and was amazed to see the water was full of boats, all heavily loaded with people and furniture.

During the afternoon Agnes refused to rest in her room and stationed herself by the window to see if she could catch a glimpse of William coming along Whyteladies Lane. 'I do hope he brings fresh

421

meat,' she said. 'I could fancy a roasted chicken or a stew of mutton. I expect he's taking so long because he's searching out some tasty morsels to tempt his old aunt.'

But William didn't come.

Following yet another supper of bean soup Agnes went to bed, muttering under her breath about his inconsiderate behaviour. 'Gone off somewhere to kick up his heels after his release, I'll be bound.'

Susannah said nothing but she thought it unlikely that William would have gone to a tavern or a bawdy house. In any case, even if he had gone pleasure-seeking, surely Jennet would have come with news? As time passed, she began to be very afraid he might have succumbed to the pestilence right at the end of his quarantine.

The sun set and the severity of the fire became more apparent. The usually black night sky was lit by the fires burning in the city, whipped up by the brisk east wind.

Susannah went to bed and tried to sleep but her mind was running over what she would say to William when he finally arrived. She fell into an uneasy doze but when she was woken by Beth's cries she saw no sign that the conflagration was burning itself out.

*   *   *

The following morning Agnes stayed in her room. 'You can call me as soon as William deigns to arrive,' she said. 'I dare say he may have a sore head from the ale house and I shall give him the sharp side of my tongue to add to his troubles.'

Susannah hoped Agnes was right. She would have preferred to know that William was in a drunken stupor in a gutter somewhere rather than stricken down with the pestilence.

To pass the time, Susannah washed her hair, rinsing it with rosewater. She sat in the garden to dry it in the sunshine. If, when, William did come she would at least be sweet-smelling. Daydreaming, she watched Beth, who lay on a blanket beside her, gazing at the roses dancing in the breeze.

Something drifted down onto the baby's face and Susannah hurriedly wiped it away, only for it to be replaced. She looked up and saw that the darkening sky was snowing flakes of ash. The smell of smoke was becoming stronger, too. Concerned that it would be harmful for Beth, she took her inside.

William still did not come.

Later, Susannah leaned out of the window to survey the activity in Whyteladies Lane, which reverberated with the grind of cartwheels on the cobbles and a continual stream of hurrying people laden with packs.

She called down to John Fuller. 'Will you catch one of the street boys and send him to give a message to Dr Ambrose?'

'If I see one I'll do so,' said John, 'but everyone from the city is on the move. The street children are earning their keep in carrying goods away from the fire.'

'Is it worse, then?'

'Raging, it is. It's burning out of control up northwards now. Cannon Street, Lombard Street and Threadneedle Street are all afire!'

'Can't they put it out?'

'The Duke of York's got people pulling down

423

the houses to make a firebreak but the wind and the heat's so great there's no stopping the sparks from jumping half a street away. I tell you this: if it can't be contained the whole city will burn. I've got family in Cheapside and it's coming too close for comfort.'

Disquieted, Susannah retreated to the attics.

Phoebe took her hand and pulled her to the window, where Joseph stood on a chair looking out over the rooftops.

The Thames was crowded with boats and barges, all heavily laden with people and their possessions. The river was bobbing with barrels, baskets and makeshift rafts.

Susannah saw a woman on a small boat struggling to hold onto a pair of virginals perched on top of a teetering pile of furniture. An upturned table bumped into the boat and the virginals slid from her outstretched hands and slipped into the water.

A mass exodus was taking place.

*   *   *

Agnes tapped at the arm of her chair with fretful fingers and drove Susannah mad with her continual questions.

'I don't *know*, Agnes!' she said at last, driven to exasperation. 'But, yes, of course it's possible that William or Jennet have been taken ill.'

'If only we weren't locked in here you could have gone to your father's shop to find out what is happening.'

'You know we can't leave here for another week!'

424

Disturbed by her mother's tone, Beth began to whimper. Susannah paced up and down the chapel with Beth on her shoulder, to soothe herself as much as the baby.

Although it was only late afternoon, the sky was darkened by a black cloud that blotted out the sun. Smoke weaselled its way into the house through any chink it could find and the smell of it clung to their clothes and hung in the air.

Phoebe carried in a tray of bread and soup and set it on the table. 'I take baby while you eat?' She took Beth from her mother's arms and nuzzled the baby's cheek. 'We find Joseph. Come now, little one.' She smiled at Susannah as she left.

'You and Phoebe seem to have sorted out your differences,' said Agnes.

'Beth would have died if Phoebe hadn't been there.'

'And Joseph would have died if you hadn't been there.'

Susannah hesitated but then decided to speak anyway, even if it was indelicate. 'I wish you had told me that Joseph is Henry's child.'

Agnes studied her with narrowed eyes. 'So Phoebe told you, then?'

'But I didn't know until Beth was born. I thought William was Joseph's father. I overheard him tell you when Phoebe first arrived. At least, I thought I overheard him say it. He said Joseph was part of the family.'

'Shouldn't listen at doors then, should you, miss?'

'No, Agnes.'

'Still, Henry left quite a muddle behind him, didn't he? Joseph is Beth's half-brother and nothing will change that. But where is William? I can't rest until I know he's safe.'

They finished their soup and sat hand in hand without talking as the last of the light faded.

Then there was a rattle of stones at the window.

'William!' Dizzy with relief, Susannah hurried to open the casement.

But it was John Fuller who stood in the lane below, in a considerable state of agitation. 'I'm leaving,' he said. 'My lodgings are in Wood Street and the fire is galloping along Cheapside. I have to go and help my wife to pack up our belongings and move the children to safety.'

'Cheapside? Has it really spread so far?'

John wiped his hand over his face. 'I should have gone before. I never thought it would take such a hold or move so fast. If I were you I'd start to pack up your own treasures ready to flee.'

'Flee? But we can't . . .'

'Stay and be burned, then! I've unlocked your door. Your quarantine's nearly over anyway and you look well enough.'

'We are well but—'

'Can't stop! May the Lord keep you!'

Susannah watched as Fuller thrust his way through the mass of people making their way down Whyteladies Lane towards the river. 'Did you hear what he said, Agnes?'

'The fire's more than half a mile away.' Agnes's face had blanched. 'Surely it won't reach us?'

'I can't imagine . . .' Susannah looked out uncertainly at the smoke cloud. Flakes of ash drifted and swirled in the gusty wind. 'But it seems the fire *is* burning out of control. Perhaps it wouldn't hurt to pack up whatever we can, just

426

in case?' If nothing else, keeping busy would take Agnes's mind off her worries about William's health.

'We'll never carry everything! What about my candelabra, for example?'

'I suppose we could bury some things in the garden?'

'Of course! I always knew you were a clever girl,' said Agnes. 'Fetch Phoebe and Mistress Oliver and they can help to pack. It's nearly dark so we'll have to bury the plate in the morning.'

Each time they thought they had finished, Agnes remembered another item that she wanted to save: the captain's globes, a metal-bound chest with Chinese plates in it, a long abandoned viol. The pile of goods became larger and Susannah despaired of ever being able to dig a hole large enough to contain it all.

It was very late by the time they went to bed. Susannah was so tired as she sat on the bed feeding Beth that her head was nodding before the baby had finished suckling. Yawning so widely that it made her eyes water, she tucked Beth into her cradle.

As she undressed, Susannah looked out at the river. Suddenly frightened, she stared at the blaze illuminating the night sky. The fire had reached Baynard's Castle, less than half a mile away.

Chapter 30

In spite of her exhaustion Susannah found it hard to sleep, her thoughts too full of worry. To make it worse, Beth seemed to sense her mother's unease and cried fitfully on and off all night.

Where *was* William? Susannah pictured his dark eyes crinkling up at the corners when she'd said something that amused him and of the love she had believed he felt for her.. She wept for what might have been and attempted to distract herself by planning her new future working again in her father's apothecary shop. But her thoughts kept sliding back to William. Was he suffering the same terrible symptoms of the plague that had killed her father? And what of Jennet, her family's faithful servant for so long? She simply couldn't wait any longer to find out what had happened, quarantine or no quarantine. She would go and find out.

By first light, Susannah had washed and dressed. The exodus along the Thames continued and the smoke cloud had increased overnight. The fire had advanced towards Bridewell, only some quarter of a mile away.

Beth had her morning feed and, tired out by her wakeful night, at last fell into a deep sleep.

Susannah took her mother's miniature from its little box, wrapped it in a handkerchief and put it in her pocket. She put on the pearl pendant and lodged it safely in her bodice. Her books, including her mother's recipe book, she tied up in a parcel with as many clothes as she could carry. She put this on the bed with her apothecary's box and left all in readiness for a hasty departure if necessary. Beth still slept peacefully so Susannah went to find Agnes.

'Has William come yet?' The old lady, her eyes shadowed with fear, looked as tired as Susannah felt.

'Not yet. We'll bury your treasures and if he

428

hasn't come by then I'm going to the shop to find out what's happening.'

'I curse my poor old legs or I'd have gone myself. But listen, we don't need to bury my things! I'd forgotten that there's an old well under the flagstones in the garden.'

Phoebe and Mistress Oliver, with Joseph running between their feet, prised up the flagstones and peered down into the well. An iron ladder was fixed to the inside and Joseph was sent down to take a look. As far as he could tell it was dry.

'Dried up back in sixteen thirty,' said Agnes, 'and the captain covered it up.'

They packed the goods into baskets and lowered them down on ropes. Then Susannah and Phoebe dragged the flagstones back over the top.

'I can't bear the waiting any longer,' said Susannah. She took Agnes's gnarled old hands gently into her own. 'I have to go and find William now.'

Agnes nodded. 'The streets will be dangerous.' Her dark eyes were fearful. 'Please, bring my William back to me,' she whispered.

Susannah turned to Phoebe, who held Beth against her shoulder, and took the baby from her. A shaft of fear ran through Susannah's heart at the thought of leaving her daughter for even a moment. But she had to find William.

She kissed Beth, breathing in the sweet smell of her, and handed her back to Phoebe. 'Will you take care of her until I return?'

'Beth is Henry's chile,' Phoebe said. 'I love her like my own.'

Susannah briefly touched her on the shoulder. 'I'll not be long.'

429

Standing in the open doorway of the Captain's House, Susannah took a moment to relish her freedom before launching herself into the press of people making their way down Whyteladies Lane towards the river.

There was agitation in the smoky air and she was shoved from side to side, bruised by handcarts and nearly knocked off her feet by crying children scurrying after their parents. One man carried a huge pack on his back, nearly bent over to the ground with the weight of it, while his wife rolled a barrel along the ground and hung onto a rope tied to a squealing pig.

Susannah forced her way through the maze of alleys and courts, dismayed to see the desperate crowd hurrying hither and thither as they carried their goods to safety. The streets were so narrow, and the houses so close together, that in some places the sheer number of people made the way impassable.

She slipped on an apple core and fell to the ground. Each time she tried to push herself up she was knocked over again by the surging horde. People shouted, children wailed and all the time there was the clack of clogs and handcart wheels on the cobbles. The noise was so great that no one seemed to hear her cries for help and she was starting to panic when a man elbowed aside the mob and dragged her to her feet.

'Thank you, sir,' she said.

'You're going the wrong way, mistress.' The man wiped the sweat off his grimy forehead. 'Turn round and go back.'

'But I must reach my father's house!'

'Everything's burning east and north of here.

430

The Duke of York and his men are blowing up the houses around Bridewell Dock to make a firebreak. Go back while you can!' He adjusted his bulky pack and set off again without a backward glance.

Susannah watched him disappear into the mêlée and hesitated before turning back in the direction of Fleet Street. She hadn't gone far when she heard the explosions, one after the other. Somewhere a woman screamed and the swarming crowd pressed so hard against her that she was flattened against the wall. The air was full of acrid gunpowder smoke, making her eyes smart, and the darkening sky was a menacing blood red.

Gradually she inched her way onwards until she came to Bridewell, where the scene of utter devastation laid out before her made her gasp. The houses that she had known all her life had gone, to be replaced by a sea of rubble. She stared around her with horror, unable even to make out where the street had once been. The ground was littered with splintered wood, plaster and thatch and the air thick with smoke and dust.

Men scrambled over the ruins and, as she watched, the few houses still standing were blown into the air with a deafening explosion.

She screamed and clapped her hands over her ears.

A man shouted at her but her ears were ringing and she was too shocked to do more than stand rooted to the ground. He ran over and shook her arm. 'You can't stay here!' He gave her a push in the direction she had come.

Stumbling her way over the wreckage, she circled the ruins but now she saw the full horror of the fire. Men were pulling down the burning buildings, shouting as they strained on ropes attached to the roof timbers by great iron hooks. The choking dust made her cough and ash and cinders rained down from the sky.

The smoke was blown aside by a sudden gust of wind and she caught a glimpse of St Bride's. Hardly able to comprehend what she was seeing, she cried out. The church where her mother was buried, where she herself had been christened and married, was burning. Vicious great orange flames licked the steeple and black smoke funnelled out of the windows into a dense cloud.

She ran towards the church, scrambling up over the mountain of debris and sliding down the other side. Bewildered people gathered in groups, watching St Bride's burn.

A weeping woman clutched her arm. 'There's no saving it! There was a water engine but no one kept it oiled and working. All too late!' she lamented. 'Whatever is to become of us miserable sinners now?'

'St Bride's? Gone?' Susannah swallowed. This was unimaginable.

'But St Paul's is saved, praise the Lord! The fire burned along Paternoster Row and Carter Lane, leaving the cathedral on an island in a sea of fire. But the fire swept down Ludgate Hill and now it's into Fleet Street.'

Susannah went cold. 'Oh, please tell me it's not in Fleet Street! My home is there.'

The woman gave her a look of terrible pity. 'Not any more, my dear.'

Susannah turned away, her knuckles pressed to her mouth. It couldn't be true! And what of William and Jennet; were they still in the apothecary shop?

432

She began to run then, instinct leading her home through an almost unrecognisable landscape. The fire roared in her ears, as loud as the iron wheels of a thousand chariots racing over cobbles. The deafening noise took her breath away as the flames crackled and rattled and spat all around her. The heat was on her face now and she had to brush smouldering cinders off her shoulders as she ran.

The wall of flame that greeted her on the south side of Fleet Street was as impassable as the fires of hell. Beaten back by the terrible heat, she was forced to enter the unfamiliar territory of Ascentia, the home of pickpockets and thieves. Twisting and turning against the tide of screaming people in the maze of dark alleyways and passages, she shoved her way forward, blindly heading towards her childhood home.

At last she saw light between the mean little tenements and found a way through into Fleet Street. The fire, whipped up by the gusting wind into a crackling, orange fury was advancing fast. The apothecary shop was some fifty yards away and her breath caught on a sob as she saw that the roof was already afire. Dread clutched at her with icy fingers; it was inevitable that her old home would be destroyed.

As she ran, the ground underneath her feet was hot and scattered with glowing embers. With every footfall, William's name echoed in her head like a silent prayer. *William, William, William.*

A stitch in her side made her slow to draw in a ragged lungful of acrid air. The sign of the Unicorn and the Dragon blazed above her now and the tears on her face evaporated in the intense heat from the adjoining house, already burning fiercely. The half

433

timbering on the first floor of the apothecary shop was glowing red, ready to ignite. She pressed her face against the shop window and looked inside but there was no one there. The door, still emblazoned with the red plague cross, was locked.

Running back from under the overhang of the first floor, she shaded her eyes against the heat of the blaze to peer up to the window above.

'William! Jennet!' Her shout was lost in the crackling of burning timber and thatch. A shower of sparks rained down upon her and she hastily flicked a glowing cinder off her singeing hair.

A shadow passed in front of the window and there was William behind the closed casement.

'William!' A great joy rose up in her heart, her legs nearly betraying her as she staggered with the relief of seeing him. Thank God he was still alive!

He pressed his hands against the glass and silently shouted at her. Flames licked at the smouldering window frames.

Then he disappeared.

The sight of him conjured up the last time she had seen her father at the window and something inside her snapped. Now that she had found him, she wasn't going to lose him. Frenziedly, she rattled the shop door and when it wouldn't open, resorted to kicking and pounding at it. Half blinded with tears and hoarse from shouting, she cast wildly around until she found a piece of timber. It burned her hands as she snatched it up and smashed the window. Heedless of the broken glass slicing through her skirt and into her thighs, she wriggled through the opening.

'William! Jennet!' She raced up the stairs two at a time but there was no sign of either of them.

She was on the landing, in the doorway of her father's smoke-filled bedchamber, hopping from foot to foot to stop the soles of her feet burning, when she glimpsed William on the other side of the bed.

'Get back!' he shouted.

Suddenly, the crackling of the fire in the roof above was drowned out by a thunderous groan. Flaming thatch and timber crashed to the floor and a blast of searing air hurled her backwards. Fanned by the wind, orange sparks fountained high up into the open sky and the roaring of the fire howled in her ears. Burning wreckage in the doorway made it impassable. Thick smoke spiralled and swirled in the bedchamber.

Susannah couldn't see William any more.

Screaming his name, she held up her arms to shield her face against the inferno. No one could possibly survive such heat. She let out a wail of anguish as she pictured William fighting to escape the flames, his body blackening and twisting in the fire until he fell to the floor and was consumed.

A choking cloud of black smoke forced her to cover her face with her skirt and the fire spat embers at her. Coughing and heaving for breath, she remembered Beth. She *must* leave before it was too late! There was nothing she could do for William now, except to grieve for him, but her baby needed her.

Then, the ceiling above the stairs exploded into flames. A glowing roof timber collapsed in a shower of sparks and fell, barring her way. Panic-stricken, she kicked it aside and tumbled down the stairs and out of the shop door, running and running until she was a safe distance away.

Gasping for breath, she leaned against the wall of the glovemaker's shop and watched as her childhood home, and William's funeral pyre, burned. Hot tears streamed down her face as she remembered William's kindness to her after Henry had died and how she had grown to love him. She remembered the passion in his voice and how he had trembled when he kissed her and then how she thought he had betrayed her. And she remembered her mother's sweet face and the loving home over the shop that had made it all the harder to accept Arabella into her place. She recalled the happy hours spent at her father's side as she learned his trade. And she realised that her dream of earning an independent living as an apothecary would remain only a dream. The shop was now entirely consumed by flames.

Her past and her future both burned before her.

'Susannah!'

She jerked round, her mouth wide with shock.

'You stupid, stupid girl!' William stood before her, his shirt singed and torn. A muscle flickered in his unshaven jaw, his anger shimmering in the scorched air. He strode forward and crushed her to him, smothering her face in smoky kisses. 'What in God's name were you thinking of?'

His body was warm and he smelled of smoke and sweat. He definitely wasn't a ghost.

'William,' sobbed Susannah, 'I thought you were dead!' She clung to him as tightly as a limpet to a rock, touching his face and breathing him in, unable to believe that she had lost, and found, him again.

He shook her until her teeth rattled, his fingers bruising her arms. 'How could you have risked *everything* by going into a burning house? Didn't

436

you hear me shouting at you to keep clear? Stupid, stupid, girl; I could have lost you!'

'I saw you on the other side of the flames; I thought you were dead!'

'I died a thousand deaths when the roof collapsed and I couldn't reach you. You disappeared in the smoke and I thought it impossible for you to escape. I'm never, never going to let you out of my sight again!' He pulled her tight to his chest and his lips came down hard and urgent on hers.

Gasping, she felt a sweet, painful blossoming in her groin and, half-swooning, she opened her mouth to his.

At last he released her and rested his forehead against hers. 'You've broken down all my defences and worked your way into my heart in such a way that I would not wish to live without you. This may not be the right time or place but I'm damned if I'm going to wait any longer. Susannah, will you marry me?'

There was a rushing in her ears and an explosion of happiness in her heart. She glanced over her shoulder at the blazing shop and the fire raging all around. She thought of her mother and her father and all the happy memories that she held. Those memories would live on, even if her home no longer existed. She looked into William's dark eyes, slightly anxious now. A deep peace descended upon her.

'I thought you'd never ask,' she said.

Chapter 31

'William! My dearest William!' Agnes's voice cracked as she called his name. She pushed herself up out of her chair, her pipe tumbling to the floor as she reached for him.

He ran and caught her frail body up in his arms, stroking the tears from her cheek with infinite tenderness. 'You didn't think I'd forgotten you, did you?' He gently deposited her back in her chair.

For once the old lady was speechless, her face working as she fought tears of joy.

William drew up a chair and hugged her bony shoulders, while she clasped his hand as if she'd never let it go.

Tactfully Susannah withdrew. She hurried to her bedchamber, where Phoebe walked the floor with a whimpering Beth in her arms.

'She miss you,' said Phoebe as Susannah gathered the babe into her arms and inhaled her milky scent. The events of the past few hours replayed themselves in her mind and the horror of what might have happened to Beth, if she hadn't returned, finally hit home. She began to shake with the aftershock.

'You find the doctor?' Phoebe's face was anxious.

'Yes, yes I did,' said Susannah through chattering teeth. 'He's well. But my father's house has burned.' She cried then and Phoebe rocked her until the storm had passed.

At last, Susannah wiped her eyes and left Beth in Phoebe's care while she went down to the kitchen.

She was overjoyed to find Jennet sitting at the kitchen table regaling Mistress Oliver with the tale of her adventures.

'But where were you, Jennet?' Susannah asked.

'The doctor sent me back here to let you know that he'd gone with the Duke of York's men to fight the fire,' said Jennet, 'but on the way I found a lost child. By the time I'd chased her family out to Highgate Village and handed her back to her mother, two days had passed.'

'And then you came all the way back here, towards the fire?'

Jennet looked up at her with fear in her face. 'I had nowhere else to go.'

'There never was a more loyal servant,' said Susannah. 'And I cannot thank you enough for what you did for my father.'

'I'll speak to the missus,' said Mistress Oliver. 'I need a good kitchen maid to replace Peg. Assuming, of course, that the Captain's House isn't burned down and we still have a kitchen.'

'The fire *is* coming closer,' said Susannah, 'and the wind still fans the flames towards us. If only the wind would change . . .' She shuddered at the thought of losing two homes in one day. 'I'll take some food to Dr Ambrose and ask him what we should do.'

She collected a tray of bread and bean soup and returned to Agnes's bedchamber.

Agnes had recovered her composure but still gripped William's hand.

'I thought you'd be hungry, William,' Susannah said.

He looked up at her with such love shining in his eyes that the world stood still for her.

439

'Spoken like a good wife,' he said.

Agnes gave him a sharp look. 'Oho! So that's the way the wind blows, is it? Have you something to tell me, William?'

'Can't you guess?' He smiled broadly, his delight plain for all to see. 'And I'm not inclined to wait long before we tie the knot.'

'So, you managed to catch him after all, miss,' cackled Agnes. 'I never thought you would but I'm very happy for you.'

Susannah blushed; Agnes's approval meant more to her than she had imagined. 'And I believe you've met your match in this one, William,' said Agnes.

'I believe so too.' He reached for Susannah's hand. 'And I'm looking forward to meeting the new addition to our family. I'll have my hands full if the babe is half as spirited as her mother.'

'You must eat first.'

'It's been days since I had more than a dry crust of bread.' He suppressed a yawn. 'I'm so hungry I could eat enough for an army.' He fell on his soup with total concentration and Susannah and Agnes watched him indulgently until he wiped out the bowl with the last of the bread. He sighed and leaned back.

'Now that you're safely home and the doors are closed behind us, it's easy to forget the fire is still raging out there,' said Susannah, 'except for the smoke in the air. Still, we've buried the silver in the old well, in case we have to escape in a hurry.'

'I can't do anything in a hurry these days,' said Agnes, her voice thin and high with fear again.

'There is the old handcart in one of the storerooms,' said William. 'We'll make you up a comfortable bed and you will be transported as elegantly as a pasha.'

'But where will we go?'

William rubbed smuts from eyes red-rimmed with exhaustion, leaving a trail of soot across his cheek. 'Westwards. Away from the fire. I'm sure Roger Somerford will find us temporary accommodation at Merryfields.'

'If only the wind would change direction,' said Agnes fretfully, 'then we might be saved.'

Susannah laid a hand on William's arm. 'You must rest. And you, too, Agnes, in case we have to leave in a hurry.'

'I won't have you out of my sight, Susannah,' warned William, clasping her hand in his.

'Then let us leave Agnes to rest. You can wash the soot away and I'll dress those burns on your hands. We'll go to the chapel; you can sleep there. I'll watch out for the fire and wake you if necessary.'

Before long, William was installed in Agnes's favourite chair with a cushion behind his head and Susannah beside him. She placed a basin of warm water on the table and carefully washed his face and hands. His eyes were closed as she wiped the grime away and she marvelled at his long, black eyelashes. She smeared the angry red burns on his palms with a marigold salve of her own making before binding them in clean linen.

As William's face began to relax Susannah stroked his hair, studying him closely. His arm twitched once or twice and then he became loose-limbed and his breathing steadied into sleep. She was still shaky with relief at his escape and she hadn't even asked him yet how he'd managed it. No matter; time for that later. She smiled to herself, the joy bubbling up inside her again. They had the

441

whole of the rest of their lives together to talk. Gently, she leaned across and kissed his forehead.

Stationing herself on the window seat, Susannah watched the smoke billowing over the rooftops as the fire edged its way ever closer. The area between Bridewell and Dorset House was aflame and, unless the wind turned towards the east, once Dorset House caught they would have to go. She drummed her fingers on the windowsill and wondered how late she dared to leave it be before she woke William.

Two hours later there was a scratching at the door. Phoebe came in carrying Beth.

Phoebe glanced at William. 'She hungry,' she whispered.

Susannah took Beth from her and Phoebe closed the door carefully behind her. William still slept, so Susannah loosened her bodice to suckle the baby. She murmured sweet nothings to her while she fed, stroking her soft cheek with her finger.

'That's as pretty a picture as ever I've seen,' said a sleepy voice.

Susannah started and hastily adjusted her chemise. 'Did we wake you?'

William yawned, stood up and stretched. 'That was the best sleep I've had for months. But now I'd like to meet your daughter.' He held out his arms. 'May I hold her?'

Bursting with pride, Susannah held Beth out to him.

He took her carefully and cradled her, rocking her gently as she screwed up her face ready to cry. 'Hush, sweeting!' He lifted her up so that her face was on a level with his own and she looked back at him through narrowed eyes. Then she blew a milky

442

bubble and the corner of her mouth lifted as if in a smile. William laughed. 'So tiny and so perfect! Have you named her yet?'

'Elizabeth, after my mother. But I shall call her Beth.'

'Would you ...' His bit his lip. 'Would you think it an imposition if I asked you to give her a second name? Since I shall be the only father she knows, I would dearly love to honour my own mother, too. Her name was Constance.'

'Elizabeth Constance.' Emotion made Susannah's voice quaver. 'It has a fine ring to it, don't you think?'

Beth began to fuss and William hoisted her onto his shoulder and walked about the room with her until she settled.

'You have a way with babies, William.'

'I always wanted children and thought that it was not to be.' He hesitated and then said, 'I don't want there to be secrets between us, Susannah. And so I must tell you that, some years ago, I was married.'

'Agnes told me about Caroline. And the baby she carried.'

'Did she now?' His eyes watched her face carefully. 'Do you mind?'

'Not now. I was tormented for a while by the thought that you'd never be able to love me for memories of her.'

'I love you far more than I ever cared for Caroline. She was pretty but capricious. And untrustworthy. I was young then and not such a good judge of character as I am now.'

'William?'

'Yes, my love?'

Her heart began to thud uncomfortably in her

chest. 'You are right; there must be no secrets between us and so I must ask for your forgiveness.'

'For what?'

She clasped her hands together to still their trembling; would the truth be too hard for William to forgive? 'I ask your forgiveness for not trusting you.' She saw a small frown begin to gather on his brow but it was too late to draw back. 'I saw you with Phoebe that last night before Father was taken ill. You were coming out of her room. And I thought . . .'

He became very still. 'You thought I had betrayed you?'

'I couldn't believe it but I *saw* you. You were both barefoot and in your night clothes. But it was the way you touched Phoebe's cheek with such tenderness that made me believe . . .' She stopped at the sight of the hurt written on his face.

'I'm wounded that you should believe such a thing of me, Susannah. Dammit, I'd told you that very evening that I loved you! Did you have no faith in me at all?' He turned away from her and went to stare out of the window at the billowing smoke. 'I never felt about Phoebe in that way. Why would I when I loved you?'

'I know that now, William. Phoebe told me the truth of the matter.'

'You should have known that without Phoebe telling you so!'

'But at the time I believed that Joseph was your son . . .'

'*My* son!' He whirled round to face her again. 'Good God, wherever did you get that impression?'

'I overheard you talking to Agnes when we first brought Phoebe and Joseph home . I thought that

444

you were telling Agnes that Joseph was your child. But now I know the truth of the matter.'

'And all these months I've been trying to protect you from the knowledge that he's Henry's son!'

'It doesn't have the power to hurt me now. In fact,' she gave him a hesitant little smile, 'I was in raptures when Phoebe told me because it meant that Joseph wasn't your child, as I believed.'

'And yet you still loved me, supposing all the while that he was?'

She nodded. 'Yes, but you can't know the torments of jealousy I suffered over Phoebe.

'In fact I do have an idea since my own imagination painted vivid pictures of you in Henry's arms.' He sighed. 'Susannah, that night when I went to tend to poor little Joseph I felt sorry for Phoebe. She had loved Henry with all her heart and he'd gone. She was alone and frightened and all she had left was her son. He'd been so violently ill she'd thought he might die too.'

'So, will you forgive me?' she asked in a small voice.

'Come here!' He caught her to him and kissed her nose. 'Your confession has answered one question for me.'

'It has?'

'I understood you were grieving for your father but I did wonder why you were often so disagreeable to me while I was in quarantine.'

'I shall try to make it up to you,' said Susannah.

'I'm sure I can find a way,' he said with a mischievous glint in his eye.

She glanced out of the window at the sun, now beginning to drop in the smoky sky. 'It's going to be difficult to run from the fire with an old lady and a baby, all in the dark.'

'And it will break Agnes's heart if the Captain's House burns. I hope we can wait until morning.'

Susannah trembled as she again pictured the apothecary shop in flames and pushed the thought firmly away; the time for grieving over that would have to come later. Frowning, she said, 'I meant to ask: what *were* you doing back in the shop? Jennet told me you'd left two days before to go with the Duke of York's men to fight the fire.'

'I did. But afterwards I returned to save your father's journals and his books.'

'His journals?'

William gave a crooked smile. 'The journals are filled with a lifetime of medical observations and his books saved my sanity while we were shut up. And I knew how important they were to you so I dug a deep hole in the yard and buried them, together with the great pestle and mortar. I don't know if they'll survive the heat but when the fire burns out we'll go back and see.'

Susannah embraced William and the sleeping baby he still cradled, her happiness bitter-sweet. 'I wish my father had known that we are to be married.'

'But he did, Susannah! I asked him for your hand before he died. He thought we would make a good match and gave us his blessing.'

Susannah held up her face to be kissed, wishing her father was there to share her joy.

'I've been making plans, oh, such plans, Susannah, but I must discuss them with you.'

'What kind of plans?' Curiosity made her forget her sadness for a moment.

'I've had a great deal of time to think. I

remembered what you said to me when I helped that poor dying boy in Bedlam. You said that, although it was only a drop in an ocean of sadness, my actions did make a difference to him. And I thought that if I can save even one tormented being and return him to good health, then I shall have achieved something worthwhile.'

Susannah nodded.

'And so I came to a decision but I need your approval. This is something not to be undertaken lightly because it would change the whole way we live.'

'In what way?'

'Next year my tenant, Roger Somerford, will leave Merryfields because he has inherited his father's estate. So we will have the opportunity to live there again.'

'At Merryfields?' Susannah put her hands to her mouth. 'Oh, William, now the apothecary shop has gone I can't imagine anywhere else I'd rather be!'

'Mmm.' William scratched his head. 'But you may not like my reasons for wanting to move there. I want to make Merryfields a place where the melancholic can come to rest and be made whole again.'

'I don't understand.'

'Some time ago you reminded me of what my mother once said; that gardening heals the soul. And Merryfields has acres of gardens. We could take in guests, those who might otherwise have been thrown into Bedlam.' He leaned forward, his voice eager. 'Not the hopelessly mad but those who have been made heartbroken by loss or who suffer from some condition that doesn't allow them to fit into society. We would provide a tranquil respite

447

from the cares of the world and encourage these guests to work in the gardens, to allow them to feel the warm earth between their fingers and watch the new shoots grow in the springtime.' His face was animated and his eyes sparkled.

Susannah gazed at Beth's sleeping face, so tenderly cupped in William's hand, while she considered his plan. At last she said, 'It's an admirable idea but I would not wish to risk the safety of . . .'

'Our children?' William smiled at Susannah's blush. 'I agree. Of course, we would have to choose our guests very carefully. And then there is another idea I think you will like.'

Susannah wondered if she could take in any more new thoughts after such a day of extraordinary events.

William's eyes blazed with triumph. 'My best idea of all is this: you shall have your own apothecary.'

'My own?'

'At Merryfields we'll need my skills as a physician but you will be at my side to help me and to dispense the medicines. And when the village hears of your apothecary the local people will come knocking on your door. I anticipate you'll be kept very busy.'

Susannah's heart was thudding with excitement. How happy her father would have been for her!

'So what do you think?'

'Yes,' she said. 'Yes, yes, yes!'

William whooped with delight, waking the baby.

Susannah placed Beth on a nest of cushions and they stood watching her while she settled back into sleep.

'I forgot to ask you,' Susannah whispered. 'How *did* you escape the fire?'

'I took a leaf out of Arabella's book,' William said with a grin as he pulled her to him. 'I scrambled out of the window and escaped over the rooftops with the flames licking at my heels!'

Susannah laughed. 'Perhaps the best thing to come out of the fire is that all Arabella's vulgar Chinese furniture has burned.'

The casement rattled in the wind as Susannah shut her eyes to escape the terrible thought of what might have been and then she felt William kiss her closed lids as gently as a butterfly's wing. She wound her arms round his neck and his unshaven chin was rough against her face. The warmth and reassuring firmness of his torso pressed against her own, together with the male scent of him, made her quiver with a sudden shaft of desire.

His arms tightened round her and his lips were warm and demanding, his breath quickening. Stumbling, they fell in a heap together onto Agnes's chair. William's hands, a little clumsy in their bandages, loosed Susannah's chemise and he bent his head to nuzzle her breast. 'My lovely, lovely Susannah,' he murmured. 'No matter what, tomorrow we'll find a parson to marry us before I go mad with longing.'

Susannah wondered if she could bear to wait until then.

A sudden gust of wind moaned in the chimney and rattled the casement again. William frowned and gently disentangled himself from Susannah. He went to the window and pressed his face to the glass to assess the progress of the fire. After a while, he said, 'Susannah?'

449

'Yes, William?' She sat up, suddenly tense again. Was it time?

'Dorset House is afire.'

Dread clutched at her. 'Then we must leave!'

'But come and look!'

'What is it?' She hurried to stand beside him.

Great flames were spouting upwards from the rooftops of Dorset House. They could hear the roar of the conflagration through the closed casement and smoke wormed its way through the cracks in the window frame. An explosion as loud as cannon fire shot a volley of orange sparks into the air and the wind caught them and whisked them away.

'The wind!' Susannah said. 'Is it changing? Those sparks blew back *towards* the fire!' The smoke whirled and eddied over the rooftops and then, very slowly, began to drift away from them.

Clinging together, they watched in silence until, at last, it seemed certain that the wind was blowing towards the east.

Gradually Susannah felt the tension easing in William's body.

'It's not my imagination, is it?' he asked.

'I don't think so,' she said. 'I do believe the fire really has stopped advancing.'

Into the Light

May 1671

Chapter 32

Susannah is running through a dark tunnel of trees, heading for the light. At the end of the tunnel she stops, blinking in the sunshine. The door to the orchard is ajar and she slips through it, the long grass soaking the hem of her skirt with dew. She halts under an apple tree and a blackbird, sitting on a branch above her, utters a warning cry and flits off to a safer perch in the plum tree.

Susannah stills her breath and listens. The air vibrates with the humming of bees and the early-morning sun is warm on her face. A duck on the river quacks on the other side of the high brick wall but she still cannot hear the sound she is listening for.

Then, in front of her, the long grass sways and Beth, her red-gold curls dancing, breaks cover.

'I see you!' calls Susannah. She runs towards her daughter who darts behind an apple tree. 'Where are you?' She makes a great play of searching behind each tree in the orchard, her expressions of dismay becoming more exaggerated as Beth's giggles become louder. 'You naughty creature, hiding from your mama! Where have you hidden yourself?' Creeping closer to the tree, she suddenly pounces.

Laughing, she snatches up the wriggling child and smothers her with kisses.

Hand in hand they leave the orchard for the garden, their shoes crunching along the gravel path lined with clipped yews. Facing them at the end of the avenue is a house built of brick the colour of faded damask roses and with high gables and tall, twisted chimneys. Merryfields.

Beth tugs on her mother's hand. 'May I make some sugar biscuits for when Father comes home?'

'He'd like that. Ask Peg or Jennet if they will help you.'

Beth blows her mother a kiss and runs off in the direction of the house.

A scattering of people are working in the gardens, some dead-heading the roses and others weeding the vegetable plot or tying up the herbs in the physic garden.

Susannah pauses to talk to a young man with a faraway expression in his eyes as he tends his vegetables.

'How are your carrots, Ben?'

'Growing fast.' He turns back to his hoeing, utterly intent upon his task.

Nearby, an old man kneels on the ground picking out stones and putting them in a bucket. He lifts a hand and smiles as she passes.

The kitchen is as busy as ever. Mistress Oliver, Peg and Jennet are preparing a feast for their master's return from London. The kitchen table is spread with pies, jellies and custards. Four chickens and a haunch of venison turn on the spit. Peg has wrapped Beth and her own daughter, a curly-haired moppet with big brown eyes, in clean aprons and is helping them to weigh out the ingredients for the sugar cakes.

The garden door opens and Emmanuel enters, carrying a basket of wood. He puts another log on the fire and then steals a kiss from his wife. 'Peg, I'm going to take Joseph fishing. See if we can catch some trout for supper.'

454

'Have you swept the paths?'

'Yes'm.'

'And cleaned out the chickens?'

He rolls his eyes, making the little girls laugh. 'Yes'm.'

'Go on with you, then,' she says. 'It's a sunny day and you'll only get under my feet.'

Joseph, grown strong and tall for ten, brings in a second basket of logs. He still bears a scar on his neck as a reminder of his escape from the pestilence. He drops his basket and he and Emmanuel depart.

Susannah knows now that she should never have doubted William's good intentions and he often teases her about it. He was no more capable of banishing Emmanuel to work in the plantations than herself and had arranged for his tenant, Roger Somerford, to find work for him, and later for Peg, too, at Merryfields. Although still young, Emmanuel and Peg are married and proving to be good and steady parents.

Susannah leaves the kitchen and walks along the corridor. She peers in through the open door of the Little Parlour and sees Mary, one of the guests, sitting on the window seat, reading poetry to Aunt Agnes. Mary had arrived at Merryfields six months before, wild-eyed and weeping after her husband and children died of a fever. She had no wish to live without them and her family had despaired of her but gradually she is recovering her spirits. Susannah stops to listen for a while and then continues along the corridor. She stops before another door and unlocks it with the key hanging from the chatelaine round her waist.

Inside, she closes her eyes and breathes deeply.

Spirits of turpentine, lavender, sulphur, liquorice and drying herbs; all the familiar scents that transport her back to her father's apothecary shop. She opens her eyes and smiles in contentment as she sees the neat shelves of gallypots and the teardrop-shaped bottles of coloured water catching the sun on the windowsill. Here are the tools of her trade which, combined with William's professional skills, maintain the health of the household and the village. But it is the great pestle and mortar that holds pride of place upon the counter, sitting next to her father's invaluable journals. After the Great Fire had burned itself out and the earth was cool enough, she and William had returned to the ruins to retrieve them.

A new city of London is rising from the ashes of the old. St Paul's had burned, after all; the heat of the fire so great that the stone exploded and the lead from the roof melted until it ran like a river in the streets. But plans are underway to build a magnificent new cathedral. The city had mourned and many people were ruined but it hadn't taken long for the Londoners with their indomitable spirit to roll up their sleeves, clear the rubble and start rebuilding. And who knows, thinks Susannah, perhaps the cleansing by fire, though as painful as cauterising the wound of an amputated limb, might ensure better health for all who lived there.

Susannah potters about for a while, tying herbs into neat bunches and making new labels for the gallypots. Writing an entry into the latest journal, she notes the ingredients for a new prescription for quinsy. She glances out of the window and sees that the sun is high in the sky. It is time. She locks the door of the apothecary behind her and sets off down the garden again.

In the orchard she opens the door in the wall and slips through onto the grassy river bank.

Emmanuel and Joseph are fishing at the far end of the landing stage with their feet dangling over the water.

Susannah sits on the grass and waits.

Presently she sees a boat approaching and shades her eyes against the sun. A moorhen splatters to the opposite bank in sudden panic, casting diamond drops in her wake.

Leaping to her feet, Susannah waves both arms.

The boatman ties up at the landing stage and William jumps out and enfolds her in his embrace. 'I've missed you,' he whispers. Then he turns back to the boat and helps a woman to disembark. 'This is our new guest, Mistress Picard,' he says, 'come to rest with us awhile.'

Mistress Pickard, distress etched in her face, looks up at Susannah with wounded eyes.

'You are very welcome,' says Susannah, taking her hand. 'Come, let me show you Merryfields.'

William carries her bags into the house leaving the two women to follow. They walk together through the garden, while Susannah talks to her of the fine library, the gardens and the other guests who are waiting to greet her.

Mistress Pickard stops under the arbour and slowly reaches out to stroke the soft petals of a dog rose and to breathe in its sweet scent.

'You may have a garden of your own if you wish,' Susannah says.

Mistress Pickard bends to scoop up a handful of soil and rubs it through her fingers. 'I should like that. My mother grew gillyflowers in her garden

457

when I was a child.'

Susannah takes Mistress Pickard to her room and leaves her to unpack and rest after her journey. Closing the door quietly behind her, she hurries along the gallery to her own bedchamber.

Inside, William is stripped to the waist and rinsing his face in a basin of warm water. He looks up at her with a smile as sweet as honey. 'There you are!'

Susannah lifts her face to receive his kiss.

'I need to clean the city dirt away before I kiss you properly.'

'Shall I wash your back?' Susannah rubs the wet soap between her palms and smoothes it over his broad shoulders, taking pleasure in the aromatic lavender scent as she eases her thumbs along the muscles next to his spine. After five years of marriage, touching his naked skin still makes her shiver with delight.

He tips his head so that she can massage away the knots of tension in the side of his neck. 'Guess who I saw in the city yesterday?' he says.

'The King?' hazards Susannah.

'Not quite.'

'Who then?'

'Arabella!'

'No!' Surprise makes the soap squeeze out of her hand and fall with a splash into the basin. 'After all this time!' Apprehension makes her voice sharp. 'But what news of my little brothers? Are they safe and well?'

'Up to all kinds of mischief, I understand. I knew you'd want to see them and Arabella has graciously said they may come and stay for a few weeks since she has arrangements to make.'

'Arrangements?'

'She was in a smart carriage with a gentleman. If I'm not mistaken he'll soon be husband number three.'

'Aunt Agnes always said that Arabella would fall on her feet.' Relief that Joshua and Samuel are well is mixed with irritation that Arabella is as self-serving as ever. She turns William to face her, forgetting Arabella as she moves her soapy hands in slow circles over his torso, the light covering of dark hair on his chest forming into spiral patterns. She drops a lingering kiss on the soft skin in the hollow above his collarbone and smiles in anticipation as she feels him quiver with pleasure under her lips.

'Susannah?'

'Mmm?' Slowly she wipes away the soap with a linen cloth and pats him dry with a clean towel. Tracing a finger over his chest, a tremor of excitement and longing grips her; the desire to reaffirm the passion they feel for each other.

He takes her face in his hands and she drowns in the love shining in his eyes. She loses herself in the fervour of his kisses as she feels his heartbeat quicken to match her own.

Loosening her laces, he murmurs words of love as he buries his face in her breast. Her petticoats fall to the floor in a silken rustle and then her bare skin is warm against his.

The sheets are cool and slightly rough against their nakedness as they slide into bed. She winds her arms about his neck, arching her back to press her breasts against him. She wants to close the space between them, to meld their bodies together for all time.

'My sweet Susannah,' he whispers. His lips are

hot on her neck as he traces her body with his hands. He runs a fingertip very slowly down her belly until he finds her secret place and she lies quivering beneath his touch, liquid with desire. William lifts her hips to his and she lets out a small gasp of pleasure as he enters her. He whispers her name as they move together, softly at first and then more urgently as their passion rises. Swelling waves of sensation ripple through Susannah's body and surge to a climax. She lets out a cry of triumph, gripping William to her breast.

He arches his back as his own pleasure takes him, sighs and sinks down beside her.

A little while later, curled up against his shoulder, listening to his steady breathing, Susannah sighs in contentment. William's love has given her the strength to mourn and move on to the new life they have made together.

He turns to look at her, his dark eyes smiling and, once again, Susannah sends up a prayer of thanks for the comfort and joy of their love.

'Now I know I am truly come home,' he says. 'But we should rise before someone comes looking for us.'

'And it would never do to find the serious and responsible doctor in bed with his wife in the middle of the afternoon.'

William kisses the tip of her nose. 'No, it wouldn't. I'd never be able to look my patients in the eye again.'

Susannah stretches luxuriously. 'Two more minutes?'

'Go on with you, you little hussy, time to get up!'

William is tying the laces on Susannah's bodice when footsteps race along the passage and the door is flung back. 'Father!' Beth races to him, her arms wide.

William glances at Susannah in amusement. 'Not a moment too soon,' he murmurs. He lifts Beth up and kisses her. 'Have you been good while I was away, my little sugar plum?'

'Very good! And I made jumbals, especially for you!' Beth hugs him tight, covering his cheek with sticky kisses.

'Has she been good enough for sugar plums, Mama?'

Susannah smiles, pinning her tumbled curls back into place. 'Yes, but only one or two, not a whole box.'

William laughs and swings Beth down to the ground. 'Come on then! But first I want to make a visit.'

'I know where we're going!' says Beth. She skips along the gallery and William and Susannah follow, hand in hand.

Beth stops outside a door where puts a finger to her lips before carefully lifting the latch.

Inside, Phoebe is singing while she rocks the cradle with her foot. She smiles a greeting and hold out her arms to Beth, who scrambles onto her knee.

William comes quietly forward and looks into the cradle at his sleeping son.

Susannah watches his features soften as her own heart swells with love. There can be no place closer to heaven on earth than her home at Merryfields with her husband and children.

William, gently stroking baby Kit's dark hair, looks up at her with a face alight with love and reaches for her hand.

Acknowledgements

Love and thanks to my husband Simon, all my lovely children and to my parents for their endless support, to Howard Barlow who believed in me, to Edward Smith and members of youwriteon.com for the reviews, to my agent Annette Green and my editor Lucy Icke at Piatkus who's helped me to make the story flower.

My gratitude to all the members of WordWatchers for their friendly encouragement and plain speaking.

And finally, my thanks to Samuel Pepys, whose diary allowed me a peep into Restoration London.